CAROLYNE AARSEN

The Rancher's Return

&

Daddy Lessons

HARLEQUIN® LOVE INSPIRED®CLASSICS

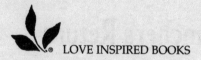

LOVE INSPIRED BOOKS

Recycling programs for this product may not exist in your area.

ISBN-13: 978-1-335-21889-6

The Rancher's Return & Daddy Lessons

Copyright © 2018 by Harlequin Books S.A.

The publisher acknowledges the copyright holder of the individual works as follows:

The Rancher's Return
Copyright © 2011 by Carolyne Aarsen

Daddy Lessons
Copyright © 2012 by Carolyne Aarsen

www.Harlequin.com

Printed in U.S.A.

CONTENTS

THE RANCHER'S RETURN   7

DADDY LESSONS   227

Carolyne Aarsen and her husband, Richard, live on a small ranch in northern Alberta, where they have raised four children and numerous foster children and are still raising cattle. Carolyne crafts her stories in an office with a large west-facing window, through which she can watch the changing seasons while struggling to make her words obey. Visit her website at carolyneaarsen.com.

Books by Carolyne Aarsen

Love Inspired

Cowboys of Cedar Ridge

Courting the Cowboy
Second-Chance Cowboy
The Cowboy's Family Christmas
A Cowboy for the Twins

Big Sky Cowboys

Wrangling the Cowboy's Heart
Trusting the Cowboy
The Cowboy's Christmas Baby

Lone Star Cowboy League

A Family for the Soldier

Refuge Ranch

Her Cowboy Hero
Reunited with the Cowboy
The Cowboy's Homecoming

Visit the Author Profile page at Harlequin.com for more titles.

THE RANCHER'S RETURN

I will say of the Lord, "He is my refuge and my fortress, my God, in whom I trust."
—*Psalms* 91:2

To Richard, my partner in joy and sorrow

Chapter One

Coming back to the ranch was harder than he'd thought.

Carter Beck swung his leg over his motorbike and yanked off his helmet. He dragged a hand over his face, calloused hands rasping over the stubble of his cheeks as he looked over the yard.

As his eyes followed the contours of the land, the hills flowing up to the rugged mountains of southern British Columbia, a sense of homesickness flickered deep in his soul. This place had been his home since his mother had moved here, a single mother expecting twins.

He hadn't been back for two years. If it hadn't been for his beloved grandmother's recent heart attack, he would still be away.

Unable to stop himself, his eyes drifted over to the corral. The memories he'd kept at bay since he left crashed into his mind. Right behind them came the wrenching pain and haunting guilt he'd spent the past twenty-three months outrunning.

The whinnying of a horse broke into his dark thoughts and snagged his attention.

A young boy astride a horse broke through the copse

of trees edging the ranch's outbuildings. He held the reins of his horse in both hands, elbows in, wrists cocked.

Just as Carter had taught him.

A wave of dizziness washed over Carter as the horse came closer.

Harry.

Even as he took a step toward the horse and rider, reality followed like ice water through his veins. The young boy wore a white cowboy hat instead of a trucker's cap.

And Carter's son was dead.

A woman astride a horse followed the boy out of the trees. The woman sat relaxed in the saddle, one hand resting on her thigh, her broad-brimmed hat hiding her face, reins held loosely in her other hand. She looked as if she belonged atop a horse, as if she was one with the animal, so easy were her motions as her horse followed the other.

When the woman saw him, she pulled up and dismounted in one fluid motion.

"Can I help you, sir?" she asked, pushing her hat back on her head, her brown eyes frowning at him as she motioned the boy to stop.

Carter felt a tinge of annoyance at her question, spoken with such a cool air. Sir? As if he was some stranger instead of the owner of the ranch she rode across? And who was she?

"Is that your motorbike, sir?" The young boy pulled off his hat, his green eyes intent on Carter's bike. "It's really cool."

His eager voice, his bright eyes, resurrected the memories that lay heavy on Carter's soul. And when the woman lifted the little boy from the saddle and gently stroked his hair back from his face with a loving motion, the weight grew.

"Yeah. It's mine."

"It's so awesome," the boy said, his breathless young voice battering away at Carter's defenses.

Carter's heart stuttered. He even sounded like Harry. Coming back to the place where his son died had been hard enough. Meeting a child the same age Harry was when he died made this even more difficult.

He forced his attention back to the woman. A light breeze picked up a strand of her long, brown hair, and as she tucked it behind her ear he caught sight of her bare left hand. No rings.

She saw him looking at her hand and lifted her chin in the faintest movement of defiance. Then she put her hand on the boy's shoulder, drawing him to her side, as if ready to defend him against anything Carter might have to say. She looked like a protective mare standing guard over her precious colt.

Carter held her gaze and for a moment, as their eyes locked, an indefinable emotion arced between them.

"My name is Carter Beck," he said quietly.

The woman's eyes widened, and he saw recognition in her expression. He caught a trace of sorrow in the softening of her features, in the gentle parting of her lips.

"I imagine you've come to see Nana... Mrs. Beck."

He frowned at her lapse. This unknown woman called his grandmother Nana?

"And you are?" he asked.

"Sorry again," she said, transferring the reins and holding out her hand. "I'm Emma Minton. This is my son, Adam. I help Wade on the ranch here. I work with the horses as well as help him with the cows and anything else that needs doing. But I'm sure you know that," she said with a light laugh that held a note of self-conscious humor.

"Nice to meet you, Emma," he said as he reluctantly took her hand. "Wade did tell me a while back he was hiring a new ranch hand. I didn't expect..."

"A woman?" Emma lifted her shoulders in a light shrug. "I worked on a ranch all my life. I know my way around horses and cows and fences and haying equipment."

"I'm sure you do. Otherwise, Wade wouldn't have hired you."

Emma angled her head to one side, as if wondering if he was being sarcastic. Then she gave him a quick nod, accepting his answer.

Carter glanced around the yard. "Where is Wade?"

"He and Miranda went to town. She had a doctor's appointment."

"Right. Of course." The last time he'd talked to Wade, his ranch foreman had told him his wife was expecting.

Emma's horse stamped impatiently, and she reached up and stroked his neck. "I should put the horses away. Good to meet you, and I'm sure we'll be seeing you around." Then without a second glance, she turned the horses around, her son trotting alongside her.

"Was that man Mr. Beck? The man who owns the ranch?" Adam's young voice floated back to him.

"Yup. That's who it was," Emma replied.

"So he's the one we have to ask about the acreage?" Adam asked.

Acreage? What acreage? He wanted to call after her to find out what she was talking about. But he was sure his grandmother heard his motorbike come into the yard and would be expecting him.

As he turned toward the house where his grandmother lived, his gaze traced over the land beyond the ranch yard. The hay fields were greener than he had ever seen them.

Beyond them he heard the water of Morrisey River splashing over the rocks, heading toward the Elk River. The river kept flowing, a steady source of water for the ranch and a constant reminder of the timelessness of the place.

Five generations of Becks had lived along this river and before that who knows how many generations of his great-great-grandmother Kamiskahk's tribe.

He felt a surprising smile pull at his mouth as other, older memories soothed away the stark ones he'd been outrunning the past two years.

Then, as he walked toward his grandmother's house, he passed the corral. He wasn't going to look, but his eyes, as if they had a will of their own, shifted to the place where the horse waterer had been. The place where his son had drowned.

His heart tripped in his chest and he pushed the memories away, the reminder of his son's death stiffening his resolve to leave this place as soon as he could.

He looked older than the picture Nana Beck had on her mantel, Emma thought, watching Carter stride away. He wore his hair longer, and his eyes were slate-blue instead of gray.

Emma had heard so much about Nana Beck's grandchild, that she felt she knew him personally.

But the tall man with the sad eyes and grim mouth didn't fit with the stories Nana had told her. The man in Nana Beck's stories laughed a lot, smiled all the time and loved his life. This man looked as if he carried the burden of the world on his shoulders. Of course, given what he had lost, Emma wasn't surprised. She felt her own heart quiver at the thought of losing Adam like Carter lost his son.

"Can I feed the other horses some of the carrots?" Adam was asking, breaking into her dark thoughts.

Emma pulled her attention away from Carter.

"Sure you can. Just make sure you don't pull out too many. We have to pick some to bring to Nana Beck." She opened the corral gate and led her horses, Diamond and Dusty, inside, Adam right behind her.

"Are we having supper there?"

Emma shook her head as she tied the horses up. "Nope. Shannon… Miss Beck said she was coming." Since Nana Beck's heart attack, Nana Beck's granddaughter, Shannon, Miranda, the foreman's wife, and Emma all took turns cooking for Nana, making sure she was eating. Today it was Shannon's turn.

"Are you going to talk to that Carter man about the acreage?"

"He just got here, honey. I think I'll give him a day or two." Emma loosened the cinches on Diamond's saddle and eased it off his back. She frowned at the cracking on the skirt of the saddle. She'd have to oil it up again, though she really should buy a new one.

And Adam needed new boots and she needed a new winter coat and she should buy a spare tire for her horse trailer. But she was saving as much as possible to add to what she had left from the sale of her father's ranch.

"Do you think he'll let us have our place?"

Emma frowned, pulling her attention away from the

constant nagging concerns and plans of everyday life and back to her son.

"It's not our place, honey." Emma pulled off the saddle blankets, as anticipation flickered through her at her and Adam's plans. "But I do hope to talk to him about it."

Wade Klauer, the foreman, had told her about the old yard site. How it had been a part of another ranch Carter had bought just before his son died. When Wade told her Carter was returning, she'd seen this as her chance to ask him to subdivide the yard site of the property. Maybe, finally, she and her son could have a home of their own.

"I'm going to get some carrots," Adam said, clambering over the corral fence. "And I won't pick too many," he added with an impish grin.

Emma laughed and blew him a kiss and then watched him run across the yard, his boots kicking up little clouds of dust.

He was so precious. And she wanted more than anything to give him a place. A home.

Up until she got pregnant, she'd spent her summers following the rodeo, barrel racing the horses her beloved mother had bought for her. Her winters were spent working wherever she found a job. But after she got pregnant, she was determined to do right by her son. And when Adam's biological father abandoned her, she moved back to her father's ranch and returned to her faith.

A year ago she met Karl and thought she'd found a reason to settle down. A man she could trust to take care of her and her son. A man who also loved ranch and country life.

But when she found him kissing her best friend, Emma ditched him. A few months later, Emma's father died. And in the aftermath, she discovered her father had been secretly gambling, using the ranch for collateral. After the ranch was sold to pay the debts, Emma was left with only a horse trailer, two horses, a pickup truck and enough money for a small down payment on another place.

As Emma drove off the ranch, her dreams and plans for her future in tatters, she knew she couldn't trust any man to take care of her and Adam.

She struggled along, working where she could, finding a place to live and board her horses. So when she saw an ad for a hired hand at the Rocking K Ranch, close to the town of Hartley Creek, she responded. The job promised a home on the ranch as part of the employment package.

As soon as Emma drove onto the Rocking K, nestled in the greening hills of southeast British Columbia, she was overcome with an immediate sense of homecoming. She knew this was where she wanted to be.

"I got some carrots," Adam called out, scurrying over to the corral, his fists full of bright orange carrots, fronds of green dangling on the ground behind him.

"Looks like you picked half a row," Emma said with an indulgent laugh as she slipped the bridles off Dusty and Diamond.

"Only some," he said with a frown. "There's lots yet." As Adam doled out the carrots to the waiting horses, his laughter drifted back to her over the afternoon air, a carefree, happy sound that warmed her heart.

When Adam was done, Emma climbed over the fence. As they walked back to the garden, she heard the door of Nana Beck's house open. Carter came out carrying a tray, which he laid down on a small glass table on the covered veranda.

He looked up and across the distance. She saw his frown. And it seemed directed at her and Adam.

* * *

"What a day to be alive," Nana Beck said, accepting the mug of tea Carter had poured. She settled into her chair on the veranda and eased out a gentle sigh.

"I'm glad you're okay," Carter said quietly, spooning a generous amount of honey into his tea. "Really glad."

"No inheritance for you and your cousins yet," she said with a wink.

"I can wait." He couldn't share her humor. He didn't want to think that his grandmother could have died while he was working up in the Northwest Territories on that pipeline job. Knowing she was okay eased a huge burden off his shoulders.

She gave him a gentle smile. "So can I." She reached over and covered his hand with hers. "I'm so glad you came home."

"I tried to come as soon as Shannon got hold of me. But I couldn't get out of the camp. We were socked in with rain, and the planes couldn't fly." He gave her a smile, guilt dogging him in spite of her assurances. "So how are you feeling?"

"The doctor said that I seem to be making a good recovery," Nana said, leaning back in her chair, her hands cradling a mug of tea. "He told me that I was lucky that Shannon was with me here on the ranch when I had the heart attack. They caught everything soon enough, so I should be back to normal very soon."

"I'm glad to hear that," Carter said. "I was worried about you."

"Were you? Really?" The faintly accusing note in his grandmother's voice resurrected another kind of guilt.

"I came back because I was worried, and I came as soon as I could." He gave her a careful smile.

"You've been away too long." Her voice held an underlying tone of sympathy he wanted to avoid.

"Only two years," he said, lounging back in his chair. He hoped he achieved the casual and in-control vibe he aimed for. He would need it around his grandmother.

Nana Beck had an innate ability to separate baloney from the truth. Carter knew he would need all his wits about him when he told her that his visit was temporary.

And that he wouldn't be talking about his son.

"Two years is a long time." She spoke quietly, but he heard the gentle reprimand in her voice. "I know why you stayed away, but I think it's a good thing you're back. I think you need to deal with your loss."

"I'm doing okay, Nana." He took a sip of tea, resting his ankle on his knee, hoping he looked more in control than he felt. He'd spent the past two years putting the past behind him. Moving on.

Then the sound of Adam's voice rang across the yard from the garden.

"So how long have the woman and her boy lived here?" He avoided his grandmother's gaze. He doubted she appreciated the sudden topic switch.

"Emma and Adam have been here about six months," she said, looking over to where Adam kneeled in the dirt of the garden beside his mother, sorting potatoes. Emma's hair, now free from her ponytail, slipped over her face as she bent over to drop potatoes in the pail. He had thought her hair was brown, but the sunlight picked out auburn highlights.

"She's a wonderful girl," his grandmother continued. "Hard worker. Very devoted to her son. She loves being here on the ranch. She grew up on one, worked on her father's ranch before she came here."

Carter dragged his attention back to his grandmother. "I'm sure she's capable, or else Wade wouldn't have hired her."

"She raised her boy without any help," his grandmother went on, obviously warming to her topic. "I believe she even rode the rodeo for a while. Of course, that was before she had her son. She's had her moments, but she's such a strong Christian girl."

Carter's only reply to his grandmother's soliloquy in praise of Emma was an absent nod.

"She's had a difficult life, but you'd never know it. She doesn't complain."

"Life's hard for many people, Nana."

"I know it is. It's been difficult watching my daughters making their mistakes. Your mom coming back here as a single mother—your aunt Denise returning as a divorced woman. Trouble was, they came here to hide. To lick their wounds. Neither have been the best example to your brother and your cousins of where to go when life is hard, as you said. So to remind you I've got something for you." Nana slowly got to her feet. When Carter got up to help her, she waved him off. She walked into the house, and the door fell closed behind her. In the quiet she left behind, Carter heard Adam say something and caught Emma's soft laugh in reply.

He closed his eyes, memories falling over themselves. His son in the yard. Harry's laugh. The way he loved riding horses—

The wham of the door pulled him out of those painful memories. Nana sat down again, her hands resting on a paper-wrapped package lying on her lap.

"Having this heart attack has been like a wake-up call for me in so many ways," she said, her voice subdued and serious. "I feel like I have been given another chance to have some kind of influence in my grandchildren's lives. So, on that note, this is for you." She gave him the package. "I want you to open it up now so I can explain what this is about."

Carter frowned but did as his Nana asked. He unwrapped a Bible. He opened the book, leafing through it as if to show Nana that he appreciated the gesture, when all it did was create another wave of anger with the God the Bible talked about.

He found the inscription page and read it.

"To Carter, from your Nana. To help you find your way back home."

He released a light laugh. Home. Did he even have one anymore? The ranch wasn't home if his son wasn't here.

Losing Sylvia when Harry was born had been hard enough to deal with. He'd been angry with God for taking away his wife so young, so soon. But he'd gotten through that.

But for God to take Harry? When Carter had been working so hard to provide and take care of him?

"There's something else." Nana gave him another small box. "This isn't as significant as the Bible, but I wanted to give this to remind you of your roots and how important they are."

With a puzzled frown, Carter took the jeweler's box and lifted the lid. Nestled inside lay a gold chain. He lifted it up, and his puzzlement grew. Hanging from the chain was a coarse gold nugget in a plain setting. It looked familiar.

Then he glanced at Nana's wrist. Empty.

"Is this one of the charms from your bracelet?" he asked quietly, letting the sun play over the gold nugget.

"Yes. It is." Nana touched it with a forefinger, making it spin in the light.

"But this is a necklace."

"I took the five charms from my bracelet and had each of them made into a necklace. I am giving one to each of the grandchildren."

"But the bracelet came from Grandpa—"

"And the nuggets on the bracelet came from your great-great-grandmother Kamiskahk."

"I brought you potatoes, Nana Beck," Adam called out, running toward them, holding up a pail.

There it was again. The name his son used to address his grandmother coming from the lips of this little boy.

It jarred him in some odd way he couldn't define.

Adam stopped when he saw what Carter held. "Wow, that's so pretty." He dropped his pail on the veranda with a "thunk" and walked toward Carter, his eyes on the necklace Carter still held up. "It sparkles."

In spite of his previous discomfort with the little boy, Carter smiled at the tone of reverence in Adam's voice.

"Gold fever is no respecter of class or age," he said, swinging it back and forth, making it shimmer in the sun.

"Is that a present for Nana Beck?" Adam asked.

"No. It's a present from me to him," Nana said, glancing from Carter to Adam.

"That's silly. Nanas don't give presents to big people."

"You're not the only one I give presents to," Nana Beck said with a smile.

Carter couldn't stop the flush of pain at the thought that his grandmother, who should be giving gifts to his son, was giving them to this little boy.

"Adam, don't bother Nana Beck right now." Emma hurried up the walk to the veranda and pulled gently back on his shoulder. She glanced from Nana to Carter, an apologetic smile on her face. "Sorry to disturb your visit. Adam was a little eager to make his delivery."

"Did you see that pretty necklace that Mr. Carter has?" Adam pointed to the necklace that Carter had laid down on the Bible in his lap. "Is it real gold?"

"Actually, it is," Nana Beck said. "I got it made from a bracelet I used to wear. Did you know the story about the bracelet, Adam?"

"There's a story?" Adam asked, his voice pipingly eager.

Carter looked away. Being around this boy grew harder each second in his presence. Harry had never heard the story about his Nana's bracelet. The story was part of Harry's legacy and history, and now this little boy, a complete stranger to him, would be hearing it.

"Adam, honey, we should go," Emma said quietly, as if she sensed Carter's pain.

"I want to hear the story," Adam said.

"Stay a moment," Nana Beck urged. "Have some tea."

"No… I don't think…" Emma protested.

"That's silly. Carter, why don't you get Emma a mug, and please bring back a juice box and a bag of gummy snacks for Adam. They're in the cupboard beside the mugs."

Carter gladly made his escape. Once in the kitchen, he rested his clenched hands on the counter, feeling an ache in the cold place in the center of his chest where his heart lay. He drew in a long, steadying breath. This was too hard. Every time Adam spoke, it was a vivid reminder of his own son.

Carter closed his eyes and made himself relax. He had seen boys the age of his son's before.

Just not on the ranch where…

Carter slammed his hands on the counter, then pushed himself straight. He had to get past this. He had to move on.

And how was that supposed to happen as long as he still owned the ranch, a visible reminder of what he had lost?

Chapter Two

"...So August Beck looked across the river and into the eyes of a lovely Kootenai native named Kamiskahk," Nana was saying, telling Emma and Adam the story of the nuggets when Carter returned to the veranda.

Nana Beck shot Carter a quick glance as he set the mug down, poured Emma a cup of tea and gave Adam the juice box and gummies he'd found in Nana's "treat cupboard."

"Thank you, Mr. Carter," Adam said, but the little boy's attention quickly shifted back to Nana.

Emma sat on the floor of the veranda, her back against the pillar, her dark hair pushed away from her face looking at ease.

"Sit down here," he said, setting the chair by her.

She held up her hand, but Carter moved the chair closer and then walked over to the railing beside his grandmother and settled himself on it, listening to the story as familiar to him as his grandmother's face.

"As August courted Kamiskahk, he discovered she had a pouch of gold nuggets that she'd gotten from her father," Nana continued, her eyes bright, warming to the story she loved to tell. "Kamiskahk's father had sworn her to secrecy, telling her that if others found out there was gold in the valley, they would take it over and things would not be good for their people."

"Why not?" Adam carefully opened the pouch of gummies and popped one in his mouth, his eyes wide.

"Because Kamiskahk's father knew how people could be seized by gold fever. So Kamiskahk kept her word, and never told anyone about the gold…except for August. And August was soon filled with gold fever. He left Kamiskahk and went looking. For months he searched, dug and panned, never finding even a trace of the gold. Then, one day, exhausted, cold, hungry and lonely, hunched over a gold pan in an icy creek, he thought of Kamiskahk and the love she held for him. He felt ashamed that he had walked away from her. August put away his shovel and his gold pan and returned to Kamiskahk's village, humbly asking her to take him back. She did, and he never asked about where the nuggets came from again."

While Nana spoke, a gentle smile slipped across Emma's face, and she leaned forward, as if to catch the story better.

Then her eyes slid from Nana to Carter. For a moment their gazes held. Her smile faded away, and he saw the humor in her brown eyes change to sympathy.

He didn't want her to feel sorry for him. He wanted to see her smile again.

"August Beck never did find out where the gold came from. What had become more important was the love August Beck learned to value over gold. He and Kamiskahk settled in this valley and had a son, Able Beck, who got the ranch and the nuggets. Able had a son named Bill Beck. My husband." Nana sat back, a satisfied smile wrinkling her lined cheeks. "I loved the story so much that Bill, my late husband, had the nuggets made into a bracelet for me."

"That's a wonderful story." Emma's voice was quiet, and her gaze slipped to the necklace lying on the Bible. "Is that made from the bracelet?"

Nana Beck picked up the necklace, threading the gold chain through her fingers. "Yes. It is." Her eyes shifted to Carter. "I wanted to give each of my grandchildren a part of that bracelet as a reminder of their heritage."

Emma cleared her throat and set her mug on the table between her and Nana Beck. "Thanks for the tea, but we should go. I promised Miranda I would help her with some sewing."

"Can I stay here, Mom?" Adam asked. "I don't want to sew."

Emma knelt down and cupped his chin in her hand. "I know you don't, but Mr. Carter hasn't seen his nana for a long time, and I'm sure they want to visit alone."

Adam heaved a sigh, and then with a toss of his head he got up. "Bye, Nana Beck," he muttered, picking up his juice box and gummies. He was about to go when Emma nudged him again.

"Thanks for the treats," he said.

"You're welcome," Nana said with an indulgent smile.

As they walked away, Adam gave Carter a wave. Then he followed his mother toward Wade and Miranda's house. Carter's old house.

Carter drew his attention back to his grandmother, who watched him with an indulgent smile. "She's a nice girl, isn't she?" Nana said. "And pretty."

Carter gave his grandmother a smile. "You're not very subtle, Nana."

She waved off his objections. "I'm too old to be subtle. I just had a heart attack. I've got things on my mind. And even though I haven't seen much of you, I know you're not happy."

Carter said nothing to that.

Nana Beck sat back in her chair with a sigh. "I've had a chance to see things differently. That's why I wanted to give you these presents now. In the future, if I'm not here, the nuggets will be a reminder of where you've come from. And the Bible will be a reminder of where you should be going."

Carter got up and set the gold nugget carefully back in the box. "So what am I supposed to do with this?"

"I want you to give it to someone important in your life," his nana said. "Someone who you care deeply about. Someone who is more important than the treasure in this world."

"Thanks for this, Nana. It's a precious keepsake." He snapped the velvet lid shut, then he carefully placed the box on the Bible. "But I don't think I'll be giving it to anyone."

"You never know what life will bring you, Carter, or where God will lead you in the future," Nana said, a quiet note of admonition in her voice.

"Well, I don't like where God has brought me so far," Carter said, looking down at the Bible. "I'm not going to trust God for my future. I'll make my own plans."

He gave Nana a level look, wishing he didn't feel a niggling sense of fear at his outspoken words.

Nana reached over and gently brushed a lock of hair back from his forehead. "Be careful what you say, Carter. I know God is still holding you in His hands."

Carter said nothing to that.

"But I also have something else to tell you," she said quietly, looking past him to the yard and the hills beyond. "I'm moving to town. Shannon has been looking for places for me in Hartley Creek."

"You want to move off the ranch?" he asked, unsure he'd heard her correctly.

"Not really. But Shannon thinks I should be closer to the hospital, and unfortunately I agree."

Carter sat back, absorbing this information. And as he did it was as if a huge weight had fallen off his shoulders. He'd never sell the ranch as long as it was Nana Beck's home. But if she was leaving, then maybe he could too. And with the ranch sold, perhaps he could leave all the painful memories of the past behind.

"So why're you shoeing horses instead of getting Greg Beattie to do your farrier work?" Carter leaned against the sun-warmed wood of the barn, watching his foreman and old friend trimming hooves. Yesterday he had spent most of his day catching up with his grandmother and visiting with his cousin Shannon. It wasn't until today that he had an opportunity to connect with Wade.

Wade pushed his glasses up his nose and then grunted as he grabbed a pair of large clippers. "I like the challenge. And Greg's been getting busier and harder to book. Lots of new acreages, and all the owners have horses." Wade made quick work of clipping the horse's hoof then let the foot down and stretched his back.

Carter swatted a fly and let his eyes drift over the yard. From here he saw everything.

Including the corral where Emma worked with a pair of horses; her son perched on the top rail of the corral fence. Part of him wanted to look away. The ranch held too many painful memories, but the corral held the harshest one of all.

His son, lying lifeless on the ground after Wade had pulled him out of the open stock tank that served as a horse waterer.

When she was pregnant, Sylvia had urged him to get rid of the large tank, saying it was too dangerous. Carter had dismissed her worries with a kiss. He and his brother and cousins had grown up with that tank. On hot days they had sat in it, cooling off in the waist-high water.

He should have...

Carter pushed the memory and guilt away, pain hard on their heels.

"This Emma girl," Carter said, "why did you hire her?"

"I told you I needed to hire another hand to replace that useless character we had before." Wade picked up the horse's hoof again and began working at it with a rasp, getting it ready for a shoe.

"I assumed you were going to hire a guy."

"She had the best qualifications." Wade shrugged. "I hope that's not a problem."

Carter looked over at the corral again. Adam now sat on top of Banjo, and Emma led him around. He heard her voice, though he couldn't make out what she said. Adam laughed and she patted his leg, grinning up at him.

She turned and looked his way, then abruptly turned around.

"It's not a problem if she knows what she's doing," Carter said, turning his attention back to Wade.

"She's good. Really good. Has a great connection with horses, and some unique ideas about pasture management." Wade tapped the horse's hoof. He dropped it again and grabbed a horseshoe from the anvil.

"So what's her story?" Carter asked while Wade nailed down the shoe. "Why would she want to work here?"

"She used to work her daddy's ranch till he gambled it away. Says she loves ranch work, and it shows. She's been a better hand than the guy I had for two weeks before I hired her." He tapped in another nail. "She wants to talk to you about subdividing an acreage off the river property. Says she wants to settle down here."

"Really?" So that's what her son was talking about when he said they had to ask him about the acreage.

"Don't sound so surprised. Some of us love it here," Wade grunted as he tapped in another nail. Then he looked up, a horrified expression on his face. "Sorry. I didn't mean it that way. I know why you've stayed away. Of course being here is hard, and I get that—"

"Can she afford to buy the acreage?" Carter asked, cutting off his friend's apology. He felt rude, but he knew where Wade was headed.

The same place he'd been going for the past year in any of their conversations and communications. The ranch was Carter's home. It was time to come back. To get over what happened.

Trouble was it wasn't so simple. It was difficult enough dealing with the "if onlys" when he was away from the ranch. If only he hadn't gone out on that gather. If only he'd stayed home instead of hiring that babysitter. If only he'd taken better care of his responsibilities, Harry wouldn't have wandered out of the house and climbed on that corral fence. Wouldn't have fallen—

"Depends what you want for it," Wade was saying, breaking into the memories that Carter had kept stifled.

"I know you've never been eager to have anyone else living in the valley, but hey, she's single, attractive, and now that you're back—"

"I'm not looking," Carter said, cutting that suggestion off midstream. "And I'm sure there's enough other guys who would be interested in Miss Minton."

Wade shrugged as he clipped off the ends of the nail protruding from the hoof wall. "Been enough of them trying to ask her out since she came here."

"I'm not surprised." Carter heard the squeal of the metal gate between the corrals and watched as Emma pulled the halters off the horses' heads then coiled up the ropes.

He understood why the single men of Hartley Creek and area would be interested. She was pretty and spunky and had a girl-next-door appeal.

"She's a great gal, but she's turned them all down flat. I think she's been burned too many times."

Silence followed his comment. But it was the comfortable silence of old friends. Carter had missed that.

In the past two years Carter had worked as a ranch hand in Northern B.C., a wrangler for a stock contractor in Peace River and, recently, laying pipe for a pipeline in the Territories. That was where he had been when his grandmother had her heart attack.

He never stayed in one place long enough to create a connection or to build a sense of community. Which had suited him just fine.

But standing here, watching Wade work, not talking, just being, he found he missed this place he knew as well as he knew his own face.

Wade looked up at him, as if sensing his melancholy. "Did you miss the place? The work?"

Carter bit his lip, not sure what to say. "I missed parts of it. I missed seeing my family. Nana, the cousins. You and Miranda."

"I missed you too, man," Wade said. To Carter's surprise, he saw the glint of moisture in his friend's eyes.

The sight of Wade's unexpected tears created an answering emotion that he fought to push down. Emotions took over, and he didn't dare go down that road. Not alone, as he was now.

"I couldn't come back, Wade. I couldn't."

"I know, but you're here now."

"You may as well know," Carter said, taking a breath and plunging in, "I'm not coming back here to stay."

Wade frowned, pushing his glasses up his nose. "What? Why not? I thought that was the reason you came back."

"My Nana's heart attack was the main reason I'm here." Carter held his friend's puzzled gaze and steeled himself to the hurt in Wade's voice. "I can't live here. I can't come back. I'm going to sell the place. Sell the Rocking K."

Chapter Three

Emma looked up from her Bible and glanced over at Adam, still sleeping in the bunk across the cabin from her. The morning sun slanted across the bed, a splash of gold.

What was she going to tell him?

Yesterday, after working with Banjo, she had come to get Elijah when Wade was done shoeing him. Then she overheard Carter's determined voice say, "I'm going to sell the place."

If Carter Beck was selling the ranch, would she still have a chance at getting the acreage? For that matter, would she still have a job? Would she and Adam have to move again?

Her questions had fluttered like crows through her mind while, on the other side of the barn, she heard Carter make his plans. He was going into town to list the property. Nana Beck was moving off the ranch. It was time.

Each word fell like an ax blow. She'd prayed so hard to be shown what to do. When she had left her father's ranch, she had made two promises to herself, that she would trust in God to guide her life, and that Adam would always be her first priority when she made her plans.

Coming to Hartley Creek and the Rocking K Ranch fit so well with both. Here she had found work she loved, had found community and, yes, some type of family. Nana Beck had taken her and Adam in and Shannon, Carter's cousin, had become a friend to her.

And Adam. Adam loved the ranch and everything about it. It was as if he blossomed here.

So what was God trying to teach her with this? Why had He brought everything together so well only to take it away?

Sorry, Lord, I don't get what is going on right now, Emma thought, closing her Bible.

Adam stirred on his bed, stretched his arms out, then turned to her, his smile dimpling his still-chubby cheeks. His hair, a tangle of blond, stuck up in all directions. "Hi, Mommy. Is it morning? Is it time to get up yet?"

"That it is." Emma smiled and set her Bible aside. She hadn't slept well and had been awake since five o'clock. She'd been reading, praying, trying to find some guidance and direction for her life.

If nothing came of her plans for the acreage, then it was up to her to figure out her next move. She took another calming breath. *Please, Lord, help me to trust in You alone,* she prayed. *Help me to know that my hope is in You.*

Adam sat up and rubbed his eyes with his knuckles. Then he bounded out of the bed onto the floor, wide awake, ready to go. Emma envied him his energy, his ability to instantly wake up when his eyes opened.

"Am I still coming with you and Wade today?" he

asked, pulling his pajama top off over his head. "When you go up to check the cows?"

"I think so. It won't be a long ride." Four days ago she and Wade had planned to take a trip to the upper pastures to check on the grass. Wade wanted to make sure they weren't overgrazing, and she had promised Adam he could come along.

"Here, let me help you with that," she said, handing him a clean T-shirt. "Once you're changed, I want you to go wash your hands and face and get ready for breakfast."

Adam tugged the brown T-shirt over his head and yanked on his blue jeans. "Can we have breakfast with Wade and Miranda? She is making pancakes and said I had to ask if we could eat there."

"But I thought we could have breakfast here." Though she knew plain toast couldn't compete with Miranda's chocolate chip pancakes, Emma treasured her alone time with Adam.

"Mom, please?" Adam drooped his shoulders, his hands clenched together in front of him, the picture of abject sorrow and pleading. "I love, love, love chocolate chip pancakes."

Adam made the best puppy dog eyes of any child she had ever known.

"Okay. But don't ask me tomorrow."

Adam launched himself at her, giving her a huge hug. "I love you, Mommy," he said, his voice muffled against her shirt.

The clutch of her son's small arms around her waist sent a powerful wave of love washing over her. "I love you too, my little guy," she murmured, brushing down his unruly hair with her hand. "Now let's go brush your hair then see if Miranda and Wade are up yet."

Once Adam was cleaned up, they headed out the door and down the wooden steps. According to Wade, they were staying in the cabin that Carter and his grandfather had built for Shannon, Carter's oldest cousin, who lived in Hartley Creek and worked as a nurse.

When their mother died, Garret and Carter moved from the little house they had shared with Noelle Beck into the main house with their grandparents. But the town cousins, Hailey, Naomi and Shannon, came up almost every weekend and for most of the summer to stay at the ranch. Bill Beck, Carter's grandfather, came up with the idea of building a cabin for each of the girls so they could have their own place to stay when they came.

Emma loved the story, and every time she walked up to the trio of cabins nestled against the pine trees, she tried to imagine five cousins spending time together, staying overnight in one of the cabins as a group, probably sharing stories. She felt a twinge of envy for what Carter had, and wondered again how he could simply walk away from all this.

Adam clung to her hand, swinging it as they walked. The sun shone overhead. A few wispy clouds trailed across the blue sky, promising another beautiful day.

"Good morning, Mr. Carter," Adam called out.

Carter stood on the porch of the far cabin, leaning on the railing and nursing a cup of coffee. The fall of dark hair across his face and the whiskers shadowing his lean jaw made it look as if he had just woken up, as well.

Her heart skipped a little at the sight.

Then she caught herself. If she reacted to seeing him, it was because he held her future in his hands. Had nothing to do with his looks, because she wasn't looking. Men were an unnecessary complication she had no desire to bring into her and Adam's life.

"Good morning yourself," Carter said, straightening.

"Did you hear the coyotes last night?" Adam asked. "I heard them, but I think they stayed away."

Carter gave him a nod and then glanced at Emma. For a moment their eyes met and as before, something indefinable thrummed between them—an awareness that created both anticipation and discomfort.

"We're going to have pancakes at Miranda's place," Adam announced. "Are you going to come too?"

Carter's gaze broke away from hers, moving to Adam.

And in that moment Emma caught a look of deep sorrow in the blue of his eyes. His mouth tightened, and she wondered where his thoughts had gone.

"I don't think so," was all he said.

Emma glanced from him to Adam and then made a quick decision. "Honey, why don't you go ahead. I'd like to talk to Mr. Carter."

Thankfully, Adam just nodded. Then with another wave to Carter, he ran across the yard, his feet kicking up clouds of dust.

Emma looked up into Carter's impassive face with its lean, almost harsh lines. She wished she felt more confident. More sure of herself. He didn't know it, but this conversation would determine her future.

"Wade said that I should talk to you about an acreage I'm interested in."

"I don't own an acreage." Carter frowned down at her, and Emma wished she had chosen a different time and place to discuss this with him. Looking up at him placed her at a disadvantage.

"No, you don't, but there's an old yard site on the ranch

that you bought before. I know that it's easier to subdivide a yard site than to create a raw acreage. So... I was wondering if you...if you would be willing to subdivide it off. I would be willing to pay the market price. I have some money left from my father's ranch for a down payment. I'd have to move a trailer onto the yard—"

Stop. Now. You're talking too fast, and you're saying too much. Try to make some sense. Emma bit her lip and braided her fingers together, taking a breath.

"So would you be willing to subdivide it?" she asked.

Carter looked into his coffee cup as he swirled it. "Sorry, Miss Minton. But I'm putting the whole ranch up for sale."

"I... I understand that. I mean, I heard that. But would you be willing to subdivide it before you sell the ranch?"

Carter shook his head. "I've already talked to a real estate agent. The place is listed. I'm sorry, I can't do anything for you."

"I see," was all she managed, each word of his evaporating the faint wisp of hope she had nurtured.

The thought of making other plans was too much to comprehend. Finding this place had been a sheer stroke of luck and grace. Where else could she live and board her horses? Give Adam the easygoing country life she'd grown up with?

She looked up at Carter again, wondering what was going through his mind, wondering if he had told his family about his plans to sell. Nana Beck had told her the history of the place, how the family was so much a part of this ranch. She knew how much Nana and Shannon loved the ranch. How could he ignore all of that?

"What does Nana Beck think of your plans?"

As soon as she blurted out the words, she wished she

could bite her tongue. It was none of her business. How many times did she have to remind herself of that?

"I apologize. That was uncalled for," she said quietly. "It's just this place…" She looked around, letting the utter peace that surrounded the property wash over her. "It's so beautiful, and I know it's been in your family a long time. That's rare." She thought of her father and how easily he had disregarded his legacy. How he had disregarded her when his life imploded. Why were men so casual with the blessings God had given them?

"I'm not going to let history dictate my choices," Carter said, taking a final sip of his coffee. He tossed the remains out. "This place means nothing to me anymore."

Carter's reply held a heaviness that underlined the sorrow she'd seen in his eyes. He sounded like a man who had come to a place where there was no other option. She assumed it had to do with losing his son. "I'm sorry about ruining your plans," he added.

Emma gave him a tight smile. "I thought asking was worth a try." She gave a light laugh as if to show him that the dreams she had spun around owning her own place meant as little to her as the coffee he had just tossed out.

He tapped his cup against his thigh, his movements jerky. "I'm also sorry about your job," he said. "Maybe the new owner could hire you."

"Don't worry about me," she said, holding up her hand as if to placate him. "I can take care of myself and my son," she added with more bravado than she felt. "Always have."

How that would happen over the next few weeks, she wasn't sure. But she had to put it in God's hands. She had to trust that somehow, something would come up.

The jangling ring of a phone sounded from the cabin, and Carter glanced back over his shoulder.

"That's my cell phone. I should answer it." Then he was gone.

Well, wasn't that a scintillating conversation. Emma spun around on her heels and strode back to Wade and Miranda's house.

Don't count on men. Don't count on men.

The words pounded through her head in time with her steps.

She would be making her own phone calls this evening. Maybe she could take tomorrow off and go into town to look for a place for her and Adam to stay. Look for a job.

Her steps faltered at the thought, but she suppressed the negatives.

Help me to let go of my fears, Lord. Help me to trust only in You.

"Carter? You won't believe this, but I think I got a buyer for the ranch."

Carter leaned against the wall of his cabin, his hands tightening on his cell phone as the words of the real estate agent sunk in.

"Already? I just talked to you yesterday." He tucked the phone under his chin as he made up the bed. He had turned down Miranda's offer to move into the house, choosing to bunk in Hailey's cabin. If he had known that Emma and her son were staying in Shannon's place, one cabin over, he would have rethought his choice.

Seeing both of them coming out of his cousin's cabin first thing this morning was an unwelcome jolt. He had assumed they were staying in the main house.

"Tell you the truth, I had a guy from Sweden, Jurgen Mallik, who came to town about six months ago, looking for property in the valley," Pete said. "We went touring around and ended up at your place. He loved it and said, as a joke, if the place ever came up he was interested. So when you came in yesterday, I called him. He definitely wants to sign up something immediately. We can do that by fax if you want. He's very excited, very interested and very well financed."

"Wow. That's quick," Carter said, surprised at the lift of panic Pete's words created.

"Quick is what you wanted." Pete was quiet a moment, and in his hesitation Carter heard again all the warnings Pete had given him yesterday. How he shouldn't rush into this. How he had to talk it over with his family. But two years of holding on to the past and waiting was hardly rushing into things. And now that Nana, one of the main reasons he had held on to the ranch, was moving, it was all the incentive he needed to get rid of the place and move on.

"So you're sure none of your cousins are interested?" Pete continued. "Not even your brother, Garret?"

Carter threw the blanket over the bed and sat down, easing out a sigh. "He said no. And he's the only one that can come close to affording it." After talking to Nana Beck yesterday, he'd made some phone calls to his brother and cousins about the ranch.

Garret wasn't interested at all. Their cousin, Naomi, was still dealing with her fiancé's cancer and didn't have enough money. Hailey would have loved to buy the ranch, but she was swimming in student loans and was desperate to pay them off. Furthermore, she knew nothing about running a ranch.

He had expected to get the strongest protest from Shannon, but when he told her his plans, she said she understood. When he asked her what Nana Beck would think, Shannon said that he had to go ahead with his own plans. Nana needed to live in town, closer to a hospital.

Which left Carter with no recourse but to go to Pete and list the property.

"So what's the next move?" Carter asked, dragging his hands over his face.

"I'll need you to come in as soon as possible and sign up a basic agreement for sale. I'll fax a copy to Jurgen, and we'll take it from there."

"Do I need to stick around for all of that?"

"Once you sign the agreement, we can do a lot by email and phone. You don't need to stick around after the initial paperwork, though it might be helpful."

An image of Emma and Adam drifted through his mind, and he shook his head as if to dislodge it. "No. I'll be leaving. The sooner I can get away from here the better."

"Let me know when you can come in to sign, and we'll be well on our way."

"One other thing," Carter said, feeling as if he owed Emma at least this. "There's a woman who works here, Emma Minton."

"Oh, yeah. I know Emma. She's a good-looking gal."

Which made Carter wonder if Pete was one of the guys who had asked her out.

As if that mattered.

"She's asked me about subdividing an acreage off the property for her and her kid. When you talk to Jurgen, could you run it by him? See if he'd be willing to subdivide it?"

Pete sucked his breath through his teeth. "I doubt it. One of the things he liked the best about the property was that he had no close neighbors. But, hey, doesn't hurt to ask."

"Just ask him and let me know." Though he had told Emma he couldn't do anything for her, he still felt he had to at least try. Then Carter said goodbye and tossed the cell phone on the bed as he glanced around the cabin. A poster of a ski hill took up one wall. Two snowboards leaned in one corner of the cabin, both cracked in half. Remnants of Hailey's wilder days when there was no ski run too difficult, no boundary that she respected, no jump she couldn't take.

He knew the other cabins, built by Carter's grandfather for each of his three girl cousins, would hold similar detritus of their lives. Another wave of second thoughts drifted in behind the memories.

Could he sell all this? Could he walk away from the history these cabins and the ranch represented? How many pillow fights had taken place in this very cabin? How many times had he and Garret snuck out of the main house where they lived with their mother to play tricks on the girls sleeping here overnight?

His eyes fell on the Bible his grandmother had given him. On top of that lay the box with the nugget. Two small things, but they carried the weight of history and expectations.

He leaned his elbows on his knees, clasping his hands as he struggled with the memories and the responsibility. He had started working on the ranch when he was only ten years old, driving the bale wagon from the fields to the yard. Over time he graduated to the tractor, and then he started baling, as well.

Together he and his grandfather had ridden miles of fence lines, Papa Bill passing on his wisdom, his knowledge and the history of the ranch.

Regret twisted his gut. Sure he had bought the Rocking K from his grandfather, paying in sweat equity and bank loans, but the ranch was passed on to him. A ranch that had been in the family for four generations.

Could he change his mind? Couldn't he simply let things go on as usual? Would Wade be willing to carry on as a manager, or would he want to have his own place eventually?

For a moment he wished he believed God heard prayers. Because that would be convenient. To ask God for some kind of guidance, some kind of sign.

But his belief in God died two years ago when he watched that small coffin being lowered into the ground, taking his purpose in life with it.

Carter pushed himself to his feet. The decision was made. It was time to move on. Pete had found him a buyer, and that was all the sign he needed. Now all he had to do was tell Wade.

And Nana Beck.

He pulled in a long breath and reminded himself this was the right thing to do. Then he left the cabin.

The sound of laughter greeted him as he pushed open the door of Wade's house.

The first thing he saw was Adam sitting at the table, his cheeks smeared with syrup, forking a piece of pancake into his mouth. Just as his son used to.

The glimmer from the past twisted, and any regrets he had about selling the farm seemed to disappear.

Adam looked up when he came into the kitchen. "Are you going to have pancakes too, Mr. Carter?"

Carter gave him a quick shake of his head, no.

But Miranda was already setting an extra plate on the table. "Of course you're going to join us," Miranda was saying. "I'll even get Emma to make a letter C for you."

Carter glanced over at the stove, where Emma was frying pancakes. Her hair was pulled away from her face, and as she flipped the pancake she glanced over at him.

The sparkle in her eyes dimmed, and she glanced away.

Not that he blamed her. He'd been less than diplomatic this morning, and he knew it. But her chitchat about Nana and history and how wonderful the ranch was twisted the guilt knife already lodged deep in his breast.

"I'm not sticking around long," he said. "How are you feeling today?" he asked. Yesterday, she had complained about a sore back, blaming it on her pregnancy.

"A bit stiff, but that's to be expected."

Carter put his hand on her shoulder and squeezed lightly. "You make sure you take it easy," he said.

Miranda waved her hand at him. "Don't fuss. I'm fine."

Carter gave her a gentle smile, then glanced over to catch Emma watching him. He turned away again. "I need to talk to Wade, by the way."

"He's having a shower right now." Miranda grabbed Carter by the arm and pulled him toward the table. "Sit down and eat. You're practically drooling. Emma, give this man some fresh pancakes."

"You'll really like them," Adam assured him with a grin just as Emma dropped a couple of pancakes on his plate.

"I smell pancakes," Wade called out, rubbing his hands

together as he came into the kitchen. "I hope Adam didn't eat them all like he usually does."

"I don't do that," Adam complained.

Wade rubbed his head, to show him he was teasing, then flashed Carter a grin. "Glad you could join us, buddy."

In spite of Wade's smile, Carter caught an underlying note of sympathy in his voice. Since he'd been back, this was the first time Carter had stepped into the house where he used to live.

Yet another reason to get away soon. Too much subtext underneath every conversation.

"Yeah. Miranda strong-armed me into staying." He kept his tone light.

"Never mess with a pregnant woman," Miranda said. "Emma, why don't you sit down and have some breakfast? I think we have enough to eat."

"I'll throw on a few more pieces of bacon," she replied.

"Got enough of that too." Wade dropped into a chair across from Carter. "Sit down. Eat."

"Do we need more coffee?" Emma asked, not moving from her place at the stove.

"What's with the excuses? If I didn't know you better, I'd guess having the boss around was making you nervous."

To Carter's surprise, he saw a flush work its way up her neck as she sat down at the table. He doubted it was caused by nerves.

More than likely annoyance.

"I'm done." Adam licked his fingers one more time then pushed his plate away. "Can I sit on your lap, Mom?"

"Of course you can," Emma said, "But first let me wipe your hands."

Carter watched as Adam made his way around the table to Emma, unable to look away. She wiped his hands and then shifted her weight so he could sit on her lap. The domestic picture in his old kitchen teased up another memory of his nana cooking for them.

He dragged his gaze back to his foreman. "Wade, I need to talk to you. About the ranch."

"Yeah, sure. What do you need to tell me?" Wade asked, squeezing the syrup bottle over his pancakes.

Carter didn't know why he glanced over at Emma again. To his surprise, she was watching him. As if she knew what he would say.

But before Carter could speak, the phone rang. Wade reached behind him, snagging the handset off its cradle.

"Wade here," he said, tucking the phone between his shoulder and his ear as he speared a piece of bacon off the plate. Then his hand froze and his eyes widened.

"What? When?" Wade dropped his fork and gripped the phone, his fingers white. "How is he…how are they?" He got up and strode out of the kitchen, peppering the phone with anxious questions.

Miranda shot out of her chair, leaving Emma, Adam and Carter alone in the kitchen.

Emma wrapped her arms around Adam, as if to shield him from the drama unfolding in the other room.

Carter felt his own disquiet rise at the concern in Wade's voice. Then silence, then more questions. Finally, a quiet goodbye. Wade and Miranda talking to each other. Then Wade came back into the kitchen.

"What's wrong?" Carter asked, dread sweeping over him at Wade's solemn expression. "What happened?"

Wade dropped the phone on the table and then dragged his hands over his face.

"That was Mom and Dad's pastor. My mom and dad were in a car accident. It's very serious." Wade blew out his breath, looking around the kitchen but not seeing anything. "I have to go. I have to be with them. I can't be here." He turned to Carter. "Can you stay? Until I come back? Take care of the ranch?"

Carter looked at Wade, his desire to get away from the ranch superseded by his friend's need.

"Of course I'll stay," he said.

Even as he spoke the words, he glanced over at Adam, still sitting on Emma's lap.

He had no choice. Wade needed him. But as soon as he could leave, he was gone.

Chapter Four

~⚬~

"Easy now. Slow it down." Carter clucked to Banjo, easing his hand down his leg and lifting his hoof. "Good job. Good horse." He patted him, then ducked under the horse's neck to do the same on the other side.

Banjo's tan hide shone from the brushing Carter gave him. He'd been working with the horse in the open paddock for the past half hour, doing some basic groundwork before he took him out. Reestablishing the relationship he'd had with this horse when he started training him three years ago.

A year before—

He cut that thought off, frustrated with the flood of memories he'd had to endure since coming back to the ranch.

His hand on Banjo's back, he glanced around at the ranch again, fighting the twist of helpless frustration. He wasn't supposed to be here. Wade was. But Wade was in the house packing up to leave, and because of that Carter was stuck here until the buyer showed up.

His eyes drifted over the familiar contours of the mountains surrounding the valley. His mother, Noelle, had moved back onto the ranch when she was expecting him and his twin brother, Garret. He never knew who his father was and, apparently, neither did his mother. At any rate, his parentage on his father's side was never discussed.

And when their mother died of cancer when Carter and Garret were ten, there was never any question of where they would live. Here. On the ranch.

Garret and Carter had grown up in the shadows of these mountains. He knew what they looked like in winter, when the cold winds surged down their snow-covered sides. In the spring when the new leaves of the aspen trees lent a counterpoint to the dark green of the spruce and fir.

He and Garret had ridden or driven down every possible game trail in and through the hills.

And when Garret went off to university to get his engineering degree, Carter had stayed behind, working on the ranch with his grandfather and eventually buying out his share.

Carter thought he'd never leave.

"How things change," he muttered, turning back to the horse. Once he was done with Banjo, he was heading out to check on the cows. In spite of his reluctance to be here, he couldn't stop a thrill of anticipation at seeing the open fields of the upper pasture. This time of the year they would be green and lush and the cattle spread out over them, calves at foot.

"He's settled down a lot the past two days."

Emma's quiet voice from the gate startled him, and as he spun around, Banjo jumped.

"Easy, boy," Carter murmured, stroking his side as he watched Emma cross the corral, leading her horses. She wore her usual blue jeans and worn cowboy boots. Today her T-shirt was blue with a rodeo logo on the front. Some remnant of her previous life. "He's got a good heart," Carter said, catching his lead rope.

"And a good nature. He's been well trained," Emma said quietly.

Carter noticed the saddles on her two horses. "Are you going out?"

"Adam and I are riding to the upper pasture."

"I'm going up there. You don't need to come along. I know where the pasture is."

Emma shot him a frown. "I'm sure you do, but I made this plan with Wade a couple of days ago. I promised Adam he could come, and he's excited to go."

"I can do this alone," he said, feeling he had to lodge one more protest. He did not want to spend any more time with the little boy than he had to.

"I'm not going to let my son down," Emma said, a hint of steel in her voice. "He's had enough disappointments for now."

Carter knew she was referring to the nonsale of the nonacreage, but it wasn't his fault the buyer probably didn't want to subdivide.

"We'll go together then," Carter said with forced nonchalance. Adam made him feel uncomfortable, but he wasn't staying behind while a stranger did the work needed on his own ranch. Though he was selling the place, he still had a stake in the ranch's well-being. And in spite of wanting to be rid of the Rocking K, a part of him wanted to see it all one last time.

Emma's horses stamped, impatient to get going.

"I'm going to water Diamond and Dusty at the river, then I'll be back," she said.

Carter looked past her and frowned again. "Where's Adam?"

"Getting some cookies for the trip. Miranda is making up a batch to take along when they leave." Emma blew out her breath in a sigh. "I sure hope Wade's parents are okay."

She was quiet a moment, as if contemplating what Wade would have to deal with. Then she turned and led her horses to the river.

Banjo snorted and danced as Emma left with the horses.

"Easy now," he murmured, but Banjo bugled a loud whinny and Diamond stopped, tugging on his lead rope as he turned his head.

Emma tried to pull him around, but he resisted, dancing sideways. Obviously, Diamond and Banjo had bonded.

"I'll come with you," Carter said, tugging on Banjo's halter rope. "My horse could use a drink, as well."

He followed her, and both Banjo and Diamond immediately settled down.

The air, trapped in the trees edging the river, was cool. A welcome respite from the heat of the afternoon. The water burbled and splashed over the rocks, and Carter felt a sigh ease out of him. "I'd forgotten how quiet it is here," he said, glancing around as his horse drank noisily from the river.

"That's why I like coming out here to water the horses," Emma said. "Though I still can't figure out why Wade won't put a waterer in the horse corral like there is for the cows. I've seen the fittings for it coming out of the ground."

"I'm the one who won't let him," Carter said, his voice hard.

Emma shot him a puzzled glance. "Why not?"

Carter didn't want to answer the question. Obviously Wade hadn't told Emma everything. Thankfully, she sensed that he didn't want to talk about it and turned her attention back to Diamond, finger combing out the tangles in his mane.

He blew, then stamped his feet, acting like a kid getting his hair brushed.

"His hooves need trimming," Carter said, angling his chin toward Diamond's feet, eager to switch to a more mundane topic of conversation.

"I know. I haven't mastered that part of farrier work yet," Emma said. "And Wade hasn't had a chance to do it."

While he watched her, she cocked her head to one side, as if waiting for something. Then she smiled. "There's the train," Emma said.

He tilted his head, listening. Then, in the distance he heard the rumbling of the coal train, and habit made him glance at his watch. Right on time.

Dusty, her other horse, tugged at the reins, as if eager to get on with the trip, but Emma stayed where she was as the second blast of the train's horn wound its way through the valley. "I love that sound. So mournful and melancholy."

Another memory slid into Carter's mind. His grandmother stopping while she was weeding the garden to listen to the same sound. She even had the same expression on her face as Emma.

"You'll get sick enough of that noise when you hear it every day, week after week." Sylvia would complain that the train horn woke her up, but Carter had grown up with the train and seldom noticed it. He had assured her that she would eventually do the same.

"I have, and I'm not," Emma said as she led her horses back up the bank. "The routine reminds a person of where he is even if he's not aware of it. Kind of anchors you."

"Routine can deaden you too," he replied.

Emma's skeptical look at his comment as she passed him made Carter think of the miles he put on his bike and truck the past two years. The constant movement from job to job, thinking that avoiding home and familiarity would ease the pain and guilt.

Instead it was as if his sorrow was replaced by a deeper longing he couldn't fill no matter how hard he rode, how many different places he worked.

"Hey, Mom. I got cookies for our trip."

Carter's heart jumped at the sound of Adam's voice calling across the yard. He clenched his jaw and struggled once again with his reaction to Emma's little boy. He'd seen children numerous times in his travels.

He'd just never seen them riding a horse. Like Harry did. Walking around his ranch like a living reminder of what Carter didn't have anymore.

Adam sat perched on the top rail of the corral, waving a paper bag dotted with grease. "They're really good."

"Don't shake that bag too hard," Emma warned with a laugh. "You'll lose the cookies."

"And I might scare the horses," he added, lowering the bag. "Can I come down?" he asked, shifting his weight toward the edge of the fence.

"Just stay there until I get Diamond and Dusty tied up," Emma said, leading the horses past Adam.

Carter held back while Emma walked her horses

through the gate, even as his gaze slipped, against his will, back to Adam, rocking back and forth on the top rail of the fence.

Carter ducked under Banjo's neck. Adam startled and pulled back.

"Mommy," he called as he flailed his arm, holding on to the bag of cookies with the other hand.

He was falling, and Emma was too far away to help. Carter reached up and snagged him around the waist, steadying him as he slipped off the fence.

"I want my mommy," Adam said, pushing at Carter with one hand, as he tried to catch his balance. Banjo shied while Carter juggled Adam and the halter rope.

"Let me get Banjo settled," Carter said to Adam, glancing over his shoulder at his horse, who was dancing around, ears back. "Hold still. I don't want you to get hurt."

Adam stopped pushing. Carter shifted him onto his hip, caught his balance and pulled the horse's head around.

"Whoa, boy. Easy now," he murmured, walking Banjo around in a circle. His horse took a quick sidestep as he shook his head and then blew. But his ears pricked up, and Carter knew he had the horse's attention. "It's okay," he murmured, reassuring the horse.

"Will my bag of cookies scare him?" Adam said in a quiet voice, now resting one hand on Carter's shoulder.

"I don't think so," Carter said, his own heart faltering at Adam's touch. It had been two years since he held a little child. Two years since a child's arm laid on his shoulder.

Adam smelled of fresh baking and warm sun and little

boy. Longing and pain rose up in Carter, and he didn't know which emotion was the strongest.

"Is everything okay?" Emma asked quietly.

"We're fine," Carter said, surprised at the tightness of his throat. When Adam saw his mother, though, he reached out for her.

Carter felt a sense of loss as Adam's weight came off his hip and the little boy's hand slipped off his shoulder. For just a moment, the emptiness had eased. For a nanosecond, his arms hadn't felt so empty.

But right behind that came the pain.

"Sorry about that," Emma said, setting Adam on the ground and then tousling his hair. "I'm sure Adam didn't mean to startle Banjo."

"No. He didn't do anything." Carter looked down at Adam, his heart beginning a heavy pounding. "I startled him, that's all. I hope Adam's okay."

Adam squinted up at him, his face scrunched up as if trying to figure Carter out. "I'm okay," he said quietly. "Thanks for helping me and for not getting mad at me."

Carter couldn't speak. How could he explain to this little boy the complications his presence created and the memories that resurfaced around him? It wasn't Adam's fault he was the same age Harry was when he died. But every time Carter saw him, the reminder of his loss plunged into his heart like a knife.

He caught Emma's enigmatic expression. As if trying to puzzle him out.

Don't bother, he wanted to tell her. *It's not worth it.*

But as their gazes caught and meshed, she gave him a careful smile, as if forgiving him his confusion.

He wasn't going to return it. He was also going to look away. But he couldn't.

Something about her called to him, and as he looked into her soft brown eyes, emotions shifted deep within him.

"Are we going now?"

Adam's voice jerked Carter back to reality and he looked away.

"That is the plan," Emma replied. "But I want to go say goodbye to Wade and Miranda first. They'll probably be gone by the time we return." She looked at Carter. "Did you want to come too?"

"I've already said goodbye," Carter said, dismissing her with a wave of his hand.

"I'll wait here with Mr. Carter." Adam flashed him a grin as if all was well between them.

"Make sure you don't eat all the cookies," Emma called back as she walked away.

"The cows are looking good," Emma said, leaning forward, her hands stacked on the saddle horn. Her eyes swept the green hills edged with fir trees, and she grinned as a half dozen calves chased each other along a fence line. Their tails were straight up and their legs stretched out. Running for no reason other than the fact that they could. Goofy creatures.

"Looks like we've got more animals on the pasture than other years," Carter said, shifting in the saddle. "I've never seen the grass so long up here before. You've done good work here."

His quiet approval warmed her heart for some silly reason. *It's because he's your boss,* she reminded herself.

"We've been doing a bit more intensive grazing this year," Emma replied, keeping her attention on the calves and not the quiet man beside her. On the ride up here he'd been quiet, watching her as if trying to figure her out.

His attention made her uncomfortable but, curiously, also created a feeling of anticipation.

"We've made the pastures smaller and moved the cows more often," she said. "Rotational grazing is more labor intensive, but I believe it lengthens the life of the pasture, which makes it possible to graze more cows on less land."

"That's a lot of fence to run."

"We use electric fencing. Run it off a solar-powered battery. That's why we come up here more often—to make sure the fence is working."

Adam's horse, Dusty, stamped, telegraphing his impatience with the lack of movement.

"Can I go up to the river?" Adam asked, cookie crumbs stuck in one corner of his mouth. "I think Dusty needs to walk a bit more, and I want to go look at that cabin." He turned to Carter. "Me and my mom found it," he explained. "It has some neat stuff in it that I want to put in the tree fort. Did you see the tree fort at the ranch, Mr. Carter?"

Carter nodded.

"I found it in the trees by the barn," Adam said, warming to his topic. "But it's not finished yet. My mom said she didn't want to do too much work on it, 'cause we might be getting the acreage. Then we can build our own fort there too. And it will be even cooler than the one we found on the ranch. And there is some really cool stuff in the cabin that I want to put in my own fort. Lanterns and stuff. Did you and your boy make that tree fort?"

Carter didn't reply, but Emma guessed, from the pensive look on Carter's face, that Adam's mention of his son hurt.

"I think Mr. Carter gets the picture," Emma said, rescuing Carter from her son's monologue. "But I don't want you going to the cabin," she warned him. "It's too far away. Just stay close, and we'll be with you in a minute." Emma wanted to check the solar panel on the fence.

"Okay, but we have to get the stuff from the cabin before someone else takes it." With that warning, Adam clucked to Dusty and, with a twist of his wrist, got him turned around.

"He seems pretty confident," Carter said, watching Adam leave.

"He's been riding horses since he was a baby," she admitted, swinging her leg over Diamond's back as she dismounted. "I used to take him up on the saddle using those buddy stirrups. He loved it. Always asked to come along when me and my dad went to check the cows. We went out a lot when I was back on the ranch." She took a breath, forcing herself to stop. Nerves, she figured. Carter's presence was a bit unsettling and she blamed her blabbering on that.

Just check the fence, she reminded herself, dropping Diamond's lead rope on the ground.

She walked over to the panel and checked the connections. All was well. Now all she needed was the tester, a small box with a digital readout that would tell her how much power was on the fence.

Carter had dismounted and was stretching his back. "It's been too long," he muttered as he took a few stiff steps.

"I'm sorry. I should have taken a break, but I didn't want to insult you by thinking you needed it," Emma said, daring a smile.

"I could have said something."

Indeed, all the way up here it had been Adam who filled the quiet with chitchat about the ranch, the horses, how the garden Miranda had put in was doing, the fair that was coming to town and, finally, the old cabin in the hills above the pasture that he wanted to get stuff from.

It wasn't lost on Emma that everything Adam said centered on the ranch. It was all he'd known since they moved here.

But Carter had remained quiet. Once in a while Emma had looked back to see if he was okay. Each time she caught him looking around, and occasionally she saw a smile. Did he miss the ranch when he was gone?

"How did you manage to teach your horse how to ground tie?" Carter asked.

Emma looked down at the lead rope she had left coiled on the ground. "Took time and patience, but Diamond figured it out eventually."

"Very impressive."

Emma bent her head over her saddlebag, wishing his compliment didn't warm her. She was supposed to be immune to him. Aloof.

But there had been a moment, when he caught Adam off the fence, that she intercepted a look of raw yearning on his face. And it hit her right in the heart, made it impossible to be indifferent to him.

She found the tester and yanked it out, but her jerky movements made the ground wire come loose. As she pulled it out, the tester's wire got twisted around the extra rope she always carried.

Everything came out in a tangle, and with a sigh she laid it on the grass by the wire fence and tugged off her gloves.

"Let me help you," Carter said, kneeling down beside her.

"It's okay. I can manage." But his nearness made her hands clumsy and unresponsive, leading to a worse mess.

"So have you made any plans for after the sale of the ranch?" she asked, latching onto the one subject guaranteed to maintain a distance between them.

"No solid plans. I'll see what happens when the time comes, same as I have for a while now." He pulled the box of the tester free from the tangle and unplugged the wire coming from it.

In that moment their hands brushed, and Emma jerked hers back.

This netted her a puzzled look from Carter. This was silly. Why was she so tense around him?

She leaned back on her heels, her hands still holding the rope she had just freed. "So you've just been moving from place to place?"

"Pretty much. I just try to find a job where they provide a place to live—either a camp job or a ranch job." Carter shot her a quick glance as he shoved the grounding portion of the tester into the grass.

Emma's hands slowed as she looked past Carter to the land flowing away from them, the mountains with their jagged lines of purple against the sky.

"I can't imagine being away from here."

Carter's eyes followed the direction of her gaze, and she saw his features relax. In that moment, she caught a sense of longing in his eyes.

"I missed it, in some ways." A melancholy smile drifted across his lips. "I grew up here, after all. As did my mother, my grandfather and his father."

"Nana Beck told me a bit of the history of the place,"

Emma said. "But when she talked about the necklace, that was the first I'd heard about August and Kamiskahk."

Carter released a light laugh. "My cousins Hailey, Shannon and Naomi liked that story more than me and Garret did when we were kids."

"Why?"

"August gave up searching for gold for the sake of a mere girl. Garret and I both said we wouldn't have done that. In fact, Garret and I even went up into the mountains once, looking for the same gold, armed with shovels and bags to carry all the gold we were going to find." Carter toyed with the contacts for the fence tester, squinting up at the mountain above them. "Of course, at age ten, girls weren't a real priority."

Emma laughed, trying to imagine two young boys hiking up the mountain, shovels over their shoulders.

"I don't imagine you found any," she said.

"Nope. Naomi was very disappointed with us when we came back empty-handed. She had imagined all the pretty things she was going to make with the gold we found. Hailey just figured we could sell it and get rich." He laughed again, and in that moment, Emma caught a glimpse of what Carter must have been like before his loss. She saw a man connected to a place and a family that he cared for.

And she also felt a twinge of jealousy at the connections he had. Cousins. Grandparents. A place that had history and continuity.

"Shannon didn't have any plans for the gold?"

"Shannon's always been the most practical of us all. She knew me and Garret would come back empty-handed. So no, she didn't have any plans." He laughed, then placed the contacts on the electric fence to test the power. "And speaking of plans, what do you plan to do, once the ranch is sold?" he asked.

Emma reluctantly returned to the present, wondering why he cared about her plans. "I guess I'll have to decide once that happens." She still planned on going into town on Thursday to look for a job and, hopefully, a place where she could board her horses.

Carter looked up at her, his eyes holding hers. "Again, I'm sorry about how this is all coming down for you."

She didn't want his sympathy, but at the same time, it still created a faint connection. She felt sorry for him, after all, and for even bigger things than the loss of a job.

"Well, that's life." She shrugged and glanced down at the meter in his hand. "How's the reading on the fence?"

Carter glanced down at the readout. "Looks good," he said. Then he rolled the wire back around the tester. "I could talk to the buyer. See if maybe you could work for him. I'm not sure Wade wants to stay on, but it might be an option for you."

"I want more than just a job out of the ranch. I'm looking for a place to settle down. A home. So Adam and I will be moving on. Again." Why did she tack that "again" on? It sounded whiny, and if there's one thing Emma knew, "whiny" turned men away faster than tears. She learned that quick enough from Adam's father and from Karl.

She pushed the bitter memories aside. That was in the past. She had to focus on the future.

"But where would you go?" Carter asked.

"I guess that's nothing you need to concern yourself with," she said, catching Diamond's rope and vaulting back into the saddle.

As soon as she got Diamond turned around, she regretted her snappy reply. His question was a way of making conversation, but it dragged out concerns and worries Emma struggled to keep suppressed.

Yet, as she headed down the trail to where Adam had gone, she wished she'd been more diplomatic.

She also wished she knew what it was about Carter that made her feel extra edgy around him.

Chapter Five

Carter pulled up on Banjo's bridle and blew out a sigh of relief. Thankfully, he had made it to the yard before Emma and Adam. Adam wanted to stop a ways back to check out some mushrooms growing along the river so Carter, seeing a way to salvage his pride, said he would meet them at the corral.

Without them as witnesses, he allowed himself to groan as he dismounted, muscles he hadn't used in years protesting every movement.

Banjo turned his head as if to ask Carter what the problem was.

"It's been too long," he muttered to Banjo, absently rubbing the horse's neck. "That kid is in better shape than I am."

He put his hands in the small of his back and stretched, then rotated his shoulders. He was tender in places he knew he would feel for the next few days. It would take a bit more riding before he could be as fluid in the saddle as Emma.

He shot a worried glance over his shoulder, but thankfully she wasn't coming up the riverbank yet.

He took a few halting steps, pain shooting up his legs, and then sighed again as he unwound Banjo's halter rope from the saddle horn. He led the horse to the corral by the tack shed, every step causing pain in one muscle or the other. He would be a hurtin' unit tomorrow.

He undid the cinch and unsaddled Banjo. By the time he got the bridle off, his horse whinnied and turned his head, signaling Emma and Adam's approach.

"Look at the cool mushroom I found, Mr. Carter. There was a whole bunch."

Carter glanced over at Adam who held up a creamy mushroom with an undulating cap. "Chanterelles are good eating," he said quietly. "And they are hard to find around here."

"Mom said she was going to cook them. With our supper."

Supper. The thought made his stomach growl. All he'd had to eat since breakfast was a couple of cookies and a granola bar that Emma had shared with him, insisting that she didn't mind.

Nana Beck had gone with Shannon to town for a doctor's appointment and to look at potential places to live, so he was on his own for dinner. Looked as if cold cereal was on the menu.

Emma dismounted in one graceful motion and then helped Adam out of the saddle. With quick, efficient movements that made Carter both envious and a bit humiliated, she tugged the cinches loose on both horses and pulled the saddles off one at a time.

He felt like an unchivalrous heel, but manhandling his own saddle onto the saddle tree in the tack shed was all he could manage.

"A bit stiff?" she asked, a smile hovering at one corner of her mouth as she dropped the saddles on their respective trees.

He was about to protest but realized it was futile.

"Oh, yeah." He dropped the saddle blanket on an empty rack and groaned again.

"Make sure you do some stretches before you go to bed tonight. A brisk walk helps too." Emma looped the cinch ropes over the horns of the saddles. "I'm sorry the ride was so long. I forgot that you hadn't ridden in a while."

Carter rubbed the tops of his legs and eased out a sigh. "Over a year ago."

"You didn't have to come," she said quietly, snagging the curry comb and brushes off a shelf.

"Until the ranch changes ownership, it's still my responsibility. But now all I want to do is go lie down in my cabin and try to work up the energy to think about dinner."

Emma picked a clump of horsehair out of the brush, avoiding his gaze. "About that… Miranda made a casserole for us. I'll go heat it up, and if you want we can eat it together in the house. I was thinking of frying up the mushrooms to go with it," she added, "if that extra incentive will change your mind."

He looked over at her and caught a dimple forming in a cheek that held a smudge of dirt. She pushed her hair back from her face, and as she held his gaze her soft brown eyes held a gentle light of understanding.

He felt a light thrum of awareness, and the thought of eating with her created a sense of anticipation. But it also meant spending time with Adam.

"Just come," she said, her voice quiet, as if she understood his reluctance. "It's only food."

She gave him a gentle smile, and as their eyes met he dismissed his other concerns. "Sounds like a plan. Thanks." Then he held out his hand for the brushes. "Give those to me. I'll finish up with the horses."

"I can do them."

He waved his hand in a "gimme" gesture. "I'm just stiff. The work will do me good."

With a light laugh, she relinquished the brushes. "Okay. Adam and I will be in the house. Give me about half an hour." Then she spun around and strode out of the shed.

In the quiet she left in her wake, second thoughts followed. Could he really sit down in his old house and have dinner with Emma and Adam? Could he really act as if everything was okay?

Carter shook his questions aside. It was time, he figured. If he was selling this ranch, it was time to lay some memories to rest, as well. Then he could walk away from this place with no second thoughts. No regrets.

Emma set the third plate on the table, wondering for the umpteenth time what got into her when she invited Carter for dinner.

Mistake. Mistake.

The words had resonated through her head with each tick of the clock on the timer counting down when the casserole would be ready.

The mushrooms were sautéing in the pan, and Adam lay sprawled on the floor behind the table. She couldn't see what he was doing, but he was humming to himself, happy.

"Today was a good day, wasn't it, buddy?" she asked.

"Yup."

"Did you enjoy the riding?"

"Yup."

"What was the best part of the day?" Open-ended questions, she reminded herself.

"The mushrooms."

"Why were they the best?"

"Because."

Emma turned off the heat under the pan and walked around the table to where Adam lay putting together a puzzle. She crouched down and grinned at him.

"Are you playing a game with me?"

He looked up at her and flashed a grin. "Yup."

She rubbed the top of his head. "I wondered what you were up to. For a minute there you sounded like Mr. Carter."

"He doesn't like to talk, does he?" Adam asked, reaching for another piece. Emma thought of the memories Carter had shared with her. He was more reserved around Adam, though.

"Mr. Carter has a lot on his mind. That's why he's so quiet," she said. "He's not like your mommy, who likes to fill the empty spaces in conversation with lots and lots of words." She picked up a puzzle piece and fitted it in an empty space, and then she pushed herself to her feet and turned around.

Carter Beck stood in the doorway, a light frown creasing his forehead, and she wondered if he had heard what she and Adam were talking about.

"Supper is ready," she said, glancing nervously at the timer, deciding to pretend he hadn't.

"Smells good in here," Carter said, taking a step farther into the kitchen. He angled his head, as if looking at Adam on the floor behind the table.

Adam got up and slipped into the chair he usually sat at. He pointed at the place setting across from him. "That's where you're supposed to sit, Mr. Carter."

Carter gave him a quick nod but glanced over at Emma. "Is there anything I can do?"

"I think I've got it under control. If you want to contribute, you can put these on the table." She handed him the bowl holding the sautéed mushrooms, then gave him a careful smile, which he returned.

She felt her cheeks flush and blamed it on the heat in the kitchen as she pulled open the oven door. The casserole bubbled, and steam slipped out from the lid.

It went on the table as well, and then there was nothing left to do but sit down.

Carter waited until she sat down. Just a small gesture, but it touched her. Whenever Karl came over to eat, he would serve himself even before she and her father sat down.

When they were all seated, there was a moment of quiet. Then, to her surprise, Adam reached across the table, one hand outstretched to Emma, the other to Carter.

Carter glanced from his hand to Emma, as if asking her what to do.

"We usually pray before our meals," she gently suggested, taking Adam's hand.

"And we hold hands," Adam added.

Carter gave a tight nod, then reached across the table and caught Adam's hand. But Adam's little gesture had put her in an uncomfortable position.

"Mom, you have to hold Mr. Carter's hand," Adam said, giving her hand a squeeze. "That's the way we always did it at Grandpa's."

"Of course," she said with a light laugh. As she put her

hand in Carter's, she felt ridiculously aware of the size of his hand and the callouses on his palms.

Then she bowed her head, trying to focus her thoughts on God and not on the rough hand that held her own.

"Thank You, Lord, for this food," she prayed, letting herself be drawn into God's presence. "Thank You for this day and the wonderful time we had outside in Your creation. Be with Miranda and Wade as they travel, and be with Wade's parents. Be with Nana Beck as she looks for a place in town. Help her to be better. Bless this food unto our bodies and help us to be thankful for all You give us and help us to love You. Amen."

She kept her head bowed for a moment longer, then slipped her hands out of Adam's and Carter's.

"So, I hope you like chicken casserole," she said with false brightness as she got up to serve the food. "Miranda's a great cook and does a fantastic job on this casserole. I've had it a bunch of times, so I'm sure you'll like it. I'm pretty sure it's hot enough. It was bubbling when I took it out of the stove, I mean, oven."

"Why are you talking so much, Mom?" Adam asked, handing Emma his plate.

Because she was nervous. Because when they were outside, there was space and distance between her and Carter and Adam.

Now they were all together in this small kitchen, and she felt as if there wasn't enough room or enough air.

But obviously she kept all this to herself while she shot her son a warning look. He frowned and opened his mouth as if to add more words of wisdom to the conversation.

"Do you want some salad?" she asked him, cutting him off.

He wrinkled his nose, thankfully distracted. "I don't like salad." He pulled his plate back, just to make sure she didn't sneak some on while he wasn't looking.

Emma held her hand out for Carter's plate, avoiding his gaze, excessively conscious of his presence and wishing for a moment she hadn't invited him. But what else could she have done? Let him sit in a cabin all by himself?

"Sure smells good," Carter said, taking his plate from Emma.

He filled the rest of his plate with salad and waited until she'd served herself to start eating. Again, a small courtesy, but it gave her a glimpse of how he treated women. He seemed at ease, which made Emma relax a bit. She was being silly. They had spent most of the day together. Why was she so conscious of him now?

Because this was such a family moment, she thought, sprinkling salt over her food. A man, a woman and a child sharing a meal together.

Her heart quavered as she set the salt shaker down. How often had she pictured herself, Karl and Adam sitting around their own kitchen table sharing a meal, just the three of them?

She stabbed her salad, glancing over at Carter, determined to act naturally. "How are the mushrooms?"

"Really good," he said, giving her a cautious smile.

"I think they taste like elastics," Adam said.

Emma laughed, and to her surprise, a smile twitched at the corner of Carter's mouth.

"Did you live here when you were little?" Adam asked Carter, stabbing a noodle from the casserole and holding it up for inspection.

Carter's only reply was a quick nod.

"Were you borned here?" Adam continued, undaunted by Carter's seeming reticence.

"Yes. I was."

"On the ranch? Here?" Adam poked his finger down at the floor.

"Actually, yeah."

"Was your boy borned here?"

"Yes." His reply was quiet, and Emma sensed Adam wasn't going to get much more out of Carter.

"Did your wife choose home birth?" she asked, trying to maintain a semblance of conversation.

"Not on purpose." Carter gave her a quick smile but turned his attention back to his food.

"I was borned in a hospital," Adam offered. He glanced at Emma. "Why wasn't I borned in a house?"

"Because your mother is a scaredy-cat and liked to have doctors and medication handy," she said, giving her son a wink so he would know she was kidding. A bit.

"You're not a scaredy-cat," Adam said, mumbling around a mouthful of pasta. He turned back to Carter, determined to engage the man one way or the other. "My mommy and I were riding and we met a bear and my mommy didn't get scared or anything. The horses got scared but my mommy told me to hang on and she made the horses get quiet again. Then the bear was gone. So my mommy is not a scaredy-cat."

This caught Carter's attention. "Really? Where was that?"

Emma glanced at Adam, half hoping he would handle the question for her, but Carter was looking at her and Adam was frowning at his plate.

"Adam and I went on a short trip to the Ya Ha Tinda, past Sundre," she said, glad to have fixed on a neutral topic. "We were up in the alpine, and a grizzly bear happened to wander across the trail."

"Really? Been a while since I've seen a grizzly. You must have been pretty tense."

"I was, but I had Adam to think about, and I couldn't afford to get too scared."

"I imagine the horses freaked."

"They spun around and were heading back down the trail, but I had to get them turned around so I could see what was happening. Thankfully, Adam hung on, and I got things sorted out. By the time I did, the bear was gone."

"Wow. That's some horsemanship." Carter sounded impressed and Emma couldn't help a flicker of pride.

She shot him a quick glance, surprised to see him looking at her. Their eyes met, held, and a tiny spark of awareness flashed between them.

Don't go there, Emma thought. *This is temporary.*

"My mommy is really brave," Adam put in, breaking the moment. "Was Harry's mommy brave?"

Carter stiffened as Adam spoke. He blinked and then looked down at his half-finished casserole. He poked some of the noodles around then dropped his knife and fork on the plate with a clatter. "You know, this was great. But I think I'm full." He shoved his chair back, the legs screeching on the worn linoleum, and strode to the counter, depositing his plate on it. "Thanks for dinner," he said absently, and then he grabbed his hat off the end of the counter and left.

"Is Mr. Carter mad?" Adam asked, lowering his hands to his lap, his lip quivering. "Did I make him mad?"

Emma suspected that he had. And she also suspected

that Carter's anger was born out of loss. But the sorrow lacing her son's voice cut her to the core.

She reached over and stroked her son's hand then took it in hers. "Mr. Carter is a very sad man. And I think that you remind him of his little boy, Harry."

This made Adam smile. "I do?" He swiped the back of his hand across his nose.

"Yes, you do. Maybe you shouldn't talk about Harry so much. Because we don't want to make Mr. Carter sad again, okay?"

Adam seemed to consider this, then nodded. "Okay."

"Now finish up your casserole and I'll let you watch *The Wind in the Willows* while I'm cleaning up."

This was all the incentive he needed. Five minutes later, his plate was licked clean, his hands washed and he lay curled up in a chair in front of Wade and Miranda's television, entertained by the adventures of Mole, Ratty and Toad.

Emma made quick work of the dishes. There was half of the casserole left, which they could have for dinner tomorrow. As she covered it up and put it in the refrigerator, she wondered whether she would repeat dinner with Carter.

Obviously Carter felt uncomfortable around Adam, and while she understood why, she didn't know how to deal with this every day. It wasn't fair to Adam, and it was too hard on her.

She lowered the dishes into the soapy water, her mind and heart at war. She needed this job, but was it worth putting Adam through all this tension? She could try to keep Adam away from Carter but how to do that and help on the ranch at the same time? Besides, once the ranch was sold, she was on her way anyhow. Why postpone the decision?

But then Carter would be left here alone. And that thought disturbed her on another level.

Dear Lord, she prayed as she scrubbed the dishes, *help me around this little mess.*

Twenty minutes later she cleaned up the last dish. She was about to leave for the living room when the phone rang.

"Is this Miranda?" a woman's voice asked when she picked up.

"No. I'm sorry, Miranda and Wade will be gone for a while. This is Emma Minton."

"The girl who works on the ranch?"

"That's right." Emma frowned. "Can I ask who is calling?"

"I'm sorry. It's Kim Groot. Miranda was telling me about you the last time I called. I'm… I'm Harry's grandmother."

Chapter Six

"You are Carter's mother-in-law?" Emma clutched the handset, wishing Carter could have taken this call. This wasn't her place. She shouldn't be the one talking to this woman.

"I've been staying in touch with Miranda, hoping to connect with Carter. She, uh, well, she called me to tell me...that Carter was back." In the pause following this, Emma heard a light sniff, followed by a wavering intake of breath. "I'm so sorry. It's just... I haven't talked to Carter since Harry's funeral. Is he...is he there?"

"I'm sorry, no." Emma leaned against the wall, clutching the handset. She felt a surge of pity for this woman who had lost so much. A daughter, a grandson and, it seemed, Carter, as well. "He's staying in one of the cabins. I can take your number and get him to call you."

A sigh followed this. "You can try. My husband and I have been trying to call him on his cell phone, but he doesn't answer."

Emma frowned, puzzled as to why Carter was avoiding Harry's grandparents. Surely he would want to talk to them?

She walked to the counter and pulled a pen and paper out of a drawer. "Give me your number and I'll mention it to him."

"I think he knows it, but I'll give you the information anyway."

Emma tucked the handset between her shoulder and ear while she scribbled down the number. "Okay. I think I've got it."

"Thanks so much," Kim said. "When you see Carter, could you please tell him that we miss him? And that we love him."

"I'll do that," she said.

She said goodbye, then wrote a note to Carter asking him to please call Kim Groot. She put Kim's number under that and tacked it to the bulletin board under the piece of paper with the number of Wade's parents' home.

She hesitated, wondering if she should call Wade and find out what was happening.

Later, she told herself. First she had other things to deal with. She went to the living room. The television was still on, but Adam lay curled up on the couch, fast asleep.

She knelt down beside him and stroked his hair away from his face, her heart growing soft at the sight of his relaxed features, his rosy cheeks. The utter innocence of her son asleep.

And his utter vulnerability.

As she fingered some hair away from his face, she thought again of the various hurts and disappointments he'd already had to deal with in his life. Karl. Her father's death. Having to leave the ranch.

And now the stress of Carter's reaction to him.

Again she reminded herself of the vow she made after Karl had left her and Adam. How she would always put

Adam's needs and care first. How his well-being was her first priority.

And if being on the ranch was causing him problems, she had to make a decision.

She wrapped an afghan around him, then bent over and fitted her arms under his knees and around his shoulders. As she went to lift him, she stumbled.

When did he get so heavy? She still thought of him as her little boy, but he wasn't so little anymore. As she shifted him in her arms, she felt a stirring of nostalgia. She felt as if only a year had passed since she could cradle him close to her chest. Now his legs and head dangled over her arms. One day he would be taller than she.

Shouldering the door open, she quashed that thought, far too aware of the responsibilities he created now. Bad enough that he would be starting school soon. She didn't need to project her worries too far in the future.

She stepped outside into the cool of the evening, his weight slowing her steps. His head lolled against her chest, and she looked down at him. He was so precious to her. He was all she had.

And it was that realization that steeled her for what she had to do next.

Once in the cabin, she managed to get his pajamas on without waking him too much. Then, when he was tucked in his bed, the blanket pulled up around his rosy cheeks, she sat a moment, watching him. He was her responsibility, and she was the only one who could protect him.

When his breathing was deep and heavy, she pushed herself to her feet, fear thrumming through her.

Please, Lord, she prayed as she stepped out of the cabin. *Please let me make the right decision. Help me to trust You and to trust that You will help me take care of my boy.*

Dusk was gathering as she walked across the yard. Golden light glowed from the windows of Carter's cabin.

She sent up another quick prayer as she walked up the steps and knocked on the door.

Carter opened the door, frowning at her. "Is everything okay?" The light of the cabin backlit him, throwing his features in shadow. He cut an imposing figure, and for a split second she wanted to change her mind. "Is Adam—"

"Adam is sleeping," she said, her hands clasped in front of her, determined to follow through on this. "Can I…can I talk to you?"

Carter stepped aside, opening the door farther. "Sure. Of course. Come in."

Emma would have preferred to talk to him outside. He still made her uncomfortable, but saying no looked rude. So she nodded and stepped inside.

"Can I get you anything," he asked as he pulled an old chair out for her. "Tea? Coffee?"

"Actually, I'm fine," she said, holding up one hand. "I'm not staying that long."

Carter shrugged then pulled out an old armchair from beside the stove for her to sit on. When Carter dropped to the edge of the bed, she sat down, as well.

"So what can I do for you?" He rested his elbows on his knees, clasping his hands as he leaned forward. His blue eyes met hers, and Emma couldn't stop a glimmer of attraction as a smile tipped up one corner of his mouth.

He seemed more relaxed than he had been around Adam, which stiffened her resolve. "I need to talk to you about Adam," she said, getting directly to the point.

Carter frowned. "Sure. What about him?"

She rubbed her hands on her thighs, trying to formulate what she wanted to say. "You seem uncomfortable around him."

Carter straightened, his gaze dropping to his hands. "What do you mean?"

"You know what I mean," Emma said, lowering her voice. Trying to sound nonconfrontational. Understanding. "It wasn't as obvious when we were out checking the cows in the pasture, but it was there, as well. Supper time was when it really came to a head."

Carter's frown deepened, but he said nothing.

"In fact, he asked me why you were angry with him."

Carter pushed himself off his bed, turning away from her. "I'm not angry with him. I…" His sentence trailed off as he tunneled his hand through his hair.

"I know you're not angry with him, but that's how he's reading your actions. And I'm guessing it was because this evening was uncomfortable for you. I'm sorry that we invited you. I mean, not sorry in the sense that I regret it for my sake…" She caught herself, stumbling along through this potential conversational minefield while Carter stood with his back to her, his hands now planted on his hips. "I… I mean for your sake. I'm sorry for your sake. It must have been difficult to see Adam sitting in the kitchen. And I'm guessing it was a stark reminder of…of your son."

She stopped there, waiting for a reaction from him.

Carter grabbed the back of his neck, still turned away from her. Still silent, but his resistance was a tangible force swirling around the cabin.

She drew in a long breath, forcing herself to continue. She had to get this out of the way.

"I know from talking to Wade and your grandmother that you haven't been back here since the accident," she said, her heart pushing heavily against her chest. "So you haven't had a chance to get used to the idea he isn't here anymore. And I'm sure seeing Adam…seeing me in that kitchen was difficult." She closed her eyes and sucked in a deep breath, desperately sending up scattered prayers. She was doing this all wrong. She was only making this worse for him.

Carter turned around, holding her gaze. "Is this why you came? To tell me that you understand what I'm going through?" His words lay heavy between them.

"Partly," she said, licking her lips, her hands like ice. "But… I had another reason."

"Like telling me how sorry you feel for me? Telling me how sad it is that I lost my son and that I'll get over it?"

Oh, Lord, what have I started?

She waited, letting the silence ease away the echoes of his voice. Then she took another breath. "I had no intention of trying to give you advice or to minimize what you've gone through. I'm only trying to tell what I'm seeing from my side of the situation and how it's—"

"Situation? What situation?"

Emma squeezed her hands into fists, praying for patience. Sure, he was a grieving father, and, sure, he lost a lot. But she had a problem to solve, and if no solution was in sight she had to make a major decision.

"While I respect your sorrow and grief, it's causing a problem for my son," Emma said, looking down at her hands, her fingers braided together on her lap. "As badly as I feel for you, my…my situation is that Adam and his well-being are my first priority. And right now, he's afraid of you. And if that doesn't change, I can't continue to work under these circumstances."

Silence followed this formal pronouncement, and Carter turned around then slowly dropped onto the bed. He grabbed his head with his hands, his fingers clenching in his hair.

"I know. I'm sorry."

His admission surprised her. Given his frustration, she thought he would simply tell her, fine. Leave.

He released his breath, then looked up at her.

"I know I'm uncomfortable around Adam. And you're right. He does remind me of…of my son." Carter looked away and pulled in another shaky breath. "And it does hurt.

"But right now, to keep the ranch going, I need you to stay. You know how things work here. I haven't been around enough to know your and Wade's system." He lifted his shoulders in a deep sigh. "I don't know how my own ranch runs. And until the buyer comes or Wade returns, I need your help."

Though she knew he referred to the ranch, on another level it felt good to know that Carter needed her.

"And I'm sorry about Adam," Carter continued. "He's a good kid. I like him…" Carter's voice faded away and his lips curved in a wistful smile. "You're doing a good job with him."

Emma waited, letting the moment settle, giving him space to deal with his own pain.

Then he looked up at her, his eyes locking on to hers. "If I promise to try to deal with all of this, will you stay?" Carter asked.

Emma held his gaze and heard the entreaty in his

voice. She struggled to balance the needs of her son with what this handsome, appealing man was asking of her.

Should she?

Emma caught her lower lip between her teeth, trying to weigh her reactions, her feelings. Part of her wanted to jump up, grab Adam and leave.

Yet the practical part of her realized that she had no other place to go. And no other real options. Yet.

"Okay," she said quietly. "If you can deal with Adam's presence, then I'll stay."

"Good. Thanks." He gave her a careful smile, his eyes still holding hers.

Emma couldn't look away. It seemed as if time slowed while awareness fluttered between them. A hesitant shift in the atmosphere that both enticed and frightened her.

She made herself look away. Made herself break the moment.

"Sylvia's mother called."

The words came out more blunt than she had hoped. But they definitely created the switch in the mood she needed.

Carter straightened and blinked, as if pulling himself from another place. "When?"

"Earlier tonight. She didn't know Miranda and Wade were gone."

"What did she want?"

The stiffness of his features made her realize her blunt pronouncement had served its purpose. And yet, the lonely part of her yearned foolishly for that small moment of closeness they shared only seconds ago.

"She wants to talk to you."

Carter got to his feet and walked to the door, then back to the bed and then to the stove. "What about?"

*You passed the message on. You're done. This isn't
your problem. This isn't your place. Just leave, already.*

But when she saw his face, the pain and sorrow that
had returned, she knew she couldn't drop Sylvia's mother
into the conversation and then leave, in spite of her need
to protect herself and Adam.

"I think she misses you," she said quietly.

"Why would she?"

Emma thought of her own lack of connections. Her
father gone. Her grandparents dead. One aunt who lived
in a retirement village in Florida. No uncles. Karl, a man
she had hoped to spend her life with, gone. The paucity
of relationships made her, for a moment, envy Carter in
spite of his loss.

"You are the only connection they have to their daughter and grandson." She pressed on, not sure why this had
become so important to her, but she wanted him to understand what he kept himself from. "I lost my mother
when I was young. I used to love it when my father would
tell me stories about her. They became my way of connecting with her. Of feeling as if the hole her absence
left wasn't as big. I think she wants to talk to you about
Harry. To share stories."

Carter shook his head, as if he couldn't believe her.
"A person has to move on. Living in the past serves no
purpose. Waste of time. Waste of emotions." Beneath his
words, Emma heard a note of yearning that called to her.

And the sorrow on his face eased past the barriers
she'd been trying to erect to keep him at a distance.

She leaned forward, trying to catch his eye. "Have
you talked to your in-laws at all?"

Carter emitted a short laugh. "I left right after the funeral. I couldn't get away from here fast enough. Why does this matter to you?"

She held his gaze and gave him a melancholy smile. "I've also gotten to know your family a bit working here on the ranch. They also lost something when Sylvia then Harry died. And they lost something when you left too. They lost your stories."

"Look, all I want is some peace in my life. And to get away from all the emotions and the crying and the pain. Now that my grandmother is moving off the ranch, I can put this part of my life behind me. Get some peace."

"And do you have peace now?"

Carter opened his mouth as if to speak, but then he shook his head. "I don't know. And talking about my son isn't going to get me what I want."

"But the longer you wait to talk about your son…" She hesitated, realizing in a moment of blinding clarity that he never mentioned Harry's name aloud. She wondered if anyone ever did in front of him, other than Adam.

She plunged ahead, "The longer you wait to talk about Harry, the harder it's going to be. It will hurt, but I think you need to get through this stage."

He said nothing to that, and Emma figured she had said enough, as well. And had spent enough time here. She had her own problems to deal with, and she had to be careful not to get pulled too deeply into Carter's.

He had to make his own decisions, and his problems weren't hers. Once the buyer came here, she would be gone and Carter would be out of her life.

She got up to leave, but the sight of this strong, silent man, sitting alone on the bed, his face in his hands, tugged at her heart.

She touched his shoulder, hoping to give him some connection. Some small comfort.

He eased out a sigh then, to her surprise, his hand came up and covered hers. The warmth of his large hand eased into the closed-off portion of her heart.

She waited a few heartbeats, reminding herself what she had wanted to say.

"You say you can't talk to your family about Harry, but you might want to think about talking to God," she said quietly.

He lowered his hand, breaking the connection, creating a momentary sense of loss. "Do you think that will help?" He looked up at her, the broken longing in his gaze calling to her. "I feel like I'm all alone in this."

Emma slipped her hands in her pockets and drew in a breath. "God never lets us go, Carter."

"How can you say that with such conviction?" The faint note of uncertainty in his voice gave her hope.

"I lost a father. I lost a fiancé. I lost hopes and dreams." *And I'm in the process of shelving a few more,* she thought.

"But the one constant in my life," she continued, "Has been my need to depend on God. To connect with Him."

Carter blinked then looked away, shoving his hand through his thick hair. "I don't know if I can start again. I've been away so long."

"God is faithful." Emma sensed his receptiveness to what she was saying. "And He wants us to be in a relationship with Him." She hesitated, wondering if she had overstepped the boundaries, but her concern for him outweighed her reticence. "It's Sunday tomorrow. Why don't you come to church? Reconnect with the people that care about you. Bring your questions to God and see if you can find a bit of the peace you've been trying to find."

Silence followed that, but Carter didn't shrug off her suggestion. Nor did he mock her declaration.

She waited a moment, then realizing she had said more than enough, went back to her cabin.

Half an hour later the sound of his motorbike roared into the night, growing quieter as he drove away. As if he was outrunning his own pain and sorrow.

Chapter Seven

Carter parked his motorbike, pulled his helmet off his head and hung it on the handlebars. He finger combed his hair and checked it in the rearview mirror of his bike. Not great, but it would have to do.

He adjusted his jacket then looked across the parking lot to the church building, gleaming in the morning sunlight.

He hesitated, examining again his reasons for being here. Nana would love it. It was what the Beck family did every Sunday. Tradition.

But even as he examined his motive, he knew something else had drawn him here this morning. The quiet comment Emma had made last night had chipped away at his resistance to God. He had gone out on a long ride last night, but he couldn't quiet the angry questions he had thrown toward heaven after Harry's death.

Emma's challenge to take those questions to the source stuck with him. So he decided to come to church this morning and face God directly. If nothing came of it, he could say he tried. And maybe, just maybe, he could find his elusive peace as Emma had said.

As he stepped through the doors, a burst of noise greeted him. Groups of people gathered in the foyer of the church, talking and laughing. Children ran among the adults, playing a rambunctious game of hide-and-seek. The door behind him opened again, and two young girls ran past him to join in the game.

He recognized a number of people. One woman close to him turned. Carter could tell the moment she recognized him. Her eyes widened, her hand fluttered to her chin and sympathy flooded her features.

Carter only gave her a tight smile, then quickly worked his way through the crowd to the sanctuary. He wasn't ready to face sympathy. Not yet.

A quick scan of the half-full pews helped him spot his grandmother and cousin. He hurried down the aisle. He slipped past a purse lying at the end of the pew and dropped onto the empty space beside his grandmother, enjoying Nana's surprised reaction.

"Carter, how wonderful to see you here." She slipped her arm through his. As she pulled him close, he caught the faintest scent of roses and hairspray, two smells he always associated with Nana and Sunday. "This makes me so happy." She drew back, her contented smile erasing all the second thoughts that had dogged him all the way here. If Nana was happy, he was happy.

Shannon leaned past Nana and gave him a quick smile and a nod of approval, her auburn, curly hair bouncing as she did. Carter was surprised to see her here. Only a month ago he knew she'd been working on decorations for the church for her wedding. When her fiancé called it off and left town, he'd been told that Shannon had stayed away from church too.

But now she was here too, and he suspected it was for the same reason he was. To make Nana Beck happy.

Though, as he settled into the bench beside Nana, he knew, beneath the desire to please his grandmother lay a deeper reason.

"You didn't bring your Bible?" Nana asked, frowning at his empty hands.

"Uh, no… I came on my motorbike."

"They have Bibles in the back." A gentle smile accompanied her suggestion, but Carter easily read the subtext.

"Save my place," he said with a wink as he got up. He walked past people coming in, giving vague smiles and replies to those who greeted him by name.

"Carter. You old pirate." A deep voice boomed across the foyer. Carter almost winced then turned to face Matt Thomas, an old school friend.

The last time Carter saw Matt, he was thinner and had hair. Now his shaved head gleamed under the bright lights of the church entrance and a goatee covered his double chin. A leather jacket blazer and black jeans strained against the extra weight across his waist. "Wow, it's been a coon's age since you've been here," Matt said, slapping Carter on the shoulder. "I heard you were back to see your grandma. How is the old matriarch? Heard she had a heart attack?"

"She's doing much better. She's here now," Carter said then gave his old friend a grin. "So what's with the biker look?"

Matt ran his hand over his shiny head. "Not all of us are blessed with shag carpeting for hair. You trying to pull a Sampson?"

"Nope. Just haven't had time for a cut."

"Next free day you have you come around to Laurie's shop. She'll have you trimmed, gelled and moussed quicker'n you can say *hair product*. Then you and me can head over to the Royal for burgers and the best fries in Hartley Creek." Matt slapped Carter on the back. "Like old times."

"That'd be good." Carter grabbed a Bible off the rack and raised it toward Matt. "Sounds like a date."

He was about to leave, thankful for the lighthearted banter he had shared with Matt.

Then Matt put his hand on his shoulder, his eyes grew moist and Carter inwardly braced himself.

And here it comes.

"Buddy, I'm so sorry about what happened to you," Matt said, moving closer as people flowed past them. "Sorry about Harry. I never had a chance to talk to you. You disappeared right after the funeral."

Carter shifted the Bible from hand to hand. "It's been a while. Two years now."

Matt squeezed a little harder. "I know, but it still must be hard. That's something you don't get over real quick. I want you to know that me and Laurie, well, we been praying for you."

Carter stopped, then looked up at his friend, surprised at how touched he was by the comment. He was moved to know that someone other than his grandmother kept his name before God.

He gave Matt a careful smile. "Thanks for that," he said.

An awkward pause followed and Carter took a step away, poking his thumb over his shoulder. "Gotta get back to my grandmother. Told her I'd be right back."

Matt nodded, but as Carter returned to the pew, he

realized a couple of things. Talking to Matt hadn't been as hard as he'd thought.

And Emma was right about her comment about community. He was looking forward to catching up with Matt, an old friend who knew him before his life fell apart.

The building had filled while he was gone, and he had to scan the now-full pews to find his grandmother.

He found her, but as he was about to step into the bench, he paused.

Emma sat at one end, rooting through the purse parked there previously. Adam sat beside her, leaning over to see what she was digging around for.

She wore a long pink sweater over a cream-colored tank top and a beige skirt. A scarf wound around her neck gave her an ethereal look. When she looked up, the happy smile she gave him went straight to his heart. Then he caught Nana watching him, and he stifled his reaction.

He slipped back into the pew. Just as he put the Bible in the empty rack in front of him, the singing group came to the front and everyone got to their feet.

The first song was unfamiliar, as was the second one, but the music was light and uplifting. A couple of times he glanced over at Emma, who smiled as she sang, obviously caught up in the music.

The song finished and Emma glanced sidelong. As their gazes met, he felt it again. A connection. A sense that something could happen between them.

She seemed secure in her faith and as their eyes held, he endured a moment of envy. At one time he'd trusted God to watch over him and his family, but that trust was choked in the aftermath of Sylvia's and then Harry's death.

He yanked his gaze away from Emma. There was no future for them. She had a son. He'd had a son once, and he couldn't take care of him. Couldn't protect him.

Easier to stay alone.

The congregation sat down and the minister asked them to turn to the Bible. He pulled his out and opened it, holding it so Nana could read with him. She gave him a quick smile then put on her reading glasses.

"He who dwells in the shadow of the most high will dwell in the shelter of the Almighty. I will say of the Lord, 'He is my refuge and my fortress, my God, in whom I trust.'"

Those words caught Carter cold. He didn't trust God. Nor could he say he had found shelter in the Almighty.

He let the rest of the words of the psalm slip past him.

The Bible reading was over and the minister began his sermon. Carter leaned back in the pew, his eyes drifting over the familiar setting. Five hundred and eighty-five tiles in the ceiling. Twenty-five panes of green glass, thirty panes of yellow glass, forty panes of blue glass in the stained-glass windows. Everything the same as it was when he was a little kid, coming here every Sunday.

The minister's pulpit was in exactly the same place it had been since he was a kid. Cross behind him on the wall. Everything was the same as when Harry's coffin sat at the front of the church.

He yanked his gaze away, and his attention was snagged by Emma. She sat with her arm around Adam, whose head lay on her lap, his legs on the pew. He was sleeping. But her focus was on the minister. Her expression held an eager look, as if she took in everything he said and heard something Carter didn't.

He caught himself turning his own attention back to what the pastor was saying, wondering what caused that rapt look on Emma's face.

"God has never promised that we wouldn't have trouble, but He has promised to be alongside us in that trouble. So that we can, in the midsts of the storms of our life say with conviction, 'It is well with my soul,'" the pastor was saying. "We need to know more than anything that peace is not the absence of trouble in our lives—peace is the presence of God."

He spoke with such conviction that Carter caught himself clinging to his words, seeking some sliver of the elusive peace he had sought since Harry died. At one time he had trusted God. Did he dare trust Him again?

But what was the alternative? Chasing after work, after money—neither of which satisfied? Running away from the pain?

Carter looked down at his hands, now clasped tightly together. He wanted to believe God was at his side, that in His presence he could find peace. He wanted to trust God again.

He didn't know if he dared.

He chanced another look at Emma, wondering what she was thinking, and was surprised to see her looking at him. She gave him a careful smile, and his heart lifted in response.

She's pretty.

And she's not for you. You are on your own.

He tore his gaze away, thankful to hear the minister announce the closing song. He got up and sang along, but he couldn't shut his mind off to what the minister had said or to Emma's presence beside him.

Why did he have the feeling the two were intertwined?

* * *

She shouldn't have come to the family lunch.

Emma fussed with her scarf, all the while conscious of Carter sitting directly across from her. Once again she wished she had turned down Shannon's invitation to join the Beck family for lunch after church.

She tried to say no. However, Adam, lured on by Nana Beck with the promise of some new farm animals for the set he always played with, wouldn't let Emma refuse.

But now having Carter sitting right across from her was disconcerting and unsettling. The last time they'd shared a meal, it hadn't ended well.

And let's not forget your little lecture of last night.

Yet even as she acknowledged her cynical alter ego, another part of her felt something else was happening. Something a bit dangerous and, if she were completely honest with herself, a bit exciting.

He's a good-looking, hurting man. You're a lonely sympathetic person. Bad combination.

"Good message this morning, wasn't it?" Nana Beck was saying as Shannon spooned out the soup.

Silence followed that comment. Emma glanced from Carter to Shannon, feeling that it was their place to reply to the comment, not hers.

Carter's attention was on his bowl and Shannon tucked a strand of auburn hair behind her ear and sat down, fussing with her gold necklace.

"I especially appreciated how the minister said not the absence of trouble but that peace is the presence of God," Nana Beck continued, undaunted by the silence that greeted her.

Another pause followed, broken only by the clink of silverware on Nana Beck's china. Emma tried not to squirm in the uncomfortable quiet. She was sure Carter was thinking about his son and Shannon was thinking about the man who had left her just before their wedding.

"I know each of us sitting here at this table has had trials and doubts," Nana added, "but I like what the pastor was saying when he quoted C.S. Lewis. 'God whispers to us in our pleasures, speaks to us in our conscience, but shouts in our pains.' I know that I prefer to be whispered to."

More silence.

Emma couldn't take it anymore. "And yet at least for me, it has been in the hard places of my life, the moments I have struggled the hardest with God, that I have felt the closest to Him."

Nana Beck shot Emma a look of gratitude. "Isn't that true. I know that after both Sylvia's then Harry's deaths, I clung to God. Though I was angry with Him and hurt, I felt His nearness in a way I hadn't felt since my husband, Bill, died."

Emma sensed that Nana Beck's reference to Harry as well as Sylvia was deliberate, and while she buttered Adam's bun, she shot Carter a covert glance to see what his reaction was.

His features were unreadable.

"I know I question God at times," Shannon put in. "I wonder why things go the way they go…" Her voice faded away, and Nana Beck caught her arm and gave it a light shake.

"You are a beautiful woman, Shannon. And you deserve much better than what that snake Arthur did to you."

Shannon shook her head, as if dislodging her memories. "Gotta admit, it's a bit hard living in Hartley Creek knowing that I'm the cliché bride-almost-left-at-the-altar. But, my problems are small compared to some." Shannon gave Carter a meaningful glance, but his attention was still on the bowl in front of him.

"What new animals did you get for the farm?" Adam piped up, his completely unrelated question breaking the awkward silence after Shannon's comment.

"I got some goats and some chickens," Nana Beck said, relief entering her voice at the change in topic. "Some of them were missing, so I bought new ones."

"Did the boy lose them?" Adam asked, swirling his spoon through the soup, chasing down a meatball.

Emma handed him a bun and shot him a warning frown, but he wasn't looking at her. He was looking directly at Carter.

"You mean Harry?" Shannon asked.

Adam ducked his head, looking down at his bowl again. "Mom said I'm not 'sposed to talk about him," was his subdued response. "She said it hurts Mr. Carter, and I don't want him to be sad again."

The atmosphere around the table held a heavy expectancy, and Emma wished her son was less forthcoming.

"I'm sorry," Emma glanced around the table. "We had a talk about…and—"

"I'm not angry with you, Adam." Carter put his spoon down, folded his elbows on the table and leaned forward, his gray-blue eyes focused on Adam. "And I'm sorry if I made you feel that way."

Emma held her breath, her gaze flicking from Adam to Carter, wondering what her son would say next.

Adam pursed his lips, as if thinking. He chased down another meatball and fished it out of the soup. Then he shot Carter a shy glance. "It's okay. My mommy said sometimes it's better to talk about things. But if you don't want to talk about Harry, I'll keep my mouth shut."

Note to self: give Adam minimal information to save maximum embarrassment.

"No, you can keep talking, Adam." Carter's smile was cautious. "I like hearing what you have to say."

Adam perked up at that. "Do you like playing with the farm animals?"

Emma groaned inwardly. Every time they came to Nana Beck's for dinner or coffee, Adam tried to con someone into playing with the farm set.

Carter gave a light shrug. "I don't know. I guess I could find out."

"Do you know the rules?"

"Honey, Mr. Carter might not like playing by your rules," Emma said gently, throwing Carter a quick smile. Adam seemed willing to ignore any discomfort he felt with Carter to gain an unwitting player.

"I know the rules Harry used to use," Carter said.

Nana Beck pulled in a quick breath, and Emma saw her glance at Shannon as if to gain confirmation of what she had just heard. But Shannon's attention was riveted on Carter and Adam, her green eyes flicking from one to the other.

"What rules did your boy use?" Adam asked, oblivious to the heightened tension in the dining room.

"He always wanted the cows of all the same color to be together in a field," Carter said, crumbling his crackers into his soup. "And the sheep and goats had to be in their own pen."

"Because they are the same," Adam said, signaling his approval. "What did he do with the chickens?"

A melancholy smile drifted over his lips. "He kind of let the chickens go wherever they wanted."

Adam frowned and shook his head. "I never let the chickens do that."

Here come Adam's rules, Emma thought, opening her mouth to intervene. She felt a foot nudge her and glanced over to Nana Beck, who gave an imperceptible shake of her head.

As Adam listed out the reasons Harry had done it wrong, the corners of Carter's mouth quirked upward. Then he glanced at Emma. She couldn't look away, inwardly pleased at his reaction to Adam's prattling.

Then, to her confusion, she felt it again. The sense that everything else slipped away in his presence. That she and he were the only people here.

She dragged her gaze away, feeling suddenly flustered. Unsure. This wasn't going the way she had pictured. This was dangerous. She shot a quick look at Adam, a visible reminder of her priority.

Carter is leaving. You are leaving. Focus on Adam.

"And the horses have to get water in the river because my mom says it's better for the horses," Adam was saying, swinging his legs back and forth as he warmed to his subject. "At my grandpa's ranch we had a big black tub to water the horses. When it was hot I would swim in it. You should get a big black tub for the horses. Then I can swim there because I can't swim in the river. Mom says it's too dangerous and I might drown."

Carter's lips had thinned at Adam's innocent prattle, and Emma knew her son had ventured too close to Carter's deepest pain.

"Are you finished with your soup?" She put her hand

on Adam's shoulder and nudged his bowl toward him with her other hand, hoping he got the hint.

Adam ducked his head and picked up his spoon again. "Do I have to finish it all?"

"Yes. Otherwise you don't get dessert," Nana Beck said.

"How is the house hunting going?" Carter's voice held a strained note as he turned his attention back to his grandmother and cousin.

"We found a smallish house," Shannon said, breaking open her bun, shifting to a safer topic. "It's close to downtown and the doctor's office."

"It has an excellent view of the ski hill," Nana Beck put in. "Hailey will love it."

"Speaking of, is my cousin making the pilgrimage home to see you, Nana?" Carter asked, his voice lightening and a smile lifting the corner of his mouth.

"She came to see me in the hospital," Nana said, her voice softening.

"Where is she now?" Carter asked.

"Working in Calgary," Shannon said.

"I wish she would come back to Hartley Creek," Nana Beck put in. "I know she loves it here." Nana shot Carter a frown. "She's going to be upset when she finds out that you're thinking of selling the ranch."

"I already talked to her, Nana. I even offered her a chance to buy the place herself."

Nana Beck snorted. "As if she could afford it on a teacher's salary." She sighed. "This place has been in our family for decades. I still can't believe—"

Shannon covered Nana Beck's hand with hers. "I know it's hard to understand, but Carter has to make up his own mind about the ranch."

Though she spoke quietly, Emma caught the glance Shannon sent Carter's way.

She felt bad for him. Though she agreed with Nana Beck, Shannon was right—it was still his decision to make and his ranch to sell or keep.

"I still think you're making a rash decision," Nana Beck said.

Carter eased out a sigh. "I'm sorry this isn't working out for you. But I can't stay here, and you want to move anyway."

Silence followed that comment.

"Before the ranch changes hands, we're going to have to organize a family get-together here," Shannon said. "Get everyone together one more time. Let us have a chance to remember old times."

It wasn't too hard to hear the melancholy tone in Shannon's voice, and Emma felt a twinge of sympathy for her and Nana Beck but also for Carter. He carried the weight of family history on his shoulders, and she sensed that the memories of each family member added to his burden.

"We've had lots of good memories here," Shannon added, cupping her hands around her mug. "Do you remember that time that Naomi and Hailey dressed up like ghosts?"

"Oh, my goodness, yes." Nana Beck shook her head, but she was smiling. "Garret screamed like a girl when he saw them rise up out of the pumpkin patch."

Laughter followed this memory.

"Then Garret got them back with that pail of water above their door, remember?" Carter said with a grin.

"Except I was the one that got drenched," Shannon said.

While the conversation skipped back and forth, recollections and old stories spilling out, Emma quickly finished up her lunch, encouraging Adam to do the same.

Though she knew all the names of Nana Beck's grandchildren and much of what they were doing, she sensed Carter, Shannon and Nana Beck would be more comfortable sharing family stories without her around.

"Thanks for lunch," she said, as soon as Adam finished the last of his soup and the bun she made him eat. She got up and brought their bowls to the counter. "Adam and I have to get going."

"But I want to play with the farm set," Adam said, wiping his mouth with his sleeve instead of the napkin.

"You can play with that another time." Emma shot him a warning glance.

"Nana Beck said she had some new animals and I didn't get dessert." His voice lifted toward the end of the sentence, coming dangerously close to whining territory.

"We can come back and play with the animals another time—"

"Nonsense. He can play with them now." Nana put her hand on Emma's arm when she came back to the table to get Adam. "I did tell him he could."

Emma was torn between keeping a promise to her son and wanting to let the Beck family spend time together without her, an interloper, around.

"I don't want to intrude," she said quietly.

"That's silly," Nana said with a frown.

Adam dragged at her hand. "Please, Mom? We can play in the living room. Real quiet."

Emma bit her lip, relenting. "Okay. Just for a little while, then we have to go."

Adam didn't wait for the rest of what she had to say. He was gone before she finished saying "Okay."

Emma followed him to the living room. Adam was pulling the box out of the bottom cupboard of the bookshelves.

As they laid out the farm set and Adam imposed his strict regimen, snatches of conversation slipped to the living room. Emma tried not to listen in, but part of her yearned for the connections and history Carter shared with his cousins. The banter and half-finished comments that didn't need to be completed because everyone knew the rest of the story.

Emma had grown up an only child who never got to know the grandparents who lived so far away. Her father had a sister who lived in Florida, also single. And that was it. The line of the family ended with her and Adam.

As she set out the pigs, according to Adam's Rules, she felt a twinge of regret. Growing up without siblings made her want a large family for her own children.

How things change, she thought, glancing at her dear son. He was her entire focus. Her life. It was just the two of them.

In spite of that declaration, her thoughts slipped to Carter and the moments they spent together. That sense of heightened awareness that was often the precursor to something else. Something more.

The sound of Carter's laugh lifted her heart.

"What are you smiling at, Mom?" Adam poked her with a plastic cow, and she jerked herself back to her son and reality.

As she looked at his dear little face, a smear of butter still streaked across his cheek, she drew on a memory. The sight of his stricken expression when she told him that Karl wasn't going to be coming to the ranch anymore. The tears that welled up in his eyes when he discovered he wasn't going to get a father.

Emma hardened her heart, even as she heard Carter laughing again in the kitchen.

He was lonely. He was complicated.

And she had to stay away.

Chapter Eight

He was leaving again.

Emma rolled over in her bed, tucking the pillow under her cheek as the roar of Carter's motorbike faded away down the valley road into the night.

Even as she congratulated herself on her wisdom to keep her heart free from the complication that was Carter, part of her felt a surge of pity for his pain. Behind that pity came another, stronger emotion.

She flopped onto her back, pushing her feelings aside, forcing herself to focus on the job she had stayed to do. Tomorrow she would ride up to the upper pasture again.

Day after that, she and Adam had to go into town for a dentist's appointment, and she should get the mail which, inevitably, meant bills to pay and the tedium of filling out applications for another job.

After that they would have to think about cutting hay and baling it. Carter could probably run the hay bine to cut the hay. She could run the baler and rake.

But would the ranch be sold before all this happened? She rolled back onto her side, struggling with her need to keep her mind busy and the concern that hung, ever present, on the edges of her mind.

And what would she do when the ranch sold? Where would she go? How would she take care of Adam? Would she have to sell Dusty and Diamond?

She dropped her hand over her eyes, sending up a prayer for…what? She wasn't sure.

Peace is not the absence of trouble, peace is the presence of God.

The quote from the pastor slipped into her mind, and behind that came another Bible passage she had read last night.

Peace I leave with you; my peace I give you. I do not give as the world gives. Do not let your hearts be troubled and do not be afraid.

Emma repeated the words, clinging to them. She had to trust that God would help her through this next phase of her life.

She repeated the Bible passage again, rolling over onto her side. Slowly, elusively, sleep found her. But just before she drifted off, her last thoughts were of slate-blue eyes and the sound of a motorbike's engine.

A light drizzle was falling when Carter strode across the yard toward his grandmother's house. The rain made it hard to tell exactly where the sun was, but Carter knew it was getting close to noon. He pulled the collar of his jacket up, wishing he had his oilskin.

He'd slept in this morning and woke up only when he heard rain on the roof of his cabin. A quick glance at his watch had shown him it was already close to noon.

He knocked on the door of his grandmother's house,

then toed his boots off. He pulled off his hat, shook off the excess water then stepped inside.

Nana Beck sat on her couch, her Bible in her lap. The sight created a flicker of guilt as he thought of the still-unopened Bible sitting beside his bed.

"How nice to see you, my dear," Nana said, motioning for him to come closer. He brushed his damp hair back, bent over and gave her a quick kiss, then gave her hands an extra squeeze.

"Goodness, your hands are cold," she said. "Do you want a cup of tea?"

"No. I had breakfast." He didn't respond to the questioning lift of her eyebrow or her quick glance at the clock. "Just wondering if you've seen Emma this morning."

Guilt stalked his every step. Last night he gave up on sleeping and had gone for a ride on his bike. He came home late and as a result had slept in. Emma's cabin was empty when he knocked on her door. She wasn't in the barn, the tack shed or the main farmhouse. Her truck was still parked in front of the machine shed by her horse trailer.

Nana frowned and shook her head. "She did say something about picking beans when she came back, though I doubt she will in this rain."

"Back? From where?"

"I'm not sure. I was taking in my clothes from the line when she and Adam came by on the horses."

"Horses?"

Nana frowned at him. "No need to sound snappy, my boy. I'm just telling you what happened."

Carter gave his grandmother an apologetic smile. "Sorry, Nana. I'm concerned. It's raining out and I can't figure where she would go on horses in this wet weather."

A smile eased away Nana's frown. "I don't think you need to worry about Emma. She's capable and independent. She's been a big help to Wade on the ranch. I think she really loves it here."

Carter saw his grandmother fold her hands on her Bible. Usually a sign that some type of lecture or scolding was coming his way.

"Shannon told me that you listed the ranch already?"

Carter thought they had covered all this yesterday over lunch. "Yes. I did. And Pete already found a buyer."

"Why so soon? Why so quick? You've only been back a few days, and you're making this huge decision?" Nana Beck's fingers tightened around each other.

Carter steeled himself to the pain in her voice. "I wanted to do this after…two years ago, Nana. As long as you still lived here, I wasn't making you move out of your home."

"But this is your home too."

The catch in her voice hooked into his heart.

Last night, as he shifted and sighed in his bed, seeking elusive sleep, he struggled with his decision. Coming back to the ranch had been harder than he thought.

Talking about Harry yesterday, first with Matt at church, then Adam, then with Shannon and Nana, had brought out painful memories. Yet, in spite of the pain, he was surprised it hadn't hurt more.

The biggest surprise was finding out how much he missed having someone to share memories with. Reliving old stories and escapades eased out good memories of the ranch. Memories he had also suppressed.

He didn't blame Emma for slipping out with Adam

while the Becks made a trek down memory lane, but he wished Emma had stayed longer. He enjoyed her company and, in spite of his own sorrow, talking about Harry, even for a moment, had helped as she had said it would.

Last night, while he lay awake, twisting and turning in his bed, an errant thought slinked around the edges of his mind. Was selling the ranch a selfish move?

He looked out the rain-streaked window of Nana's house to the corral. The horse trough was gone, but the memory wasn't. And on the heels of that memory, the guilt swept in.

He couldn't live with these reminders every day.

He shoved his hand through his hair as he exhaled heavily. "I'm sorry, Nana. I feel like I should put this part of my life behind me. It hurts too much."

Nana's eyes brimmed with tears as she got up. "I'm so sorry for you, my boy. I've been praying every day that you would be able to live with the memories. That you would forgive yourself. When you said you were coming back, I was so hoping you would stay."

Carter picked up his hat and turned it around in his hands, his second thoughts of last night niggling at him. "I really feel I need to move on." He bent over and gave her another kiss. "I'd better see if I can find Emma and Adam. Find out why she didn't let me know what she was doing." He didn't want to admit this to his grandmother, but he was a bit worried.

"Give her a little slack," Nana said quietly. "She's used to doing a lot on her own."

"Maybe she has, but she should still let me know when she's going to be gone."

"Of course she should."

Did he imagine that little smirk on his grandmother's face?

"By the way, have you heard anything from Wade?" she asked, thankfully moving on to another topic.

"Yeah, he called me on my cell phone. His father is in stable condition, but his mother will need some surgery. Wade is doing okay, but he's a little frazzled."

His grandmother clucked in sympathy. "Then we'll need to remember them in our prayers."

Carter felt a twinge of envy. Prayers. It had been some time since he had talked to God other than in anger. He wished he could be as trusting as his grandmother seemed to be about God's listening ear.

"You do that, Nana. Meantime, I better go see what Emma has been up to."

"Don't you be getting angry with her," Nana admonished.

Carter couldn't help a faint smile at his grandmother's defense of Emma.

"I won't." He dropped his hat on his head and strode across the yard to the tack shed.

He snagged a halter off a peg, then headed to the horse pasture. He whistled for the horses, but they didn't come.

Frowning, he climbed over the fence and walked toward them.

Banjo lifted his head at Carter's approach. Then, with a whinny, he turned and trotted in the opposite direction.

The other horses whinnied, then followed their leader.

He whistled again, but Banjo wasn't listening.

"Ungrateful critter," he muttered, threading the halter rope through his hands. He watched the horses, figuring his next move. He wasn't going to chase them around the pasture. The trick was to get the horses to come to him.

Just as he was planning his strategy, the horses stopped, whinnied and trotted toward the fence.

Carter looked in the same direction and saw Emma and Adam on their horses, coming down the trail from the upper pasture.

"Hey, Mr. Carter," Adam called out, the leather of his saddle squeaking, standing in his stirrups as they approached. His bright yellow jacket and black pants made him look like a bumblebee. "Did you finally wake up?"

The "finally" cut. A bit. But Carter just nodded.

The horses came alongside and Emma reined them in. She wore a brown cowboy hat today and an oilskin jacket and worn leather chaps. Water dripped off her hat, but she was smiling.

Carter's mind flashed back to a trip he had made with Sylvia when they first were married. They had ridden up and around the hills behind the ranch, and it began to rain. Sylvia, normally easygoing, had complained all the way down. When they got back she said she wasn't going out riding again unless Carter could guarantee sunny weather.

Emma, however, didn't seem daunted by the moisture or the fact that she had mud spatters on her chaps, coat and face.

"Where did you go?" he asked, forcing his attention back to the subject he wanted to talk to her about.

"Up to the higher pasture. Didn't you read the note I put on your door?"

Carter frowned. He hadn't bothered to check his door. Didn't even think she might have left him a note.

"No. I didn't."

"I think we'll have to move the cows in a few days. I wanted to make sure they were okay until then."

"Why didn't you wake me up?" He set his hands on his hips, trying to look as if he was in charge.

"I heard you leave late last night. I thought you would still be tired." She gave him a careful smile as she dismounted.

Carter sighed as a trickle of rain worked its way down his back. "You're my ranch hand, not my mother."

The edge in his voice came from a mixture of frustration with a horse he couldn't catch and guilt that this woman and her son were able to take care of his ranch without him.

At any rate, his curt tone made her smile disappear and her lips thin. He felt like a heel. His grandmother had just warned him about getting angry with her.

"Okay. Next time I'll ask before I make the same decisions I've been making since I was hired." Her voice took on a prim tone. She swiped a gloved hand across the moisture trickling down her face, smearing the bits of mud across her cheek. Which ruined the confident and in-charge effect he guessed she was going for.

Which in turn made him smile.

She glared at him, her brown eyes snapping. "What's so funny, Carter? Is it so hard to imagine me in charge?"

"No. Not at all. It's just—" How was he to regroup from this?

"I've been taking care of the cows since I got here," she said, gripping Diamond's reins, not giving him a chance. "The whole pasture-management scheme was mine. Wade, thankfully, was able to trust me to do what I'd been doing for four years on my father's ranch. I know what I'm doing."

He held up his hand in a placating gesture. Where did this prickly attitude come from? "I'm not a chauvinist, Emma. I appreciate what you've done here. It just felt weird to get up and find out you were off doing what I should have been doing."

She blinked, glancing back at Adam, who was still on his horse, a puzzled frown pulling his eyebrows together.

"Again. I'm sorry," she mumbled. "I thought since you're selling the place, it wouldn't matter what I did..." She let the sentence trail off.

"I'm selling this place as a turnkey operation, and I want to make sure that I know what's happening on the ranch when I talk to the potential buyer."

Even as he mouthed those words, a part of his mind accused him of lying. No, the reason he cared went deeper. Went back to his youth. To growing up on this place. To all the memories that were such a part of him and had only recently come out again. The memories he had from before Harry died.

"Speaking of the buyer," Emma said, her voice lowering. "Did you find anything out about subdividing the acreage from the new owner?"

Carter rubbed his chin, feeling a flicker of regret as he recalled his last conversation with Pete. "Apparently the new owner wants to keep the land untouched. He likes the isolation and isn't interested in breaking off parcels of the ranch." He caught the sorrow in her eyes. "I'm sorry, Emma. I wish I could tell you something different."

"That's okay." Emma's quiet words showed Carter how much of a disappointment this was to her. But he could do nothing. It was out of his hands.

She turned away and walked over to her son to help him out of the saddle. As soon as Adam's feet hit the ground, he scooted over to Carter, eyes bright. "My mom said that if the weather is nice, when we go to move the cows, we're going to have a picnic."

Carter knelt down so that he was face-to-face with him. "A picnic sounds like a great idea," he said, giving the boy a quick smile.

Adam put his hand on Carter's shoulder. "Can you come with us?"

The touch of Adam's hand created a mixture of emotions. Sorrow for his lost son, but also a connection with this little boy who looked at him with such trust.

"That would be nice," he said quietly, holding Adam's gaze. Then, as if of its own will, Carter's hand reached up and covered Adam's. To his surprise the sorrow eased away, replaced by a surprising tenderness toward Adam.

Adam's grin lit up his mud-streaked face. "Maybe my mom will let me take pop."

"That would be nice too," Carter said. He pointed at Adam's face. "But you're going to have to wash your face before we go."

Adam frowned then lifted his shoulder and wiped a trickle of water off his cheek, making the smear bigger. "Is it gone?"

Carter laughed then pulled out his hanky and wiped Adam's cheek. Then as he straightened, he caught Emma smiling at him, her eyes soft.

As their gazes held, his emotions shifted into a new place. A question arose in his mind. Could they...

His first reaction was to withdraw. But the question wouldn't go away.

Then he gave in to an impulse and reached over and gently wiped the mud off her face, as well. "There. Now you're all clean too." As he gave her a wink, he took advantage of her momentary bewilderment to gather up the reins of the horses and lead them away.

"So you pay the bills online now?" Carter asked, frowning at the computer.

Emma moved the mouse, gave it a click and tried not to notice how close Carter sat. He had to, she reasoned, to see the monitor better, but it still was too close for her comfort.

She smelled the rain on his clothes, the faint scent of horses on his blue jeans.

The hint of spicy aftershave lotion from his cheeks.

The same smell that was on the hanky he used to wipe her face. Why had he done that?

She swallowed and forced her attention back to the computer. Focus. Focus.

"Our banker told us it was perfectly safe," Emma said opening the banking site and plugging in the password. She had to try three times before she got it right.

"All the account information is here." Emma hit the Okay button again. Thankfully this time it was right and a new screen flashed up on the monitor.

In the background she heard the soundtrack of the movie Adam was watching. A bribe so she could pay the bills she had picked up in town this morning.

One of the reasons she had gone to town was to get the mail she knew would be piling up. The other was to look for a place to live, a job and a place to board her horses.

The easiest part of the excursion was getting the mail. Three of the jobs she had circled in the newspaper from the week before were filled. The fourth place was looking for someone with more education than she had. Not one of the jobs was in her field of expertise—horses and ranching.

She had tried to let go of her concern and hope that something, somewhere would come up.

"And working on this site is safe?" Carter asked as she clicked into the checking account.

He reached across her and pulled a pen out of the holder in front of her.

Droplets of moisture were captured in the waves of his thick hair. She had to clench her fists to keep herself from brushing them away.

What was wrong with her? Why was she so jumpy around him lately?

So aware of him?

"Emma? Did you hear me?"

She jerked her attention back to the computer screen and away from him. "Yeah. I did. Sorry. It's perfectly safe." She drew in a quick breath. "Plus it's convenient. Much easier to do this way. We don't have to get to town on time to meet the deadlines. It also saves a bunch of postage, which all helps. But, yeah, the bank account is well, healthy."

And you are babbling like an idiot.

Carter shot her a puzzled look. "Why are you so nervous?"

"I'm not nervous," she said with a shaky laugh.

"You talk more when you are."

Emma took refuge in sarcasm. "So now you're the Emma expert?"

Carter said nothing, and the only sounds in the ensuing silence were strains of music coming from the living room. Sounded as if the movie was ending.

He held her gaze, and a faint smile curved up one corner of his mouth. "What's wrong, Emma?"

You're what's wrong, she wanted to say. *You're a distraction and a problem.* Her son in the next room was a potent reminder of what was at stake for her if she made bad choices. He depended on her to take care of him.

Getting distracted by an attractive, wounded man was not in Adam's best interests. Especially not a man who had no intention of sticking around.

Been there. Done that.

"I've just got…things on my mind." She caught herself. No whining, either.

Carter leaned an elbow on the table but didn't look away. "Like what?"

She kept her eyes on the computer screen. "It's not your worry." She clicked on the Pay Bill button and flipped through the bills in front of her, looking for the next one to pay.

"Is it a job you're worried about? Your future?"

Her hand paused. The concern in his voice was almost her undoing. How long had it been since anyone, including her father and even Karl, her once-fiancé, had even been concerned about her? Had cared enough to ask?

"It's a factor," she said, pulling out the envelope she was looking for and ripping it open. "I'll be fine. I can manage."

"You do that well," Carter said quietly.

"Open envelopes?" she asked, deliberately misunderstanding him.

"Act like everything is fine. Like you're in control."

Emma clutched the paper then lowered it to the desk trying to mask her awareness of him. "I've never believed I'm in control. I don't think any of us are."

Just look at him. Act as if you're not aware of his height. The breadth of his shoulders.

The largeness of him that made a girl feel safe. Protected.

That's a pipe dream, and you know it. You can't trust men.

"No, I don't suppose we are," Carter said quietly, looking directly at her. Then he tilted his mouth up in a smile and, to her surprise and dismay, reached over and brushed his fingers over her cheek.

She tried to stop the rush of warmth washing up her neck, heating her cheeks. He had done that before. When he wiped the mud off her face. What was he trying to do to her?

"You had a piece of lint stuck to your face," he said, holding up his fingers to show her.

"Oh. I see." She turned back to the computer, hoping he didn't notice her shaking fingers. She typed in a number in the box to pay the bill, corrected it and tried again.

"So then, once the bill is paid, I enter the amount in the checkbook," she said quietly, hoping she sounded in control. In charge. "That way, if Wade takes the checkbook to town, he knows exactly how much is still in the account."

"That's easier than the way I did it," he said with a rueful grin. "Sylvia always said I did things backward."

Emma was surprised. This was the first time she'd heard him mention his wife's name. "Did she ever do the books?"

Carter laughed and shook his head. "She was a good woman, but she always said she could add up four numbers five times and come up with six different answers."

"I saw a picture of her at Nana Beck's," she said, capitalizing on his memory. "She was a beautiful woman."

Carter's sigh held more melancholy than sadness. "She was. Inside and out. She was a real example to me of Christian love. I sometimes wonder what Harry would have been like if she'd been around." A tiny break entered his voice as he spoke of his son.

His sorrow touched Emma's nurturing soul. She reached over and covered his hand with hers.

"I'm so sorry, Carter," she said quietly. "Sorry for all you've lost."

He held her gaze and gave her a wistful smile as his hand squeezed hers in return. "I'm sorry too."

Their gazes held again. But she felt a shift in the atmosphere. A change from sadness to something deeper.

Attraction. Understanding. A sense of coming home.

Look away. Look away. This is trouble.

But Emma couldn't.

"Mom, the movie is done," Adam announced, hopping into the kitchen and bringing energy, enthusiasm and reality with him.

Emma yanked her hands away from Carter's and swallowed down the anticipation brewing in her chest.

"Can I have a cookie?" Adam asked.

Emma nodded absently, furiously clicking on another button, suddenly wishing Carter would let her finish up alone.

Adam wandered to her side and wiggled his way between Emma and Carter, his hands full of cookies. "Can I sit on your lap, Mom?" he asked.

"In a minute, buddy." She frowned at the cookies in his hand. "Why did you take four?"

He laid two on the desk. "One for you and one for Mr. Carter."

"Two for you, I noticed," Carter said with a surprising grin.

"Yup. 'Cause I'm the cookie getter." Adam took a bite of his cookie and released a dramatic sigh. "How come I can't sit on your lap?"

"Because I can't work on the computer and hold you at the same time."

"I can't see." Adam turned to Carter. "Can I sit on your lap? Sometimes, when Mommy is done on the computer she lets me play a game. Or look at the horse pictures."

Emma's gaze flew to Carter, even as she nudged her son, hoping to catch his attention. She wished she had let Adam sit on her knees, because she knew Carter would turn him down.

But Carter was looking at Adam, his mouth curved in a rueful smile.

Then, to her surprise and amazement, he lifted Adam up on his lap.

As Adam settled against Carter, Emma felt a whirlwind of emotions. Astonishment that Carter would willingly take Adam and hold him.

And, threaded through that, a sense of confusion she couldn't pin down. She didn't want Adam to connect with Carter this way. She didn't want her son to be tied in with the man who was, even now, making Emma's hands clumsy and making her heart lift. The scene was too much like a family setting. Mother, father, son. All cozy and comfortable.

Guarding her heart was how she had to take care of Adam. Carter was outrunning his past by leaving when the ranch sold. This would never work. Adam could not experience another disruption in his young life.

"When you're finished can we look at the pictures?" Adam was saying.

"Yes. And then you can sit on my lap," she said with a false brightness as she slit open another envelope. She flew through the rest of the bills, flipping and clicking and hoping she input the correct amounts. She wanted to be done so she could split up this too-cozy tableau.

She closed the bank site then opened up the photo program. Wade had made a file of horse pictures, and Adam loved looking at them.

But her hands were clumsy and she hit the wrong file. As she reached for Adam, a movie opened up. A little boy waved at the camera from on top of a horse.

Harry.

Wade led the horse and in the background Emma heard Carter's voice, probably from behind the camera. "Make sure you hold on, Harry. Don't show off too much."

The movie showed Wade bringing Harry closer to the camera, and Emma couldn't look away even as she clicked and clicked, trying to shut the program down.

Harry was a younger version of Carter. Same thick, wavy hair. Same blue eyes. Same crooked smile.

She heard a sharp intake of breath from Carter and then…finally…thankfully, the movie disappeared. An intense silence followed. Emma was sure everyone heard the heavy pounding of her heart.

Then Adam turned to Carter. "I'm sad that your little boy can't be here." The simple words slashed the quiet.

Emma was afraid to look at Carter, to see his reaction. But her gaze slipped to his face anyway, and to her surprise, moisture glimmered in his eyes.

"I'm sad too," was all Carter said, his voice quiet.

"Maybe if you pray, God will help you feel better," Adam replied with the simple confidence of his innocent faith.

Carter's smile was warm and Emma's heart tumbled in her chest as Carter brushed his hand over Adam's hair. "Maybe," he said. Then he gently set Adam aside, mumbled a hurried "Excuse me," and left.

When the door clicked behind him, Emma felt tears prick her eyelids. Seeing Carter's son, alive and smiling, made his loss tangible. Painful.

What must Carter be going through right now?

Ten minutes later she got the answer as she heard the rumble of Carter's motorbike starting up then, in spite of the rain, leaving.

His life is too messy, she reminded herself, stifling the momentary attraction she had just experienced. *Adam doesn't need more complications and disappointments. You're the only one who can take care of him.*

Yet, even as she talked herself through her usual litany, a yearning for the momentary connection she and Carter shared thrummed through her.

What was she supposed to do about that?

Chapter Nine

"Can we take some cookies along?" Adam leaned on the counter watching Emma making sandwiches.

It was early morning, and she and Adam were putting together the picnic in Miranda and Wade's house—Carter's old house, she thought.

"Sorry, buddy, they're all gone," she said absently, half her attention on her son, the other on how many sandwiches she should make. "But you can take some chips."

Yesterday, after Carter left, the rain quit and the sun came out, promising a better day. Today they had to go up to move the cows. She could only assume Carter was coming along. Especially after his speech about him still being the owner of the ranch.

Would the situation be awkward?

"But I really like cookies," Adam grumped. "So can I take pop instead?"

"Why don't we take our water bottles?" she suggested. "That way if you empty it, you can fill the bottle up in the stream." Thankfully Adam didn't counter that offer.

To make up for the lack of cookies, Emma put in an extra bag of chips and added two more chocolate bars.

A quick glance at the clock showed her she had time to spare.

"Let's go and see Nana Beck," she said, lifting Adam off the chair. "Make sure she's doing okay."

"Why is Nana moving off the ranch?" Adam asked as Emma pushed the chair back under the table.

"She's not been feeling well and she wants to live closer to the hospital, which means moving to town."

"I don't think she should move." Adam shoved his hands in his pockets and shot Emma a petulant look. "I don't think we should move."

Emma's heart faltered at the sadness in her son's voice. She knelt down and brushed his hair back from his face, then wiped a remnant of breakfast from the corner of his mouth. "Things change, son. And Mr. Carter is selling the ranch."

"Can't we work for the other man? The man buying the ranch?"

Emma thought of what Carter had told her about the acreage then, with a light sigh, shook her head. "Sorry, Adam. I want to find a place where we can live for good. A place we can own."

Adam frowned. "We have a place to live. The cabin."

"It's not the same." He was only five. He didn't understand the need to put down roots. The need to have a place no one could take away. He trusted her to take care of that for him.

She gave him a quick kiss to forestall more questions then pushed herself to her feet. "Let's go see Nana Beck." Then find Carter.

They stepped out into warm, inviting sunshine, so welcome after two days of drizzle and rain. Adam ran ahead of her, singing at the top of his lungs some song he had learned at Sunday school.

He flapped his arms, turning in circles, laughing at his own antics. The sight of him running so free gave her heart a tug. Come September he'd be going to kindergarten. After that, full-time school.

She wanted to stop time and bottle it. To hold these moments close. He was her precious little boy, and she wanted to keep him to herself as long as she could.

"Someone is in a good mood."

Emma jumped at the sound of Carter's voice behind her. He had caught up to her, his hands in the pockets of an old oilskin jacket, chaps covering his legs.

"We still on for moving the cows?" he asked, shooting her a sidelong glance.

Emma tried to gauge his mood. She hadn't seen him since he left yesterday. When he had finally returned, it was 7:00 p.m. and he had gone directly to Nana Beck's house.

Now, he acted as if yesterday hadn't happened.

"I was taking Adam to see if Nana Beck needed anything," she said, trying to keep her voice casual. "Then I was going to get you."

He held up a hand, as if to stop her. "Don't worry. I won't run the old 'I'm the owner of this ranch' schtick like I did the last time."

She nodded, slipping her hands in her pockets, unsure of what she should say. Then she figured, go with ordinary. Act as if nothing happened.

"So where were you just now?" she asked, glancing at the water beaded up on his leather chaps.

"I took Elijah out for a ride. Figured he needed a bit of extra work. We went down the trail leading to the river."

"You thinking of taking him along this morning?"

"When we go move the cows?" Carter shook his head, his eyes still on Adam. "For that I'll need a more seasoned horse. Which one works better with your horses?"

She angled him a questioning look, wondering if he was just trying to make her feel important after her little spiel of the other day.

"Banjo. Definitely," she said, playing along for now. "Plus, he's more docile, which is better with the cows."

"In other words, a plug."

Emma laughed as she walked up the steps to Nana Beck's house. "I wasn't going to say that, but—"

"He won't win the Triple Crown." Carter finished her sentence.

Their eyes met and humor flashed between them. "He's a good horse. Solid and dependable. Which is more important in my books than flash and dash."

Carter's mouth curved into a crooked smile. "That's good to know."

Then as she reached for the door, he caught her by the shoulder and turned her back to face him. Emma fought the urge to pull back, sensing he wanted to tell her something.

"I want to apologize for taking off yesterday and leaving you with the books. It was just…" His slate-blue eyes held hers, and in their depths she saw his pain. At the same time, she caught something else. Something she couldn't define.

"I understand," she said quietly, carefully stepping back from him. "I'm so sorry about the movie. I can't imagine how hard it was to see Harry that way."

He slowly drew in a breath, looking away from her.

"I didn't expect…didn't think I'd see him, hear him…" His voice broke and Emma's heart broke too.

"He looked like you," she said quietly.

Carter nodded then released a short laugh, but it didn't have the same bitter tone it would have the first time she met him. "My cousin Shannon always said Harry looked more like me than Garret did. Though Sylvia's mom and dad said he looked like Sylvia's father."

"I guess a person sees who they want to see."

"So who do people say Adam looks like?"

His question created a twinge of envy. "He doesn't look much like me or my father, but neither does he look like his father. Of course, I have no clue if he looks anything like Adam's grandfather. I never met him."

Carter frowned, and in that moment she felt a deep sense of shame at her messy past.

She lifted her shoulder in what she hoped was a casual shrug. "When Adam's father found out I was pregnant, he took off. I haven't gotten so much as a phone call or text message from him or his family since then."

"I'm sorry," he said, lightly touching her shoulder. She wanted to feel comforted, but instead it brought out the stark contrast between her and Sylvia. Sylvia who had family and community.

Emma, who had a sordid and shameful past as compared with Carter's history and roots.

She pushed the memory and comparisons aside. "So who do you think Harry looked like?" she asked, moving back to their previous topic.

"I always thought he looked more like Naomi, my other cousin," Carter said, a pensive smile curving his lips.

"Naomi of the middle cabin?"

"That Naomi." Carter pulled his hat off his head then gave her a quick smile.

Emma shook her head, deliberately keeping her tone light. "I haven't met Naomi, but if Harry looked like her, then she is more your twin than Garret is."

Carter's laugh was genuine. "Garret and I don't look that much alike for twins."

"I noticed that."

"Where?"

"In the pictures Nana has up on the wall." Nana Beck had an entire gallery devoted to her family, though pictures of the grandchildren far outnumbered the pictures of her daughters, Denise and Noelle.

"You've seen the photos?"

"And the albums," Emma said, adding a wink. "I know all your secrets."

Carter laughed again. Then, as their gazes met, a mellow smile still tugged up one corner of his mouth. "Thanks. For listening. For letting me talk. It's been hard, coming back. But the past few days have been… interesting. Don't know how else to say it. Seeing Harry yesterday was tough, but somehow, not as tough as I'd imagined."

"I'm thinking you've never had a chance to talk about him. Any of the people you've been around didn't know him and even if they did know you lost a son, they couldn't empathize."

"But you can."

"I know loss," she said softly. "But I haven't had to deal with what you've had to. I'm sure it's been a long, hard road for you the past few years."

Carter shook his head slowly. "When Sylvia died I thought that God gave me my quota of pain. Guess not."

"I don't think a God who promises us that He will always be with us is a God who doles out pain and sorrow."

Carter shrugged at that. Then he touched her shoulder again. It was a simple graze of his hand, but it sent a tingle down her spine. "Thanks for listening and for talking. You seem to know what to say, when."

His quiet words settled into her soul.

She waited, then unsure of what to say next, she opened the door of Nana Beck's house. After toeing off her boots, she followed Adam's happy chatter and the homey smell of cookies baking to the kitchen.

Adam had already pushed a chair against the counter, supervising Nana Beck removing cookies from the cookie sheet.

"Are some of them for us?" he asked, his chubby elbows planted on the counter as he watched. "Because we don't have any cookies for our picnic, and I really like cookies."

"Of course some of them are for you. You can't have a picnic without cookies." Nana turned, and her blue eyes lit up behind her glasses when she saw Carter and Emma. "So you two finally came in."

You two. As if they were a couple.

Emma dismissed the little tingle her words gave her and beckoned to Adam. "We have to get the horses ready, mister."

Adam glanced from Emma to Carter. "Is Mr. Carter coming with us?"

"We can't move those cows by ourselves," Emma said.

Adam pumped a fist in celebration. "We get to have cookies," he announced as he scooted off the chair. Then he turned to Nana, a worried look on his face. "Do the cookies have to cool or can we take them now?"

Nana Beck held up a paper bag. "I packed some already for you guys." She handed them to Adam. "Now you make sure they don't get broken, or they won't taste as good."

"That's silly," Adam said. "My mommy says that if a cookie is broken, you get more to eat."

"Are you going to be okay?" Emma asked Nana Beck as Adam opened the bag and counted the number of cookies inside.

"I'm feeling great. I had an urge to do some baking. I'll sit down after this." She wiped her hands on a rag, looking from Emma to Carter then to Adam. "Shannon is bringing me lunch this afternoon, so I won't be by myself for very long."

"Okay, then," Emma said. "You have a good day." She turned to Carter. "I'll get our lunch and meet you at the corrals."

His smile was simply to acknowledge what she said, but it still gave her spirits a peculiar quiver.

She put her hand on Adam's head, still bent over the bag, and steered him toward the porch. As they walked to the house, her footsteps quickened and her smile grew, though she didn't want to analyze why.

"Is there power on the line?" Emma's voice drifted across the open field.

Carter looked down at the tester that he had just put against the electric wire he and Emma had spent an hour stringing up as a fence for the cows. "Full power," he called back.

He gathered up the tester and put it back in his saddlebag, waiting for Emma. She got on her horse and rode toward him, glancing back now and again at the cows they had just moved.

Her hat hung from her neck by a leather strap. The wind picked up her hair, tossing it around her face. Carter smiled at how natural she looked sitting on that horse.

When they herded the cows to the other field, it was sheer pleasure to see her horse responding to her slight shifts in the saddle, her gentle touch on the reins and the nudges of her feet on her horse's side. All smoothly done without flash or dash, as she had said earlier.

While she rode she lowered the reins, gathered her hair up and tied it back in a ponytail with a few quick twists.

Too bad. Carter liked it better when she let her hair down, when it framed her face in loose, brown waves.

He buckled up the saddlebag, trying to stifle his response to her. For the past few days he'd catch himself thinking about her. Worrying about her and her son, and what they would do once he sold the ranch. Adam so clearly loved being on the ranch. It bothered him to think of the little guy living in town.

Yesterday, after getting over seeing Harry in the video, he'd gone into town, to see Pete at the real estate office.

Things were coming together, Pete had told him. The buyer's financing had come through, but Carter still had a few days to stop the deal. If he didn't come into the office to sign the paper revoking the sale by the date and time set out in the agreement, then it was a done deal, Pete reminded him.

Now, standing up on the mountain, watching Emma come toward him on the horse, looking as if she belonged here, the second thoughts shadowing him were gaining substance.

She fit here. He realized that what he felt for her was

deeper than mere looks. She was a devoted mother, a hard worker. A caring person. And his attraction to her increased each moment they spent together.

A tempting thought drifted on the edge of his consciousness.

What if he stayed? What if he changed his mind about selling the ranch?

He caught himself as Emma pulled up beside him.

"I think we have some very happy cows," Emma said as she swung down from the saddle. "They should be good for a couple of weeks yet. All that rain certainly helped."

"I can't believe how much grass we still have up here," Carter said, resting an arm on the pommel of his saddle. He dragged his gaze away from her, back to the cows.

Their red-brown bodies gleamed in the sun, sleek and fat, as they munched on the new grass. The calves raced around, checking out the perimeter of this new pasture. One touched the fence, let out a throaty bawl and then raced back toward its mother, the rest of the calves right behind. Carter laughed at the sight.

"That's what the rotational grazing has done," Emma said, threading the reins of her horse through her hand. "Next year I'd hoped to find a different way to feed the cows the hay over the winter. I've done some research on it—" She caught herself and looked away. "Anyhow, it was a good theory."

"We can have our picnic here," Adam called out from the copse of trees he'd been scouting out for the past few minutes.

"Shall we go?" Emma asked, picking up Dusty's reins from where Adam had dropped them. Without a backward look, she led both horses away.

In a matter of minutes Emma had a blanket spread out and was handing Adam various containers.

"Is there anything I can do?" Carter asked.

"We've got it under control." Emma glanced up at him then away, as if she was suddenly awkward around him. All the way up here she'd been quiet, and he wondered if he'd said too much on the porch.

He tied up the horses, and when he came back it looked as if everything was ready.

Carter sat down on the edge of the blanket, glancing from Emma to Adam. What were they waiting for?

"So. We're here. Let's pray," Emma said, nudging Adam. He pulled his cowboy hat off and Carter, surprised at this little moment, followed suit.

"Thank You, Lord, for the beautiful sunshine and the rain," Emma prayed. "Thank You for smoothing our path as we moved the cows. Thank You for this food and for a chance to be outside in Your amazing creation. Help us in our times of sadness and sorrow to know that You take care of us. Amen."

Carter kept his head lowered a moment, moved by her prayer. Simple yet sincere. Comfortable even. He felt close to God as she had prayed.

"So, here are the sandwiches. I didn't know what kind you liked, so I made a variety," Emma was saying as she snapped the lids off containers. "There's water in a bottle for you."

"If you need more to drink, you can take it out of the creek," Adam said. "But you don't want to go where the cows go. Because that's gross."

"Of course it is," Carter said with a grin, taking a sandwich out of the container. He took a bite and smiled at Emma. "Miranda had some homemade bread left?"

"Actually, I made it."

"Really?"

"Why do you sound surprised?" An injured tone crept into her voice.

"Sorry. I assumed that you were more of an animal person than a domestic one," Carter said, trying to back-pedal and failing miserably. Animal person? Really?

"I kept house for me and my father," Emma replied, taking a bite out of her sandwich. "I can do domestic too."

"It's just you're so good with horses and animals, I can't see you with an apron on working in the kitchen." He stopped there and finished off his sandwich in the awkward silence. Then he dusted off the crumbs from his shirt and heaved a sigh. "Okay, I think no matter what I do I'm going to say the wrong thing here. So why don't I just apologize in advance and hope it covers any other dumb thing I might say for the rest of the afternoon."

Her burst of laughter was a welcome surprise.

"It's okay. I shouldn't be so touchy. So I apologize too."

"Is there a best-before date on your apology? I'm wondering if it will cover the next few weeks of dumb things Carter might say.'"

This netted him some more laughter. Which brought out a sparkle in her eyes and a flush in her cheeks.

Which made her even more attractive than before.

He turned his attention back to the lunch spread out before him.

"So Adam, what should I have next?"

Adam tapped his fingers on his chin, considering. Then he picked up another container. "My mom's potato salad is really good."

"Potato salad it is, cowboy."

As they ate, any previous discomfort faded and the

conversation drifted along. Adam told Carter about the tree house. Emma and Carter talked about the calf crop. The hay crop. Nana Beck's health. Carter's family.

Halfway through the conversation Adam moved onto his side, closed his eyes and promptly fell asleep. Emma shifted off the blanket and covered him up with the rest of it.

"He didn't sleep well last night," Emma said quietly, getting up. "I'd like to move away so we don't wake him." She walked over to a large spruce tree and sat down.

Adam snorted and Emma looked back, checking on him, but he settled down again and soon they could hear his heavy, steady breathing.

"Sorry about this," Emma said quietly. "I knew he was tired, but he insisted on coming along. I'd kinda like to let him sleep for a bit, if that's okay."

Carter gave her an indulgent smile. "I don't mind staying a while longer. I like it up here. It's peaceful. Quiet." And he enjoyed being with her.

Emma pushed her hair away from her face and, leaning forward, wrapped her arms around her knees. "I love it up here too. I feel like I've left all the troubles and worries down there. At the ranch. Up here, it's just Adam, the horses and me trying to find the picture your Nana Beck calls The Shadow Woman."

Carter squinted across the valley, trying to find the shadow.

"The conditions have to be right…but it looks like they are today. See that rock face?" Carter pointed across the valley to the farthest mountain. "The sheer bluff above the trees to the right of that huge cleft? The shadow is on that rock face."

He shot her a quick glance, but she frowned and shook

her head. So he moved a bit closer, pointing it out. As their shoulders touched, he caught a hint of almonds blended with the faintest scent of leather. Her hair, lifted by the wind, tickled his cheek.

He dragged his attention back to the shadow. "See those two dark holes? Those are two caves, her eyes. The rock jutting out makes her nose."

He looked over at her again and now they were side by side, but she was still frowning. "That long shadow—that's her hair, and then below the caves—" He leaned a bit closer, following the shadow with his forefinger, pointing it out.

"Oh. Of course. I see it now. I see it." Emma clapped her hands in a girlish gesture. "And that's her dress. The one that the man in the legend bought her."

"The man she is waiting for," Carter added.

Emma grinned, looking well satisfied with herself. "I finally found it. I've been looking since I came here."

"Like I said the conditions have to be exactly right. She's easier to see in the summer and up here, easier yet." Carter smiled. "I used to feel sorry for her, forever waiting for her love to come back."

"I'm glad that your family story has a happier ending." Emma smiled and leaned back against the tree. "Though I think your Nana feels like her story won't have a happy ending until all of her grandchildren are back. Even Shannon talks about moving away, after Arthur called off the wedding."

"It's been tough on her. Shannon told me every time she had to cancel some part of the wedding, she felt ashamed again." Carter blew out a sigh, feeling a flash of sympathy for his cousin.

"I know exactly how she feels," Emma said quietly,

twisting a blade of grass around her fingers as she looked at the shadow on the mountain. "It's not easy finding out that someone you trusted wasn't worthy of that trust." But before he could comment on that, she gave a light laugh. "What about the rest of the kids? Hailey, Garret, Naomi? Do you think any of them will come back again?"

Carter pursed his lips, thinking. "I know Hailey was thinking of coming back after Nana's heart attack. To be around Nana for a while. Naomi hasn't been able to get here yet and is feeling horrible about that. When Garret came to see Nana in the hospital, he talked about coming back to Hartley Creek for good. But we'll see."

"And you're moving." Then she waved her hand, as if to erase what she had just said. "I'm sorry, I didn't mean to make you feel guilty about your plans."

Carter paused, looking at Emma, then took a chance. "If I follow through on them."

Emma's eyes widened. Then she looked down, as if afraid to let Carter see what she was thinking. "What… what do you mean?" she asked, her voice quiet.

"I don't know what I want anymore." The words spilled out before he could stop them.

Emma's eyes sprang to his. "What are you saying?" she asked as he moved nearer.

Then they were face-to-face, so close that their breaths mingled.

A strand of hair stuck against her mouth. Carter reached up to brush it away the same time Emma did. Their hands met, and before he realized what he was doing, Carter caught her hand in his.

He saw her swallow, look down. But she didn't let go. Nor did she move away.

The silence surrounded them, creating a bubble of

solitude. Maybe it was loneliness, maybe it was the attraction Carter felt brewing between them. Maybe it was more than that.

He dismissed his thoughts, leaned closer and their lips met. Touched. Withdrew. Then met again.

Then his arms were around her, holding her close. Hers were around him, one hand clutching the back of his neck, the other pressing against his back.

She tasted like cookie. Like sweetness. Like Emma.

He knew he should stop, yet it felt so right. As if it was the right step in the right direction.

For the first time in years, Carter Beck felt as if he had truly come home.

Chapter Ten

Pull away. Now. Stop this before you lose yourself.

Emma let her one hand drift away from Carter's neck to his shoulder. She gave a gentle, halfhearted push, and when Carter drew back, she felt bereft in spite of her self-talk.

Then she looked up at him, lost herself in his eyes, and this time she was the one who leaned in. Her lips brushed across his, generating a yearning that could be satisfied only with another kiss. With being held close to him.

Adam murmured, and like a splash of cold water, his presence intruded into the moment.

She pulled away, pressing her hands to her heated cheeks. What was she doing?

"I'm sorry," she muttered. "I shouldn't have let this happen."

Carter put his hand under her chin and turned her face up to his. "You didn't 'let' this happen," he said. "I started it."

"I know, but I let you…and I shouldn't…"

She wanted to look away, but his hand still held her

chin and, if she were honest, her protests were more symbolic than anything.

The past few days with Carter had been a mixture of emotions and feelings she couldn't sort out. This kiss they shared only added to her confusion.

Then his vague comment about not knowing what he wanted? It raised a hope in her she didn't dare latch onto.

Carter's fingers caressed her cheek, but then, thankfully, he lowered his hand.

"Traditionally, this is where the guy apologizes for the kiss, but the only thing I should feel sorry about is that I'm not sorry." A crooked grin followed this admission, and Emma felt her feeble resistance shift.

Emma glanced from him back to Adam, reminding herself of her priority.

"He's still sleeping," Carter said.

"It's not that." She looked down at her hands with their broken nails, her mind casting about for the right way to express her reasons. "Adam depends on me to take care of him and to provide for him. I'm the only person in his life. He doesn't have aunts or uncles or cousins or grandparents. It's only me. And I have to make sure that all my decisions are what's best for him."

Carter said nothing to that, and Emma kept her gaze on her hands, her heart thrumming in her chest with a mixture of anticipation and concern. "Right now your plans are to sell the ranch and leave."

"What if I tell you that things might change? What if I tell you that I might—"

"Mom? Where are you?"

Adam's plaintive voice cut into what he was going to say, the reality of his presence underlining what she had told Carter.

Emma jumped to her feet and ran to Adam's side. He was sitting up, stretching his arms, and when he saw her he grinned. "Did you eat all the cookies?"

"No, honey. There are lots left." Emma went to grab the bag, but when she did, she was disappointed to see her hands trembling. She balled her hands into fists and tried again. "Here you go, buddy," she said, giving him a cookie. She set the bag aside and pulled him onto her lap, holding him close as she always did after his nap.

Focus. Adam is the nucleus of your life. He depends completely on every decision you make. Don't get distracted.

Even as she formulated that thought, she shot a quick glance toward Carter who was watching her and Adam. His "what-ifs" rang through her mind, bringing more confusion.

And she knew that Carter was becoming more than a distraction. He was becoming intertwined in her and Adam's lives.

Carter and his horse topped the rise, and then below him lay the ranch buildings.

Behind him he heard the plop of Emma's and Adam's horses' hooves on the trail still wet from the rains of the past few days, the jingle of their bridles, the squeak of the saddles as they shifted with their horses' movements.

Even more than that, it was as if he felt them behind him. Felt their very presence.

He tugged on the brim of his hat and blew out a breath. What had he done back there? What had he started?

He resisted the urge to look back over his shoulder, to catch Emma's eye. Ever since the kiss, she had avoided looking at him. As if she regretted their moment of intimacy.

He guided Banjo down the trail, easing up on the reins as he slipped then caught his footing.

All the way back from the picnic, Emma said nothing. Adam, seemingly oblivious to the tension between Emma and Carter had chatted about the weather, the horses. How his mom said he could ride in the tractor with Wade when he cut the hay and wondering how many bales they might get.

Each comment about the ranch hit like a tiny lash. Carter doubted that Emma and Adam would be around when haying time came. He understood from Pete that the buyer was anxious, well financed and ready to take over the ranch very soon.

The thought he had tentatively expressed to Emma blew back into his mind. What if he didn't sell the place? What if he decided he wanted to come back here? Start ranching again?

With Emma and Adam?

Carter shot a glance back at Emma, and in that moment she looked over at him. Then a flush colored her cheeks and she looked away. What was she thinking?

When they got back to the ranch, he knew they needed to talk more. She needed to know that his kiss wasn't simply a casual thing. And he wanted—no, needed—to know her reaction. He didn't dare build a potential future on such a flimsy foundation as a kiss.

She's pretty. You kissed. What does it matter?

The trouble was, it did.

Emma was more than an attractive woman. She was a mother with a mother's responsibilities. He had to take Adam's needs into consideration as, he was sure, Emma did. Could he take on this little boy, as well? He couldn't make that decision lightly.

He glanced over at Adam, who grinned back at him, and Carter felt that warmth again. That sense of connection. Then his gaze drifted to Emma, who was watching him with puzzlement in her expression.

He squared his shoulders then turned, looking at the ranch buildings as they came closer. He and his grandfather had put up the hay shed, the shop and the small garage by the house. His great-grandfather had built the barn and the corrals and the house he had lived in.

With every step of Banjo's hooves toward the ranch, history pulled at him. Memories slipped into his mind. Naomi and Shannon screaming as Garret and Carter dumped them into the river. Hailey trying to snowboard off the roof of the hay shed and breaking her leg.

Papa Beck taking them on a wagon ride every year after haying was done. The wagon ride was one of the highlights of the year for the cousins. That, and Christmas when everyone came together at the ranch, singing carols with Papa and Nana Beck, unwrapping presents, eating way too many cinnamon buns.

The memories rolled over one another, braided snatches of voices, songs. Good memories folding over the sad ones.

Did he have to sell this place? Did he have to leave?

Peace is not the absence of trouble, peace is the presence of God.

He turned Banjo's head to make the last turn down the hill to the ranch as he thought again what the pastor had said on Sunday.

Dear God, he prayed, struggling to find the right words to address someone he hadn't talked to in a long while. *I don't know what to think. Show me what to do.*

Behind that prayer came a measure of peace. A sense of wait-and-see. He had time yet. He didn't have to make a decision today. Or tomorrow.

He and Emma could explore where things were going. He wanted to spend more time with Adam, too. To find a place for the boy in his life. If, indeed, that was the direction he and Emma would go.

"Who is visiting Nana Beck?"

Adam's voice startled him out of his thoughts. Adam was pointing at Nana's house, and Emma's attention was on Adam.

Tonight, he thought, tonight he wanted to talk to her.

He turned back to the house, and from here he saw the two figures Adam had referred to, sitting on the deck of his grandmother's house. Probably someone from church.

He reined his horse right, toward the corrals, and rode past the pasture. Banjo whinnied and the other horses called back then ran to join them.

"Yeah, yeah, I'm sure you missed these guys horribly," Carter said as he dismounted by the hitching rail.

To his surprise, he wasn't near as stiff as before. Getting used to riding again, he thought with a satisfied smile while looping the reins over Banjo's head.

"Those people are coming over here," Adam was saying as Emma helped him off the saddle.

The man walking toward them was tall, thin, with close-cropped graying hair and a net of wrinkles around his deep-blue eyes. His suit coat hung loose on his narrow shoulders, and his blue jeans were crisp and new over his cowboy boots.

The woman was short, plump, with curly hair framing her face. She wore a long skirt, a T-shirt and flip-flops.

As Sylvia always did.

"Do you know who they are?" Emma asked, glancing sidelong at Carter.

Carter's heart slowed, then began racing.

"Yeah. Those are Sylvia's parents. Harry's grandparents." His voice choked on the last sentence.

What were they doing here? How come they didn't tell him they were coming? What was he supposed to do with them?

"I'll take care of Banjo," Emma said quietly, coming to stand beside him.

He glanced down at her, then back at Sylvia's parents. The last time he saw them was across Harry's grave. After the agonizing reception in the church, he had raced home, thrown his things together, given Wade a few muttered instructions with promises for more to come later, hopped on his motorbike and left. He hadn't seen them since.

Carter dragged his attention back to Emma, his emotions a whirlwind of confusion, guilt and yet…his heart softened a moment as his eyes met hers.

Too easily he recalled what it was like to hold her in his arms. That feeling of everything being right in his world, if only for a moment.

"That's…that's okay. I'll deal with it."

"I'm sure you'll want to talk to them." Emma reached over and took Banjo's reins. "I know they want to talk to you. Very badly."

Carter held on to the reins, catching her attention. "The only person I want to talk to right now is you."

She blinked, but then her eyes lowered. "I don't know… I'm not sure."

"Neither am I," he said, an urgency entering his voice as he heard Kim Groot calling his name. "But what happened up there was more than just a kiss. You and I both know that."

She shot him a quick look, and in her eyes he caught a hint of uncertainty, which gave him hope. "Maybe, but right now you have other things to deal with."

"Later, then. We'll talk later."

She gave him a shy smile, a quick nod, and then before he could say anything more, the past caught up to the present.

"Carter." Kim Groot's voice fluttered across the moment and then Kim enveloped him in an awkward hug, her tears wetting his shirt.

He lifted his free hand and patted her on the shoulder, unsure of what was expected of him. Over Kim's head he saw Sylvia's father, Frank, reach up and swipe a hand over his eyes.

Emma eased away from him, leading Banjo, Dusty and Diamond to the pasture.

"Oh, son, it has been too long," Kim was saying as she stepped back and wiped away the moisture running down her cheeks. She looked up at him, her green eyes, so much like Sylvia's, red and glistening with tears.

Frank moved closer, laying his hand on Carter's shoulder. "Sorry for dropping in on you like this, but we haven't talked to you. Haven't seen you since—" His voice broke again, and Carter felt slowly drawn back to a storm of emotions he had tried to avoid for the past two years.

"Since the funeral," he said quietly, surprised at how calm and even his voice sounded.

Frank nodded, drawing in a shaky breath. He pulled a worn hanky out of his pocket and handed it to Kim.

She wiped her eyes, blew her nose and gave Carter a wavery smile.

"Like Frank said, I'm sorry for doing this to you, but I did call. Some girl answered."

"Emma," Carter said. "That's Emma who was here a moment ago." Emma who was now putting the horses away in the corral. Emma whom he had just kissed. Emma who was confusing him more than he had ever been confused before.

"Who is the little boy?"

As Carter dragged his attention away from Emma, he caught a peculiar inflection in Kim's voice and a frown on her face. Carter recognized the emotion. He had felt the same way when he first saw Adam on the ranch.

As if the child was an interloper.

"That's Adam. Her son."

"So she's married?"

"No."

Kim nodded slowly, as if pondering this situation. Carter wasn't sure what to make of her frown or the way her lips were pressed together. He wanted to defend Emma. To explain what she was really like.

"She seems to know how to handle horses," Frank said.

"She's good with them. And she loves the ranch."

"Sylvia loved the ranch so much," Kim said, a defensive note in her voice. "And I know she loved riding."

Frank frowned. "What do you mean? Sylvia was uncomfortable around the horses."

"No, she wasn't, was she, Carter?"

Carter's mind raced, trying to find a diplomatic way to answer his mother-in-law. Sylvia was an amazing woman and a wonderful wife, but she went riding with him only once or twice.

"How are you doing, Carter?" Frank asked, thankfully rescuing him from answering.

"I'm doing okay," he said quietly, shoving his gloves in his back pocket.

"We missed you, son," Frank said, his voice gentle. "It's been a long hard road for us, and we wanted to talk to you once in a while. Just to see how you were doing."

"But we couldn't because you were gone," Kim added, curving her arm through her husband's. "You're the only connection that remains to Harry and Sylvia. You're all we have left of our grandson and beautiful daughter." She sniffed and drew in a long breath. "She was so precious to us. She's been gone five years, but at times I still expect to see her coming through the door of our house singing those hymns she loved. She was such an example to me, so strong in her faith. I still don't understand why God took her away from us."

Carter didn't either, but he found he didn't want to talk about Sylvia. Not out here. Not in front of Emma.

"And then to lose Harry." Kim reached over and laid her hand on his arm. "If we feel the loss so keenly, you must feel it even more."

Each word Kim spoke laid another brick of guilt on his shoulders. The guilt of a man who couldn't keep his wife from dying. Who couldn't keep his son safe.

He thought about the kiss he and Emma shared. The feeling that overwhelmed him when he held her in his arms. He hadn't felt that way in so long.

But Kim's words haunted him.

How could he consider taking care of Emma or Adam?

Chapter Eleven

So what was she supposed to do? Sit and wait for Carter to come to her? Go to him?

Emma fidgeted in the easy chair tucked in one corner of her and Adam's cabin, her book forgotten on her lap. Adam snored lightly in his bed, the fresh air and excitement catching up to him.

Carter's in-laws had left over an hour ago. But still Carter didn't come. He had said he needed to talk to her. So where was he? Had seeing Sylvia's parents reminded him of his past too much, putting any future plans in jeopardy?

She rubbed her forehead, pressing away a headache that threatened. Too many thoughts roiling through her head. Too much to figure out. At one time she had a plan. A purpose. A goal.

Now she felt as if her life had been tossed upside down. As if God was playing some joke on her.

And Carter was becoming…what? Important to her? Special?

Her fingers drifted to her lips as if trying to find the kiss she had given him.

Oh, Emma, you are such a silly fool. Didn't you learn your lesson with Karl? With Adam's father?

But in the deepest places of her heart she sensed Carter was different. The fact that he grieved for his son, grieved for his wife, though hard to watch, showed her that relationships were important to him. He wouldn't have kissed her if he didn't mean it. Wouldn't have treated that lightly.

He's a guy. You know you can't depend on them. Where is he now? He said he wanted to talk to you, but where is he?

Emma tossed her book aside and reached for her Bible, hoping to find solace there. But as she turned the pages, the words blurred into each other.

She wanted to draw nourishment from scripture, but her mind kept slipping to what she and Carter had shared this afternoon.

Then a knock on the door sent her heart into overdrive.

She waited a moment, sent up a prayer for strength and opened the door of the cabin. Carter stood there on her deck, the light behind him casting shadows on his face. She couldn't read his expression.

She glanced back at Adam then stepped outside and closed the door, shutting off the light coming from the cabin. Carter became a darkened outline against the remnants of daylight.

"What do you want?" she asked, struggling and failing to sound in control.

Carter blew out a sigh and shoved one hand through his hair. "I want to talk to you."

Emma's heart fluttered at his admission, but the hoarse sound of his voice sent a chill of foreboding, chasing the momentary excitement away.

"Can we sit down?" he asked, walking over to a wooden bench.

Emma hesitated, then perched on the side of the bench closest to the window so she could watch Adam and be reminded of her first responsibility.

Carter eased himself down beside her.

He leaned forward, his elbows resting on his knees, his hands clasped between his legs,

"So, how were Kim and Frank Groot?" she asked, determined to be in charge of the conversation.

Carter pinched the bridge of his nose with his thumb and forefinger, kneading it slowly. "When you told me I should talk to them, I had hoped it would be on my time." He released a sigh into the gathering dark. "It was hard seeing them." Carter's voice faltered, and Emma felt a surge of pity for him as quiet fell between them again. This time Emma said nothing and waited for him to bridge the gap his silence had created.

"Did anyone tell you how Harry died?" Carter asked.

Emma shook her head. Wade had only said that Harry had died on the ranch. Nana Beck didn't tell her much more than that, and Emma hadn't pried.

"Remember how you commented on the fact that I didn't have a horse waterer on the place?"

She simply nodded.

"I had one once. A big plastic tub. The kind you attach a hose to and a switch shuts the hose off when the water level gets high enough."

"My dad had a couple of them on the yard." She wasn't crazy about them, but they were cheaper than putting in an underground heated waterer.

Carter dragged his hand over his face then exhaled slowly. "Wade and I had to go up to the high pasture and gather up some stray cows. Nana Beck usually babysat Harry, but she had the flu so I got someone to come in. She was an older woman who used to live down the road. She fell asleep on the couch. My son… Harry wasn't even in bed yet. He walked out of the house and went over to the corral to look at the horses. Probably feed them some carrots." He gave a short laugh. "He used to do that all the time. I noticed Adam does too."

Silence followed his comment, and Emma waited.

He drew in a shaky breath. "No one knows what happened. Whether he hit his head, or fell or one of the horses scared him. Wade came on the yard first and found him facedown in the waterer." He stopped there, staring straight ahead.

The heaviness of his words fell between them, creating a chasm she didn't know how to bridge with words. Finally, she realized nothing she said would make a difference. So she took his cold hands and wrapped hers around them.

His fingers tightened as he drew in a ragged breath. He clung to her hand, then turned it over in his grasp. "I should have been here. I should have stayed home. Should have let Wade take care of the cows himself. Harry was my responsibility, and I should have been here to…to save him."

His voice broke, and it was that mournful sound that eased away the flimsy barriers she tried to erect against him.

She cupped his chin in her hand and turned his face to her. "It was an accident."

"But he was my son. He counted on me to take care of him. I promised Sylvia I would take care of him."

"How were you supposed to stop what happened?"

He said nothing, but in the light of the cabin she caught the sheen of tears in his eyes.

"You took care of him. You got someone to come and watch him. What happened was a tragedy. An accident you couldn't have prevented."

Carter's eyes drifted shut and his tears slid down his cheeks, flowing over Emma's hand. "He was my son. My son." The words were ripped from the deepest part of him.

Emma slid her arms around his shoulders, wishing she was stronger, bigger. How could she help him in his grief when her arms barely went around him? How could she support him when he towered over her?

Then Carter laid his head on her shoulder, his arms clinging to her. And as his silent tears flowed, she knew all she had to do was be here. His shoulders shook and she held him, realizing his tears were cleansing, as well.

Seeing this strong, self-assured man crying brought tears to her own eyes. Yet, his utter vulnerability dove into her soul. His tears, shed in front of her, were as intimate as the kiss they had shared. Nothing would be the same between them after today.

"It's okay," she murmured, holding him as tightly as she could, thankful she could be here for him. "It's okay."

He drew a deep breath, then slowly straightened, leaving her feeling incomplete. He palmed away his tears, removing the evidence of his weakness.

He couldn't look at her, but she kept her hand on his shoulder and caught his other hand in hers.

"I'm sorry," he whispered, his voice still hoarse with grief. "I don't know what happened there. I haven't cried since the funeral."

She stroked his unruly hair back from his forehead.

"That's probably why," she said, her voice quiet, her hand lingering a moment on his head.

"But it's been two years." His voice held an edge of disappointed anger, as if frustrated with his lack of self-control. "Why now?"

She cupped his face and turned it toward her. His eyes, red now, looked haunted, but in contrast the lines bracketing his mouth had softened. "Could it be because you didn't allow your family to enter in your grief?"

Carter's shoulders lifted as he breathed in. Then he exhaled slowly, as if expelling the grief he had just experienced.

"I couldn't face it. I couldn't think about it, let alone talk about it. I lost Sylvia and then I lost Harry. It seemed easier to shut the memories off. To push them down and bury them. To pull back from my family."

"When you do that, grief will have its way," Emma said quietly, reluctantly pulling her hand away, his whiskers rasping on her skin. "After my father died, I was so angry with him but I still missed him so badly. At first I didn't want to cry, but the tears came anyhow. It's as if grief requires a certain amount of tears. If they are not shed, grief follows and shadows us until it is paid its due."

Carter gave a short laugh. "It certainly followed and shadowed me." His fingers pressed tightly against hers, as if drawing strength from her.

"Now that you're back I'm sure the pain is back."

His only response was a nod and a tightening of his jaw.

"Maybe seeing Sylvia's parents—Harry's grandparents—triggered the sorrow?"

Carter drew in another breath then his mouth lifted

in a wry smile. "Maybe. We talked and I realized it was like you said. They wanted to share stories. To talk."

"Was that difficult?"

"At first, yeah. I thought I didn't want to talk about him ever again. And yet..." His words drifted off and then, to her surprise, his mouth curved in a wry smile. "It hurt and it was hard to watch their grief, but at the same time, it was like I was allowed to still say he was my son. I was allowed to bring back the good memories. The things that made me smile and gave me joy."

"Why wouldn't you?"

Carter lifted his shoulder in a shrug. "Because I didn't think I deserved to."

"I know you were a good father, Carter." Emma spoke quietly, a note of conviction in her voice. "You loved your son. Your tears showed me that. Even the fact that you stayed away because it hurt to be here shows how much you love and miss him." She had to stop, her own thoughts casting back to Adam's father. How quickly he neglected his responsibility. Or Karl. How easily he abandoned her. Or her father.

Panic trembled through her even as his hands held hers. Carter wasn't like that, she reminded herself. Carter was a good man.

Why do you think you need to defend him? I thought you were trying to stay away from him?

"You took care of your son even while you were still running the ranch," she said, trying to stop the negative voice in her head. "You manned up. You took your responsibility seriously and you took care of him. And even though you knew it would hurt to be here again, you came back when Nana needed you."

He looked down at her, his gray eyes clear, intent. "You sound like you're defending me."

"Maybe I am," she said quietly. "Maybe I need to remind myself that there are good men in the world."

"I don't know if I'm a good man..." Carter's words eased away and his grip tightened on her hand. "But I know that you're a good woman."

His words flew into her heart and settled there.

And confused her. She struggled to keep a bit of distance. She couldn't get pulled into this.

"I know that God knows your heart in spite of how you see yourself," she said quietly.

"I used to think God didn't care about me," Carter said. "I used to think I was on my own."

"And now?"

Carter released a light laugh. "I don't know. I know that when I was in church I fought with anger with God over what happened and yet..." He shook his head, as if confused.

"Yet?" she prompted.

"It was good to realize that God is still there no matter what I may think. That He is still trying to be a part of my life. I feel like I have to try to find my way back to Him."

"It's not hard," Emma said quietly.

"I don't know where to start."

"I could pray with you. That would be a start."

Carter's mouth shifted into a wry smile. "You could," he agreed.

Emma twined her fingers through his then lowered her head. "Dear Lord, thank You for Carter. For his doubts and for his anger with You. Because it means that he cares about You. Lord, You know the pain he's carrying. Please let him know that You understand what it is like to lose a son." She faltered there, wondering if she had gone too far, then she felt Carter's hands tighten on hers and she carried on. "Thank You, Lord, for his searching. Let him know that he will be restless until he finds his rest in You. Help all of us to know where our hope and peace lie. With You. Not with this world." She paused, letting the moment settle. Then she lifted her head.

Carter was looking at her, a bemused expression on his face. "You talk so easily to God," he said.

"I didn't always. I've had my own struggles with God and with my life and the direction it was going." She looked down at their intertwined hands, feeling as if things had shifted again. Shifted and deepened. "But I learned that no matter where I go, God has been there before and He promises me that He will never leave me. I've clung to that promise in spite of some of the things that happened to me." She stopped there, hoping he didn't think she was preaching at him, yet wanting him to know that her faith in God was not dependent on her actions, but on God's faithfulness. And His love.

"You're quite a woman, Emma Minton," Carter said quietly, lifting his hand to cup her face. "Thank you for praying with me."

She wasn't sure what to say so she kept quiet, but the touch of his hand on her face distracted her.

Then his thumb made gentle circles on her cheek, each movement shifting her awareness of him.

"I'm glad I kissed you this afternoon." His hand stopped its enticing movement then slipped to the back of her neck and anchored itself there.

"I'm glad you kissed me too." She raised her face, their gazes locking. She felt as if she sank into his eyes.

"I want to kiss you again," he whispered.

The practical part of Emma called out warnings. Reminded her that this was tenuous. That nothing about either of their lives was settled or sure.

But the lonely part of her, the part that yearned for what Carter gave, made her move closer. She set her hand on his shoulder then angled her head so that when their lips met, it was a perfect fit.

He pulled away and she murmured her protest, but he brushed light, gentle kisses on her cheeks. Her forehead. Her eyelids.

She couldn't breathe. His kisses had literally stolen her breath.

Then he drew her head down to his shoulder, cradling it there and pulling her close to him.

Emma let her head rest on his shoulder. Let his arms hold her close. Let herself be held up. She had been in charge of her and Adam so long, having someone support her filled a deep need she didn't dare acknowledge.

"I don't know what's happening, Emma," Carter whispered against her hair, his breath warm and enticing. "But I know it feels right. Like my life has turned around and the things I once wanted aren't so important."

His questions ignited an ember of hope.

But her own questions and concerns kept it tamped down. Tomorrow would bring more questions. More searching. More maybes.

For now the chill of the evening made itself known. Emma shivered and eased away from the sanctuary of Carter's arms. "I should go in," she whispered, her cheeks warm in spite of the cold. She looked up at him, then, because she could, stroked his face and ran her hand through his thick hair.

He caught her hand, pressed a kiss to the back of it. "I'll see you tomorrow."

The promise in his voice sent a thrill of anticipation racing through her.

"It's Sunday tomorrow," she said quietly, though she wasn't sure why she felt she had to bring that up.

"Do you need a ride to church? I'm bringing Nana in her car."

His suggestion created such a perfect domestic scene in her mind. Man. Woman. Child. Grandmother. All coming to church together in one vehicle.

In spite of his kisses, in spite of what they had shared, a part of her wanted to hold back and protect her independence. Just in case.

"I'll take my truck," was all she said.

To her surprise he simply nodded as he got up, drawing her to her feet. "Then we'll see you tomorrow."

He walked with her the few steps to the door of the cabin. "Good night Emma. Thank you for being you," he whispered as he brushed a kiss across her forehead.

Then before his kiss cooled on her face, he was down the stairs, jogging across the yard to his own cabin.

Emma waited a moment, unwilling to return to the cabin. This time was like a place apart from her ordinary life. As soon as she opened the door, she would be faced with her responsibilities.

Just a few minutes more, she thought, her finger tracing her lips, resurrecting the memory of Carter's kiss.

Tomorrow she could figure out where to put this. Tomorrow she could be a responsible mom again. Tomorrow her other worries would crowd in and threaten this peace.

For this moment she wanted to be a woman kissed by

a wonderful man. A woman growing more attracted to a man with nebulous plans.

She stopped herself there.

A tendril of worry began working itself up from her subconscious. Was she being irresponsible? She had no idea what lay ahead, and Carter's comments were nothing to make plans around.

Do not worry about tomorrow for tomorrow will worry about itself.

The passage from Matthew settled her thoughts, and as she looked up a falling star streaked across the evening sky, like a tiny benediction. Emma smiled at the sight, and with that memory resting in her mind, she opened the door and stepped into the cabin.

"Miss Minton. Miss Minton."

Emma pulled her attention away from the woman she was talking to in the foyer of the church and turned just as a slight man limped toward her. The overhead lights shone on his balding head, which was offset by the bushiness of his beard and mustache.

"Mr. Devieber, how are you doing?" Emma flashed him a bright smile as he came to a halt in front of her. Scott Devieber owned a bed-and-breakfast on the edge of Hartley Creek, and on a whim she had gone there and applied for a position the last time she was in town. The biggest plus was the fact that the B and B was situated on six acres of fenced pasture. "How is business?"

Scott stroked his beard as he nodded his head. "Well. Now. That's what I need to talk to you about." He eased out a sigh, shifted his weight, neither of which boded well for what he supposed he had to say. "I had hoped to call you earlier, but because you don't have a cell phone,

I gotta tell you now." His pause only underlined what Emma knew was coming next. "Sorry, Emma. I'm sure you're a great worker, but I can't hire you."

And you had to tell me this on Sunday right after a service where I was encouraged to trust in the Lord?

With intense purpose, Emma kept her smile in place. "That's too bad, Mr. Devieber. Did you fill the position?" When she had applied it was vacant, and in a follow-up phone call Mr. Devieber assured her that she had a good chance at the job.

"Actually, I have a niece coming to visit me from New Zealand. She's looking for work. Says she wants to spend the winter skiing here." He lifted his hands in a "what can I do" gesture.

"Of course. I understand," Emma said brightly, though inside another hope died. Another worry twisted its way through the peace the church service had granted her.

What was she supposed to do? How was she going to take care of Adam? Where were they going to live, and what was she going to do with her beloved horses?

"But I trust in you O Lord; I say, 'You are my God.' My times are in your hands..."

The words of the Bible verse the minister had read this morning wound their way around her panicky soul.

"I hope she enjoys her time here," Emma said, struggling to be upbeat and positive. "I know that the ski hill is amazing." Not that she knew from personal experience. She hadn't had the time or money to go skiing.

"I'm sorry. I know this position would have worked well for you and your horses. But I'm sure you'll find something." He stroked his beard, gave her another apologetic look then left.

Scratch that faint hope, Emma thought. She turned in

time to see Adam slouching toward her, his head down, his hands shoved in the pocket of his red hoodie.

"What's the matter, son?" she asked, crouching down to his height, no mean feat in her narrow skirt. "You look sad."

"Allister can't come over," he said, heaving a deep sigh. "I wanted him to help with the tree fort. I'm so disappointed."

In spite of her own disappointments, Emma grinned at his word choice. He was getting older, she thought with a gentle pang. This September he would be starting school.

Where? How?

Emma quashed the frantic questions.

"I'm disappointed too," Emma said, stroking his head lightly. "But you know, maybe you and I can work on the tree fort ourselves."

Adam shrugged at her suggestion.

"What? I'm a good builder," she said with mock injury.

Adam pushed his toe against the carpet of the church foyer. "Not as good as Allister. He has a hammer."

"Who has a hammer?"

Carter's deep voice behind her created a trickle of anticipation.

She got up slowly, unconsciously fiddling with the white silk flower she had, on a whim, pinned on her red blouse. Now it seemed ostentatious and a little foolish.

She caught his gaze flicking from the flower to her. Did his eyes brighten, or was that just her imagination?

"Allister. My friend," Adam grumped. "He was going to help me with the tree fort. But now he can't come." This was followed with another theatrical sigh.

Carter turned his attention to Adam, and he smiled, as well. "Maybe I'll have to help you."

Emma hoped her surprise didn't show on her face. She knew Carter and Harry had started the tree fort, and now he was willing to help her son work on it?

"That would be so, so cool." Adam's face lit up like a kid at Christmas.

"Don't you need to cut the hay this week?" Emma asked.

"Yeah, but I'm sure I can take some time to help Adam." Carter's eyes crinkled at the corners as their gazes met, and a smile crawled across his lips.

Emma felt her own answering smile, and it was as if the people milling around them in the foyer slipped away and the world had shrunk down to only the two of them.

"That would be great," she said quietly.

Emma wanted to ask him if he was okay working on a project he had started with Harry, but now was not the time. Maybe later.

Later. The possibilities of that word created a tiny thrill of expectation.

"So, my dears, what are you all doing for lunch?" Nana Beck joined them, her bright eyes flicking around the group.

Emma caught a gleam in the elderly woman's eye as she zeroed in on Emma and Carter. *Don't blush. Don't blush.*

But the more aware she became of her reaction, the harder it became to suppress.

And the gleam in Nana Beck's eyes grew.

"Shannon wants us to come for dinner," Nana announced. "And don't you even think about protesting, Emma Minton. You and Adam are invited too." She leveled Emma a glance that brooked no argument. Before Emma could either accept or decline, an older woman tugged on Nana's arm, drawing her attention away from Emma and Carter.

"Sorry about that," Carter was saying. "But you know Nana. If you want to go home, that's okay."

Emma was thankful for the out he gave her, yet some ornery part of her wished he insisted she come.

Then he moved a bit closer and brushed his hand along her arm. "But I'd kind of like it if you did come."

That was all the encouragement she needed.

"Are you sure you want the door here?" Carter called out.

Emma shaded her face against the lowering sun and looked up at Carter standing astride the uprights of the tree fort, shadows of branches crisscrossing over his shirt.

"That looks good to me," she called out. "What do you think, Adam?"

Adam squinted up at Carter, his hand on his hips, looking like a little adult as he considered. "I think so," he said with a quick nod.

"Starting to saw," Carter announced, yanking on the starting cord of the chain saw. Chips of wood spat out as the saw bit into the solid wall of the fort, and minutes later Carter had cut an opening.

"Are you guys almost done here?" Emma asked Adam. "It's your bedtime."

"Can't I stay up a bit longer?" Adam whined. "I want to finish making the door."

"That's not going to happen tonight, sport." Carter lowered the chain saw by a rope then clambered down the ladder he had built last night. For the past three days Carter had worked in the evenings, helping Adam as he had promised. And each day his smile grew bigger and Adam's anticipation ran higher.

And the tiny spark of hope ignited that night on the porch with Carter grew in Emma's chest. Carter had never said anything more about his plans, but she got the sense that both of them were hovering on the edge of a change. A shift in direction.

Once down on the ground, Carter looked up at the sky and the gathering clouds. "Glad we got that hay cut today," he said. "Looks like rain's coming." He gave her a quick smile then, as casual as can be, he ran his forefinger down her cheek.

His offhand familiarity formed a mixture of perplexing emotions.

The past week with Carter was time out of time. A step back from her world of worry and concern and fear for the future. It was as if she and Carter had an unspoken pact to see where they were going without talking about it.

They worked together and ate together at Nana Beck's in the evening. After dinner they sat around and visited. After Adam went to bed, Carter would come by and he and Emma would sit on the deck and talk.

They talked about the ranch. About Sylvia. And even about Harry once in a while. Carter's voice still held a trace of pain when they did, but each time Harry's name came up, Carter seemed more at peace.

And each time they talked, Emma let herself experience the potential of possibilities. Of hesitant maybes.

"I hope it doesn't rain too long," Emma said, struggling to keep herself grounded. "I want to get some more beans picked this week."

"Nana sure appreciates the fresh produce," Carter said. "And she enjoys our dinners together."

Emma looked up at him. "I do too. Nana is a special person. I'm glad she's feeling better. Do you think she'll change her mind about moving into town?"

"I don't think so." Carter's expression grew serious, and he caught one corner of his lip between his teeth. "And about that. I need to talk to you later," he said, his voice holding a curious note.

"Sure. Of course." She felt puzzled at his sudden switch in topic, but the intensity of his expression and the way he held her gaze sent a storm of worry swirling through her head. They'd been talking for the past few evenings. What could he say to her tonight that he hadn't said in previous nights?

"Looking forward to it," she said, keeping her tone light. Playful.

He just looked at her, and the storm grew.

Then he picked up the chain saw and walked toward the machine shed.

"Mom, do I have to go to bed? Can I work a bit more?" Adam picked up a hammer and a handful of nails.

Emma snapped her attention back to her son. "No, son, tomorrow is another day."

"But…"

"No buts. You need to go to bed. Now let's put the tools away."

"I don't want to go to bed." Adam's lower lip quivered, which showed Emma that bed was not an option, it was a necessity.

"Of course you don't." Emma gently removed the hammer from his hand. "It's hard to go to bed when there's so many fun things to do."

"Tomorrow can we go up to the hills to get the lanterns out of the cabin? For my fort?"

"No. I don't think so."

"But in a couple of days Carter will be gone, and I want him to finish the tree fort before he goes."

"What?" Emma felt her heart slow and turn over. "What do you mean Carter will be gone?"

"I heard him say to Nana that he had to go. So we have to get the stuff tomorrow. *Have to.* So we can finish before he goes." Adam tugged on her hand as if for emphasis.

Emma swallowed as her heart raced in her chest. Her cheeks burned as reaction set in. Carter. Saying he had to leave?

This didn't ring true with Carter's current behavior. *Men can't be trusted. Men can't be trusted.*

The old voice returned and, with it, her usual doubts.

But he had kissed her. He talked about making changes. He wanted to speak to her tonight. Surely it wasn't to tell her he was leaving? Not after what they had shared?

"That's why I want to finish the fort," Adam was saying, his voice taking on a petulant whine. "And go get the stuff from the cabin."

Emma dragged her attention away from the voices whirring around her head, playing on her uncertainty and the delicate balance she struggled to maintain the past few days.

"No, Adam. You have to go to bed now."

He stamped his foot in the ground, his hands clenched into little fists. "I want to go now. Right now."

"Stop it, Adam. We're not going anywhere right now. It's time for you to go to bed." She reached for his hand, but he spun away and ran toward the river. What was wrong with him?

"Adam, come back here." Her voice grew extra firm.

Adam slowed down then stopped and turned around, tears shining in his eyes. "I have to get the lantern. Because then I can put a light in the fort. So people who are lost can find it."

Her heart jolted at his little declaration. What was going through his head? Was he worried about Carter leaving?

"Adam, honey, I know you want to get the lantern. But we can't do it tonight, and we can't do it tomorrow. I promise you when we have a chance, you and I will ride up and get it."

Adam frowned at that, as if he didn't believe her. Truth to tell, she didn't blame him. She didn't know what she was allowed to think about or plan for, either.

Please, Lord. Help me to take one moment at a time.

She waited for Adam, and finally he trudged back to her, his head hanging and his feet dragging. After half an hour of coaxing him, she tucked Adam in bed. Thankfully, he fell asleep while she said his evening prayers with him.

Emma wasn't sure what had gotten into him, but he seemed determined to get that lantern.

She waited until she knew he was well asleep, reading her Bible to still the voices of uncertainty Adam's little comment had whipped up.

Peace is not the absence of trouble, peace is the presence of God.

Emma clung to that saying and held it close. As she did, she reminded herself that her hope was primarily in God. Not in the circumstances of her life.

Adam snorted then rolled over, his arms flopping to the side. Utterly innocent, trusting and utterly dependent on her.

Emma put the Bible away, pressed a kiss to his warm cheek, then slipped out of the cabin. Usually Carter came to her cabin, but after what Adam had told her she felt restless and edgy and unable to sit still.

So instead of waiting for Carter to come to her, she would go to him.

A light rain drizzled down as she walked across the yard. Lights were on in Nana Beck's house, but Carter's cabin was dark.

As she came closer, the door of Nana's house flew open and music and noise spilled out, followed by an unfamiliar woman. "C'mon, Carter, let me check out my cabin. I can't believe you moved into it."

The woman was tall and slender, and a spill of reddish hair flowed down her back. Hailey, Emma guessed, recognizing the hair from pictures Nana Beck had shown her. Carter's cousin and Shannon's sister.

Emma held back, unsure of what to do.

She heard Shannon say something, followed by a comment from Carter. Though she couldn't understand what they said, it was apparent some type of family reunion was going on. Hailey, she knew, hadn't been around for years.

Unwilling to disturb them, she returned to her cabin. She slipped quietly inside and went to bed herself, taking her book and attaching a small reading light to it so she wouldn't wake Adam. Obviously, Carter wouldn't be talking to her tonight.

But what had he wanted to say to her?

Chapter Twelve

Emma rolled onto her side, snuggling deeper in the blankets. The only sound in the cabin was the steady drum of rain, which had poured down, hard, all night. Obviously the plans for the day would be put on hold. Which meant she and Adam could sleep a little longer.

She hoped it wouldn't cause too many problems for Carter and the hay crop.

The thought of Carter sent a tiny shock through her system.

He had said he wanted to talk to her, and though he'd had his cousins visit, she had waited for a couple of hours, clinging to a faint hope that he might come when they were gone. But when the sound of Shannon's car faded into the distance, Carter didn't come knocking on her door. When she had finally fallen asleep, it was to dream of her and Carter kissing. Her and Carter arguing. Carter driving away on his motorbike.

Emma gave up on grabbing some more sleep, sat up in bed and swung her legs over the edge, her feet looking for her slippers as she slipped her housecoat over her pajamas.

Maybe today she would find out what he wanted, she thought, rubbing her eyes then pushing herself off the bed.

Stifling a yawn, she padded across the cold cabin floor to Adam's bed, but as she got close her heart stuttered in her chest.

Adam wasn't in his bed.

"Adam? Adam?" She tried not to let panic take root. "Adam, are you hiding?" she called out, her gaze racing around the cabin, looking for possible hiding spots.

But there was no answering giggle. No sound of a body moving anywhere in the cabin.

It took her mere seconds to plunge her legs into her jeans, stab her arms in a T-shirt and sweater. As she did, she noticed that Adam's boots were gone, as was his rain slicker.

Relax, relax, she told herself as she tugged on her boots and snatched her own slicker off the peg. Maybe he went to Nana Beck's house. Or Carter's cabin. Or the tree fort. Yes, probably the tree fort.

She grabbed her hat, slapped it on her head and ran outside.

Water poured off the roof, splashing into puddles beside the cabin as she scanned the yard, misted with rain. No sign of Adam. In the mud at the foot of the stairs she saw a set of footprints leading in the opposite direction of the tree fort, so Adam probably wasn't there. And three steps later, the footprints disappeared in the mud.

Slow down, she told herself, buttoning up her slicker, her hands numb with fear. *Don't make this bigger than it has to be. Take it one step at a time. He wouldn't have gone far.*

She jogged across the yard to Nana Beck's house and knocked on the door.

Nana came to the door, looking bright, trim and happier than Emma had seen her in a while. Then her cheerfulness faded into concern. "What's wrong, my dear? You look worried."

"Have you seen Adam?" Emma asked breathlessly, needing to get right to the point.

"Not since yesterday afternoon."

The first sliver of icy panic pierced her self-control. "Is Carter here?"

"I believe he's in his cabin yet, though I'm surprised. I thought for sure he would be up and about early this morning. He said he had to get to town today. Said he had something important to do, though he was all secretive about it."

Part of what she said registered in Emma's mind, but all she understood for now was that Adam wasn't here.

"Thanks, Nana. I gotta go." Emma took a step back and spun around, clattering down the stairs, dread clenching her heart in an icy fist.

"If I see Adam, I'll tell him you're looking for him," Nana called out as Emma raced across the yard to Carter's cabin.

Please, Lord, let him be there. Please Lord, she prayed as she slipped and slid in the mud gathering on the yard. She ran up the steps to Carter's cabin and pounded on the door. No answer.

She raised her hand to pound again, and the door opened.

Carter stood framed in the doorway, dressed and looking as if he was ready to go out. He wore pressed blue jeans and an ironed khaki shirt and his motorcycle chaps hung over his arm.

His cheeks shone from a recent shaving, and his hair was tamed and neatly brushed.

Where was he going in this weather?

The question was banished as Emma's gaze slipped past Carter into the cabin. No little boy hove into view. No voice called out for her.

"Emma, what's wrong?" Carter tossed the chaps aside and caught her by the arms. "Your face is white as a sheet."

"Is Adam here? Have you seen him?"

Carter's grip tightened. "Not this morning. Why?"

"He's not in his bed. He's not at Nana Beck's. I didn't see him on the yard. I have no idea where he could be." She heard her voice growing more shrill and hysterical with each word, but she couldn't stop herself.

Carter's face blanched, and Emma knew exactly what he was thinking. "Okay. We need to go looking." He grabbed his slicker and hat and put them on.

"You're sure he's not at the tree fort?" Carter asked as he stepped out of the cabin.

"I saw his footprints in the mud in front of the cabin leading the other way."

Carter dropped his hat on his head and ran down the steps, glancing around the yard. "Adam. Adam, come here right now," he called.

The only sound she heard was the rain splattering on the yard and the far-off whinny of the horses.

"Looks like he came here." Carter pointed to the mark of a small boot in the wet ground. "But then, it looks like he went away again, but not back to your cabin."

He kept his eyes on the ground, following the footsteps.

"Did he say anything last night?" Carter asked. "Anything about going anywhere today?"

He sounded so calm. So in charge.

But Emma saw the anxiety in the lines bracketing his mouth.

"No. He just said he wanted to finish the fort today because…" Her voice faltered there. One thing at a time. Find Adam. Deal with Carter later.

Carter chewed at his lip, his eyes skittering around the yard, his hands resting on his hips, his frown deepening. "Yesterday he talked about going up to that old abandoned prospector cabin and getting some stuff out of there." He walked away from Emma, his eyes on the ground.

All Emma wanted to do was run to the corral and grab a horse, jump on it and ride off. Call 911. Do something. Anything. Find her son.

But she had no plan, and she sensed Carter did.

"Here. His prints again." Carter knelt down and pointed to another set of footprints leading away from the yard. "Looks like he's heading up to the hills." Carter turned back to the yard. "Let's saddle up the horses. You take Diamond and I'll take Elijah. He's faster than Banjo."

Finally. A job to do.

She squelched her other fears. Because to go up to the hills, Adam had to cross the river.

Emma headed to the tack shed, slipping in the mud. It seemed to take hours to saddle up the horses with fingers clumsy with fear and cold. Then, finally they were up and riding away from the ranch.

They came to the river, and fear clutched Emma with an icy hand. *Please, Lord, don't let him have fallen into the river. Please, Lord, keep him safe. Please, Lord, let us find him. Please.*

Carter stopped by the river and rode away from the bridge downstream. Then he passed Emma and rode upstream.

Then without a word to Emma, he led his horse across the footbridge, Elijah's shod hooves beating out a muffled rhythm on the wooden bridge. Emma followed.

"Are you sure that's where he would be going?" Emma called out as they rode up the hill. What if Adam had left the yard going down the road? What if they were heading away from him?

Carter didn't answer, his head down, water dripping off his hat onto his broad shoulders. Then a few feet after they got off the bridge, he pointed down. As Emma rode by, she saw it too. The remains of a print in the dirt.

Her son's boot.

Carter flexed his fingers inside his sodden gloves, unclenched his teeth, lowered his shoulders. At least Adam had made it safely across the river. As far as he could guess, the boy had gone to the cabin. They would find him there, give him trouble for making them so scared. They would have a reunion, and then he could talk to Emma about his plans.

Carter stifled his panic as he shifted in his saddle, looking back.

Emma hunched over the saddle, looking down at the trail, water dripping off her hat. As if sensing his gaze on her, she looked up, but her cheeks were pale and her eyes shone with a frantic light.

He wanted to reassure her that everything would be

all right. But his own worries were like a howling storm that he struggled to stay on top of.

Please, Lord. Please, Lord.

His prayers were no more than this two-word plea as he pushed Elijah on up the trail that grew more muddy with each passing minute. It couldn't happen again. He couldn't lose another—

There. Another track. Fainter now.

Please, Lord.

He needed to keep his wits about him and keep himself calm and in control. He had to reassure himself that Adam was okay. He couldn't panic. Emma depended on him.

Old doubts and fears spiraled up and with them even more desperate prayers.

You're not the right person for the job. You were gone when Harry died. You couldn't keep Sylvia safe.

This is different. You're doing something about this. You're going to look for him.

The rain battered at them when they were in the open and dripped relentlessly off the trees when they were sheltered. Carter's shirt underneath his slicker grew damp, and his pants were now completely soaked. He should have taken the time to get his leather chaps.

There hadn't been time. There had only been fear and the thought that time was running out.

He nudged Elijah in the ribs, and his horse pushed forward again, head down, feet churning in the mud of the trail.

After what felt like hours, the trail turned out into the open area where the cows were pastured. Carter's mind flicked back to that perfect afternoon as they watched the calves racing across the pasture. As he held Emma in his arms and kissed her.

The day his life had made a drastic shift.

Now he was riding up in these same hills looking for her son, struggling to keep his own worries for the boy at bay.

He pushed on.

Finally he saw the break in the trees, and a few moments later Carter pulled up to the cabin, slid off his horse and tied him up with a few quick twists of the halter rope.

He arrived at the door almost the same time as Emma.

"Adam," she called out as Carter yanked open the door.

The interior of the cabin was gloomy and dank, and Carter had to strain his eyes to see.

A collapsed wooden bed sat in one corner of the cabin, a table pushed up against the wall. A few muddy footprints were on the floor, and water dripped into the cabin from the various holes in the roof.

Carter couldn't see Adam.

"Adam. Adam." Emma's voice, hoarse with fear, echoed in the empty building.

She turned to Carter, catching him by the arms. "Where is he? Where is Adam?"

Carter wanted to pull her into his arms. To hold her close and protect her, but right now they had other concerns.

His gaze swept over the cabin. Think. Think.

Then he noticed that the lanterns that Adam had wanted so badly for the tree fort were gone.

"He's been here." Carter struggled to absorb the information. To sift through it and figure out where Adam could be.

"But where is he now? We didn't see him on the trail. What if he wandered off the trail and we passed him?"

Carter laid his finger on her lips, stopping the spill of panic. "He would have heard us, or the horses would have seen him. He wouldn't have gone off the trail. He didn't on the way up here, he wouldn't have on the way back."

Her face was wet, and he suspected not all the moisture on her cheeks were rain.

"We'll find him, Emma. I promise you."

Please, Lord. Please, Lord.

Emma choked back a sob and dashed her hand over her face. Then she pulled in a quavering breath and glanced around the cabin.

"So where would he have gone?"

Carter had to still his own rising fear as he tried to think. He glanced around the cabin again then stepped outside.

Please, Lord. Please, Lord. Let us find him.

He concentrated on the ground, looking for a clue. Under the trees around the cabin the ground wasn't as wet.

Then he saw it. Another footprint. This one didn't head down the trail back to the ranch. It went up.

"Did you ever tell Adam about the abandoned mine up in the hills?" he asked Emma.

"Wade did when we first came up here. I think he pointed it out to him."

Bingo.

"I think I know where Adam is."

Emma clung to the confidence in Carter's voice even harder than she clung to the saddle horn as they worked their way up the narrow mountain trail. The horses slipped and slid but kept on going.

Rain dripped from her hat brim down the back of her neck, and her pants were so wet and chilled she couldn't feel her thighs.

None of it mattered. All she wanted was to see Adam, to know that he was safe. Their little battle of last night seemed so small and petty now. Why didn't she go up with him to the cabin last night? It would have taken an hour with the horses.

Because he was exhausted and needed his sleep.

So why didn't you go get the lantern?

Because I couldn't leave him alone.

Her mental conversations flipped back and forth between rational reasoning and unreasoning fear.

Please, Lord, let him be okay. Please don't take him from me too.

Her prayer held a note of desperation, and as she prayed she lifted her head, her eyes glued to Carter's back. He looked straight ahead, urging his horse on, as if he couldn't get to the site fast enough.

"There it is," Carter called out, raising his voice above the rain falling on the trees. He pointed as he looked back, and Emma saw it too. The cave opening.

Carter was already out of the saddle, tying up his horse before Emma, cold and stiff and wet, could even lift her leg out of the stirrup. She dismounted, dropped the reins, then charged up the incline behind Carter.

He was in the cave before she scrambled to the opening.

"He's here, Emma. He's here." Carter's voice sounded shaky. "He's all right."

It was only adrenaline that got Emma to the cave, because the relief flooding through her loosened her bones. She staggered into the cave behind Carter, looking wildly around in the half-light. Then she saw a bundle curled up against the wall.

"Adam. Oh, Adam." She stumbled toward him, but Carter was there already, checking him over.

"He's okay," Carter said, sitting back on his haunches, his hands falling to his sides as if they were too heavy to hold up.

Emma crouched down beside her son, then lifted him into her arms. He groaned. Then his eyes opened and he smiled.

"Mommy. I got the lantern."

"Did you? That's great." She pulled him tightly against her, rocking him, tears of relief and gratitude spilling from her eyes.

"Thank You, Lord," she whispered, stroking Adam's head, kissing his cool cheeks. "Thank You."

Adam pulled back. "Why are you crying, Mommy?"

Emma sniffed and swiped her gloved hand over her eyes. "Because I thought you were lost," she said, her fear slowly melting away now that she knew he was safe. "I woke up this morning and you weren't in your bed. I thought something bad had happened."

Adam lowered his head. "I just wanted to get the lantern, and you said you wouldn't. So I thought I would get it before you woked up."

"Oh, honey," Emma said, her voice wobbly with relief.

"You should have told us," Carter said. "That was very dangerous for you to come up here all by yourself."

Emma caught the strained tone of Carter's voice. As if this was too close to his own loss.

"I'm sorry," Adam mumbled. "I won't do it again."

"Why did you come up here?" Carter asked.

"It was raining and the cabin was wet. I remembered Wade told me about the cave."

"It's okay, honey. We found you," she said, her own voice trembling with relief. "I'm so glad you stayed here," she said. "That you didn't go wandering off." She drew gently back and stroked his hair away from his face. "I was so worried about you."

"I'm sorry, Mommy." He bit his lip, and Emma could see that he was close to tears himself. She forced herself to stand and pulled him up with her.

"I know you are, but you know what? Now we have to go back to the ranch."

Adam spun his head around, looking. "My lantern. Where's my lantern? We have to go get it."

"We need to go right back to the ranch," Carter said, the firm note in his voice brooking no argument. "We can come back for that another time."

"But I came up here to get the lantern."

"Adam—"

Carter and Emma spoke at the same time. Carter held up his hand. "Sorry. I didn't mean to—"

"It's okay." Emma gave him a smile of understanding. She didn't mind his interjection. In spite of the tension they had just experienced, his behavior with Adam created another connection with Carter. It was as if, for the first time in her life, she had help and support in taking care of her son.

Emma zipped up Adam's jacket, hoping it would be warm enough. "Okay. Let's go," she said, tugging his hat down on his head.

They stepped out into the rain which, if anything, had increased in the past few minutes. Thankfully the trip down would take less time than it took coming up—and with a lot less stress.

"Adam should probably ride with you on the trip home," Carter suggested. "I don't trust Elijah with two people."

Emma nodded and climbed into the saddle. She sat back as far as she could then held out her arms for Adam. Carter set him in front of Emma. Diamond jigged a bit but settled as Emma tugged lightly on the reins. Carter smiled up at her, and she read a promise in his eyes. When they came back to the ranch, they would talk.

Once Carter was in the saddle, Emma turned and led the way down the mountain back to the ranch. They were going home. The thought made her smile.

The trail had gotten muddier since they had gone up, and Diamond slid a few times. But Emma trusted him to keep his footing and for the most part let him have his head.

But all the while they rode she felt Carter behind them, protecting them, watching out for them.

After what felt like an eternity, the trail made one more turn and then, through a break in the trees, she saw the ranch.

"See, honey. We're almost home," she said to Adam, shivering with relief and the cold. "We just have to cross the river and we're home."

They got to the creek, and Emma's heart dropped like a stone.

The bridge was washed out and the river, once a benign babbling stream of water had swollen to almost twice its size and had become a raging swirl of logs and muddied water.

Carter pulled up beside her, and Emma read the concern on his face. He glanced upstream then down. "This is the best place to cross," he said, raising his voice above the noise of the creek and the rain. "Farther up it's too narrow, and farther down it gets too rocky and steep."

"I'll go first," Emma called out, pushing down her own trepidation. "Diamond is sure-footed."

Carter still didn't look convinced, but they both knew there was no other option. He put his hand on her arm, his own fingers blue with cold. "You be careful. I'll be praying for you."

Emma gave him a tight smile, sent up her own prayer for safety, then nudged Diamond in the side and loosened the reins to give him more freedom.

Diamond shook his head then, when Emma nudged him again, took a tentative step into the water. Emma tried not to look at the water gushing past them, her heart fluttering in her chest, her breath coming in quick gasps. She felt the force of the swelling water against Diamond's body as he took one cautious step after another.

Just a few more feet, she thought, trying not to urge him on. Just a bit more.

"Emma. Watch out," Carter shouted, his voice urgent.

She turned in time to see the log surging toward them. Before she could react, it hit Diamond. He lost his footing, and Emma and Adam were plunged into the icy water.

Chapter Thirteen

There was no time to think. No time to plan.

Carter threw off his slicker and plunged into the river. The cold sucked the air out of him, and it was all he could do to keep his head above the water.

A wave washed over him and he came up, sputtering, his eyes filmed with dirty water.

Where were they? Where did they go?

There. Downstream. Too far.

He saw Emma's head bobbing, her arm flailing. Where was Adam?

Please, Lord. Please not again.

He dug his arms in the water, pulling, swimming and then, miraculously, he was closer. With one final lunge, he caught Emma by the jacket.

He couldn't talk. Couldn't say anything above the roar of the water. He kicked and swam, trying to find purchase on the slippery rocks.

They inched closer to the bank with each stroke of his arm, each kick of his feet. Was it soon enough?

The river made a tight turn farther downstream, then

plunged down a series of rocky rapids. They had to get to shore before the turn.

One more pull. One more kick. Emma swam too.

He caught an overhanging branch with his free arm, but the force of the river almost tore the branch out of his hand.

He held on, praying, sputtering as water washed over them. And inch by inch, he hauled his precious burden closer to shore.

Emma finally managed to get her feet under her. She was up to her thighs in the water and the flowing stream pulled at her slicker, but she was safe. Carter looked back out to the water.

He couldn't see Adam.

Carter's fear became a black, whirling vortex.

Emma was pulled sideways, but she managed to grab a branch from the tree Carter had caught, and she rose up out of the water again.

And Carter saw she was holding Adam by his jacket.

"Is he okay?" Carter gasped as they moved forward foot by foot, working their way up the tree's branches.

Emma only nodded, water streaming down her face, her eyes two dark brown bruises in her chalk-white face as they worked their way to shore.

Then, finally, the water's force lessened. They were up to their knees, then their ankles and then Carter could help Emma lift Adam up and onto the soggy grass of the bank.

He lay quiet, then he sat up, coughed and sputtered, and Carter's bones went rubbery with relief.

"Carter? Mom?" Adam called out, looking wildly around, water streaming down his face. He blinked and rubbed his eyes, and then Emma crouched down beside him, her hair plastered to her face, her lips blue with the cold.

Carter had never seen a more beautiful sight in his life.

"We're here," Emma said then coughed herself. "We're all here."

Carter caught Adam and held him close, rocking him, and then tears, warm against his ice-cold cheeks, poured down his face. "I'm so glad you're okay, little guy. So glad."

Emma knelt beside him and he grabbed her with his free arm, pulling them all together in a circle of life. They embraced and laughed and cried. There were not enough emotions to express what they had just gone through.

Then Emma caught Carter's face in her hands and pressed a cold, wet kiss on his mouth. "Thank you. Thank you," she sobbed, her voice hoarse, her eyes red with tears and river water.

Carter kissed her back. He couldn't hold her close enough. Couldn't kiss her enough. They were all here. They were all alive. *Thank You, Lord,* he prayed. *Thank You.*

He could say nothing more.

"I was really scared," Adam said as Emma toweled him off, steam from the warm bath still hovering in the room. "I thought I was going to be drownded."

Emma shut her mind off to the images flooding her mind because of his innocent comment. She had to pin her attention to the here. The now. Concentrate on rubbing the moisture out of her precious son's hair, wrapping the towel around his warm, pink body.

His wriggling, living body. He was okay. Everything was okay. Carter had saved them.

"You're nice and clean now," she said with a forced smile. "That mud from our walk all washed off you."

After they came out of the river, the three of them had walked for a few hundred yards, shivering and holding each other up, the horses following docilely behind them.

Emma still couldn't believe that Diamond had managed to scramble to shore or that Elijah had forded the river on his own. All that was another reason for thanks.

By the time they arrived at the ranch, they weren't shivering as hard, but the chill had settled deep in Emma's bones.

Carter had tried to make Emma take a shower at his grandmother's place while he took care of Adam, but she didn't want to let Adam out of her sight.

"There, now you look as shiny as a new penny," she said, bending over to plant a kiss on his forehead.

"When can we get my lantern?" Adam asked.

After everything that happened, all he could talk about was a lantern?

He's only five, she reminded herself. *He moves past and moves on.*

"We're not getting it for a long time," Emma replied, fear making her voice more authoritative than usual.

Now that everyone was okay and they were safe and warm, she felt the need to lay down the law.

"You shouldn't have taken off like that." She kept her voice quiet but firm.

Adam dropped his head. "I said I was sorry."

Emma knelt down and tilted his face up to hers. "I know you are, honey. But I was so scared when I woke up and didn't see you there. You know that you never, ever go out of the cabin without me."

Adam kept his eyes averted, and though Emma could see he was sorry, she felt she had to drive this point home.

It could have ended so badly. It could have been so much worse. An icy shiver trickled down her spine at the memory of what they had just survived.

"This is important, Adam. You know what I'm saying, don't you?"

Adam gave a tiny nod, and Emma saw tears welling up in his eyes. She steeled herself to his sorrow.

"Because you went out without me and didn't tell anyone, we are not going to be working on the tree fort for the rest of the week."

Adam blinked and a tear, released from his eye, trickled down his cheek. He sniffed and wiped his face with the back of his hand.

"Carter isn't going to be here anyway," he said quietly.

Emma didn't want to think about what Adam was saying. Carter had given her no indication he was leaving.

Like you had much time for chitchat.

But surely he would have said something. Even on the way back to the ranch?

Yeah, something like, it's been fun saving your life and all, but I got to do what I got to do?

"Then *I'm* not going to be helping you with your tree fort," Emma corrected, trying to still the panic that hovered. Carter wasn't leaving. She was sure of that.

She pushed herself to her feet and brought him out to the living room, determined to carry on. "You're allowed to watch *Backyardigans* while I have a quick shower."

She stopped and tightened her grip on his shoulder, which made Adam look up at her in concern.

"You're not leaving the house, are you?"

"I won't do it again, Mommy," he said, suddenly subdued. "I don't want to be scared like that again."

A picture flashed through her mind. Adam falling off the horse, her swimming after him. The panic that paralyzed her even after she caught his coat.

Then Carter's hand grabbed her, and their relentless surging down the river stopped. She closed her eyes, preferring to focus on that moment when she and Carter held Adam and each other on the riverbank. After he had saved their lives.

She went back to the bathroom and made quick work of her own shower. The hot water washing over her removed the memory of the cold and the fear. She deliberately pushed back the doubts that Adam's words had planted in her mind. Until she heard from Carter herself, she wasn't going to speculate on what was happening after this.

Adam still sat on the couch when she came back, toweling off her hair. He was watching the show, smiling faintly at the antics of the cartoon characters.

She sat quietly beside him, brushing her hair, her own mind wandering to Carter in Nana Beck's house. Should she go to him? Wait for him to come here?

Ten minutes passed. Twenty. Thirty.

Surely he was done now. Surely Nana Beck would realize he would want to come here to make sure they were okay.

Emma closed her eyes, reliving that moment when he kissed her. When she kissed him back.

I want to talk to you.

His voice resonated through her head, adding to her growing concern. He wouldn't leave now, would he? Not when the assurance of a future hung between them, unspoken but present.

Finally she couldn't stand it any longer. "Put on your coat, mister," she said to her son. "We're going to find Carter."

When they stepped out of the house, the rain had quit, but rivulets of water flowed into the flower garden.

They ran across the yard, splashing through the puddles. Each step held apprehension and created an inevitable movement toward something she might not want to face.

They knocked on Nana's door and, without waiting for a reply, stepped inside.

The homey scent of coffee and cookies baking comforted her, creating a sense of normalcy. A solid reassurance in a frightening and emotional morning.

"Hello," Emma called out in her brightest, happiest voice. As she shucked off her coat, she glanced quickly around the entrance.

She didn't see Carter's boots or his coat, and as they walked into the kitchen, she didn't see him.

Nana Beck was already coming toward them, her arms spread wide, her eyes registering her concern.

"Oh, my dear children," she said, hugging first Emma then Adam, the comforting scent of vanilla and chocolate wafting around them. "Carter told me what happened. You must have been so frightened. I'm so thankful you're okay." She pressed her hand to her heart, and Emma was afraid that she might have another attack.

"We're fine. It's okay," she assured her, grasping her by the shoulder. "Really."

Nana's eyes glistened. "I'm so thankful. So thankful."

She drew in an unsteady breath, then forced a smile to her face. "Do you want some hot chocolate and cookies?"

What Emma really wanted was Carter, but she wasn't telling Nana Beck that. Emma glanced around the kitchen again as maybe, by some weird chance, Carter was hiding in a room somewhere.

Nana set a kettle of water on the stove and then put out two mugs. One for her and one for Adam.

Emma couldn't stand the tension one second longer.

"Where's Carter? He told me he was going to wash up here."

Nana nodded. "He did. And then he left."

"He left? For his cabin?" Emma couldn't keep the sharp note out of her voice.

"He said he had to go to town. I thought he told you?"

"No. He didn't tell me a thing."

"Well, now. That's a puzzle." Nana Beck's words and her accompanying frown sent Emma's heart plunging into her stomach. Why didn't he stop to talk to her? Why did he leave right away?

She and Adam stayed long enough to eat cookies and drink the chocolate. As soon as was polite, Emma retreated to her cabin and her worries.

Chapter Fourteen

"I don't want to bake bread. I want to go to work on my tree fort." Adam dropped into a chair by the kitchen table of Wade and Miranda's house and heaved out a sigh.

"I know you do, but it's going to be dark in a while, and I have to get this bread done," Emma said, trying to keep her voice soothing as she sent yet another glance out the window at the setting sun.

Carter was gone on his bike again.

Unbidden came the feeling of his arms around her after he had pulled her and Adam out of the river. Too easily, she again felt the blinding fear and choking panic.

Carter had saved them. And then Carter had left. He'd been gone all afternoon. It was seven o'clock now, and he still hadn't returned.

Don't trust men, don't trust men.

Emma felt a cold place in the center of her chest that had once harbored affection. Attraction. Maybe even love. Now, all that lived there was the pain of being left behind. Again.

She had trusted Carter. She had opened up to him and let him into her life. Now he was gone without a word.

She poured water into the bowl Miranda always used for bread, measured out the yeast and put in the sugar, just like Miranda had taught her.

She wasn't even sure why she was doing this. But she had to keep herself busy, as she had all afternoon. After they left Nana Beck's, she and Adam had cleaned out their cabin. Then they came to the house and tidied it up.

Busy work, Emma thought, taking the eggs out of the refrigerator.

"I'm bored," Adam whined, swinging his feet. "I don't know what to do."

"You can help me make bread," she said with a falsely bright smile.

"That's boring." He draped himself over the table, dropping his chin on his arms. "When is Carter coming back?"

Emma bit back a snappy response to that as she measured out the oil. She wanted Carter to come back too. So she could give him a piece of her mind.

And then, so she could quit. She needed to get on with her own life, and when he came back—whenever that would be—she and Adam were going to leave. She couldn't be with a man who ran whenever things got difficult.

But he pulled you from the river. He saved your life.

And what else could he have done? Why didn't he stay to see how she and Adam were doing? To talk about what happened to them? To help her deal with it?

In spite of her questions and her frustration with Carter, the thought of leaving him sent a shaft of pain into her heart. Into her very soul.

Carter. His face swam into her mind, and right behind that came a wave of sorrow mixed with anger.

How could he just walk away after all that had happened? Was he too scared to face them? Had he shown them too much of himself? Was he pulling back emotionally, as well as physically?

Her eyes closed as her heart and mind battled with each other. Karl's betrayal had hurt, but she had gotten through it.

She knew, deep in her soul, that Carter's absence after what they had just shared hurt far more.

Please, Lord, help me to find my peace in You. Help me to trust in You only. Only You are faithful.

She waited a moment, reaching for the peace that she had prayed for. Drawing in a long, slow breath, she straightened.

Keep going. Do what comes next. Get through this. Keep busy.

Then, as she took the flour out of the pantry, she heard a noise that lifted her heart. Was that a bike?

She shook her head, angry at how easily her hope was resurrected.

The noise grew and became the distinctive sound of a motorbike. Her heart jumped as she dropped the bag of flour on the counter, then leaned over the sink to look out the window.

There he was, parking his bike and pulling off his helmet.

Just like he had the first time she saw him. Only, then she didn't know who he was. Now, the sight of that thick, wavy hair catching the light from the setting sun, that shadowed jaw and his slate-blue eyes brought a flush to her cheeks and sent anticipation singing through her veins.

She pulled back from the window, clenching her fists, trying to pull her emotions to a more neutral place.

The door opened, and Adam's head shot up.

"Carter! You're back!" Adam shot out of the chair and threw himself at the tall figure that entered the house, his presence taking over the kitchen.

Carter bent over and caught Adam under his arms, swung him up in the air then, to Emma's surprise, pulled him close in a fierce hug.

Then, dropping Adam onto his hip, he turned to Emma.

"Hey, there," he said, his voice quiet. "How are you? Feeling okay?"

Her eyes blurred and her throat thickened, and she turned away so he couldn't see how his presence and the concern in his voice affected her.

"I'm fine. So is Adam." She cracked open the eggs with unnecessary force, almost sending the contents of the bowl spewing over the counter.

"That was really scary when we were in the water," Adam said, wrapping his arms around Carter's neck. "I'm so glad you saved us."

Emma glanced over in time to see Carter hold Adam close, his eyes closed, his arms wrapped tightly around the little body. The sight of him holding her son created a tiny bloom of warmth, thawing the chill that she had wrapped herself in for protection. "I'm glad too, buddy," Carter said.

Adam put up with the hug for a minute, but then pulled away, his eyes holding Carter's. "Were you scared?"

Emma caught fear in Carter's broken gaze. Then he nodded. "Yes. I was scared."

"But you were really brave," Adam said.

"So were you," Carter replied, then let his eyes rest on Emma. "And so was your mother."

"Where did you go after you brought us back? My mommy was mad at you for going away."

Emma tore her gaze away from Carter, but didn't bother to reprimand her son. He was only telling the truth.

"Adam, can you go tell Nana Beck that I'm here?" Carter said quietly, setting Adam on the floor. "Ask her to give you some of her cookies and wait for me there."

Adam glanced from Emma to Carter, unsure whether to follow the instructions. Not that Emma blamed him. Hadn't she spent all day reminding him that he wasn't to go anywhere without her?

"I'll go with you. To make sure you get there okay," Carter said. "It's getting dark out there."

So Carter and Adam left, and for a few moments Emma was alone to try to gather her thoughts and scattered emotions.

She pressed her hands to her heated cheeks, angry at the tears that threatened, a sign of how much Carter had come to mean to her in the past few weeks.

Keep it together, she scolded herself. *Don't cave.*

A few minutes later, Carter was back. He stood in the doorway of the kitchen of his old house, and, in spite of her confusion in his presence, she felt a flicker of sympathy for him. How hard it must be to see a woman and a child, the same age as his son, in his house.

Would Harry and Sylvia's memories always hang over this place? Could he ever forget them and simply see her and Adam?

"Can I come in?" Carter asked, his voice quiet.

Emma nodded and beat the eggs into the oil. But

Carter didn't go to the table and sit on the chair. He came to stand beside her, resting his hip against the counter, looking down on her.

"I'm sorry," was all he said. "I'm sorry I had to leave."

Emma swallowed a knot of sorrow, wishing his presence didn't affect her so. Then, unable to keep her eyes down, she looked over at him.

"Why did you have to leave? And why did you stay away?" The questions burst out of her, edged with frustration and sorrow.

Carter waited a moment, as if gathering his thoughts in the face of her emotions. "I had to go to the real-estate agent," he said. "And I had to get there as soon as possible. I'm sorry I wasn't here for you, but I had to do something very important."

She turned her attention back to the flour she was measuring out. "What was so important?"

Carter released a heavy sigh. "When I put the ranch up for sale, Pete gave me an escape clause. I had until noon today to call if I wanted to cancel the sale. But I missed that call."

Emma's hands slowed as she tried to absorb what he was telling her.

"What do you mean you missed the call?"

Carter took the measuring cup out of her hands and set it on the countertop. He took her hands in his and pressed them. "When you came to my cabin this morning, I was leaving for town, remember?"

Emma's mind ticked back, recalling Carter's pressed shirt, his new jeans. He had been dressed to go out. "But that was when Adam was missing." Things fell into place. "And we went out to get him." She stopped there, the

memory of what had happened too fresh and frighten-
ingly real.

"When we got back to the ranch, I was already late.
I wanted to talk to Pete about canceling the sale, but by
then, it was past noon. I went into town, hoping that
I could talk to him face-to-face, work something out.
Change things."

Emma's confusion settled and reality took its place.
"You wanted to cancel the sale of the ranch? Why?"

Carter reached up and fingered a strand of hair away
from her face, his fingers trailing down her cheek, then
coming to rest on her shoulder. "I didn't want to let it
go. I wanted it to be mine. For you and Adam and me."

She held his gaze, unable to speak, as his words settled
like oil on the troubled waters of her soul.

"When I found out I couldn't stop the sale," he continued, "I tried to come up with another plan. To fix what
I had broken." His eyes traveled over her face, regret
etched on his features. "I wanted to make a home for us."

Weakness invaded Emma's limbs as hope unfurled in
her chest. "A home? Here?"

Carter nodded, his hands moving to her waist, holding her up.

Emma bit her lip, his touch confusing and comforting her at the same time. "I thought…when you left…
that you weren't coming back."

Desolation crept over Carter's features. "Did you think
I would leave you like Adam's father left you?"

His words lay bare her deepest fears. "I trusted him
to take care of us," she said, looking down at her hands.
"Trusted him to do the right thing. Then, one day, he just
left. And Adam and I were alone."

His hands tightened their grip on her waist. "I'm so

sorry. I should have called you, but when we got to the ranch and I realized the time, I was in such a hurry to get to town that I left my phone behind. Then, when I found out I couldn't stop the sale, I was too upset to call. I never even thought that you would assume I was leaving for good." He tipped her chin up with a finger. "I was coming back. I figured you would know that."

Emma couldn't hold his gaze, her own shame intruding on the moment. "Every man in my life, other than Adam, has let me down. I was afraid you had done the same."

"Even after I rescued you?"

She was surprised to hear the faint note of humor in his voice, but as her gaze slid to his, she caught a hint of fear in his eyes, a hint of the fear she had heard in his voice when he pulled them out of the river.

"Even after you rescued me," she echoed.

Silence followed her comment, then Carter spoke. "I know I wasn't the best person when you first met me, but I've changed. And you're the one who helped me make that change. I've come to care for you and Adam more than I ever thought I could. I didn't want to fall for you. Didn't want to let you into my life, but you found a way in." He slipped his hands to the small of her back, closing the small distance between them. "When you and Adam fell into the river, I thought I'd lost you both. I thought that was it." His voice stumbled over the words, as if reliving the pain the moment had caused. "Then, when I jumped in and saved you, I knew it wasn't over. I hadn't lost someone else I cared so deeply for."

Was it true? Did he care deeply for her?

Then she looked up at him, and in his eyes, she saw a yearning that sent her heart hammering.

But he had more to say.

"You scared me, Emma. You and Adam. But when we came to the other side, I knew, more than anything, that I had to find a way to keep us together. To keep us on the ranch that I know you love, and that I've always loved—just not always appreciated. That's why I left. I left for you. For us."

His words, spoken with such authority, eased into her lost and lonely soul.

"I want you to trust me, Emma. To trust that I will take care of you. I can only hope that you believe me."

Emma felt a prickling behind her eyes as she clung to his words. She drew in an unsteady breath, struggling to find her way through this new, unfamiliar place. "I'm sorry I thought you left me. I… I haven't had a lot of reasons to trust men. Adam's father left as soon as he found out I was pregnant. My father let me down by gambling away our ranch, leaving Adam and me with nothing. My old boyfriend cheated on me. When I came here, I didn't trust men, and didn't want to." Her sudden resolve faltered as old fears and distrusts intruded.

Carter said nothing for a moment, as if honoring her confession. "I'm sorry you thought that of me," he said quietly. "I don't know what to say to make you believe you can trust me." He stopped there and his hand came up and traced the line of her cheek. His touch was tentative, as if unsure of her reaction.

Emma looked up at him as other pictures imposed themselves. Carter in church. Carter holding Adam as if he was his own. Carter trusting her enough with his sorrow to cry in her arms, letting her see his broken places.

Carter risking his own life to save her and her son.

Emma felt her body relax, as if she'd been struggling

to carry a weight and could finally release her burden. She looked back up at Carter and felt as if she was balanced on a precipice, that things could shift either way depending on what she said or did next.

In a moment of blinding clarity, she knew which way she wanted to go. Maybe it was too soon, but she knew if she didn't tell him now, she never would.

"I trust you, Carter Beck," she said, sincerity ringing in her voice, "with me and my son. I trust you with our lives, and I trust you with our hearts."

The silence following her declaration grew large, heavy, and for a moment Emma wondered if she had said too much. Exposed her heart too fully.

Then he swept her in his arms, cradled her head in his hand and kissed her. Hard. Then again. Then more gently, as if sealing a promise.

He drew her close, laying her head against his chest, his chin resting on her head. His chest lifted in a sigh, and Emma closed her eyes, contentment washing over her.

She wanted time to stop right here. Right now. She didn't want to think what may lay ahead or what they would have to deal with once the ranch sold.

Carter rubbed his chin over her head. "Thank you," he whispered. "Thank you for trusting me."

She drew back and, smiling up at him, brushed a lock of hair back from his forehead, as if sealing a claim on him. "I didn't think I could put my trust in a man again. But, yes, I trust you."

He kissed her again, then rested his hands on her shoulders, his expression growing serious. "And I love you."

Emma stared as the words, one by one, dropped into her weary soul.

"Did...did I hear you right?"

Carter stroked her hair back from her face, his fingers lingering on her cheek as his mouth lifted in a wistful smile. "Yeah. You did." He released a short laugh that held a note of melancholy but absolutely no bitterness. "I didn't think I'd ever say those words again. But you kind of snuck up on me."

She didn't want to cry, but she felt her throat thicken and her eyes grow warm. She blinked, trying to find her footing in this new place.

Carter caught his lower lip between his teeth. "Um... now would be a good time to say something."

"I love you too." She couldn't stop the words and didn't want to. "You opened up my heart and soul again, and I trust you with both," she said quietly.

Carter pressed another kiss to her lips then drew her close against him. He laid his hand on her head, stroking her hair with his thumb. "I dared to make plans again. Dared to hope we could make a life on this ranch. I'm so sorry I couldn't stop the sale."

Regret flickered, but only for a moment. Emma wrapped her arms around his waist, holding him close.

"I'm sorry too, but you know, right now I'm thankful for what we have. Right here. You and me and Adam. I'm thankful for all the blessings God has given us. Anything else is only gravy. Extra." She pulled back to gauge his reaction to what she had just said.

Carter's mouth lifted in a wry smile, but Emma saw he wasn't convinced.

"I mean it, Carter," she insisted. "I know it sounds corny, but we have each other, and that's the best starting point."

"I'll have the money from the sale of the ranch. We

could start somewhere else…" He shook his head slowly. "I can't believe it's happening. I wish… I wish I hadn't…"

Emma said nothing but pressed her fingers against his lips. "It doesn't matter, Carter. Like I said, we have each other, and that's more than we had even a few weeks ago when you still owned the ranch."

He cupped her shoulders in his hands. "I feel like my life has spun in a completely different direction since then."

"So has mine. But I'm comforted that we're facing that direction together." Regret was still etched on his face. What could she say to assure him? She covered his hands with hers, her gaze seeking his and holding it. "The ranch is just a place. A home and a business."

"You already lost one home and business," Carter said, his voice urgent. "When you had to sell your father's ranch. Now I'm bringing that same disappointment back into your life. I know how much you loved this place, and now I took that away from you too."

"You gave me so much more," she said quietly. "Anyone can build a house. A business. A ranch. But what we have now, what you've just given me, is the most important foundation for any life together. When your great-great-grandfather made his choice, he didn't choose for money. He chose for love. When you chose to help me go find Adam, you made the right choice too. Because if you hadn't…" Her voice faltered as the frightening images flickered through her mind again.

He drew her close, as if to shelter her from the memories.

"I'm so thankful to the Lord for saving us," she continued, speaking from the shelter of his arms. "For using you to save us."

They were quiet a moment, as if letting the moment settle into their minds and their lives.

Emma didn't want to move on. She wished it would never end.

Then the door of the kitchen slammed open and Adam burst into the room. He skidded to a halt when he saw Carter and Emma. He looked from one to the other, and as he did Emma felt her heart falter.

Then he grinned and ran toward them, his arms open wide. "Hug me too, hug me too," he called out, and Carter and Emma bent over and swept him into their arms, completing the circle.

"Well, I'd say that's about time."

Nana Beck's wry voice made them all look up. She stood in the doorway, her arms folded over her midsection, looking smug and well pleased with herself.

Emma endured a moment of guilt. After all, she now stood in the kitchen of the house that had once belonged to Sylvia, her arms around her husband.

But Nana Beck's smile was like a blessing on the moment. A stamp of approval that swept away any misgivings Emma had.

"We were just coming over—"

"Of course you were," Nana Beck said, giving Emma a quick wink. "But Adam was getting impatient and I was getting curious. So now we're here." Nana moved into the kitchen and sat on a nearby chair. "And you might want to do something about that bread dough," she said, angling her head toward the bowl now overflowing with risen dough.

She laughed and reluctantly released herself from Carter's arms. Adam, however, stayed there gladly, asking Carter about the fort and when they were going to work on it again.

Emma stifled her own regret as she and Carter exchanged melancholy glances. But she gave him an encouraging smile before she turned her attention back to her bread. What was done was done. As she had told Carter, they had each other, and that was truly what mattered, wasn't it?

She put a kettle of water on the stove to make some tea. As she returned to her bread, the phone rang.

Carter caught it on the third ring, and as Emma punched down the dough, she couldn't help listening. Carter's replies were terse, and she didn't get much out of what he said.

Then he hung up the phone, staring at it for a moment. He drew in a long, slow breath, then turned to Emma.

"That was Pete. The buyer is coming tomorrow to look over the ranch."

Chapter Fifteen

❦

"Why have you not laid a water line to the corrals? For your horses." Jurgen Mallik, the buyer of the ranch, tugged on his glaringly white cowboy hat as he stood in the corral, looking around.

Jurgen was spare of build with graying blond hair hanging well below the brim of his cowboy hat. His jeans were new-store crisp, and his blue-and-white plaid shirt still held the fold lines from the packaging Carter suspected it had just come from.

"There is a water line. It's not hooked up to a waterer, though." Carter was surprised how easily the words came out. The underlying pain still lay in his soul, but it was as if it had settled and the edges worn smooth. He caught Emma's look of concern and gave her a quick smile to let her know it was okay. She moved a bit closer to him, as if to make sure.

"You have said you have a manager who has been helping you to take care of this place?" Jurgen asked in his heavily accented English.

"He's out of town on a family emergency now, but he'll be back in a couple of weeks." Carter dropped his hat on his head, hoping he didn't sound as out of breath as he was. Jurgen had come twenty minutes earlier than Pete had told Carter yesterday. Eager to see the place, he had said, apologizing when he had shown up.

Emma, however, chatted with him while they waited. Which was okay with Carter. She knew more about the current ranching operations than he did.

"Wade has been taking care of the ranch while Carter was gone," Pete hastened to explain. "I'm sure he'd be willing to stay on as manager once you take over."

Pete angled a questioning look Carter's way, as if to verify.

"Is this true? Would your man be able to help me with this ranch?" Jurgen asked.

"I can't speak for Wade. You'd have to talk to him about that, but I'm sure he would be pleased to know that he could still work here." Carter was glad Jurgen would be willing to keep Wade on. That had been one of his concerns for his good friend. "You might want to look at hiring an extra hand, though, until you know the ranch well enough to manage it yourself," Carter said.

Jurgen frowned as he looked at Emma. "I understand you work here. You would not be staying on?"

Emma's hand surreptitiously slipped into Carter's. "I don't think so."

Her hesitant words gave Carter pause. After his declaration, they hadn't had much opportunity to talk. To decide where things were going between them. To make any plans. He had his own ideas, but he could hardly expect Emma would immediately fall in with them simply because he had told her he loved her.

Jurgen's eyes slipped to their hands. "I see," he said, though his frown told them otherwise. "So now I have seen the house and the corrals. Now I would like to see the cows."

"They're in the upper pasture," Carter said. "We would have to ride up to them." He glanced over Jurgen's clothes, the cowboy boots so new the soles were probably unscuffed.

"I expect that," Jurgen said. "I have ridden horses before."

Carter doubted that, but he kept his doubts to himself.

"Have you ridden English or Western?" Emma asked.

"English," Jurgen replied. "But the Western saddles are sturdier. I am confident I can hold my seat."

"I can let him ride Diamond," Emma said, as if sensing Carter's hesitation. "We can use Wade's saddle."

This seemed to be the best plan.

"Did you want to come up with us?" Carter asked Pete as Emma got the halters from the tack shed.

He held up his hands, a look of horror on his face. "You kidding me? I'll go see if I can scam some cookies from your grandmother. How long will you be?"

"Maybe half an hour. Probably more."

"Take your time." Pete shot them a quick smile, then beat a hasty retreat.

"So this Emma girl. She is your girlfriend?" Jurgen asked as Carter pulled two saddles off the trees in the tack shed.

Again Carter felt a faint niggle of dissatisfaction. He wanted to lay a claim on Emma, but in spite of what she had said to him yesterday, he still felt as if he had to get part of his own life in order before he did.

And the biggest part was what to do after the ranch was sold. He wanted to know he could provide for her and Adam. Take care of them.

How was he supposed to do that when his future and future employment were surrounded by so much uncertainty?

"We care for each other," was all he said as he laid the saddles by the hitching post.

He looked up to see Emma coming toward them, leading three horses through the grass. The sun burnished her brown hair, bringing out a reddish tinge. She was talking to the horses, her voice low, quiet and confident.

This was where she belonged, Carter thought, his heart growing heavy in his chest. If only...

He cut that thought off. The new owner of the ranch stood in front of him, waiting to be shown the rest of the place. Carter had spent enough time in the past. It was now time to move on.

Twenty minutes later they were mounted up, and Emma led them out of the pasture toward the river.

"Pete tells me the ranch has been in your family for four generations," Jurgen was saying as they rode side by side down the trail.

"That's true. My great-great-grandfather started this place, and it's been passed on." Carter tried to keep his voice even, his tone light, but regret hung like a cloud in the background. Why had he been so hasty? Why hadn't he waited?

"I asked Pete why you are selling this place. He only told me that you had experienced a loss."

"My son. He drowned in a stock waterer in the corral two years ago." Again Carter felt the pain of the words, but as he spoke them he looked ahead and saw Emma sitting straight in the saddle, her hand resting on her thigh. She didn't wear a hat this time, but her pose so easily resurrected his first memory of her.

How much had changed since then. Emma had brought such healing into his life.

As they splashed across the river, much lower now than a few days ago, Emma looked back, giving him a tentative smile, as if quietly thanking him again for saving her and Adam. He returned the smile, and in that moment his regret slipped away.

They would make it, he thought. It didn't matter where he, Emma and Adam lived or what they did. They would make it because they would be together.

"I am so sorry to hear about your son," Jurgen said quietly as the horses walked up the other bank of the river. "That is a huge loss and difficult to recuperate from."

"It was, but I'm thankful for Emma and her son, Adam," Carter replied. "They've given me a new reason to carry on."

Jurgen said nothing after that. The trail narrowed and they rode single file. Once in a while Emma turned around and pointed something out to Jurgen. A mountain they saw through the trees. An old wagon trail, since overgrown. Rubbings on the tree from elk trying to shed the velvet from their antlers.

The sun played hide-and-seek behind the clouds, but as they broke out of the trees into the open fields of the upper pastures, the clouds dissipated. Golden sun poured down from a blue sky and lit up the valley below like a promise.

"Nydelig utsikt," Jurgen said, his voice full of awe as he brought Diamond to a halt. He leaned forward, his eyes looking over the valley as shadows of clouds chased each other over the green-clad slopes of the mountains

sweeping away from them. The dumbfounded expression on his face said more than his words had.

"I don't think we need a translation of that," Emma said as she brought Dusty up beside Carter's horse. "I remember feeling exactly the same way when I first saw this."

Carter gave her a melancholy smile then, giving in to an impulse, brushed her hair back from her face. His fingers lingered a moment on her cheek, and she reached up and captured his hand in hers.

"I'm so sorry. I wish things were different."

She squeezed his hand, her expression growing serious. "No. Please. Don't say that. We've both spent enough time in the past. I don't want you to look back."

He cupped her cheek with his hand, and his smile shifted. "How did I get so blessed to have you come into my life?"

"How many acres—" Jurgen stopped, and Carter dragged his attention away from Emma.

"I'm sorry," Carter said, lowering his hand. "What were you going to ask?"

Jurgen's eyes slid from Carter to Emma, as if trying to puzzle out their relationship.

"I was wondering how many acres you have up here. For pasture. And how many cows the pasture can carry."

Carter shot Emma an inquiring glance. "Why don't you take care of this?" he asked. "You're the one who came up with the rotational-grazing plan."

"Rotational grazing?" Jurgen frowned again.

Emma swung off her saddle. "Come with me," she said. "I'll explain."

Jurgen dismounted and followed Emma, but Carter stayed behind, looking out over the valley. Thankfully it was too early in the day to see The Shadow Woman. He was afraid that if she made an appearance, he would see rebuke in her features.

In spite of Emma's brave words, mourning of another sort settled in his soul. Mourning for the loss of a place where he grew up. A place that had been a source of refuge for him and his brother. A place where he and his cousins had grown up.

Naomi had called him early this morning and had expressed her regret at the loss of the ranch, but she had echoed what Emma had said. The ranch was just a place. People were what counted.

And yet…

Carter tried to slough off his momentary funk.

Forgive me, Lord, he prayed. *Help me to be thankful in all circumstances.*

Then he looked back at Emma, and he realized how blessed he really was.

"…we get better usage of the land and the cows are healthier," she was saying, obviously selling Jurgen on her new project.

Carter came up beside Emma, and she flashed him a quick smile. He caught her hand in his, giving it a gentle squeeze.

"What is the name of that mountain? Across the valley?" Jurgen asked.

"The Three Sisters," Emma and Carter said at the same time.

"Of course," Jurgen said with a slow nod. "Three peaks. Three sisters."

"My cousins always said those mountains belonged to them," Carter said with a laugh.

"You have cousins?"

"Hailey, Naomi and Shannon," Carter said, pointing to each of the peaks as he listed off his cousins' names.

"The girls all had their own cabin at the ranch, as well," Emma put in. "Those were the cabins you were asking about before Carter joined us."

"So your family spent much time here."

"Whenever we could." More regret twisted his gut. He took a deep breath and struggled to push it aside.

"They did not want to buy this place?" Jurgen asked, pulling his hat off his head, looking over the valley again.

"Couldn't afford it."

"Your price is reasonable."

Carter shrugged. At the time he listed it, he just wanted to be rid of it.

And now?

"Carter isn't a greedy man," Emma said, giving him a quick smile, as if she understood what had gone through his head at the time.

"You two. You don't want to live on this place?" Jurgen's voice held a note of puzzlement.

Emma bit her lip and looked away, and again Carter felt as if he had taken something precious from her. All he could do was slip his arm around her shoulder.

"It is what it is," was all Emma said as she leaned into him, accepting his silent solace.

"Is there anything else you wanted to see?" Carter asked Jurgen, bringing the conversation back to the practical and the immediate.

Jurgen sighed as he worked his hat around his hands. "You two love this place, don't you?"

Emma and Carter locked gazes, sharing a forlorn look.

"I think you do," Jurgen said, answering his own question before Carter formulated a suitable response. "And I think you two care for each other, as well. Have you known each other long?"

Carter shook his head. "We met after I came back to the ranch. About the same time I put the place up for sale."

The only sound that followed his comment was a breeze soughing through the grass, easing away the heat of the sun.

Dusty snorted and Diamond whinnied in response. The horses were growing restless.

"We should probably get back to the ranch," Carter said, turning away and picking up Diamond's reins. He handed them to Jurgen and waited until he and Emma both mounted up before getting on Banjo.

The ride back to the ranch was quiet. Carter was in the lead with Emma bringing up the rear.

As they approached the ranch yard, the horses left behind whinnied. The door of Nana Beck's house flew open and Adam scooted out, running toward the corral to meet them.

Pete, obviously alerted to their presence by Adam's sudden departure, was close behind him. The two of them were waiting when they rode into the corral, Pete standing close to the fence, Adam astride its top beam.

"Did you have a good ride, Mr. Mallik?" Adam called out as they rode by.

"Very nice. Thank you, Adam," Jurgen replied.

"The ranch is really beautiful, isn't it?" Adam added.

"Very beautiful."

"I have a tree fort I could show you. Me and Carter were working on it. But now I won't be able to. 'Cause you're buying the ranch. I'm sad that we can't live here anymore and so is my mommy. She loves it here. Says it's the best home we ever had."

Carter saw Emma frown at Adam and give him a tight shake of her head, as if asking him to stop. Adam got the message and puffed out his cheeks in a sigh of resignation.

"So? What did you think?" Pete asked Jurgen as he slowly dismounted.

"It is a beautiful place. More than beautiful," Jurgen said as he handed Emma Diamond's halter rope. "But I am of mixed feelings. *Confused,* I think is the word."

"What's to be confused about?" Pete said with a forced laugh, his hands spread out. "The price is perfect. The place is perfect. You've seen it before."

Jurgen scratched his forehead with his index finger, his frown deepening. "I think this is not right, my purchase of this place." He looked over at Carter then toward Emma, who was loosening the cinch of Diamond's saddle with quick, efficient movements.

"What's not right? You did sign all the necessary papers." Pete's voice held a note of warning, and Carter felt tiny pinpricks of apprehension at Pete's concern.

Jurgen sighed and looked over at Carter. "You had a big loss, when your son died here. Then you left and never came back, correct?"

Carter nodded, the pinpricks growing, wondering where Jurgen had gotten this information.

"Your friend Emma told me how sad this made you. While we waited for you earlier," Jurgen said, answering Carter's unspoken question. "But now you seem happy."

Carter's confusion grew. "Yes. I am happy." His gaze drifted toward Emma, who was laughing at something Adam said. As if sensing his regard, she looked his way and, as often happened, an awareness of each other arced between them.

Jurgen followed the direction of his gaze. "This place, you both love it very much."

His voice was matter-of-fact.

"Yes. We do."

"I am thinking you wouldn't choose to sell it now, would you?"

Carter's gaze flew back to Jurgen, a sense of disquiet rising up inside him. "What do you mean?"

"You wanted to wipe away the reminder of your lost son. This was why you wanted to sell. Before you and Emma fall in love." Jurgen's gaze was riveted on Carter, as if trying to delve into Carter's psyche.

Behind him he saw Pete raise his hands in a gesture of surrender.

What was going on?

"Would you sell it now?"

Carter's disquiet morphed into the tiniest beginnings of hope. "No. I wouldn't sell it now."

Jurgen nodded as if that was the answer he was waiting for. Then he looked around the yard, slowly, as if committing each building, each part of the landscape, into memory. "This is a beautiful place with much memory. Much history. I would be happy to own it." Then he looked back at Carter. "But I cannot take this away from you. From Emma and her son. I think this can be a place for you to heal." He turned back to Pete. "I am thinking I want to withdraw my offer. If I am able to. Legally."

"I am thinking you can probably do whatever you want," Pete said in a wry voice, throwing up his hands in a gesture of defeat.

Carter's heart slowed as he tried to absorb what Jurgen was saying.

Jurgen turned back to Carter. "I am hoping you will not sell this place to someone else. But I think you won't."

Carter stared at him, the import of what he said registering word by word.

"You're not buying the place?" was all he could manage, his heart pounding in earnest against his rib cage.

Jurgen shook his head, his mouth curved in a melancholy smile. "I do not want to, how to say, take advantage of your sorrow. I think you are not so sorrowful now." Jurgen extended his hand to Carter.

Carter, still reeling from the shock of what Jurgen had said, could offer only a limp handshake.

"Thanks. Thank you," was all he could stutter out. "Thank you so much."

He stood a moment, surprise and awe rooting him to the spot. Then as everything came together, he said a quick goodbye and ran toward Emma and Adam.

Toward his future.

Chapter Sixteen

❧

"Next time we go on a picnic, I would like to go to the upper pasture," Nana Beck said as she set the cooler down on the blanket Emma had spread out.

It was a glorious Sunday afternoon. When Carter had suggested a family picnic at the old yard site that Emma had, at one time, wanted to buy, she was puzzled but agreed. Then Hailey found out and decided she and Nana would join them.

Though Carter had looked less than impressed, Emma hadn't spent much time with Hailey and looked forward to knowing her better. She seemed spunky and full of fun.

"You have to ride a horse then." Adam dropped down beside the basket, his expression expectant as Nana lifted the lid of the cooler.

"Nana can ride a horse just fine," Hailey said, setting out the plates, her gray eyes flicking from Carter to Emma as if still trying to figure out their relationship. "She taught me how to ride."

"Did she teach you how to snowboard?" Adam asked.

Ever since Adam had seen the broken snowboards

in Carter's cabin, he had been curious about the owner. Carter had obliged by telling him stories of his cousin's many escapades.

"Actually, it was Carter," Hailey said with an exaggerated wink for Emma. "He can shred with the best of them."

"Don't try to pin your kamikaze snowboard routine on me," Carter said with fake indignation as he snapped open a lawn chair. "I didn't even like snowboarding that much."

He set the chair down, and with a wave toward Emma gave a short bow. "Your throne, madam."

"I like how this man thinks," Hailey said with a laugh.

A flush warmed Emma's face as Carter bent over to place a kiss on her cheeks. He touched her nose with his finger and winked at her. "Have a seat, my dear."

Behind the flush came a rush of love so complete, so full, it threatened to overwhelm her. She wasn't so independent that she didn't like having a man fuss over her from time to time. "Thanks. I think I will."

Carter brought over a second chair to her grandmother, and as she sat down Nana Beck looked around, her smile wide with pleasure. "Isn't this nice. Too bad Shannon couldn't join us."

"Cluck, cluck," Hailey said with a laugh as she dropped down on the blanket beside Adam. "Nana won't be happy until all her little chicks come home to roost."

"Where they belong," Nana said. "But for now I am so grateful to God that three of my chicks are back in Hartley Creek. And that Jurgen changed his mind about buying the ranch. I prayed for a miracle, but I didn't think it would come this way."

Carter sat down beside Emma and laid his hand on

her knee. "It was a miracle," he agreed. "And I'm thankful for it."

"No such things as miracles," Hailey said, her voice taking on a surprisingly tough edge.

"Oh, yes, there are," Nana said, patting Hailey on the shoulder. "You'll see. Someday."

Hailey's only answer was a light shrug.

Emma leaned back in the chair, unwilling to let Hailey's little negative comment ruin the moment for her. The sun shone like a blessing on the moment, and Adam was happier than she'd seen him in months.

As for herself, she sat beside the man she loved.

"Ironic that you picked this place to have a picnic," Hailey said to Carter. "Wasn't this the homestead Emma wanted you to subdivide for her?"

"It was."

"So why did you want us to have the picnic here?"

"I planned a picnic for just her and me and Adam. And I wanted to have it here because I wanted to bring things full circle."

"What are you talking about?" Hailey asked.

Carter scratched the side of his nose, then pulled his hat off and laid it to one side.

"Uh-oh. I see a serious face," Hailey said.

Carter laid his finger over his lips. "To everything there is a season, and now is the time for quiet. You weren't supposed to be here, so pretend, for the next few moments, like you're not."

Hailey frowned, and as Carter pulled out two tiny boxes from his shirt pocket, Emma felt her heart quicken.

She hardly dared breathe. Hardly dared let her mind go too far ahead.

Carter turned to her and, to her amazement, got down on one knee.

Emma looked down into Carter's gentle blue eyes, wondering why she had ever thought them cold when they shone with such warmth now.

"I think I like where this is going," Hailey whispered to Adam.

"Where is it going?" he whispered back.

"Wait and see," Nana said. "Hush, now."

Carter took her hand in his and everything and everyone else faded away until it was just Carter and her.

"Emma, I love you. More than I ever thought I could love a person again." Emma's heart tripped in her chest at the expression of devotion on his face. He opened the first box. Inside she saw the wink of a diamond, and tears threatened.

"Emma Minton, will you marry me?"

She nodded, blinking away her tears.

Then she was in his arms, his mouth pressed against hers, and a faint breeze picked up and swirled around them like a benediction.

Her heart felt like bursting, and she couldn't hold him close enough, couldn't be held close enough.

"Thank You, Lord," she whispered in Carter's ear.

She drew back, and Carter slipped the ring on her finger. The diamond winked in the sun, like a promise.

"I love you, Emma," he said, his voice breaking. "And I'll try to be worthy of the trust you said you placed in me." Carter turned her hand over and pressed a kiss to her palm, as if sealing that promise.

"I love you too," she said, her voice breaking. "I love you so much." It was all she could say.

"Is that where this is going?" Adam asked.

Carter turned to Adam and gestured for him to come over. Adam scrambled to his feet and ran over. Carter caught him in a one-armed hug and pulled him close. Adam pointed. "What's in that box?"

"Let's see," Carter replied. He let go of Adam.

Carter opened the other box and pulled out a golden necklace. From it dangled the gold pendant Emma had seen shortly after Carter had come back to the ranch. "You were there when Nana told the story about this pendant," Carter said quietly, unclasping the necklace. "I want you to have this as a reminder of the choices my grandfather made. And as a reminder that you are now part of this family. Woven into the stories and the legends."

He placed the necklace around Emma's neck and kissed her again.

"I love a happy ending," Hailey said in a choked voice.

"I do too," Nana replied.

"Is this the end of the picnic?" Adam asked sadly.

"No, Adam. It's just the beginning." Carter pulled Emma close and wrapped Adam into the three-way embrace.

Emma returned the hug, trying to take it all in. Trying to absorb that she and Adam were now a part of Carter's life, present and future.

As he drew away, her eyes flitted from Adam to Hailey to Nana Beck, her heart full of love, joy. And below all that, a comforting thread of peace.

This was a homecoming.

She and Carter and Adam—they had all found home.

* * * * *

DADDY LESSONS

Oh, the depths of the riches of the wisdom and knowledge of God! How unsearchable his judgments, and his paths beyond tracing out!
—*Romans* 11:33

As a writer I am so thankful that I don't work alone.
I want to thank my editor, Tina James, for her
hard work and patient guidance in shaping my stories.

Chapter One

"C'mon, honey, we've got to get going. You don't want to be late for your first day of school." Dan Morrow tossed his daughter's backpack over his shoulder and reached for Natasha to help her down from the truck.

Bright orange buses pulled up along the sidewalk of Hartley Creek Elementary School, spilling out their loads of children. Some ran, some walked and some trudged up the sidewalk, their winter coats wide open, ignoring the chilly wind swirling snow around the school yard.

British Columbia mountain weather, Dan thought with a shudder.

But Natasha sat on the truck seat, her hands folded over her stomach, her brown hair hiding her face and falling down the front of her bright red winter jacket.

"My tummy still hurts," she said, peeking through her hair, adding a wince in case he didn't believe her. "And I still miss my mommy." Natasha sniffed, her brown eyes shimmering with tears.

Despite her performance of variations on the same theme for the past few minutes, his heart still twisted at her words. Though he and Lydia had been divorced for five years, Dan was still dealing with his ex-wife's recent death. He couldn't imagine what his little girl, who had lived with Lydia up until her death a month ago, was going through.

He pressed a kiss to Natasha's head. "I know you're sad, honey," he said, tucking her hair behind her ear so he could see her face. "But school is starting and you don't want to be late, do you?" He made his voice reasonable and soothing, hoping she would move.

The bell sounded and the last of the stragglers entered the school. Dan tossed a quick glance toward the grade one classroom directly ahead of him. Kids moved past the frosted windows, getting settled into their desks. A taller figure stopped, looking out the window. Even from here, he caught the red-gold shine of Hailey Deacon's hair, that little tilt of her head that told him she was watching them. He'd seen her stop before to look out the window and watch them as soon as they pulled into the parking lot.

He tried not to let his heart flip the way it always did whenever he saw her, back when they were dating.

Since he and Natasha had come back to Hartley Creek, he'd managed to avoid Hailey, his old girlfriend. But she worked as a teacher's aide in the grade one class his daughter was supposed to attend. A first meeting between them was inevitable.

Dan turned back to Natasha, his concern for his daughter taking priority.

"I don't want to go." Her raised voice echoed over the now-empty school yard. "I want to stay with you."

"I know, but you have to start school. And I need to get back to work at Grandpa's hardware store."

He was about to tug on Natasha's arm again when a glint of reflected light from the school's door caught his attention. The door fell closed and there she was, her coat open, her hair flowing like a copper flag behind her.

As she came closer he saw the concern on her delicate features, the frown above her gray eyes. His heart flipped again.

Everything has changed, he reminded himself, turning back to Natasha. *You were married. You've got a daughter. You lost your chance with her. Stay out of the past.*

"We're going now," he said to his daughter, trying to sound as if he was in charge.

But Natasha just looked ahead, her arms clasped tightly over her stomach.

"Sorry to barge in," Hailey was saying. "But I noticed from the window you were having some trouble."

Dan steeled himself, then turned to face his old girlfriend. She brushed a strand of hair back from her face as a hesitant smile played around the edges of her mouth. She looked as beautiful as she ever had. Maybe even more so. Old emotions seeped up from where he thought they were buried. He pushed them down. He had no right to get distracted.

"Natasha is upset," he said curtly. "She doesn't want to go to school."

"Of course she's sad," Hailey replied, coming around to stand beside him. Then Hailey gave him a sympathetic look that almost found its way through the barriers he had thrown up. "I'm sorry to hear about your wife."

"Ex-wife."

She pulled back from him, his tone obviously accomplishing what he wanted—to keep her at arm's length and protect himself.

"I heard about that too." She attempted another smile, then turned back to Natasha.

Dan looked down at the top of Hailey's head. She still parted her hair in that jagged line, still let it hang free over her shoulders, still wore perfume that smelled like oranges.

He clenched his fists and turned his wavering attention back to his daughter.

"Hello, Natasha, my name is Miss Deacon." Hailey held her hand out. "I'll be helping you in school this morning."

She had pitched her voice to the same low, reassuring level she used when she taught children how to ski and snowboard on the ski hill.

"I don't want to go to school," Natasha said, turning to Dan, her voice breaking. Her cries tore at Dan's heart. He couldn't leave her like this. But neither could he take Natasha back to the apartment above the hardware store. His father was recuperating from an extreme case of bronchial pneumonia. His mother worked at his hardware store and couldn't watch Natasha. Dan didn't know anyone who could babysit during the day.

He cleared his throat, embarrassed that Hailey had to witness his lack of control over his daughter. "I'm sorry, Natasha, but it's time for school."

He tried to get his arms around her to lift her out of the truck, but she swung out at him. "I don't want to go. Don't make me go." Her feet flailed in their heavy winter boots, hitting him in the arm. She wasn't going willingly.

Now what should he do? Drag her into the building?

"Dan, can I talk to you?" Hailey asked, catching his arm.

He shot her a puzzled glance and Hailey immediately released him, rubbing her hand against her pants, as if wiping away his touch.

As they walked away from the truck, Natasha's cries grew louder and more demanding.

"If I can get her into the classroom, I'm sure she'll be okay," Dan insisted. "She just needs to know who's in charge. Her mother always let her do whatever she wanted."

Hailey sighed and he got the impression she didn't

agree with him. Big surprise. Hailey had always been the kind of girl who went her own way, did her own thing.

And you're judging her after all the things you did?

The old guilt rose up again, a feeling that nagged at him as much as his self-reproach over his brother's death seven years ago.

"Natasha has had a lot to deal with in the last few weeks," Hailey was saying. "Things have happened to her she had no control over and now she's trying to find a way to take back some of that lost control. This is how she'll do it."

She sounded reasonable and, thankfully, practical. They were simply two adults discussing what to do about a little girl.

"But I need to get to work," he said, glancing back at Natasha. "My mother needs me at the store now that Dad isn't doing so well."

"I know that and you should go." Hailey put her hand on his arm again. He was sure her gesture was automatic, but even through the thickness of his jacket her touch still managed to hit him square in the gut.

This time he jerked away.

"How will that work?" he asked, shoving his hands in the pockets of his jacket.

"The store isn't that far from here." Hailey folded her arms over her chest. "I suggest you leave the truck here and walk to the store. I'll stay here with her until she's ready to come inside."

Dan frowned, glancing from Natasha back to Hailey. "Don't you need to get to the classroom?"

"Right now, my priority is your daughter. She won't sit in that truck all day and even if she does that's okay. Tomorrow we might have to do it again, but eventually she'll get tired of sitting outside. If we let her make the decision, hopefully she'll feel as if she has some say in the matter. Once that happens, she can slowly move into a routine which will help her in the healing process."

"It seems like a lot of trouble," he said, glancing over at Natasha, who had quieted down and was watching them with interest. "What if it takes all day?"

"I'm not that busy in the classroom today. Two days of the week I only work half-time. Today is one of those days."

"So what do you do the other half of those days?"

As soon as he spoke he felt like hitting himself on the forehead. That was none of his business.

He was also surprised to see a faint flush color Hailey's cheeks. "I volunteer at the ski hill. Visit my Nana."

Her comment reminded him of her reason for her temporary return to Hartley Creek. "I heard about her heart attack. I'm sorry. I knew you and your sisters are very close to her. How is she feeling?"

Hailey tipped her head down, fingering a gold necklace hanging around her neck. "She's doing very well. Thanks for asking."

The little hitch in her voice kindled concern for her and resurrected memories and emotions he thought he'd dealt with long ago.

He blinked, mentally pushing them away. Natasha and her care was his priority right now. Hailey didn't even make the list. Besides, he had heard she was leaving town at the end of the school year.

He shifted his weight, trying to decide what to do, then glanced at his watch and his decision was made for him. Time was running out.

"Okay. I'll leave you with her," he said with a resigned sigh. "But if you need me, call me at the store." He reached in his shirt pocket for his pen and the pad of paper he always carried around.

She held up her hand in a stop gesture. "I know the number."

Of course she would remember. When they were dating, he worked at his father's store after school and she would call him every day.

He shook off the memory as he glanced past her to his daughter, who still watched them with an intent gaze as if trying to figure out what they were talking about.

"Just so you know, she's incredibly stubborn and strong-willed." His heart shifted at the sight of her, so small, sitting in the truck, her feet straight out. "But she really needs a routine in her life and the sooner the better." Then he turned back to Hailey. "You call me if she gets upset or needs me."

"I will," Hailey promised.

Still he hesitated. He'd had to walk away from Natasha so many times; he didn't want to do it again. At least this time he would see her in a few hours instead of a few weeks.

"I should say goodbye to her before I go," he said.

Natasha's expression grew hopeful when he approached the truck. He bent over and gave her a quick kiss and a hug. "I'm going to the store, honey. You can stay here in the truck, like you wanted."

Puzzlement creased her forehead as Dan straightened. She seemed unsure of this new twist in her plans.

He stepped away, fighting his own urge to give in to her. He zipped up his coat and walked toward Hailey. "You'll let me know how things go?"

"I'll make sure she's okay."

Dan gave her a tight nod, but before he left, their gazes met and held and it seemed as if the intervening years slipped away. Seven years of living away from Hartley

Creek and a failed marriage drifted away like smoke with one look into those gray-blue eyes.

Then the past slid into the present and with it came reality.

He had Natasha, his greatest blessing and the only positive consequence of his marriage.

"Talk to you later," was his gruff response as he steeled himself against old emotions.

At one time he had loved Hailey. At one time they'd made plans. Then Austin's death had crashed into their lives and with it had come a flood of guilt. Dan had promised his parents, who didn't like for their sons to go snowboarding, that he would watch over Austin. He'd failed them when Austin died on a run he should never have started.

And then Hailey had broken up with him.

He straightened his shoulders. Hailey belonged to his past, not his present.

"Adam, come here," Hailey called out to the little boy who was about to run out of the school with no coat, no hat and no scarf. The temperature hovered around minus ten with the wind. The kid's ears would freeze and his mother, Emma Minton, would be annoyed.

Adam sighed, and turned around, trudging back to her, dragging his coat and his backpack. "Why do I have to put on my coat? It gets so hot in the bus."

Hailey knelt down. "If something happens, we want you to be properly dressed."

As she helped him with his coat, the doors at the end of the noisy hallway opened up again. A tall figure strode around the much smaller bodies, shifting to avoid the headlong rush of children released from the confines of the class.

Although she had seen Dan Morrow every afternoon for the past week, each time an echo of her old feelings lifted her heart.

He was taller than he had been in high school; his shoulders had filled out and broadened. His blond hair had darkened, his face had gained a few more lines, but it was his gaze that snagged and held her attention.

His deep-set eyes used to mesmerize and melt her heart. Now they looked at her with a calm indifference that hurt her more than anger would have.

You broke up with him because he wanted to leave. Why do you care how he looks at you?

The question mocked her as she forced her attention back to Adam, who was squirming like a snake.

Dan reached for the door to the class, but Hailey held out a hand to stop him. "Natasha's teacher, Miss Tolsma, wants to talk to you before you take Natasha home," she said.

"Why?"

Hailey hesitated, then angled him a quick glance. "Today was not…not Natasha's best day," she said, deliberately keeping her comment vague in front of Adam, Natasha's classmate.

"At least she got out of the truck right away today," Dan said, with a hopeful note in his voice. He shot a quick glance through the window in the classroom door at his daughter, who sat perched at the edge of a tiny chair, clutching her backpack.

Hailey followed his glance and suppressed a sigh as she zipped up Adam's coat.

It was Friday afternoon and school was done for the week. As he had the past four days, Dan had come to pick Natasha up. Megan Tolsma had asked Hailey to tell Dan she needed to talk to him. However, Megan was still in a staff meeting, leaving Hailey to fill the awkward silence between her and Dan with idle chitchat.

At one time Hailey could have regaled Dan with stories about people they knew. Passed on a bit of gossip. Talked about the snow conditions on the mountain.

Now their history and the silence of the past seven years yawned like a chasm between them, and above that space floated memories of Austin's death. The tragic event that pushed them apart. That sent Dan west to Vancouver and Hailey in the opposite direction.

Dan drummed his fingers against his thigh, obviously also aware of the awkwardness trembling between them.

Hailey dragged her attention back to Adam. "Are you still coming to the ranch next week?" Adam asked as Hailey tugged a toque on his head. "Mommy made your favorite chocolate cupcakes and put them in the freezer so me and Carter won't eat them."

"I'm excited for cupcakes," she said, hoping Dan didn't hear the waver in her voice.

Please, Lord, she prayed, *help me get over this. I don't want to feel so confused around him. This has to get easier.*

It's that whole first love thing, she reminded herself. You never really forget the drama and emotions of that first love. She just had to try.

Yet, as she wrapped Adam's scarf around his neck, she knew her reaction to Dan was beyond that of former high school sweethearts. Dan had been part of her dreams and the promise of a settled and secure future—something she had lacked with a mother who always wanted to be anywhere but Hartley Creek. And a father who had left her and her sisters long ago.

While she tied up the ends of the scarf, Adam turned his attention back to Dan.

"Are you Natasha's daddy?"

"Yes. Are you friends with her?" Dan asked back.

"I want to be, but she doesn't play with me. She's not fun."

Hailey tugged on Adam's scarf to get his attention. "Remember? We only say good things about our friends," she said, adding in a warning frown when Adam met her gaze.

"She's not my friend yet," Adam protested. "She won't play with me because all she does is cry."

She needed to work on the potency of her frown, Hailey thought. Obviously it had no effect on Adam. As Hailey glanced back at Dan she caught a shadow of pain cross his expression.

All week she and Megan had tried to be diplomatic with Dan in their discussions about Natasha. Dan kept insisting Natasha only needed a few more days to get used to the routine.

But Natasha needed more than a few more days to settle in. They hadn't told him yet that Natasha had spent all of today hunched over her knapsack, her hair hanging over her face, silent tears streaming down her cheeks.

Megan was saving that information for the parent-teacher meeting this afternoon.

Hailey pushed herself to her feet. "Out you go, buddy. Say hi to your mom and Carter for me," she said, sending Adam out the door, watching to make sure he got to the bus. When she saw the principal of the school urging Adam on, she turned back to Dan.

"So, how does that kid know your cousin Carter?" Dan asked.

"His mother, Emma, and my cousin Carter are engaged."

"Glad to hear that," Dan said, slipping his hands in the

back pockets of his jeans. "Carter's had it pretty rough the past few years. What with losing his wife and then his little boy."

Hailey tried not to read too much into his knowledge of her family. Carter was her cousin, but he was also a part of the Hartley Creek community. Dan's mother and father would have kept Dan abreast of what was going on.

"Carter's happy now."

Dan nodded, then blew out a sigh. "What did that little guy mean when he said all Natasha does is cry?"

"Today wasn't a good day for Natasha." That was all she felt comfortable telling him.

"She'll have her good and bad days, I guess," Dan replied. The look he gave Hailey seemed to contain both challenge and hope.

She swallowed, unable to look away, wondering if he ever thought of their last time together and the fight they had. Had he done the same thing as she had done in the months that followed? Relive that conversation over and over? Say things differently?

After Austin died, Dan had pulled back. She had understood that and had given him room to grieve. Then, when he finally asked to get together again it was to tell her that he wanted to move away from Hartley Creek. When she asked him why he said only that he needed space.

As she'd faced him down, Hailey had relived the pain she felt when she'd watched her father silently pack his suitcase, then walk past her and out of the house. She had been eight years old then and vividly remembered her helplessness.

Added to the past memory was the reality that four months before Austin's accident, when Hailey had just graduated from high school, her mother, Denise, decided her youngest daughter was old enough to fend for herself. Her sisters, Naomi and Shannon, were out of the house already, so Denise packed up and moved away from Hartley Creek, leaving Hailey behind.

Then Dan wanted to leave her too?

It was all too much. This time she would be in charge, Hailey had thought. This time she wasn't going to be left behind. So she'd broken up with him.

Part of her had hoped, even yearned, that he would plead with her not to break up. That he would change his mind and want to stay in Hartley Creek with her.

But nothing.

The first six months he was gone, she nurtured the faint hope he would return. When she heard about his marriage to Lydia she knew their relationship had ended.

Though the sting of that betrayal had stayed with her a long time, the memory of the love she had held for him lingered.

And now, looking into his eyes, that old memory grew stronger and she was reluctantly drawn into his gaze.

She couldn't do this. Not here. Not now.

Relief flooded her when she saw Megan striding down the hall.

"Here's Miss Tolsma," she said, reaching blindly for the handle of the classroom door. "I'll sit with Natasha, until you're finished."

Then she turned and retreated into the room, closing the door firmly on Dan and on the past.

She'd found out the hard way the only way to stay in control of your own life was to stay in control of your plans.

No way was Dan disrupting them.

Chapter Two

Natasha sat in the little chair in the corner, still clutching her knapsack, her chin resting on the top of it, her brown hair hiding her face.

At least she wasn't crying anymore.

Hailey sat down beside her, perched awkwardly on a chair made for six-year-old bottoms. She folded her hands on her lap, saying nothing, simply being there for the little girl.

As if finally sensing her presence, Natasha looked up. Her red-rimmed eyes and tear-stained cheeks plucked at Hailey's heartstrings.

Natasha dragged her coat sleeve across her face, drying her eyes. "Is my daddy come yet?"

"He's talking to Miss Tolsma for a few minutes. As soon as they're done he'll come to get you."

"I want to be with my daddy. I don't want to be in this school." Natasha looked down at her knapsack, fiddling with a tiny stuffed rabbit hanging from the zipper pull.

"I'm sure your daddy wants to be with you too." Hailey laid her hand on Natasha's tiny shoulder.

Natasha shook her head. Hailey heard her draw in a trembling breath and her shoulders shook with silent sorrow, as if she had no hope her cries would be acknowledged.

Hailey's heart broke for the little girl adrift without her mother and living in an unfamiliar place.

"You know your daddy loves you very much," Hailey said, giving the little girl's hand a squeeze. "He wants to take very good care of you and he wants you to learn. That's why he put you in school."

Natasha's silent cries only increased. Hailey couldn't stand watching her. She pulled the little girl onto her lap. Natasha made a token protest, then wilted against Hailey, her arms twined around her neck.

Hailey wrapped her arms around the tiny, slender body, rocking slowly back and forth and making shushing noises. Natasha burrowed her head in Hailey's neck.

"I don't want to be sad," she murmured, sniffing.

"I know you miss your mom and this place is different. It's okay to be sad about that."

Natasha drew in a shuddering breath. "Daddy said I shouldn't talk about my mommy," she said. "Because it makes me cry."

Hailey felt torn. She didn't want to go against Dan's parenting, but she also wanted to look out for Natasha.

"You can talk about your mommy to me, if you want," Hailey said. "You can tell me anything you want about her."

Natasha considered this, then lay against Hailey again. "I really like you," she whispered.

"I like you too," Hailey replied, stroking Natasha's damp hair away from her face. She clung to the little girl. Dan's little girl.

What if Austin's accident hadn't happened? What if Dan had stayed in Hartley Creek? Would the little girl in her arms be her and Dan's?

The light touch of a hand on her shoulder made her jump. Hailey yanked herself back from her meandering thoughts, then just about fell off the chair when she turned and saw Dan pull his hand back from her.

A frown pulled his eyebrows together as he looked down at her.

"She was so upset…she was crying… I didn't know what to do." Hailey stumbled through her excuses, wondering why she felt she had to explain her behavior.

But Dan's direct gaze made her feel as if she had stepped over some invisible boundary.

He bent over and lifted Natasha away from Hailey and the little girl tucked herself into his arms. He stroked her hair just as Hailey had, tucking Natasha's head under his chin as he held her close.

Just as Hailey had.

"It's okay, honey," he murmured to his daughter. "We're making this better for you."

Hailey glanced over to Megan standing by the front doorway to the class, one arm crossed over her chest, her other hand tucked under her chin while she watched Dan and his little girl.

Hailey beat a retreat to her friend's side.

"Did you figure something out?" Hailey asked.

Megan ran her forefinger across her chin, as if drawing out her thoughts. Then she turned to Hailey. "We've decided that Natasha would do better with a tutor who could work with her in her home."

Hailey looked back to Dan, now perched on the edge of the small table, still holding his daughter.

"Good idea, but where will you find a tutor in Hartley Creek?" she asked, watching as Dan rocked slowly back and forth, comforting his daughter.

As a father has compassion on his children…

The Bible verse that had comforted her so often in the dark days following Austin's accident slipped into her mind.

Dan was a good father, so unlike her own.

Megan turned away from Dan to Hailey, lowering her voice. "I'm thinking this might be a good job for you."

Hailey's attention jerked away from Dan to her friend. "What, what?"

"Shush. Use your church voice," Megan whispered, holding her finger to her lips. "You and I both know that this little girl needs more help than any of the children in the classroom. When I saw you holding her on your lap, I knew you were exactly the right person for this job."

"I don't think so." She couldn't see Dan on a regular basis. That would put too heavy a strain on her emotions.

"But think of Natasha," Megan urged. "That little girl is overwrought. She recently lost her mother. She needs some kind of direction and she has obviously formed an attachment to you."

Hailey pressed her lips together as her sympathy for Natasha swayed her reasoning.

Megan sensed her wavering and put her hand on Hailey's shoulder. "I think you're exactly the right person for the job," she said.

Hailey shrugged, her reluctance battling with her sympathy for Natasha. "You can think all you want, but I'm sure Dan won't go for your plan."

"We'll see," was all Megan would say.

They walked over to where Dan sat, still holding Natasha. The little girl lay quietly in his arms.

Dan looked up when they came close, a raw hope in his eyes.

"I have a temporary solution to your problem." Megan

gave Dan a bright smile. "I've talked to Hailey about your situation and she is willing to tutor your daughter."

Dan's gaze flicked over Hailey and then returned to Megan. "I don't think that's an option," was his blunt response.

"I feel it's a reasonable solution," Megan replied, brushing aside his objections. "Hailey and Natasha obviously have some kind of bond."

Dan's only reply was to lift Natasha, stand up and settle her on his hip. Then he glanced over at Hailey. For a moment, as their eyes met, she caught a flicker of older emotions, a hearkening back to another time. Her heart faltered in response.

"This won't work," he said, then turned and walked away.

Hailey watched him leave, the definite tone in his voice cutting her to the core. Though Hailey had known Dan wouldn't agree, she didn't think he would be so adamant about it.

She wondered why she cared. Her response to him showed her she wasn't over Dan Morrow at all. And if she wasn't over Dan, she certainly shouldn't be teaching his daughter.

"Natasha, don't play with that, honey." Dan took the cardboard-and-cellophane box holding the baby doll away from his daughter.

It was Saturday afternoon and he and his mother had spent most of the day doing damage control, keeping his daughter from running up and down the aisles, fingering the china displays and playing with the toys in the store. Patricia, the store's only employee, manned the register.

"But it's pretty and I don't have a doll like that." Natasha stuck out her lip in a classic pout as she dropped onto the wooden floor, her green fairy dress puddling around her in a mass of glittery chiffon and satin.

Dan carefully closed the box and put it back up on the shelf with the rest of the toys. "Come with me to the front," he said, taking his daughter's hand. "Patricia said she has a game for you to play."

She jerked her hand away just as his cell phone rang out. Without bothering to check the caller, he pulled it from his pocket and answered it.

"We've been trying to call you for the past two days," a voice accused him.

At the sound of the woman's voice Dan's heart sank. Lydia's mother. Carla Anderson.

"I want the doll," Natasha called out, pulling away from Dan as he tried to control her and use his phone. Thankfully the store had hit a lull and Dan didn't have to deal with any customers right now.

"Is that Natasha?" Carla asked, her voice raising an octave. "What is wrong with her?"

"She's fine." The only thing wrong with her was she wasn't getting what she wanted. "And what can I do for you, Carla?" he asked, forcing himself to smile. He'd read somewhere that if you smile even if you don't feel like it, your voice sounds more pleasant. And he needed that pleasant tone right now. Every conversation with his mother-in-law since Lydia's death had been a battle over who would take care of Natasha. He had custody, but Lydia's parents brought it up at every turn.

In the weeks after Lydia's death Dan deliberately kept everyone out of his daughter's life just so he could cement his relationship with Natasha. He wanted to give her stability, create a connection. He'd had such little time with his daughter when Lydia was alive. However, in Dan's opinion that had meant keeping everyone, even his own parents, at arm's length for those first critical weeks after Lydia's death.

Now he lived in Hartley Creek and Carla and Alfred were still in Vancouver, and they'd been pushing harder and harder with each phone call.

"I want to talk to Natasha," Carla was saying. "I haven't talked to her for a couple of days."

Dan looked down at his sniffling daughter, then at the checkout counter. His mother was bagging some items for Miranda Klauer. The store was quiet, so he had time to supervise the phone call.

"Okay. I'll put her on," Dan said, as he took Natasha's hand and walked toward the door leading to his and Natasha's apartment above the store. They stepped into the stairwell and closed the door, leaving it open a crack so he could give them some privacy and yet keep an eye on what was going on outside.

"It's your gramma," he said to his daughter, lowering the phone and covering the mouthpiece. "She wants to talk to you. Do you want to talk to her?"

Natasha gave a halfhearted nod and Dan gave her the phone.

She lifted it, frowning just a bit, as if unsure what she would hear.

"Hi, Grandmother… I'm fine… Yes, I love my daddy. And he loves me." Natasha sat down on the first stair, fidgeting with a piece of her skirt as she listened to her grandmother. "My Gramma and Grandpa Deacon are really nice too… It's cold here but I don't have to go to school." Natasha looked over at Dan, puzzlement crossing her features. "Because my daddy said so… My daddy can homeschool me, like my mommy did." Her frown deepened with each pause in the conversation as she listened to what her grandmother was saying. "But I like being with my daddy and I don't want to live with you—"

Fury rose up in Dan and he had to stop himself from snatching the phone away from Natasha. "I need to talk to Grandmother Anderson," he said, keeping his voice calm as he held out his hand.

Thankfully, Natasha willingly gave the phone up.

Dan took in a deep breath, then another, then raised the phone to his ear.

"We have all kinds of fun toys and I can take you to the park all the time because it's not cold here," Carla Anderson was saying.

"This is Dan." His words came out clipped and he didn't bother smiling this time. "What are you doing?"

A pause greeted his angry question, then Carla cleared her throat. "I was merely pointing out to Natasha the advantages of residing with us. And I think they are numerous."

Dan massaged the bridge of his nose, praying for patience, praying he didn't lose it in front of Natasha, who was watching him from her perch on the stair.

"We are not having this discussion now." He pitched his voice low, hoping he sounded nonthreatening. Hoping the fear twisting his gut didn't come out in his voice.

He'd spent almost six years of Natasha's short life battling with his ex-wife to get her to respect Dan's court-ordered weekend visits with his daughter. He had struggled not to run to court every time Lydia had decided this weekend she might take Natasha out of town, or Natasha was too sick to come, or any other lame excuse. He didn't want Natasha to become a pawn in their battle. But it had been difficult not to succumb when a month could go by with no visit.

Sad as Lydia's death had been, in one way, for Dan,

it had been a relief from the constant tension of battling over visits with his daughter.

Then, shortly after the funeral, he'd received a phone call from Lydia's brother, a lawyer, warning Dan that his parents wanted to sue for custody of Natasha. Since then the battle lines had been drawn and Mr. and Mrs. Anderson had slowly advanced, revealing their strategy one methodical step at a time.

The past few days their tactic had been to convince Natasha she wanted to live with them.

"We're not giving up on Natasha." Carla warned. "We have much to give her."

Dan bit back an angry reply. Mr. and Mrs. Anderson owned a condo in Hawaii, a twenty-six-foot yacht anchored in the Victoria Harbor, a small private plane and a home just outside of Vancouver with more square footage than both his parents' hardware store and the grocery store beside it.

"She's my daughter," he said, "and I will take care of her."

"That may be, but she said she's not going to school. How is that taking care of her?"

Dan should have known Carla wouldn't have missed one beat in Natasha's conversation. "She's having a hard time adjusting." No sooner had the words left his lips than he felt like banging his head on the wall behind him. Why give them any kind of ammunition? What kind of idiot was he?

"You do realize your daughter needs to attend school. That is still required," Carla replied, a note of triumph in her voice.

The all-too-familiar panic rose up in him as he felt himself backed into a corner. He glanced over at Natasha. She was smiling at him, rocking back and forth on the stair. He wasn't letting her go. Never.

Mrs. Anderson was still talking. "If you aren't responsible enough to take care of her schooling, perhaps we will have to—"

"I'm getting a tutor," he snapped, cutting her off midthreat. He leaned back against the wall behind him, the old cliché of being stuck between a rock and a hard place suddenly becoming very real. Could he hire Hailey? See her every day?

Maybe there was another way. Someone else to tutor Natasha.

"I see." Mrs. Anderson's clipped tone showed him that he had, for now, caused her to retreat. "Then I guess we'll have to see how things pan out for her."

"Yes, we will." Dan experienced a momentary reprieve and, to his disappointment, one of his knees began to bounce, an involuntary reaction to stress. He pushed it down and forced a smile that came more naturally this time. "And now I'm saying goodbye." He ended the call before Mrs. Anderson could ask to speak to Natasha again.

He laid his head back against the wall, closing his eyes.

"Are you tired, Daddy?" Natasha asked him, tugging on his hand.

He looked down at her, feeling the weight of his responsibilities. He was tired. Tired of trying to balance all the emotions his homecoming had created. Tired of trying to do it all himself.

In spite of what he had told Natasha's grandmother, however, he wasn't sure he was ready to have Hailey tutor his daughter every day. Surely he could find someone else to do the job.

"No, honey. I'm fine." He dropped his phone in his pocket and took her hand. "Now, let's go see if Gramma needs any help."

Hailey smoothed her hair, pressed her lips together and then caught herself mid-preen as she walked out of the cloakroom. It's church, silly. And like last week, Dan won't be here anyway.

In spite of her self-chiding, she still tugged on the wide leather belt cinching her knit dress, pressed her lips together to even out her lipstick, then threaded her way through the people gathered in the foyer, toward the doors leading to the sanctuary.

She paused in the doorway, glancing around the church, looking for a place to sit. Shannon was working at the hospital this morning and her Nana wanted to sleep in, so neither of them would be here this morning.

She caught sight of her cousin Carter's dark head bent over his fiancée, Emma, her son, Adam, sitting on his lap. People sat on either side of them, so it didn't look like there was room for her there.

"Miss Deacon. Miss Deacon," Natasha's voice called out over the buzz of conversation from the lobby. Hailey's heart skipped its next beat.

She turned to see Dan's tall figure moving through the people gathered in the foyer. His dark blond hair still glistened with moisture, as if he had stepped right out of the shower, gotten dressed and come here. As Natasha pulled him closer she also saw a line of blood trickling from a cut on his cheek. Probably shaved as quickly as he had dressed.

"Miss Deacon, you come to church too?" Natasha asked, beaming with pleasure.

"Yes. I do." Hailey returned her smile, yet couldn't stop her eyes from drifting toward Dan.

He wore a blue blazer over a light blue shirt. No tie, and jeans with cowboy boots. Just as he always did. And just as before, one point of his collar was tucked under the lapel of his blazer and the other lay overtop.

Hailey had to stop herself from reaching out to straighten it. As she always did.

"Hello, Hailey," he said.

Hailey hoped her smile looked as polite and emotionless as his. Then she noticed the trickle of blood heading dangerously close to his collar.

"You're bleeding," Hailey said, pointing to his face.

Dan grimaced and lifted his hand to the wrong cheek. Without thinking Hailey pulled a tissue out of her purse and pressed it to his face. She felt the warmth of his cheek through the tissue.

Dan, however, pulled back, smearing the blood.

"Sorry. So sorry," she said, angry at how breathless she sounded. "It's just the blood was going to stain the collar of your shirt. I thought I should stop it. I didn't mean—"

Stop now, she chastised herself as she handed him the tissue again.

He took it from her and slowly wiped his cheek. "I should go to the washroom and clean this up," he said. "Would you mind watching Natasha for me?" he asked.

Hailey gave a tight shake of her head, pulling her gaze away from him. She drew in a long, careful breath. *Please Lord, help me through this,* she prayed. *I'll be seeing him from time to time. Just let me get my silly emotions settled down.*

As Dan left, Natasha caught Hailey's hand in hers, clinging to it. "I wanted to wear my fairy wings to church so I could look like an angel, but my Daddy said I couldn't."

Hailey dragged her attention from Dan's retreating back to the little girl.

Natasha swung Hailey's hand as if they had known each other for years instead of only a few days.

"I think you look like an angel now," Hailey returned.

"I don't like this dress, but my daddy said I had to wear it." Natasha pulled at the dress, her blue cotton tied at the waist. White tights and black patent leather shoes finished the look.

"You look really nice," Hailey said, but from the look of Natasha's sloppy ponytail she suspected Dan hadn't had much luck with her hair.

"My daddy said we had to hurry to get to church so we could sit with Gramma and Grandpa, but I want to sit with you," Natasha said, looking up at Hailey.

"You better wait to see what your daddy says," Hailey returned. Knowing the tension surrounding them each time they got together, she doubted Dan would give in to that request.

People moved past, smiling at her and Natasha. A few stopped to chat, but most walked directly into the sanctuary. Finally Dan appeared again. The cut on his cheek was only a tiny red line and seemed to have stopped bleeding.

Without looking at her, Dan reached for Natasha's hand. "We should go, sweetie," he said.

But Natasha wouldn't let go of Hailey. "I want to sit with Miss Deacon."

"I'm sure Miss Deacon has her own place to sit," he said, motioning her forward.

But Natasha wouldn't move.

Hailey saw Dan press his lips together and tried to

release Natasha's death grip on her own fingers. "You should go with your daddy," she said.

Natasha's lips thinned and she gave a quick shake of her head as she gave Hailey a determined look. "I want to sit with you." Her voice rose on that last word and people already seated in the sanctuary were looking back at them. Some looked concerned, some grinned, and Hailey sensed Dan's growing frustration.

Dan tried one more time to take Natasha away.

"I want to be with Miss Deacon," she called out as Dan took her hand firmly in his.

A few more heads turned and a few titters flew around the sanctuary. And in case neither Dan nor Hailey understood Natasha's determination, she emphasized her little pique with a stamp of her foot.

Hailey looked over Natasha's head at Dan. "I don't mind if you and her sit with me," she said, giving him a gracious way to give in to Natasha.

Dan drummed his fingers on his thigh, then gave a reluctant nod of his head. "Okay. I guess we can."

In spite of the tension of the moment Hailey couldn't stop a tiny frisson of pleasure at the thought of sitting with him. She dragged her attention back to Natasha. "I guess we'll need to find an empty spot," she said to the little girl. Then without another glance at Dan, she turned and walked down the aisle, searching for a place near the back where they wouldn't be too obvious.

As they passed Carter and Emma, she caught Carter looking at her and Natasha. Hailey averted her glance, but not soon enough to miss the smirk on her cousin's face. A flush heated her cheeks, but she kept her head up and finally found a spot at the end of a pew. Hailey slipped into the empty space, Natasha right behind her. And Dan right behind Natasha.

Hailey settled into the pew and, as Natasha slipped her arm into hers, tried not to look over at Dan. Thankfully the service started and the first song was announced. Hailey reached for the songbook at the same time as Dan. As their fingers brushed, she pulled her own hand back, curling her fingers against her palm.

Dan simply opened the book to the correct page and held it out for her to follow along.

Please help me get through this service, she prayed as she folded her hands together and sang along. *Please help me to stay focused on You, Lord, and not be distracted by Dan.*

When the song was over Hailey sat down and kept her gaze forward, concentrating on the worship team. The pastor. Anything but the man sitting a couple of feet away.

Natasha leaned contentedly against Hailey, swinging her feet back and forth, her arm tucked in Hailey's. By the time the pastor started preaching, however, Hailey felt Natasha's body grow heavier and heard her breathing slow.

She shot a quick glance down at the girl, surprised to see her eyes closed. Dan seemed to have noticed too. He reached over to take her from Hailey, but even in her sleep, Natasha clung to Hailey, shifted, then laid her head on Hailey's lap.

Hailey looked down at the little girl's face, so relaxed and innocent in sleep. Her heart faltered and she couldn't stop her hand from lightly brushing the child's hair back from her face, then letting her hand rest on Natasha's shoulder. She looked over at Dan at the same time he looked at her, and in his eyes she caught a fleeting glimpse of sadness. It's not my fault, she wanted to say, as she did not understand the strange attachment the young girl seemed to have to her.

Dan held her gaze a moment, then looked down at Natasha. He reached over and put his hand on her arm, as if laying his own claim to the little girl.

The service flowed on and still Natasha slept, her warmth and vulnerability creating a surprising feeling of protectiveness in Hailey.

But, to her shame, in spite of focusing her attention on the pastor, she was far too aware of Dan's hand resting only inches from hers.

Chapter Three

The chords of the last song rang through the sanctuary and Dan waited a moment, too many emotions storming the defenses he'd spent seven years putting in place.

All through the service he'd been far too conscious of Hailey. Her movements. The way she would curl her hair around her finger. The way she would smile at a point the minister had made.

Sometimes it seemed that the past seven years were just a drift of smoke, but then all he had to do was look at his daughter and realize that, between him and Hailey, everything had changed.

Now, as Natasha lay with her head on Hailey's lap, part of him wanted to snatch Natasha away from Hailey, pull his little girl to himself. Pull himself into the present.

But part of him also felt a disturbing sense of rightness. Hailey had always wanted to be a mother. She had always talked about having a large family. Six kids. Maybe more.

Dan gave himself a mental shake, erasing past emotions and history that had come back to haunt the present. What he felt for Hailey didn't belong here and now.

However, right now he had another reality to deal with. Natasha's schooling.

Hailey gently shook Natasha, trying to wake her up, but she wouldn't even open her eyes.

Dan sat down again. "Just leave her," he said quietly. "I need to talk to you anyway." He glanced over his shoulder at the people leaving the sanctuary. He couldn't see his parents, which was just as well. He needed a moment with Hailey. Alone.

As he waited, the buzz of conversation from the exiting congregation was punctuated with bursts of laughter. Light streamed over the emptying pews from the stained glass windows, bathing everyone in a multicolored glow.

Not much had changed here, he thought.

"What do you want to talk to me about?" Hailey asked, shooting him a puzzled frown.

Dan didn't say anything right away. In a few moments they could speak in private. Finally, the last people left the foyer and only then did Dan turn to Hailey.

"I have a favor to ask of you," he said, keeping his voice low so he wouldn't wake Natasha.

"Sure. What is it?"

Dan tapped his fingers on the back of the wooden pew, realizing how silly he was about to look, given his initial resistance to Hailey tutoring his daughter.

But that was before the in-laws' phone call. Before the pressure to come up with a solution had pushed him to this place. Before he had realized there was no one else to do the job.

"I was wondering if you're still willing to tutor Natasha," he said.

"What? Why now?"

Dan pursed his lips, trying to think of how to tell her, then decided to go with the easiest response. The truth.

"Ever since Lydia died, her parents have been pushing to get custody of Natasha. When they found out she wasn't going to school, they saw it as ammunition." He couldn't stop the bitter tone that crept into his voice. Or the anger. He paused a moment to settle himself, then looked over at Hailey. "Truth is, I'm stuck. I need a tutor, and because you're a qualified teacher, that makes it easier to prove I'm doing the right thing with Natasha's schooling." He didn't add that he couldn't find anyone else.

Before Hailey's glance slid away from him, he caught a glimpse of pain in her gray eyes.

He didn't want to analyze why she might feel that way. He felt as if he was using her, but when it came to his daughter he would do anything.

"I'll pay you," he added, hoping, praying she wouldn't turn him down. "I don't expect you to do this for free."

Hailey raised her hand as if to say stop. "Don't worry about that. I'll tutor her."

The tension in Dan's shoulders released. "Great. I appreciate that. I will pay you, though. At least as much as you're making at the school."

Hailey gently stroked Natasha's hair. Dan was surprised to see a slight tremor in her fingers. "Did you want me to start tomorrow?" she asked.

"That would be best."

Hailey pulled in a long, slow breath, then turned back to him. "Are you sure about this?"

Her direct question accentuated his own concerns but he knew he had no choice.

"I have to be," was all he could say to her.

Her eyes held his and in her expression he saw all the misgivings he also had entertained.

It would work, he told himself. A lot had happened between then and now. They were different people now.

Besides, it was only for a while. Once Natasha had eased back into regular classroom life, he wouldn't need Hailey's help anymore.

And once the school year was over, Hailey would be leaving Hartley Creek anyway.

"Are you sure it's a good idea to be tutoring Dan's girl?" Shannon closed a cupboard door in her kitchen and set a bowl beside the stove. "That won't be awkward?" Hailey's sister tossed her long, wavy hair away from her face as she dumped a pan of green beans into the bowl. Then she reached past Hailey for the nutmeg.

Hailey blew out a sigh as she carved up the chicken for the dinner she and Shannon were preparing for Nana in Shannon's apartment. "Hopefully not. I mean we're both adults. Besides, when he married Lydia he made it clear he had moved on."

"But still—"

"Have you heard anything more from Naomi?" Hailey didn't want to talk about her and Dan's past. She had shed enough tears over Dan's decisions and Shannon had been witness to most of them. Hailey had her own life now and Dan wasn't a part of it. "Last I talked to her, the oncologist said Billy had maybe another month?"

Shannon shook her head. "Poor Naomi. When she and Billy got engaged, who could have imagined this would happen?"

"Do you think she'll be back for Carter and Emma's wedding?"

"I hope so." Shannon frowned as she sprinkled nutmeg over the bowl of steaming beans. "Our poor sister has had to deal with so much, it would be good for her to be around family."

"Hopefully Garret will be done with that engineering job in Dubai by then."

"I hope so too. I'm looking forward to having everyone back for a while."

"What do you mean, for a while?" Nana Beck's quiet voice interrupted the sisters' conversation. She settled herself in the folding chair beside the plastic table that took up one corner of Shannon's minuscule kitchen.

"You know I have a teaching job in Calgary come September," Hailey said, laying a drumstick on the plate she was filling up.

"I still don't believe you can't find a job closer to home," Nana complained.

Hailey gave her grandmother a placating smile. "Calgary is only a three-hour drive away. I'll be back to visit."

Nana smoothed back her gray hair. "At least I've got three of my grandchildren together for now. And Carter seems so happy now that he and Emma are making their wedding plans."

"Yeah. Lucky Carter." Hailey felt truly happy for her cousin, but Dan's return to town reminded her of her own might-have-beens.

"You'll find someone, don't worry," Nana assured her, as if she could read her granddaughter's mind. "Maybe in Calgary. Or maybe here. Now that Dan Morrow is back. You two were such a sweet couple."

Hailey caught Shannon's sympathetic glance at their grandmother's lack of subtlety. Her sister, more than anyone, knew exactly how much Dan's desertion had hurt her.

"Lots of other fish in the sea, Nana," Shannon said. "And sometimes you need to try another sea."

Nana Beck sighed at that. "Well, I keep praying for all you grandchildren. That you will all make better choices than my daughters did. That you will make the kind of choice your great-great-grandfather August Beck did."

Shannon walked over to their grandmother and dropped a light kiss on her forehead. "That means a lot to us, Nana." She gave her grandmother the bowl of beans. "Why don't you put this on the table in the dining room and when Hailey is finished butchering that chicken, we can eat."

"I've got things under control," Hailey protested, even as she struggled to cut the breast away from the bone.

Shannon put her hand on Hailey's shoulder and gave her a knowing look. "I sure hope so, little sister."

Hailey caught the questioning subtext in her sister's comment and looked away.

She sure hoped she had things under control. Seeing Dan every day would create a challenge to keeping her heart whole.

But she had to. She just had to keep thinking of leaving Hartley Creek and starting over in a new job in a new city. It was the only way she would get through the next few months.

Hailey shifted her backpack on her shoulder, then took the first steps up the flight of wooden stairs hugging the brick wall at the back of Hartley Creek Hardware Store. A cutting winter wind whistled around her ears and through the open zipper of her down-filled jacket. She wrested the sides of her coat together, as memories emerged with each step up the stairs.

When she and Dan were dating they would take turns doing homework at each other's place. When her mother was gone, which was frequently, Hailey would come to

Dan's place. They would sit beside each other, papers spread over the table, a plate of fresh-baked cookies in front of them.

Mostly, though, she and Dan would just hold hands under the table and whisper to each other. They would make up scenarios and weave plans.

Dan would become a partner with his father in the store. Hailey would work at the ski hill until the kids came.

Hailey's steps faltered as she made her way up the stairs, her hand clinging to the wooden rail.

Okay, Lord. I know doing this will bring up many memories, but that's long over. Done. We were just kids then. We've both moved on to different places. We're both different people. Please help me remember that.

She waited a moment, as if to give the prayer time to wing its way upward, then she followed it up the rest of the stairs. She rapped on the door, then hugged her coat around her, glancing over her shoulder at the mountains surrounding the town.

From here she could barely make out the The Shadow Woman. The contours of her face and body would show up better in the latter part of summer and even more clearly from just the right spot on Carter's ranch, the old family place.

Melancholy drifted through her. By August, she would be leaving Hartley Creek.

The creak of the door opening made her turn around.

Once again, Dan stood in front of her. She caught the piney scent of his aftershave, the same one he always wore. The kind she had bought him when he'd started shaving.

His hair, still damp from the shower, curled a bit. He

wore it shorter than he used to but the look suited his strong features and deep-set eyes.

"Hey," was all he said, adding a curt nod. "Natasha will be right out. She's cleaning up her bedroom."

He stepped aside for Hailey to come in and as she looked around the apartment, she felt the brush of nostalgia. Her eyes flitted over the gray recliner, the overstuffed green couch and love seat, all facing the television perched on a worn wooden stand. Beyond that, through the arched doorway to the dining room, she saw the same heavy wooden table and matching chairs with their padded brocade seats.

The same pictures still hung on the walls, the same knick-knacks filled the bookshelf along one wall of the living room.

"Looks like your parents still live here," she said, dropping her backpack on the metal table in the front hallway and removing her jacket.

"Mom and Dad wanted a fresh start when they moved out," Dan said, reaching for her coat. "They took only a few things to the new house."

As Dan took her coat, their fingers brushed. Just a light touch, inconsequential in any other circumstance, with any other person. Trouble was, Dan wasn't just any other person.

Just as she had at church yesterday, she jerked her hand back, wrapping it around the other. "You probably want to get back to work." Thankfully, her voice sounded brisk and businesslike, betraying none of the emotions that arose in his presence.

"Mom and Patricia have been downstairs for half an hour already," Dan said as he hung her coat up in the cupboard beside the door. "I need to get going."

Hailey nodded as she picked up her backpack with the

assignments Megan had planned for Natasha. "I imagine the dining room is the best place to work."

"That's what I thought." Dan shifted his feet, his hands in the front pockets of his pants, and Hailey wondered if the same memories of their past slipped through his mind. "I just want to tell you I appreciate you coming here. I know it keeps you from helping Megan."

"I'm sure Natasha will be back at school in no time," Hailey said with a breeziness she didn't quite feel. "So Megan won't be without my help for long."

"I hope so. I'll get Natasha." Dan took a step back and then headed down the long, narrow hallway just off the living room.

She ambled over the worn carpet, then through the arched doorway to the dining room. The table was cleared off and she set her knapsack down on its polished wooden surface. Hailey zipped open the knapsack, glancing around as she pulled out her papers and books. The glass-fronted armoire in the dining room still held the same plates, teacups and serving bowls. Why had Mrs. Morrow left so much behind?

Then Hailey's eyes fell on the row of school photographs marching along the facing wall.

Pictures of Dan ranged from a pudgy, freckle-faced kindergartner with a gap-toothed grin to the serious senior. Already in grade twelve he showed a hint of the man he had now become, with his deep-set eyes and strong chin.

Hailey was surprised at the little lift his pictures gave her. At the memories they evoked.

She turned her attention to the row of pictures below Dan's. Austin's narrow features grinned back at her from the school photos, his blue eyes sparkling with the mischief that typified his outlook on life, the complete opposite of his older, more serious brother.

But Austin's series ended with a photograph from grade eleven. The year he died. Regret for might-have-beens twisted her stomach, then she turned, putting the pictures behind her.

"Miss Deacon, you came." The bright voice of Natasha banished the memory. As the little girl bounded into the room, her brown hair bounced behind her.

Today Natasha wore a lime-green T-shirt tucked into torn blue jeans. A pair of sparkly yellow angel wings completed the look.

Obviously the little girl had chosen some of her own clothes today.

"Wow. Don't you look spiffy," Hailey said, trying not to smile too hard at her ensemble.

"These are my favorite wings," Natasha announced as she lifted the wand in her hand and performed an awkward twirl, almost knocking over a plant stand in the process.

"Natasha, please, no dancing in the house," Dan said, catching the rocking houseplant and setting it out of reach of her wings. "I'd like you to go take off your fairy wings."

Quick as a flash Natasha's good mood morphed into a sullen glare. "I like my wings and you said I couldn't wear them to school. But this isn't school."

"This is *like* school," Dan said, kneeling down in front of her. "And I want you to behave for Miss Deacon."

Natasha caught the end of her hair and twirled it around her finger, her attention on the books on the table and not on what her father was saying. "Are those mine?" she asked.

"Yes. They are." Hailey glanced at her watch. "And it's almost time for us to start."

"But first the fairy wings come off," Dan insisted.

"I want to keep them on," she protested, wiggling away from him.

Dan cradled her face in his hands and turned her to face him. "Sorry, honey, but now it's time for school, not time for pretending. Now I have to go to work and you have to stay up here, but I'll be back at lunchtime, okay?"

Natasha pouted but then it seemed the fight went out of her. "Okay, Daddy. But you'll be right downstairs, won't you?"

Dan nodded, tucking a tangle of hair behind her ear. Then he brushed a gentle kiss over her forehead. "Love you, munchkin," he said as he slipped the wings off her shoulders.

"Love you, punchkin," she repeated with a giggle.

Dan set the wings aside and smoothed her hair again, smiling at her, the love for his daughter softening his features.

Hailey swallowed as she watched the scene between them. She always knew Dan would make a good father.

Her heart twisted a moment with old sorrow and old regrets and a flurry of other questions. Why had Dan married Lydia? Why had he moved on so quickly from her to another woman?

She pressed her eyes shut a moment, as if to close her mind to the past.

It was none of her business, she reminded herself.

And it was a bleak reminder that what she and Dan had was dead and gone.

Chapter Four

"I don't want to do math now. I hate math." Natasha pushed her chair away from the table, the wooden legs screeching over the worn linoleum. She folded her arms over her chest as she pushed out her lower lip.

For the past hour Hailey had been working with Natasha on math problems and all they had to show for the time were some princess doodles on the bottom of the page and one measly solved problem. Which made Hailey wonder how much homeschooling Lydia had done.

"Don't say hate. Say instead that you don't *like* math," Hailey corrected, picking up the pencil Natasha had tossed on the table. "We want to save the word *hate* for really big things."

Natasha shot her a puzzled glance. "What big things?"

Hailey held the pencil out to Natasha, waiting for her to take it. "Big things like sin and killing and saying bad things about God."

Natasha pursed her lips, as if pondering this, then tossed her brown hair over her shoulder and took the pencil from Hailey.

"My mommy said there's no such thing as God," Natasha said, doodling a princess in one corner of the paper.

Hailey wasn't sure what to say as she watched Natasha add a crown to the princess's head. She didn't want to disparage Natasha's memory of her mother, but she was fairly sure Dan disagreed with Lydia's beliefs. He'd always had a strong faith in God. At least he had until the day of Austin's death.

Natasha wiggled a bit, then put her pencil down. "I have to go the bathroom," she said, slipping off her chair before Hailey could stop her.

Hailey let her go. Finding routine would take time with a little girl who didn't seem to know the meaning of the word.

As Hailey gathered up the pencils Natasha had scattered over the table, her eyes were drawn to the pictures on the wall of Austin and Dan.

She drew in a long, slow breath, stifling the painful memories resurrected by Austin's face. So easily she remembered the day Austin died.

The three of them, Dan, Hailey and Austin, had been snowboarding together. Hailey had gotten separated from Dan and Austin in the lineup for the chairlift and, by the time she got to the top of the hill, only Dan was waiting for her. He told her that Austin had gone off on his own.

Dan and Hailey had spent most of the afternoon on the runs at the top of the mountain, and they got to the bottom only to find out that Austin had gone out of bounds on a black diamond run and had gone over a rocky ledge.

He had died instantly.

And right after that Dan and Hailey's relationship had fallen apart.

"I'm done," Natasha announced, coming back to the room.

The little girl's voice broke into the thoughts flashing through Hailey's mind. She pulled her hands over her face as if wiping them away. She needed to get out of this apartment and the memories it evoked. And from the way Natasha had been struggling to concentrate the past hour, she needed to go out too.

Hailey made a quick decision.

"You know what we're going to do?" Hailey asked, gathering up the papers and the pencils. "We're going to do some schoolwork downstairs."

Natasha jumped up eagerly, then frowned. "My daddy said he doesn't want me in the store. He said I make problems."

"I'll be with you." Hailey picked up a folder and slipped the papers inside.

"But my daddy—" Natasha protested again.

"I'll talk to your daddy and help him to understand," Hailey said with more assurance than she felt.

All morning the little girl had been unable to concentrate on even the simplest problems. Maybe a different method of teaching was in order. And Hailey had just the idea of how this was to be done.

"First I have to put on my wings," Natasha said.

Hailey didn't bother to stop her. One step at a time, she reminded herself.

A few moments later, wings firmly in place, she and Natasha were headed down the narrow stairs inside the apartment leading to the store below.

"We have to be quiet," Hailey whispered. "We don't want your daddy to get angry with us."

Hailey pushed open the door and was greeted by the buzz of conversation and the chiming of the cash register as Dan's mother rang up another sale.

The wooden floor creaked under her feet as she and Natasha crept toward the bins at the back of the store, where Hailey knew they wouldn't be in anyone's way. She couldn't see Patricia or Dan. So far, so good.

"The Makita is a good choice," she heard Dan's deep voice say on the other side of the aisle. "You won't regret it."

"That's my daddy," Natasha called out and pulled her hand free before Hailey could stop her. Natasha's glittery wings bounced as she jogged down the aisle. As she rounded the corner, one wing caught the edge of a toolbox and stopped her headlong rush. As Natasha lost her balance, the box toppled toward her and knocked her over. She sat a moment, looking shocked, and then her wounded cries reverberated through the store.

"Natasha. What are you doing here? Where's Miss Deacon?"

Hailey caught up to Natasha at the same time as Dan, not surprised at the suppressed anger in his voice. Hailey pulled the box off Natasha and Dan pulled his now-sobbing daughter up into his arms. He brushed her tangled hair off her face, looking her over as she kept crying.

"I think she's more scared than hurt," Hailey said over Natasha's wails, trying to put the box back on the shelf.

"What is she doing down here?" Dan asked as he tucked Natasha's head against his neck. Then, behind Dan, Hailey caught the curious glance of the customer Dan had been helping. Great. Carter's gray eyes sparkled with mischief and the smirk on her cousin's face told her that whatever happened here would be reported posthaste to Nana, her sister Shannon and Carter's fiancée, Emma.

"Thanks for the help, Dan," Carter said. "I'll go pay for this."

"Let me know how that drill works out for you," Dan replied, the scowl on his face showing Hailey how bothered he was at this interruption.

Carter winked at Hailey, then left, his cowboy boots echoing on the wooden floor.

"So why are you here?" Dan set Natasha on the floor, his scowl deepening. "I hired you so I wouldn't have to deal with these kinds of distractions."

"Natasha has been having difficulty staying focused, so I thought we could try some hands-on problem solving." Hailey strived to sound as though she was in control of the situation.

"I thought your job was to get her to stay focused?" Dan growled.

Hailey put on her most pleasant expression and nodded. "This is a transition time."

Dan's hazel eyes narrowed. "I still don't see how bringing her down here and disrupting things will help her."

Hailey forced herself to stay calm and not get pulled into the challenge she saw in his gaze. "I'll make sure she stays out of your way and doesn't bother customers. It's just for a few moments, to give her a bit of a break."

Dan shook his head. "I prefer if you keep her upstairs. She has to learn to stay on task. That's what I hired you for."

"You also hired me to use my judgment, right?" She forced a smile, hoping she didn't sound as contrary as she felt.

Dan didn't return her smile. "I hired you to do what I want. Right now I want you to take her upstairs and work with her there. Goofing around in the store won't help her make the transition."

He held her gaze a beat, as if to reinforce what he'd said.

Though every part of her rebelled, Hailey guessed this was not the time and place to argue with him.

Natasha pulled on her hand. "Can we go do my school-work now?"

Lowering her shoulders Hailey took a deep breath to relax. She'd have to find a better time to have this discussion with Dan. But they would have it. He had hired her to do a job and if he didn't like her methods, then he would have to find someone else.

"We're going back upstairs, sweetie," Hailey said, putting her hands on Natasha's shoulders.

"I don't like it in the 'partment. I want to be here with my daddy."

Well, your daddy doesn't want you to be here with him.

Hailey knew that wasn't entirely true. Dan had his own ideas of how Natasha should be schooled but, unfortunately, they didn't coincide with hers.

"I like this sandwich." Natasha grinned as she looked up from the plate Hailey had set in front of her. "How did you make it look like a rabbit?"

"Your grandmother has a great big cookie cutter in the shape of a rabbit," Hailey said. She remembered when Dan's mother had brought the cookie cutter up from the store. Dan and Austin had teased Mrs. Morrow about the humongous cookies she would be making with them and how fat they would all get eating rabbit cookies.

The memory teased up other emotions, which she fought down with a sense of dismay. Was this how it would be for the rest of her time teaching Natasha? Old memories and old emotions constantly assaulting her?

She took a quick breath. *Just get through it.*

"Aren't you making a sandwich?" Natasha asked, swinging her feet as she picked up her rabbit.

"Not for me. I'm going to eat with some friends at a café," Hailey said, just as the stairway door creaked open.

Dan stepped into the apartment, talking on his cell phone. "I needed that order yesterday," he said as he bent over Natasha's head and gave her a kiss.

When Hailey got back from the kitchen with the sandwich she had made for him, he had finished his phone call.

"How was your morning, munchkin?" Dan asked, sitting down beside Natasha as Hailey set a plate in front of him. "Did you get lots of work done?"

"I got bored and then I got sad." Natasha delivered the comment with a sorrowful look Dan's way, and just in case he didn't get that, she added a dramatic sniff.

"What were you sad about?"

"My mommy."

Dan pulled the corner of his lip between his teeth, then pointed to the plate in front of her. "But look at the cool sandwich Miss Deacon made for you. It looks like…a rabbit?" He shot Hailey a puzzled look.

"I used that old cookie cutter of your mother's."

"She still has it around?" Dan's mouth quirked up in a grin, which didn't help Hailey's equilibrium around him. She'd thought he would still be upset with her for taking Natasha downstairs. It appeared she'd been forgiven.

"I thought it would make her sandwich more interesting," Hailey returned, wrapping her purple sweater around herself. "So, if you guys are good, I'm heading down to Mug Shots for lunch."

Dan's puzzled expression held a touch of relief. The awkwardness between them was palpable and she guessed he would be more comfortable if she left.

"Sure. Thanks a lot for the sandwich. You didn't have to do that."

"I didn't mind," Hailey said, walking to the cupboard to get her coat.

"No. You can't go," Natasha cried out. "You have to stay and eat with us. Daddy always says it's important to eat together."

Hailey gave the little girl a gentle smile as she pulled her coat on. "Your dad was talking about families eating together," she said, pulling her hair free from the collar. "Which you are doing right now. You and your daddy are a family."

Natasha turned to Dan, grabbing his arm and giving it a tug. "Tell her she has to stay. Tell her, Daddy."

Conflicting emotions flitted across Dan's features.

Hailey held up her hand, forestalling his answer and giving him an out. "No. I should go. I have some friends waiting for me I want to visit with." Not entirely true, but there was bound to be someone she knew hanging around Mug Shots.

As she zipped up her jacket, Dan's cell phone rang.

Dan answered it, then, as he spoke, glanced up at Hailey, frowning. "Yeah, I guess I can," he said. He ended the call, then eased out a sigh as he held her eyes. "That was Jess Schroder. I need to meet him down at the lumberyard in twenty minutes."

Hailey bit her lip as she checked the clock. "That doesn't give me enough time to get to the coffee shop, eat and come back." She hesitated a moment more, then accepted the inevitable. "I guess I better eat lunch here," she said, unzipping her coat.

"Sorry about that," Dan said. "I'll make sure you get a break tomorrow."

She just nodded, then returned to the kitchen to make a sandwich for herself. She took her time, not sure she wanted to sit down at the table with Dan and Natasha. The situation smacked of domesticity.

She brought her sandwich to the table, sat down, then

bowed her head, her hair falling like a curtain around her flushed cheeks. *Dear Lord, just help me get through this,* she prayed. *Help me act around Dan like I would around any other guy. And bless this food, please, and thanks for all the blessings I have.*

She waited a moment, as if to let the prayer settle. When she looked up she caught Dan's enigmatic expression. She knew what he was thinking. At one time church, God and praying had not figured prominently in her life.

I'm not the irresponsible and goofy girl I used to be, she wanted to say.

Though she kept her thoughts to herself, she was unable to look away, unable to stop the tender stirring in her chest of older emotions. Older attractions.

"Why were you looking at your sandwich?" Natasha asked.

Hailey broke the connection, smiling at Natasha's confusion. "I was praying a blessing on my food."

"Why?" Natasha pressed, biting off the ear of her bunny sandwich.

Hailey cut her bread in two, then carefully laid her knife down, considering her answer. "It's because everything we have comes from God and so does our food. So I like to thank Him for it."

"How come we don't do that, Daddy?"

"Because I don't always think of it," was his quiet response. "But we should."

Hailey kept her attention on her sandwich, perplexed at the change in their situation. At one time she'd been the one who didn't pray and seldom went to church. Now, it seemed, Dan was the one who had moved away from the faith he'd been raised with.

"My mommy never prayed either," Natasha was saying. "Is that bad?"

Hailey coughed, then took a quick drink of water to cover up her reaction. "Your mommy probably had other things to think about and other things to do."

"My mommy did lots of things." Natasha examined her sandwich as if deciding which part of the rabbit to remove next. She swung her legs, then bit off the tail. "Like reading and sewing and driving and having long naps in the sunshine. I always had to be quiet then."

Dan put his hand on Natasha's arm. "We don't need to talk about Mommy," he said, his voice quiet.

Natasha gave him a puzzled glance. "Miss Deacon said it was good to talk about Mommy."

Dan shot a frown in Hailey's direction. "Did you tell her that?" he asked, a stern note edging his voice.

Once again she felt as if he was questioning her methods. And once again he was doing it in front of Natasha. They needed to have a teacher-parent "chat" about this later on, but in the meantime she needed to deal with this latest situation.

Hailey set her sandwich down, trying to decide how to approach this, reminding herself to be diplomatic.

"It's healthy to verbalize the past," Hailey said, using words Natasha might not understand.

"But that brings up extreme emotions."

Hailey lifted one slender shoulder in a light shrug, knowing Dan referred to the periodic meltdowns his daughter had gone through. "Expressing those emotions is not a negative, considering the timeline of the loss. But more importantly, burying the past is not healthy. These difficulties have a way of manifesting themselves sooner or later and not always in positive interactions," she replied.

As soon as she saw Dan's stricken expression, chills feathered down her spine. She was speaking about Natasha's losing her mother, but she wondered if her comment resurrected thoughts of Austin.

Since Austin's death, she and Dan had never had the chance to talk about him. Their last conversation had been full of pain and anger and the resoluteness of Dan's decision to leave.

Once again the old questions rose up, the second-guessing that haunted her after she walked away from Dan. What if she hadn't forced him? What if she had been more understanding?

She dismissed the questions, pulling her gaze away from Dan, realizing the futility of returning to the past in this situation. At the time she'd made the best decision for herself. She couldn't have predicted what had happened after she'd broken up with Dan.

Maybe Dan was right. Maybe some things were better left in the past. Maybe moving on and forgetting was the practical thing to do.

"As far as verbalizing memories of Lydia are concerned," she continued, determined not to let the current point of discussion on the table be dropped, "I feel strongly that I am correct, based on various psychological studies that I've read on the subject during my time in university." This time she locked eyes with his determined look, playing her education as her final card.

He blinked, then looked over at Natasha. The confused expression on the little girl's face told Hailey that, thankfully, she didn't understand what they were discussing.

"Okay, so how would this work?" Dan asked.

Hailey sensed his wavering in the question and pressed on, still looking at him.

"I would let her determine the direction of the conversation. Allow some fantasy elements, play along a bit, but then steer the topic back to the present."

Dan simply nodded, drumming his fingers on the table. "And if it never stops?" His comments seemed to challenge her but beneath them Hailey caught a hint of fear.

"I think you will discover that in time, that will ease away. But time and expressing the sorrow are equally important factors."

"We'll need to talk more about this," he said, lowering his voice.

"Are you guys talking about me?" Natasha piped up, her eager gaze flicking from Dan to Hailey.

Dan cleared his throat. "Yes, we are," he said. "And we're talking about your mommy."

Well, that was a bit of progress, Hailey thought. She turned her attention back to Natasha. "Why don't you tell us some of the things your mommy liked to do?" she asked, taking the conversational initiative.

The huge smile spreading across Natasha's face only reinforced what Hailey had been trying to say to Dan. "We would go swimming in the creek," she said, waving the rest of her sandwich. "She liked to splash me. We would go to the ocean and she would dance with me in my princess costume on the beach. Sometimes we would play hide-and-go-seek." Natasha put her sandwich down, leaning forward, her eyes bright as the memories spilled out. "One time we played it in a grocery store. That was so fun. And Mommy bought popcorn for supper and we went on a secret trip with Mommy's friend, Harold, and Daddy was mad because he wasn't invited."

Dan cleared his throat and Hailey couldn't help quickly glancing his way. His lips were pressed together as if stifling his own comments.

While Natasha talked, however, Hailey got a clear picture of what Natasha's life was like with Lydia. Erratic, interesting and nothing like Dan's well-ordered, agenda-driven lifestyle that could drive Hailey crazy sometimes.

More questions bubbled to the surface of her consciousness. How had Lydia and Dan met? How had he ended up marrying someone so completely different? Or had that been her appeal?

Then Natasha sighed and her features melted into a sad uncertainty, as if the memories reinforced what she had lost.

She sniffed and a few tears drifted down her cheek, shining in the light cast by the lamp above them. "I miss my mom," she said, her voice hoarse with pain.

Dan shot Hailey a knowing glance, as if Natasha's sadness punctuated his previous protests, but Hailey didn't flinch. She knew she was right to encourage Natasha to talk about her mother and that tears were a natural result of bringing up those memories.

Dan drew his daughter into the shelter of his arms, laying his head on hers. Once again Hailey couldn't look away from the obvious love Dan had for his little girl. It created a throb of regret for the relationship she'd never had with her own father.

This little girl does not realize how blessed she is, Hailey thought, getting up to tug a few tissues from the box that Dan's mother always had sitting on the refrigerator. When she got back Dan was talking to Natasha in low, comforting tones. She wasn't crying anymore, but she stayed ensconced on her father's lap.

Hailey handed Dan the tissues. He wiped Natasha's eyes, then dropped a light kiss on the top of her head. "Are you going to be okay, munchkin?" he asked, his voice low.

She nodded as she drew in a wavering breath. "Can

I go get my princess wand? I think it can make me feel happy."

Dan nodded and she slipped off the chair, trudging down the hall.

Sorrow pinched Dan's face as he watched her go. Then, with another sigh, he pushed himself away from the table, picked up his and Natasha's plates and walked to the kitchen.

Hailey took her own plate and followed him.

"In time, it will get better," she assured him, setting her plate on the counter. "I still believe she needs to articulate what she's dealing with."

"It's hard to watch," Dan said, his voice breaking a little as he leaned back, his hands resting behind him on the edge of the countertop.

Hearing him speak his own pain was hard for her as well. She felt an onslaught of pity for him and had to clench her fists to prevent herself from reaching out and comforting him.

So she stayed where she was, the few feet between them looming as large as Hartley Creek Canyon. They had to keep their lives separate. She had her plans in place and she wasn't wavering from them because an old boyfriend had come back to town.

He's more than an old boyfriend, her conscience accused her.

But she ignored the insidious voice and, as if underlining the distance between them, she took a step away. "I'll wait until you're done for the day before I leave," she said, keeping her voice even and professional.

Dan shook his head. "You're a tutor, not a nanny."

"I know, but you can't have Natasha running around downstairs unsupervised and I don't mind watching her until the store is closed." Hailey was pleased with how reasonable she sounded.

Dan's frown deepened but Hailey knew that, for now, he had few options.

"Okay. Thanks again for helping me out." He waited a moment, as if he wanted to say more, but then pushed himself away from the counter.

"Before you go," she said, "I need to talk to you about my teaching methods with Natasha."

Dan shot her a resigned look and, crossing his arms, rested his hip against the counter again. "Go ahead."

He didn't sound very encouraging, but Hailey, feeling a bit flush from her previous small victory, pushed on.

"I know you might not agree with my methods and what I'm doing, but I really need to emphasize that I'm a trained teacher. I may not be a psychologist, but I understand how to deal with students who won't fit with the usual pattern of classroom discipline."

My goodness, listen to me, she thought. I sound like I'm lecturing him. And from the way he lifted one eyebrow at her, she knew he agreed.

She spread her hands. "All I'm trying to say is, you want me to teach Natasha. Trust me to do it my way."

Dan caught the corner of his lower lip between his teeth. "But really? In the store?"

"I told you I would be discreet and I think it's important for Natasha to know that she can see you from time to time."

"And how will that work when she's back at school?"

"But, you see, we're not putting her back in the school until we know she can make the transition. Make the move," Hailey corrected.

"I know what transition means," Dan said dryly.

"Sorry. I just sounded too much like a teacher."

Dan released a gentle laugh. "I guess I have to keep reminding myself that you are one. A teacher, that is."

"I have new skills. What can I say." She attempted a smile, pleased to see one in return.

He laughed again. "I guess that happens when you don't see each other for seven years." Then he grew serious. "I still can't believe it's been that long."

His quiet admission hooked like a barb in her heart.

"Well, it has been," she said with a brisk note in her voice, reminding herself of Natasha and Lydia and all the events that had come between them during those seven years. "It's a cliché, but true. Time does march on. Natasha is six years old, after all." She looked directly at him, reminding him of his obligations.

Dan held her gaze then, and it was as if a shutter fell over his features. "That she is." He pushed himself away from the counter. "And as far as working with her in the store is concerned, go ahead. Just keep it reasonable."

Hailey's shoulders lowered. She didn't even realize she'd been holding them up.

"But if I feel like I don't think it's helping her and it's causing a problem…" Dan let the sentence trail off as if he was unsure what he would do when the time came.

"I'll keep things under control," Hailey promised.

Dan gave her an oblique look and, as he walked away, Hailey blew out a long, slow breath.

Round one—Hailey Deacon.

She hoped she wouldn't have to cross swords with him again. It seemed as if every time they faced each other the awkwardness between them grew.

She wasn't sure she could continue to deal with that.

Chapter Five

"So now I want you to divide them up into piles of three and then count them." Hailey brushed her hair back over her shoulder, the overhead lights enhancing its red-gold shine.

Dan leaned against the metal railing dividing the small appliances from the hardware, watching the two of them, Hailey's red head bent over his daughter's darker one.

Natasha's lips were pursed and her forehead wrinkled in concentration as she dutifully rearranged the bolts that Hailey had laid out on the table beside the scale where they weighed items for sale.

Natasha grinned when she was done. "I have four piles."

"So let's write that down," Hailey said, handing Natasha a pencil. "Four plus three is—"

"Seven." Natasha's triumphant look pulled a reluctant smile from Dan.

Dan's initial reluctance to have Hailey and Natasha downstairs was borne out when he caught himself stopping by the back of the store for the fourth time. And it wasn't just Natasha he watched.

When Dan had seen Natasha barreling around that

corner the other day, he'd struggled to keep his frustration down. He had assumed Hailey was teaching his daughter structure and balance. Instead Natasha was running around the store wearing fairy wings and carrying one of the many so-called magic wands Lydia had given her.

When Hailey had insisted this was part of her teaching strategy, Dan had had his doubts. But watching them together, his doubts had shifted from worrying about Natasha in the store to worrying about Hailey in the store.

She was a distraction that he wasn't sure he could deal with.

Hailey made Natasha count the bolts again as she dropped them back in the bin, then made her count the bins as they spun the revolving rack around, looking for something else to work with. She spoke softly but Dan didn't miss an underlying firmness to her tone.

"So how is the teaching going?" he heard his mother saying.

Dan glanced back at his mother. She was watching Natasha and Hailey, a bemused expression on her face.

"I think they're just about done. It's lunchtime."

His mother gave him a wry look. "I suppose you're eating upstairs again?"

"Did you have lunch already?" Dan asked, forestalling the impending questions. His mother loved Hailey and she had made no secret that she saw Hailey as a future daughter.

His own feelings for Hailey were confused enough and growing more so every day. He didn't need his mother rooting for his old girlfriend and mixing him up even more.

"I did," his mother said, her expression growing pensive as she watched Hailey and Natasha. "She really has a knack for working with Natasha, doesn't she?" his mother said. "She's one of those natural teachers. She seems to know exactly what Natasha needs."

"And how is Dad feeling today?" he asked, derailing his mother's train of thought before it could pick up too much steam.

"He said he wants to come to the store tomorrow for a few hours," his mother said with a light shrug of her narrow shoulders, thankfully getting the hint.

"Don't let him push too hard. I've got things under control," Dan said.

His mother gave him another quizzical look and unease stirred through him.

"Do you? Really?" The reflective note in her voice wasn't lost on him, but he didn't respond. "You know how glad your father and I are that you and Natasha are home. You really need to be here."

Apprehension trickled down his back at the serious note in her voice and the way her eyes held his, as if trying to say more than her words could convey. He recognized the look and the tone. After Austin's funeral, she would often pull him aside, using the same voice, as she tried to take his emotional temperature.

"And I'm glad to be home." Dan flashed her a smile. "I also appreciate Dad letting me buy into the business," he added, hoping to divert her now as he had tried to divert her then.

"That had always been the plan," she said, her voice growing quieter. "Even before you left Hartley Creek." She folded her arms over her chest. "But that's not what I want to talk about."

"I'm kind of busy right now, Mom." He pushed away from the railing, trying to get away from the sorrow he saw building in her eyes.

But she caught his arm and gave it a gentle tug. "Please don't keep shutting us out."

It was the plaintive note in her voice that stopped him from moving away, but he didn't turn to face her.

"I want you to know that your father and I love you..." She halted, her voice breaking. "But we sense a darkness in you that we can't break through. You know that you can tell us anything."

Dan shook his head even as her words settled in his soul, striking his guilt with deadly accuracy. "There's nothing to tell, Mom." He shot her a tight smile over his shoulder. "The past is over. Done. I've moved on."

"I know we have," his mother said, tightening her grip on his arm, "but I'm not so sure you have. I feel as if there are unhealed wounds you carry yet." She glanced back at Hailey. "And I have a feeling that Hailey is the one who can help you with that. Help you move from that bleak place I know you go to sometimes."

Dan followed the direction of his mother's gaze, the ache in his heart easing a bit as he watched Hailey. As she flicked her hair over her shoulder it seemed to catch the light and beam it onto them like a promise.

"She's good for you. She always was," his mother was saying.

Dan watched the interplay between Hailey and his daughter, the ache in his heart easing a bit as they laughed together. Then he pulled himself to the present.

"I'm not sure I'm good for her," was his cryptic reply.

A short buzz from the front door signaled the entrance of a customer and, thankfully, brought an end to the conversation.

"We'll talk again," his mother said, then strode to the front, her short bob swinging with every step down the crowded aisle of the store. When she came to the end, she turned and gave him a rueful smile, then disappeared.

He clenched his fists, fighting down his confusion. Reality was he'd had his chance with Hailey and he'd blown it. He didn't deserve her in so many ways. Now his focus was Natasha and he had better remind himself of that.

"Daddy, look. I'm adding," Natasha called out.

Dan turned in time to see Natasha come running over, her fairy wings bobbing behind her as she caught his hand. "Come see," she insisted, dragging him around the divider to where she and Hailey had been working. She pointed to the various piles she had created and the papers beneath each pile. "This says four plus three is seven. And this says three plus three is six. And this says six plus one is seven." She pointed out a few other problems, the pleased note in her voice lifting his spirits.

"That's really good, Natasha. You're getting so smart."

Natasha clasped her hands together, squirming with pleasure at his praise. "Miss Deacon says I'm a really fast learner."

"That's great. You'll be back to school in no time."

Natasha shot him a panicked glance and pulled away from him. "No. I can't go to school. I have to stay with Miss Deacon."

"Someday you'll be back in school," he said, unable to keep the gruff tone out of his voice. "Remember, Miss Deacon is only teaching you for a while," he said, keeping his eyes on his daughter. His mother's comments, though well-meant, had only served to resurrect his old shame and guilt.

Natasha looked stricken, then turned to Hailey as if seeking confirmation. "You're going to teach me all the time, aren't you?"

"I'll teach you as long as you need me," Hailey said,

being far more diplomatic than he'd been. "Now, let's clean up this stuff and we can go upstairs and I'll get lunch ready." She turned to him. "Are you joining us for lunch?" she asked, her smile soft and gentle.

It hit him like a punch to the stomach.

"Yeah. But just for a bit," he said, his voice stern.

Her puzzled look made him feel like a heel, but he had to stay in control. Keep Hailey at a distance. *She's only around until Natasha goes to school,* he reminded himself. *Come summer, she'll be gone and out of your life.*

So why did that idea create this bleak hollow in his stomach?

"There you go. You got them all right," Hailey said, going over Natasha's work.

Natasha held up the paper. "I know. I'm pretty smart."

"And you're pretty pretty."

Dan's voice behind her raised the small hairs on Hailey's neck, sent a shiver trickling down her spine.

And put her heart into overdrive. She pushed the emotions down, reminding herself to stay professional.

Yet as he came to stand beside Natasha she shot a quick glance his way. Just as he had this morning, he avoided her glance. "Wow, you made a really nice duck," Dan said to his daughter.

"And I made a robot." Natasha pulled up the other connect-the-dots pictures she'd been working on. "That one wasn't hard because it didn't have lots of numbers."

"What else did you do this morning, besides come into the store?" Dan asked, keeping his attention on Natasha, avoiding Hailey's gaze as she set the table.

"Miss Deacon and I did some reading and she said we could do art, but I want to go in the store with her again after lunch."

"You two had some time down there already. Miss Deacon should keep you up here for the rest of the day," was his brusque reply.

Hailey couldn't stop her eyes from moving to Dan, but as soon as their gazes connected his shifted away. It was as if he had retreated again. But why?

Natasha seemed to pick up on the tension thrumming through the atmosphere and was strangely subdued, her eyes flickering from Dan to Hailey.

To Hailey's surprise, when they were all served Dan took Natasha's hand. "I think we should pray," he said quietly.

"Just like Hailey does," Natasha said in an overly bright voice.

Dan simply nodded. "Yes, just like Hailey does." He bowed his head and prayed a simple prayer. Before she raised her head, Hailey silently added one of her own.

Please, Lord, help me to understand what is happening with Dan.

In spite of her prayer, the unspoken strain between Dan and Hailey continued through lunch. Thankfully, everyone made short work of their meal.

As soon as Natasha was done, she pushed her plate away. "Did I eat enough?" she asked, glancing from Hailey to Dan as if not sure who she should be asking.

"Yes, you did."

"Of course."

Dan and Hailey spoke at once and Hailey felt like smacking herself. Natasha was Dan's daughter, not hers.

"Can I go play in my room with my new princesses that I got from my other gramma?" Natasha asked as pushed her chair back against the table. Lydia's parents had sent a parcel of gifts for Natasha, which Hailey had used to reward the girl for getting her work done this morning.

This time Hailey said nothing, but neither did Dan.

Natasha's confusion showed on her face. "Did I ask something bad?"

"No, honey. You didn't," Dan said finally. "If it's okay with Miss Deacon, you can go play with your dolls for a while."

"Of course you can," Hailey quickly added. "You worked very hard this morning."

Natasha sent them one more puzzled look, then walked down the hallway to her bedroom.

Dan shot to his feet and grabbed his plate, striding to the kitchen with it as if he could hardly wait to leave as well.

Hailey waited a moment, then realized she couldn't stand this anymore. Something had changed and she couldn't identify when or how. She wondered if his seeing her and Natasha in the store this morning had bothered him more than he wanted to admit.

If that was the case, she needed to talk to him. She wasn't letting Dan change her mind about her teaching methods.

She followed him to the kitchen where he was scraping the remainders of his lunch off his plate into the sink.

"Is everything okay?"

"Yeah, of course."

Hailey bit her lip at his abrupt response. "You don't sound like everything is okay. I understood you were okay with Natasha coming down to the store."

"I don't have a huge problem with it. She seems to enjoy working downstairs." Dan rinsed his plate with quick movements, then dropped it and the utensils into the dishwasher.

Hailey's confusion grew. "But you looked angry this morning, when I was finished with Natasha. And just now you said you don't want her downstairs."

"Well, it's just, she needs routine." He washed his hands, then reluctantly turned back to her.

"We talked about this," she said, thoroughly puzzled now. "I feel like we're going in circles. I need to be clear on this. Is it okay if I bring Natasha down to the store or not?"

"My mother isn't comfortable with the idea," was his strange reply.

Hailey's puzzlement shifted to frustration. "That's odd. While I was working with Natasha your mom specifically spoke with me, telling me how happy she was that I was working with Natasha. She said nothing about having a problem with me being down in the store."

Dan looked away and didn't say anything.

"What's going on, Dan? This morning everything seemed fine and now it's like we're back to you not trusting me and my methods."

Dan blew out a sigh and shook his head. "I trust you."

"So what's the problem then?"

He pulled his hands over his face and then looked directly at her. "I don't know what's wrong. Everything. Nothing. I used to know exactly what I wanted, but now…" He finished his sentence with a shrug.

"I'm sure coming back home has been hard for you," Hailey said, folding her arms across her midsection. "It must bring back memories, both good and bad."

As she held his gaze she sensed a shift in the atmosphere. A sense of restlessness. Of half-formed thoughts that neither of them dared speak.

"It has." He blew out his breath, as if deflating, and leaned back against the counter behind him.

And to her surprise, he looked as confused and be-wildered as she felt.

"Do you want to talk about it?"

Dan slowly shook his head. "It wouldn't do any good."

Hailey frowned. "What do you mean? If something is bothering you about what I'm doing with Natasha, I want to have it out in the open. That's the only way this is going to work."

He gave her a melancholy smile. "It's not about how you are teaching Natasha. You're doing a great job with her. She's come a long ways since you started working with her and I appreciate that."

Hailey's confusion only increased. "So why is there this tension between us?"

Dan sighed again but this time Hailey waited for him to talk.

Finally he looked up at her. "I think it's that I feel as if so much of the stuff I thought I dealt with is still hang-ing around."

"Stuff like what?"

"Stuff like you and me. How we used to be a couple." Dan paused, his hazel eyes seeming to pierce hers as her heart skipped a beat. What was he trying to say? Where was he going?

"I promised myself when I came back to Hartley Creek that I would keep my focus on my daughter," he contin-ued. "And I don't need any distractions from that."

His statement plunged into her soul like a shard of ice. The intensity of her hurt surprised her. He saw her as a distraction.

Yet why should it bother her? She didn't want any dis-tractions either. She had the course of her life set out. This stay in Hartley Creek was merely for her grandmother's sake. If she was honest with herself, Dan's presence was a complication for her as well.

"I think the reality is, like you said, we used to be a couple," she said, choosing her words as carefully as a rock climber chooses his precarious handholds. "And that can cause uneasiness that can be a distraction too. But we may as well be adult about it, realize our old relationship was there and move on." She forced a smile as she looked up at him again, disappointed at how his blunt pronouncement had made her heart ache. "I want to be comfortable teaching your daughter without all the tension that seems to follow us."

Dan leaned against the counter behind him, tapping his fingers against the edge. Then he looked over at her again. "You're probably right. It will make things easier if we recognize we had a past and move on. Like you said, we're adults. We were so young then."

"We were," Hailey said, with an airy wave, struggling to sound more offhand than she felt. "My goodness, just high school kids."

"Sort of cliché, isn't it?" Dan said quietly.

Hailey released a light laugh. "A bit. But that's okay. Our lives are not as original as we'd like to think."

A moment of silence followed her statement.

Then Hailey reached for her plate and put it in the dishwasher, hoping he didn't notice her trembling hands. "I'm glad we got that out of the way. Now I can get back to work and you can get back to work and we can be normal around each other." She was pleased at how practical she sounded. How grounded.

How mature.

Dan cleared his throat, then said, "You know, I'm sorry for the way things went after Austin died." His voice was quiet.

His words hovered in the silence between them. This was the first time he'd acknowledged the horrible event that had divided their lives into a before and an after.

Regret and sorrow for what might have been twisted her stomach but she couldn't allow it to stay and take hold.

"I'm sorry too," was her guarded response.

"But, like you said, that's in the past," Dan replied. "We should be able to move on and act normal around each other. We used to be friends."

"Still are, I hope," she said, injecting a falsely hearty tone into her voice.

"Still are." He put his hand on her shoulder. The same kind of casual gesture friends use with each other.

But when he looked at her all her intentions slid away and with them, the intervening years.

Dan's eyes held a shadow of regret but even as their gazes held, something else shifted in his features. A shadow of sorrow flitted across his face and for a moment his hand tightened.

Then he blinked, as if coming back from past to present, and he lowered his hand.

"See you later," he said quietly. Then he turned down the stairs leading to the store, closing the door behind them.

Hailey waited a moment, gathering her own scattered wits even as part of her mind mocked her.

Really? Normal? Around a guy who makes your heart shift into overdrive whenever those hazel eyes connect with yours?

She dismissed the voice. She and Dan could get past this. It would take time before they could treat each other as dispassionately as they would any other person in their lives. She had loved him so much, she thought, her heart aching with the memory. He had been everything to her. Reducing all that to mere friendship wasn't impossible.

But neither was it going to be easy.

"That soup tasted really good, Hailey. Thanks so much," Dan said, wiping his mouth with the napkin she had laid out.

Hailey flashed him a quick smile and he leaned back in his chair, a surprising feeling of well-being washing over him. For five days in a row he hadn't had to make lunch. For five days he hadn't had to worry about Natasha.

For five days he and Hailey had been able to act surprisingly ordinary around each other. He could do this, he thought. Acknowledge they had been good friends and get through the next few days until Natasha was back in school. Once Hailey left town, he could find a new rhythm for himself and Natasha, a new way of doing things and living their life.

The easing of tension also had much to do with his mother, who had backed off the past few days. She hadn't dropped any of her heavy hints about Hailey, which had only served to bring up his own memories of what he and Hailey had once shared.

"Glad you enjoyed it," Hailey said, getting up and reaching for his bowl.

"Natasha and I will take care of this. You've done enough." He reached out and caught her hand.

Her fingers were cool to the touch. As soft as they ever had been.

She jerked her hand back as a frown pinched her brow. "That's okay. I don't mind," she said.

Dan felt a flicker of dismay at his reaction to her. Hardly the reaction of "just friends."

Only a matter of time, he reminded himself. After all, they had both talked about this weirdness between them and brought it out into the open. It would go away. What they had was in the past and going back served no purpose. It was time they moved on.

"C'mon, Natasha, let's start cleaning up," he said, gathering the plates and bowls.

Natasha jumped up and eagerly helped him carry the dishes to the kitchen.

"Miss Deacon is going to the ranch on Sunday night," she said as she laid the plates on the counter. "She's going to have chocolate cupcakes." Natasha gave him a beatific smile. "I love chocolate cupcakes."

"I do too," Dan said, humoring her as he set the dishes in the dishwasher.

Hailey brought the soup pot to the kitchen and set it on the counter. "There's enough here for supper tonight and tomorrow night if you're really stuck," she said.

"That's great." Dan released a slow smile. "I don't mind soup two nights in a row if I don't have to make it."

"I don't want to have soup two times," Natasha stated, then scooted around him to where Hailey was spooning the leftover soup into a plastic container. "Can I come with you to the ranch on Sunday instead? Can I have supper with you and your friends?"

"Natasha, don't be a beggar," Dan said. "Miss Deacon will want to spend time with her friends by herself."

Dan suspected she was going to a family get-together at her cousin Carter's ranch. He remembered going there from time to time when he and Hailey were dating.

"Actually, I'd like to talk to you about that," Hailey said, snapping a lid on a plastic container. "Natasha, can you go into the dining room and finish up that problem we were working on? When you're done we can go downstairs and do some more word matching."

Natasha glanced from Dan to Hailey, as if trying to puzzle out what they might need to discuss. Then, thankfully, she skipped into the dining room, her ponytail bouncing behind her.

Hailey waited until Natasha was settled at the table, then turned back to Dan. Her actions piqued his curiosity. What could she have to say that she didn't want Natasha to hear?

"Remember Adam from Natasha's class? Emma's boy?" Hailey asked. "When Emma invited me to come for supper she suggested Natasha could come as well."

His gut instinct was to say no. He didn't want to have Natasha gone while he hung around the apartment by himself.

"I thought it would be a good opportunity for Natasha and Adam to spend some time together," Hailey continued. "It could help Natasha's transition to the classroom."

Dan glanced through the doorway to the dining room. Natasha appeared engrossed in her work and was not paying attention to them. Nonetheless, he drew a bit closer to Hailey and lowered his voice. "Is he the boy who talked about her crying all the time?" Dan wasn't sure he wanted his daughter spending time with a kid who didn't seem to like her.

"He said that because he was worried about her, that's all."

He looked down at Hailey, her face barely a foot from his. Her gray eyes, her pale skin, all framed by a riot of red hair, sent a surprising flash of attraction through him.

A familiar attraction.

Dan's fingers rasped against his whiskers as he considered the idea. "I've spent enough time sitting by myself over the weekends. I'm not sure I want her away so soon."

Hailey looked away, breaking the connection between them. "Okay. Then why don't you come along?"

This caught him by surprise. He paused, trying the idea on for size. While he would have preferred to have his daughter at home with him, he wasn't sure he wanted to take this opportunity away from her either.

"I suppose I could," he said. "But are you sure it would be okay with your cousin?"

"Future cousin," Hailey corrected. "But yes, I am. It's just dinner. Emma and Carter would love to have you."

"Okay. Then I'll come. Besides, I wouldn't mind catching up with Carter some more. Find out how that drill has been working out for him."

Hailey tugged her sweater over her hands, wrapping her arms around her middle. "Okay, then, I'll phone Emma and tell her you're coming." The hesitancy in her voice resurrected his doubts.

It would be fine, he reasoned. Carter wasn't just Hailey's cousin. He had also, at one time, been a friend.

It would be like old times.

Which could, potentially, be a problem.

Chapter Six

"I am excited to go to a ranch. Have you ever been to a ranch, Daddy?" Natasha bounced on the seat of Dan's truck, her excitement easing away Hailey's concerns about having asked them both along to Carter and Emma's place.

When Dan had agreed to come as well, Hailey had been surprised. Her offer to him had been a courtesy. She hadn't thought he would take her up on it.

She had arrived at church late this morning because she'd had to walk, and had caught only a glimpse of Dan and Natasha as she left. They'd been occupied talking to an older couple and hadn't seen Hailey so she hadn't had a chance to go over their plans.

When Dan called after church to double-check the time, her relief that the trip was still on was frustrating. She guessed the "normal" she wanted to achieve with Dan would take time yet.

"I've been to this ranch," Dan said as he turned the truck onto the road heading out of Hartley Creek toward the Rocking K. "I even rode a horse there!"

"If you want to call that riding," Hailey couldn't help

adding, trying to keep things light. Just a couple of old friends reminiscing.

"Only got bucked off once," Dan said.

"You got bucked off a horse?" Natasha was all ears. "Why?"

"Because your daddy forgot to tighten the cinch like someone told him to," Hailey said, her smile widening at the memory. She could still see Dan sailing through the air and flattening the undergrowth when he landed.

"Someone wasn't very specific in her instructions," Dan added, giving her a knowing look.

"Or someone wasn't listening."

"Maybe someone wasn't."

Hailey held his laughing gaze, then turned to watch the snow-covered fields edging the road. Beyond the fields the frozen river snaked along like a silver thread unspooling from the mountains, rising up to cradle the valley. The sun hovered above the mountains, burnishing the hills with a golden color.

A quick glance in the rearview mirror showed her the ski hill overlooking the town, the lights from the lifts starting to appear in the late-afternoon light. Early this morning she'd heard the muted thump of avalanche bombs going off on the hill, which meant the powder on the upper runs would be epic. So she had hitched a ride with Megan to the hill and taken a few runs.

While they were skiing, Megan had mentioned to Hailey that the grade one class would be going every afternoon to the ski hill for lessons. She had said it would be a good opportunity for Natasha to spend time with her future classmates in a more casual setting.

Though Megan had encouraged Hailey to talk to Dan about it, Hailey was hesitant to mention the skiing lessons. She wasn't sure how Dan would react to his daughter going skiing on Misty Ridge.

"Do you think I can ride a horse when we are at the ranch?" Natasha was asking.

Hailey turned her attention back to the little girl. "It's a bit cold for riding, but maybe next time you can."

"That would be so fun," Natasha said. "Then I can tell my mommy that I rode—" Her voice broke abruptly and she looked down, fiddling with the pom-poms on the end of her scarf.

Hailey's heart broke for the little girl but to her surprise, no tears came. Natasha simply heaved out a heavy sigh, then said with a plaintive voice, "I don't think I can tell my mommy, can I?"

Hailey slid her arm over the girl's shoulders to comfort her. Dan had the same idea, however, and for a moment both of them held Natasha, their arms overlapping. But neither of them flinched and neither of them pulled back.

Hailey couldn't help another glance over at Dan, pleased with this new shift between them.

It was as if getting away from the store and getting out into the countryside had eased away the disquiet that surrounded him.

She welcomed the change because it made her more relaxed as well.

"I like your pretty necklace," Natasha was saying, eyeing the gold chain Hailey was unconsciously fingering.

Hailey held it up, smiling. "Thank you. I got this from my Nana," she said.

"Is it special?" Natasha asked.

"Very special. It came from a bracelet my Nana had. The bracelet had five gold nuggets that came from my great-great-grandmother. Her name was Kamiskahk."

"That's a funny name," Natasha said.

"It's a Kootenai name," Dan added. "You should tell Natasha the story. It's very interesting."

Hailey shot Dan a surprised look, then remembered that he knew the story of Kamiskahk as well. Her Nana had told him when Dan had asked her about the bracelet that she always wore.

Another link between them.

"Can you tell me the story?" Natasha asked.

"Kamiskahk's father hadn't told anyone else in the tribe about the gold nuggets and he told his daughter to keep them a secret when he gave them to her. Then my great-great-grandfather, August Beck, came to the valley. He met Kamiskahk and fell in love."

"Did he get hurt?" Natasha asked, her eyes wide.

"Maybe a bit," Hailey said with a laugh. When she looked at Dan it was to discover him looking at her. She forced herself to hold his gaze then gave him a quick smile, pleased to see him return it.

See? They could do normal.

"Anyway, August found out about the nuggets," Hailey continued. "And he got gold fever."

"I got fever once," Natasha put in. "My mommy said it would go away, but it didn't. I had to go to the hospital."

Another glimpse of the little girl's life with her mother. Which made Hailey wonder, yet again, what kind of woman Lydia had been. And what had Dan seen in her?

That was none of her business. That was Dan's life and Dan's past and she had no right to that. Not anymore.

"Well, gold fever isn't really like being sick. It means he wanted to find gold very badly and he'd do almost anything for it," Hailey said, carrying on with her story. "So August left the village and went looking for the gold. He spent weeks and months but couldn't find any. Then one day he felt cold and tired and he started thinking about

Kamiskahk. And he realized he had made a mistake but he was too ashamed to go back and admit it."

"Did he ever go back?" Natasha asked, leaning closer and touching the gold nugget at the end of the necklace.

"Yes, he finally did make the right choice. And he and Kamiskahk got married and they had a boy named Able, who had a boy named Bill, who married my Nana Beck. And the gold nuggets were passed down and my grandpa Bill made them into a bracelet for my Nana. And my Nana then got a necklace made out of each nugget and she gave them to her five grandchildren. And I'm one of the grandchildren."

Natasha nodded, her attention riveted on the necklace.

"I always liked that story," Dan said, slowing down to make the final turn to the ranch. "I'm just curious, what made your Nana decide to break the bracelet apart? I know she treasured it."

Hailey twined the chain around her finger, thinking of the evening her Nana had given it to her, along with the Bible. How Nana had hoped she would take the story seriously and be encouraged to make the right choices in her life, just as August had.

"I guess she wasn't sure about giving it to either of her daughters. Carter and Garret's mom died when the boys were little and I know she and my mom weren't close. I guess she decided to skip a generation. And it worked out pretty good. Five kids, five nuggets."

"That's a great legacy," Dan said, looking at her across the cab. "You're lucky to have it."

As Hailey held his gaze, other parts of her legacy came to mind. How her father had left her and her sisters. How her mother had moved away, leaving Hailey, seemingly without a second thought.

How Dan had also left her.

Hailey pulled her gaze away. "Yes. I am. But I'm also very thankful that my Nana gave it to me. I'm thankful we still have her with us."

"Will she be here tonight?" Dan asked.

"Oh yes. Wherever two or more grandchildren are gathered, Nana is there."

Dan looked like he was about to say more but then Natasha leaned forward, straining against her seat belt, pointing. "Is that it? Is that the ranch?"

They had rounded a corner and were approaching a group of buildings. The snow crunched beneath their tires as they slowed down.

The barns and corrals lay to one side of the large yard. On the other were two houses, one smaller than the other. Smoke poured out of the chimneys of both houses, and lights shone from the windows with a welcoming glow. A few cars were parked in front of the larger house, where Emma and Adam lived.

"What are those little houses?" Natasha asked, pointing to the three structures beyond the large red barn and the corrals.

"Those are cabins," Hailey said as Dan parked beside Shannon's little car. When Shannon had found out Hailey was coming, she'd offered her a ride. When Hailey had told her sister she would be riding with Dan and Natasha, she'd endured a long, meaningful pause more expressive than anything Shannon could have said. Hailey hoped her sister would keep her negative comments to herself tonight. Shannon had made no secret of the fact that she thought Hailey was playing with fire, spending so much time with Dan.

"Who lives there?" Natasha asked, yanking at her seat belt.

"Carter lives in one of them," Hailey said, helping her

unbuckle the belt. "But before that, me and my sisters would stay in them whenever we came to visit our Nana, Grandpa, and Garret and Carter. They all lived in the big house, the one we're going to right now."

"Can we go to the cabins? Can we see inside?" Natasha asked, tugging on her toque and mitts, as if fully expecting to go look at them right away.

"We first have to go to the house. But maybe later I can show you my old cabin." Hailey stepped out of the truck into the chilly air. As she did, wistfulness plucked her heart. She'd visited the ranch a couple of times since she'd been back, of course, but each time a new set of memories surfaced. The games she and her cousins played, the hikes they made, the hot dog roasts and the horseback trips.

And this time, memories of the few visits she and Dan had made here assaulted her. She choked those thoughts down. They belonged in the past.

Smoke wafted out of the nearest cabin, and a weak light shone from its window. After Emma and Carter got engaged, she'd moved to the big house and Carter had moved into the cabin Emma had been staying in when she was simply a hired hand on the ranch.

So much had changed for Carter, she thought, hugging herself. Once he'd been so broken, but Emma and her boy had healed him.

She forced herself not to look at Natasha or Dan. Theirs was a different story, she reminded herself. She and Dan had had their chance. Too many events were crowded between then and now.

Besides, she had her own plans.

An undisturbed blanket of snow covered Naomi's cabin. No one had visited it since winter had come. While she looked at the cabin, Hailey sent up a prayer for her sister keeping watch over her dying fiancé.

Beside Naomi's was Hailey's cabin. The path leading up to it still held the vague shapes of her footprints from the last time she'd been here. She had shoveled the snow off the veranda then and had sat there for a while, letting herself get drawn into the innocence of the past. The simplicity of her life at that time.

Natasha tugged on her hand, pulling her out of her reverie. "Let's go to the house and ask Mr. Beck if I can ride a horse."

Hailey was about to reply when Dan came around the front of the truck and knelt down in the snow in front of her. "We're not asking Mr. Beck anything," he said, catching her by the shoulders and turning her to him as he established some ground rules for his daughter. "That's rude, okay?"

Natasha glanced up at Hailey as if to ask her to advocate for her.

"We're here to visit," Hailey said. "So I think your daddy is right."

Natasha pushed her lip out in a pout. "I mean it, Natasha," Dan reiterated. "No asking."

Natasha sighed, then nodded as she took Hailey's hand, then Dan's. Together they led her to the house, the snow squeaking under their feet as they walked. Hailey tried not to look over at Dan and the little domestic scene they had created, the two of them walking with Natasha between them.

The door of the house swung opened as soon as they stepped onto the veranda. Emma stood framed in the doorway, the light behind her burnishing her dark hair. She wore a loose sweater over blue jeans and bare feet, in spite of the cold. "Come in, come in," Emma called out, waving them into the house.

Hailey pulled Natasha along behind her and as they entered the house warmth washed over them, laced with the mouthwatering smells of supper cooking. Laughter bursting from the living room beyond the kitchen added to the cozy ambience.

"Carter, Shannon and Nana are trying to play a new game Shannon bought at a garage sale," Emma explained as she took Dan and Natasha's coats and hung them up in a closet in the porch. "Go inside, Dan. Make yourself at home. Natasha, Adam has been waiting for you. He's in the living room setting up the farm set."

Dan nodded, then walked into the kitchen, Natasha right on his heels. Hailey went to follow when Emma caught her by the arm, pulling her back.

"So?" Emma asked, the single word dripping with innuendo. She tucked a strand of her long, dark hair behind an ear, her brown eyes brimming with curiosity. Emma had been around the family long enough to know Hailey's history, romantic and otherwise, and was obviously curious about Dan's presence here.

Hailey held her eager gaze, then said, "How are the wedding plans coming?"

Emma tilted her head to one side, hoop earrings flashing in the light of the porch, then she grinned. "I just find it interesting that Dan came along," she said, ignoring Hailey's attempt to head her off at the conversational impasse.

Hailey's only answer was to crane her neck to see where Dan was, making sure he couldn't hear her. Then she turned back to her future cousin-in-law and lowered her voice. "This is the deal. I'm only telling you once. Dan is very protective of his daughter and he didn't want her coming along by herself. That's it. That's the whole reason and the only reason he's here." She underlined this with a slice of her hand. "Yes, we used to date. Yes, we used to be serious. But I broke up with him and now he's a widower with a little girl. What we had is beyond ancient history. The Mesopotamians are modern compared to what me and Dan had. Okay?"

Emma pursed her lips and folded her hands as she considered Hailey. Then she sighed in resignation. "Okay. I get it."

"Thanks." At least that was settled.

"But I still think there's something going on."

Hailey simply rolled her eyes, spun around and strode into the house. Seriously! Family!

"I imagine you're happy with the cattle prices right now," Dan said to Carter as he leaned back against the couch.

Dinner was over and under orders from the women, he and Carter had been sent to the living room while they cleaned up the dishes and made tea and coffee. A fire crackled in the large stone fireplace, sending out welcome waves of warmth.

"Not complaining," Carter agreed, lounging back in his recliner, his wavy hair a dark contrast against the beige upholstery. "It's helped us turn a favorable corner."

"And it's meant Carter can afford to keep me in the manner to which I'm accustomed," Emma said, setting out a tray of teacups and coffee mugs on the low table in the living room.

"What manner is that?" Hailey asked with a laugh as she spooned some sugar into a teacup and handed it to Nana.

"Oh, you know, barefoot, in the kitchen," Emma said with a wink toward Carter.

"I hope the third part of that very rude statement will come true someday," Nana said, stirring her tea, her graying hair setting off her slate-blue eyes.

"One thing at a time, Nana," Emma said, holding out a mug for Dan. "Coffee?"

"Sounds good." He took it and Emma held out the sugar bowl.

"He only takes cream," Hailey said handing him the pitcher.

He felt an instant of surprise that she remembered.

"And how are wedding plans coming?" Shannon asked Emma. "Will Garret be back in time to stand up for you, Carter?"

"He better be," Carter growled. "He said the job in Dubai would be done by then."

"I'm sure he'll be back," Hailey said. "Garret always does what he promises."

"Used to, anyway," Carter said, looking down at his coffee.

No one responded to that enigmatic comment and the women were drawn into wedding talk. Dan was content to sit back and watch the interaction.

All during dinner the conversations would bypass each other, interweave, join up and double back. Sentences would be started by one, finished by another. A single word would elicit peals of laughter.

Emma and Dan would look at each other and shrug.

Dan couldn't help a tinge of envy at Hailey's connection with her cousins. His parents had moved to Hartley Creek as a young couple, leaving family behind in Houston, Texas, and Windsor, Ontario. Because the store kept his parents busy six days a week and most weeks of the year, they didn't often get away to visit extended family.

So for the majority of his life it had been just him and Austin.

And now it was just him and Natasha.

He took a quick sip of coffee, then coughed. Too hot.

"You okay?" Hailey asked, throwing him a questioning look.

"Fine. Just fine." He held his hand up to assure her.

"And how is your father doing, Dan?" Nana was asking. "Is he recuperating?"

"He's doing okay. Still gets tired quickly," Dan said. "The doctor said he's never seen such a bad case of pneumonia, but he's getting stronger every day."

"I know your parents are very glad to have you back," Nana said, glancing around her own brood. "We do miss our children after a while. And I know your parents were never the same after your brother died on the ski hill."

"No. I guess they weren't," Dan muttered, cradling his coffee mug in his hands, her innocent comment agitating a storm of old feelings.

"I know how hard it was for me to bury my daughter Noelle, Carter and Garret's mother. I'm sure your parents felt the same." Nana Beck lifted her hand in a gesture of helplessness. "It was difficult to see your parents deal with all their grief. They became shadows of their former selves."

"Daddy, come and see what me and Adam did," Natasha called out. "We're making a farm."

Dan put his mug down so fast the contents sloshed around, almost spilling. "I should... I should go see what's she's been doing," Dan said, seizing the opportunity to leave an increasingly uncomfortable conversation.

"Of course. Of course," Nana said, waving him off.

"I'm so sorry if what I said hurt you. I didn't mean anything."

"No, it's fine." Dan moved to where his daughter sat. As he crouched down beside her on the carpet, the heat from the fireplace warmed a chill that had gripped him. "So, what are you kids doing here?"

"See, we've got all the goats together because Adam said that's how it's supposed to be," Natasha said, pointing to a plastic pen. "And over here are the chickens. They have to be close to the barn so they can go inside quick if a coyote comes."

"Or a fox," Adam intoned as he moved a few sheep around.

"I never seen a fox," Natasha said.

"They are bad for chickens."

Dan let their chatter wash over him. He felt a bit rude for leaving Nana so quickly, but her comments about his parents cut him deep and hard. Her words had ignited the guilt that seemed to be his constant companion since he'd seen that covered sled coming off the ski hill, holding his brother's body.

He hooked the tractor to a baler for Adam, then helped Natasha move the barn. After a few moments he glanced over at the adults and caught Hailey looking at him.

Her wistful smile made his heartbeat tick upward and when she got up to join them, his emotions tipped into anticipation.

"This looks amazing," Hailey said, standing over them.

"My daddy is a good farmer," Natasha replied, intent on the fence she was assembling for the horses.

"I'm sure he is," Hailey said. But she didn't sit down with them. "I just thought I'd let you know, I'm heading over to my cabin to pick up a few things. And anytime you want to go, Dan, is fine with me."

Natasha's head spun around at that. "Can I come? Can I see the cabin?" She clambered to her feet.

Dan caught his daughter by the arm. "No, honey. I think Miss Deacon wants to go by herself."

Natasha's lower lip started moving out and she sent a pleading look Hailey's way.

But Dan wasn't giving in to her. Not in front of Hailey's family. Besides, it was time his daughter heard the word no.

Hailey sent Dan a look that clearly telegraphed it was okay with her, but Dan shook his head. "Natasha can stay here. You go." He glanced at his watch. "I wouldn't mind to be back in town soon. I need to stop in at my parents' place as well." He hadn't seen his father since day before yesterday and wanted to let him know how things were going at the store.

"Okay, if I'm not back in time, come and get me." And then Hailey turned and left.

Dan wasn't going to watch her, but he couldn't keep his eyes off her slim figure, moving with an easy grace, her hair a copper fall, swinging with every step.

"Daddy, why are you staring at Miss Deacon?" Natasha asked.

Dan quickly averted his gaze, hoping the rest of Hailey's family hadn't heard what she'd said.

But more than that, hoping Hailey hadn't heard what she'd said.

Stay focused, he reminded himself as he tried to keep his attention on what his daughter was doing. *You can't afford to get distracted.*

And yet, even as he told himself this, he couldn't erase the picture of Hailey from his mind.

Chapter Seven

Hailey shivered in the chill of the cabin and turned up the temperature on the little heater, wondering why she bothered. By the time the cabin was warm it would be time to go.

But at least for now, it took some of the bite off the cold air.

She glanced around the cabin, memories crowding each other. She'd had so many good times here.

She got on her knees and reached under the bed, ignoring the rolling dust bunnies as she pulled out a shoe box. She set it on the bed and brushed the dust off.

Pain stabbed through her when she saw the writing on the lid.

Letters and notes from Dan, with a date scribbled beneath the title.

She knew she should toss the box aside to be discarded. But in spite of herself she rested her hand on the box, her lips pressed together as memories assaulted her.

When she'd made the decision to move away from Hartley Creek, she'd thrown away what she could and moved the rest to her cabin here. It wasn't much. A few boxes of photos, some CDs, some books and memorabilia. A couple of old snowboards that, at one time, she had scrimped and saved for and hadn't been able to part with, even after she'd broken them.

And in the box below her hand, some of the notes she and Dan had sent each other throughout high school and after he'd graduated.

The date scribbled on the lid was four days before Austin's accident. A month before Dan left Hartley Creek.

With a decisive movement, she set the box aside, then went under the bed again and found the box she'd come looking for. This one held some old CDs she wanted to hear again. A few movies she could watch again. Stuff. She set it aside, found another box that held books and set them both by the door. Hopefully, Dan wouldn't mind putting them in the back of the truck. She glanced around the cabin. In a few months she would be moving again and anything she left behind would be here for a long time.

She was about to go, but her eyes shifted to the box on the bed. She had to find a way to get rid of it. Maybe Carter could burn the letters.

What if he looked through them?

She snatched the box off the bed and quickly brought it to the pile by the door. This she had to do herself. But if she was taking them back to Hartley Creek in Dan's truck she'd have to bag the box up, or find a way to seal it shut so the lid wouldn't come off in transport. Maybe Emma had something in the house she could use.

Before she left, however, she walked back to the corner where her old snowboards stood. Bright red and orange flames decorated one of them.

She picked it up, grinning at the huge crack between the two bindings on the board, remembering how it had happened. She and Megan had just carved through some awesome powder and ended up on the edge of a double black diamond, squinting against the sun dancing off a thick layer of snow that had fallen the night before. Below them lay the town of Hartley Creek, bisected by the river. Dan had taken his brother Austin down an easier run and was waiting for them at the bottom of the hill. Hailey knew if she didn't get down soon, Dan would be up the chairlift again and she would have a hard time finding him. So she'd taken Megan's dare.

Halfway down she hit some exposed rock, tumbled, turned over, hit another rock with her board and that was the end of snowboarding that day. When she'd finally caught up with Dan he'd been furious. That was when Hailey knew he really cared for her.

They'd started going steady after that.

Hailey was about to set the board back against the wall when a knock on the door startled her. She jumped around, dropping the snowboard with a clatter.

"Can I come in?" Dan called out.

Hailey was surprised by the tremor in her chest at the sound of his deep voice. She smoothed her hair away from her face, then caught herself preening. With a shake of her head she walked to the door and opened it.

To her surprise he stood by himself on the deck, shadows flickering over his face from the single bulb hanging from the ceiling behind Hailey.

"Where's Natasha?" she asked as he stepped into the cabin.

"She got distracted by a video game she and Adam are playing." Dan looked past her and grinned. "Are those your old snowboards?" he asked.

"I should throw them away, but haven't been able to." Hailey shoved her hands in the back pocket of her blue jeans, suddenly far too aware of how small the cabin had become when Dan had come inside.

Why had he come?

Probably just to hurry her along. He had said he wanted to leave early.

But he picked up the board she had set aside, seemingly not in any rush to go yet. "I remember this one. Didn't you name it Red Lightning?"

Hailey shrugged, surprised he remembered and a little embarrassed at the same time. "I know. Not exactly original or accurate."

"I remember how the sales guy at Edge of the Sky laughed at you when you christened it with that bottle of water."

"Was a big day for me," Hailey answered, letting his easy comments pull her back into the drift of old memories. "My first brand-new snowboard, and a Burton to boot. I can't remember how many kids I babysat or how many dishes I washed at the Royal to pay for it."

"Lots, I'm sure. Boards are expensive." Dan picked it up, his long fingers tracing the crack running across the bottom. He grinned as he set it aside. "You were a bit of a daredevil on the hill. I remember how hard I had to push myself to keep up with you." His smile was relaxed, easy, and as their eyes met it was as if the events and relationships of the past few years shifted to the side and they were simply Dan and Hailey again.

Silence hovered between them but this time it was the quiet comfort of old friends. Which is what they were.

Hailey had known Dan since she had moved to Hartley Creek. Though he was a year older, in a small town that didn't matter as much, and they'd grown up together.

"I'm glad Natasha is enjoying playing with Adam," Hailey said, pushing the snowboard Dan had just set down into the corner again. "That will make her transition into school easier."

"That's good for her. Natasha hadn't had much chance to play with other kids when she lived with Lydia. Or, for that matter, when she came to visit me."

Hailey pulled in one corner of her lip. "Did Lydia really do any homeschooling with Natasha?"

Dan shook his head, releasing a bitter laugh. "I think you've seen the results of that. Lydia had all these grand ideas, but she wasn't good on the follow-up."

Hailey pulled her coat around her, surprised that Dan had been the one to bring up his ex-wife. Other than the brief mention of Lydia's parents, it was as if they had an unspoken agreement not to talk about her.

But Hailey's curiosity was piqued, especially hearing Dan's tone when he spoke of her.

"Your divorce must have been difficult for you as well as Natasha."

Dan gave her a wry look. "Actually, this sounds a bit harsh, but it was a bit of a relief."

This was news to Hailey. "Why?"

Dan scratched his temple with one finger and eased out a sigh. Then, to her surprise, he sat down on the stool behind him. Hailey took the hint and lowered herself to the bed, waiting.

"Lydia and I didn't have the best marriage. It started for the wrong reasons." He wove his fingers together, tapping his thumbs against each other, the grimness of his features throwing his eyes into shadow. He said nothing for a moment and Hailey had to stifle the questions bubbling beneath the surface. "You may as well know… Lydia and I…" He paused, his attention on his hands, avoiding her gaze. "When I left Hartley Creek I felt depressed. I didn't live the life I should have." He lifted his shoulder in a shrug. "There's no excuse for it, but

I hung out with a bad crowd. Partied too much. Made some dumb mistakes."

Hailey pressed her lips together, sensing they were edging toward unknown territory. Moving toward a place from which, once entered, there would be no turning back.

A frisson of fear trickled down her spine. Did she want to go there? Would it change things between her and Dan?

Right now she had her life mapped out. And, apparently, Dan had his own goals too. And neither figured in the other's future plans.

And yet, all those questions she had agonized over when she found out about Lydia still hovered at the edges of her consciousness. Maybe, if they could be answered, it would ease some of the lingering brokenness that she had carried all this time, even make it easier for her to leave when the time came.

"What happened, Dan?" Hailey slipped the question into the quiet following his initial admission.

He said nothing at first and even the shadows behind them seemed to hold their breath, waiting.

Dan squeezed his hands together. "Like I said, I made some bad decisions. Some big mistakes. I was lonely and still trying to deal with all the...all the stuff that happened back here." He stopped, then looked up at Hailey. "Lydia and I ended up together one night. She got pregnant. I knew I had to step up to my responsibilities, so I told her we had to get married. And we did. Then, two years after Natasha was born, Lydia left me and filed for divorce."

As he spoke, it was as if something deep within her was torn up by the roots. All her old thoughts, bitterness and sorrow had been grounded in wrong perceptions. False conclusions.

"That's why you married her? Because of Natasha?" She had to say it again, to hear the confirmation from him.

Dan nodded, looking down at his hands, his mouth set in angry lines. "Yes. That's why. It wasn't because I loved Lydia. It was because I wanted to do what was right. To fix my mistakes."

As Hailey's breath left her lungs, she became aware she'd been holding it.

"I'm not sorry I did that," Dan added. "I knew I had to man up to my responsibilities. My regret is for the mistakes I made that required me to marry her."

Regret. He felt regret for mistakes.

Hailey rocked back and forth; Dan's admission had created a seismic shift reverberating backward through her memories and through her life.

He hadn't married Lydia because he loved her.

Which made Hailey wonder how Dan had felt about her when he'd left.

Dan's eyes were full of sorrow and pain as his gaze caught hers. "I'm sorry you had to hear this, Hailey. I'm not proud of what I did."

"But you did the right thing," Hailey said, pressing her hands to her heated cheeks. "You absolutely did the right thing. And now you have Natasha and I'm sure you don't regret that."

Dan's grateful smile dove into her heart and settled there.

"No. I don't," he said quietly. "I guess God hadn't given up on me. He found a way to make her a blessing to me."

The only sound in the ensuing silence was the hum of the heater. The cabin walls isolated them from the rest of the world, creating a momentary haven.

Outside lay responsibilities and decisions. But right here and right now it was just the two of them dealing with the brokenness that had come between them.

"I'm glad you told me about Lydia," Hailey said, rubbing her hands up and down her denim-clad legs. "Really glad."

Dan blew out a long, slow sigh. "Not easy to admit the stupid mistakes a person does, but I knew if we ever met again I'd have to tell you. Especially because at one time we were close."

At one time. The words had a finality to them that created a pang of wistfulness.

"Yes, we were," Hailey said, getting to her feet, looking over at the snowboard, then at the boxes beside the door. "And now we should probably get back to the house before people think you got lost."

Or before they think something else.

Dan stood at the same time and then they were inches apart. Hailey swallowed, her mind telling her to move but her heart wanting this moment of closeness.

"Hailey, I'm so sorry," Dan whispered. Then he lifted his hand and rested it on her shoulder. Squeezed ever so slightly.

Even through her jacket she felt his warmth. Then, without thinking why, she lifted her shoulder, and pressed her cheek against his hand.

Dan's hand squeezed tighter, and then his other hand moved to her other shoulder, pulling her closer. Her hand lifted and rested on his chest, her fingers curling against the rough material of his wool jacket.

She moved nearer.

Emotions old and new roiled around them, pulling, pushing, woven through with a sense of waiting. Anticipation.

A sharp rap on the door splintered the moment.

Hailey jumped back, her cheeks flaming. Dan lowered his hand and moved away.

"Come in," Hailey called out, shoving her hands in her pocket as she strode toward the door.

Emma put her face inside, glancing from Hailey to Dan. "Natasha was wondering where Dan had gone. She wants to show him something on the computer."

"Of course," Hailey said, clenching her hands inside her pockets. "We'll be right there. Dan was helping me figure out which boxes I can put in the truck. I guess it's okay if I leave the snowboards here unless they're in the way?" She heard the nervousness in her voice. Way to sound guilty, she chided herself.

The glint of humor in Emma's brown eyes told Hailey she thought the same thing.

"There's no rush. I just wanted to make sure Dan found the right cabin and wasn't wandering around the yard."

Then, with a discreet wink to Hailey, Emma closed the door, leaving Dan and Hailey behind.

"We should probably head back to town," Dan said, looking everywhere but at Hailey. "I promised my parents I'd stop in tonight with Natasha."

"Of course. I'll get these boxes to the truck and see you at the house." Hailey didn't look at Dan as he closed the door behind himself but she was sure he saw her flushed cheeks.

Stupid fair complexion, she thought, gathering up the boxes. Dead giveaway every time.

Dead giveaway of what? He's not supposed to mean anything to you anymore.

Hailey shook her head as if to dislodge the accusing voice. He didn't. That moment with Dan had been born of an intimate conversation. It was an aberration.

So why did Hailey feel as if they were on the edge of something else?

Chapter Eight

"No. I don't want her going on the ski hill." Dan knelt on the floor and ripped open the box of drill bits he had brought up from the back room.

It was a Monday morning. The lunch rush was over and his mother was taking care of the lone customer in the store.

Which was probably why Hailey sprung this on him now.

"It will be a good opportunity for her to connect with the other kids." Hailey stood beside him and from the corner of her eye he saw her pursed lips, her head tipped to one side as if she was trying to figure him out.

Not that he blamed her. Lately he couldn't figure himself out either. One moment he was telling himself that he and Hailey had moved on. That they were mature adults who could interact like any other mature adults.

The next he was almost kissing her in her old cabin at the ranch.

"She can do that when she's back in school," Dan retorted, pulling out a couple of blister packages.

"We talked about transition," Hailey said. "I think this

could be another good step for her to integrate back into the class in a nonthreatening environment."

"I'd hardly call Misty Ridge a nonthreatening environment." As Dan stood, he couldn't stop a thrum of anxiety at the thought of his daughter on the ski hill. "She's too young yet," he said, looking over Hailey's shoulder. Natasha was working in the back of the store again, sorting some nuts and bolts. Dan couldn't figure out why she seemed to enjoy that so much, but Hailey was able to show results by doing it. And he wasn't going to argue with results.

But he was going to argue with Hailey's proposition. He turned his attention back to her. "She's never been on the ski hill, or any ski hill for that matter."

"The younger she can start the better it will be for her." Hailey sounded reasonable, but he couldn't get his emotions past the thought of his daughter skiing on Misty Ridge.

"Better for what?" he said, turning back to sorting the drill bits. Why had Hailey sprung this on him while he was working and distracted? Had she hoped he would simply agree and leave it at that?

"It would be better for her confidence and for her skills."

"She doesn't need to learn how to ski or snowboard." As Dan hung the blister pack of three-eighths-inch bits on the peg he realized how silly he sounded.

"Considering that the ski hill is a scant ten-minute drive from town, I would think sooner or later she'll end up on Misty Ridge," Hailey said. "May as well equip her with the skills she needs as early as possible."

As much as he hated the idea, Dan also knew she was right. And he also knew that in a town like Hartley Creek, where skiing and snowboarding were imbedded in the culture of the town, it was inevitable Natasha would get drawn into it.

"I still don't like it," he insisted.

"She had so much fun with Adam at the ranch," Hailey said, pressing on as if she sensed his wavering. "This would be a logical next step. Besides, like I said, it is a nonthreatening situation for her and for her classmates."

"You know I don't like the idea and I'm sure you know why," he finally admitted.

"Of course I know why," she said. "I was there that day too, remember?"

He looked over at her and as his gaze held her gray-blue eyes it was as if he had shifted back in time and they were back up on the mountain. She was leading the way in her usual kamikaze style, daring him to follow her down that double black diamond run. Daring him to follow her into the roped-off areas that held a whiff of danger. He felt the same tickle in the pit of his stomach he experienced when he stood on the edge of a difficult slope. A sense of expectation and exhilaration.

But mixed in with that, a sense of fear.

Because he also remembered her reaction when they'd gotten the news about Austin's death. How she had stumbled backward. Fallen down and then started weeping inconsolably. She had suffered almost as huge a loss as he had. Her grief had been almost as deep as his.

And he had to carry that with him as well.

Hailey took a step closer, laying her hand on his arm. "How about I take her on Monday, just for the day? Now that your dad is better, you can come out and see for yourself how things go with her."

Her hand felt warm and soft, and as he looked down at her face he caught again the orange scent of her perfume. She stood so close that he could see the faint scar along her cheekbone, and before he could stop himself he'd reached up and touched it.

"Remember when you got this," he said, his finger lightly tracing its outline.

"It was just a bump," she said.

"But I remember how scared I was when I saw you fall." He reluctantly lowered his hand.

Hailey looked down, a faint blush creeping up her neck.

"There's danger everywhere," Hailey said, lowering her voice, creating a cocoon of intimacy in the aisle of the store. "Statistically, driving Natasha around in your truck is more dangerous than taking her on the ski hill."

She sounded so rational and it became harder to argue with her.

"We'll be on the learner's hill. What could happen there?"

Dan realized he was being overdramatic. And Hailey's reasonable arguments made him look as though he was being stubborn for the sake of proving his point.

"Okay," he said, turning away from her. "We'll start with one day. And if Dad is feeling okay, I'm coming out to see how things go."

Hailey almost bounced, she was so pleased. "You got 'er. One day."

"So when does this start?"

Hailey bit her lip. "Tomorrow."

"Already?"

"I was hoping to ask you sooner, but then we went to the ranch and I thought I'd see how that went." She stopped and her blush grew.

They both knew how that had gone.

"Dan, I've got a customer who wants your help," Mrs. Morrow's voice called out, one aisle over.

Hailey took a quick step back, then flashed him another smile, spun around and almost skipped back to Natasha.

Her mission was obviously accomplished, Dan thought with a wry grin as he set the box down and went to help his mother.

"Make sure you dig in with one ski more than the other," Hailey said to Natasha. "Remember, like I told you, you have to make a wedge with your skis, right? Like a piece of pizza."

Natasha bit her lip, concentrating on her skis.

While she got ready, Hailey glanced up the hill. The top ridge was a white jagged edge against a hard, blue sky.

Overnight, ten inches of fresh powder had fallen up on the high runs. Hailey could see tiny, antlike figures zipping back and forth across the runs, or hurtling down others. She yearned to be there for a moment.

Hailey pulled her attention back to Natasha and the other children she was working with, Adam and Deanna. The rest of the grade one class was divided among the other four instructors. Though they'd been on the hill for almost two hours, the first half of their time had been taken up with showing the kids how to handle the equipment, taking skis on and off and the importance of safety. It was only in the past half hour that Hailey had been able to do hands-on instruction.

"Remember to keep your hands on your knees, like I showed you in the scooter drills," Hailey reminded the group. "Make your pizza with your skis as you're going down the hill. If you push harder with one ski than the other, you'll make a turn."

"Is this how I'm 'posed to do it, Miss Deacon?"

Deanna called out as she slid down the hill and came to a stop in front of Hailey.

"Yes, exactly like that. Good job." Hailey clapped her gloved hands together.

Adam followed suit, also earning Hailey's praise. Finally, as if afraid of being outdone, Natasha took the plunge.

She wobbled a bit but regained control and then also came to a stop beside Adam. She shot Hailey a triumphant look and Hailey praised her loudly and effusively.

Then Natasha looked past Hailey. "Hey, Daddy. I'm skiing."

"I see that, munchkin."

Dan's voice calling out across the hill sent a light shiver dancing down Hailey's spine. She turned in time to see Dan, wearing his old snowboarding jacket, blue jeans and winter boots, trudging across the snow-covered hill to join them. His head was bare and his cheeks ruddy.

Time wheeled back and Hailey experienced the familiar surge of expectation she felt whenever they'd gone boarding together.

Where were they going today? What new jumps would they try? Would they dare to duck out of bounds?

"Miss Deacon, can we do that again?" Deanna called.

Hailey spun her head around, pulling herself back to the present. "Of course we can, Deanna. I'll go a bit farther down and you, Adam and Natasha can come ski down to me."

She ignored Dan as she demonstrated a snowplow turn to the children.

Dan stood to one side, watching as Natasha made the first attempt. She seemed far more confident. And when she came to a stop by Hailey she turned and waved to Dan. "I'm skiing lots, Daddy," she said again.

"Yes, you are," Dan said.

"Can we try the hill with the T-bar?" Adam asked.

Hailey glanced at her watch. "Sorry, Adam, I have to get you guys back to the bus in a few minutes."

"Can I stay and practice some more?" Natasha asked. "My dad can help me."

"Don't you have to go back with the other kids?" Dan asked.

"Me and Hailey came in her car," Natasha replied. "I don't have to take the bus."

"Okay, then. I'll help you."

Hailey shot Dan a thankful look, happy to see the interaction between daughter and father. Especially on the ski hill.

She took Adam and Deanna back to the rental chalet to turn in their equipment, then stayed with Megan to get the class onto the bus. When the bus had left, Hailey returned to the learner slope, pleased to see Dan and Natasha still working together.

"This is so much fun," Natasha called out to Hailey as she negotiated another turn. But in her enthusiasm, she overestimated, caught her edge too deep and fell over in a cloud of snow.

Dan immediately ran to her side, and Natasha managed to get her skis under her, only to end up sliding farther down the hill. "Stop, Natasha," Dan called, going after her. But as soon as Natasha regained control, she made another turn and scooted off in the opposite direction.

"I'm skiing, I'm skiing," she called out, her voice full of pride.

"Your dad told you to stop now," Hailey called out. The hill had such a gentle slope that if Natasha didn't stop on her own, the terrain would slow her down soon enough.

"I don't want to stop," Natasha said, keeping her hands on her knees as Hailey had showed her.

But topography worked against Natasha's wishes and a few seconds later she glided to a halt right in front of Hailey. Dan caught up to them and the scowl on his face spoke volumes.

"You skied really good, Natasha," Hailey said before Dan could speak. "But when your dad or I tell you to stop, you have to listen."

Natasha grinned, glancing from Dan to Hailey. But when she didn't see an answering smile on either Hailey or Dan's face, her own joy seemed to fade away.

"But I wanted to ski." Natasha lowered her head.

"I know that. But in order to learn to ski properly and safely you have to learn to listen," Hailey continued, crouching down to maintain eye contact. "If you don't, we can't ski anymore."

Natasha's gaze flew from Hailey to Dan. "I don't want to stop skiing. I want to go again. Can I?"

To her surprise, a smile crept across his lips. "You can go again," he said. "But you have to listen to Miss Deacon."

"I will. I will." Natasha clapped her mittened hands together, then skied over to the Magic Carpet, the moving sidewalk that relayed her up the beginner run. As she stepped onto the plastic matting that moved up the hill, Dan walked alongside her, then watched as she got off at the top by herself.

Hailey's heart swelled at the sight. Dan, on the ski hill. Sure, it wasn't even the bunny run, but his presence showed a small acceptance of the slope.

From time to time, their eyes would meet and each

time his gaze lingered a little longer. Hailey wasn't sure what was happening and right now she didn't care. They were having fun.

Just like a little family.

An hour later, Natasha's cheeks were flaming-red from exertion, Dan was slowing down and the sunlight was waning. The lifts at the top of the hill weren't running, the vacant seats swung gently up in the ever-present breeze.

The day was winding down. The liftee at the top of the hill waved to Hailey. "I'm shutting the Magic Carpet down," she announced. Hailey waved back to show her she had heard.

When Natasha made her final turn at the bottom of the hill, Hailey delivered the bad news. "It's time to go, sweetie."

To her surprise Natasha only nodded. "We had fun, didn't we?" she said, tugging her helmet off.

"We sure did." Dan brushed some snow off his knees from when he had fallen down after Natasha had run into him.

"I'm so, so hungry," Natasha said, looking from Dan to Hailey, as if expecting that they would immediately produce hamburgers or fries.

"Then we better do something about that," Dan replied. "But first we have to get you back to the rentals so you can return your skis."

"Can you please pull me, Miss Deacon?" Natasha held out a mittened hand. Hailey caught it and towed her along, snow squeaking under the hard soles of her ski boots. Natasha squealed with pleasure, Dan trailing along behind.

Fifteen minutes later the skis and boots had been returned and Dan, Hailey and Natasha walked out into the cooling air.

"So can I take Natasha here tomorrow again?" Hailey asked.

Dan looked her way and, again, a faint frisson of attraction hummed between them. Just like old times.

Even as that thought entered her head, she knew things between them had changed. Newer emotions had become part of the mix, shifting her perceptions.

"I think so," Dan said.

Hailey shoved her hands in the pockets of her jacket, releasing a smile. "Then I'll see you tomorrow," she said, taking a step back, removing herself from the two of them.

"Can we go there and get something to eat?" Natasha asked, pointing to the flashing neon sign of the restaurant beside the main chalet. "I'm so, so hungry."

"I guess we could," Dan said. "I think I have my wallet with me."

"Can Miss Deacon come with us?" Natasha said, looking from Hailey to her father. "Can she, Daddy? Can she have supper with us?"

Hailey shook her head, giving Dan an out. "I should go. You just enjoy your time together."

"No, you come with us," Natasha insisted. "You have to eat too."

"Why don't you join us?" Dan asked.

She knew she shouldn't, but the thought of returning to an empty apartment after spending such a wonderful afternoon with Natasha and Dan didn't appeal to her.

And the tender smile Dan gave her was all the encouragement she needed.

"Okay. I'll come. But I'm paying for myself," she insisted.

Dan's smile grew. "What else is new?"

She knew he referred to the fact that she had always paid her share of the bill when they were dating. "It's how I roll," she said with a casual shrug.

"I'm really hungry," Natasha repeated, in case anyone might have missed it the first time. She grabbed Hailey's hand and, leaning forward, pulled the two adults across the brick square toward the restaurant. To their left loomed the log chalet, lights streaming from inside, music pouring out the large door whenever it opened. Then a voice with a drawling New Zealand accent called Hailey's name.

"Hailey, you're finally back," a tall, lanky man exclaimed. His bright purple jacket and black snow pants made a swishing sound as he loped toward them. He stopped and swept his hair out of eyes. "Where you been? I haven't seen you in yonks."

"Erik. Wow. You're still coming here," Hailey replied, grinning at her old snowboarding friend. "I thought you would have quit years ago."

"Wouldn't miss it. It's beaut. Oh Hailey, I missed your goofy grin!" He grabbed Hailey in a tight hug and lifted her off the ground.

Erik dropped Hailey, then slapped Dan on the back. "And Dan, so good to see you too. Wow, this is brilliant. The gang is back."

"Good to see you, Erik." Dan's greeting sounded more restrained than Erik's.

Erik had shown up for the first time at Misty Ridge when Hailey was in grade ten. He had just graduated college in New Zealand and was traveling the world on his parents' dime. He came to Hartley Creek in November and stayed the entire winter, working just enough to pay for his snowboarding.

The population of Hartley Creek swelled in the winter with people like Erik. People who came to Hartley Creek from all over the world to snowboard the epic runs at Misty Ridge and work at any available job to support their passion.

Erik had connected with Dan and Hailey and had snowboarded with them whenever he could. And flirted with Hailey whenever he could. It had been a small source of tension between Dan and Hailey. She had tried to tell Dan that it meant nothing, but Dan wasn't always so sure.

Erik dropped his hands on his hips, grinning. "So, Dan and Hailey. Still together. Some things never change."

"What is he saying?" Natasha asked, before Hailey could correct Erik. "Why does he call you Den and Highly?"

Erik grinned at Natasha, then crouched down to her level. "It's me Kiwi accent, darlin'. And what's your name?"

"Nime?" Natasha asked, looking puzzled.

Hailey laughed. "Your name, honey. He's asking you what your name is."

"It's Natasha," she said, pulling a bit closer to Dan. Obviously Erik's charm was as ineffective on the daughter as it was on the father.

Erik shot his dark gaze from Dan to Hailey, then straightened, his grin growing. "So you two finally tied the knot and got a little nipper out of the deal." Before anyone could correct him, Erik clapped Dan on the shoulder. "I guess the best man did win, mate."

"We're not…not together," Dan said, slipping his arm around Natasha's shoulder.

"And what are you doing now?" Hailey asked, before Erik could make the awkward situation even more awkward. "You had an accounting degree, didn't you?"

Erik turned back to Hailey and she could see his smile shifting. "I work for myself. Just enough to pay for coming here every year. It's flash." Then he put his hand on Hailey's shoulder. "We have to go boarding again. Duck under the ropes. Take a ride on the wild side." He angled his head toward her as he gave her a slow-release smile and added a wink. Erik could turn the charm on like a tap.

"I think I'll give that a pass," Hailey returned.

"You gonna pike out on me? Too bad."

"What bed?" Natasha chimed in.

Hailey couldn't help a laugh. "You have a good evening," she said to Erik. "And enjoy the fresh powder."

"Yeah. It's gnarly." He sighed, then patted Hailey on the shoulder. "You change your mind, darlin', you know where to find me. And if you ever need company for supper, I'd be chuffed."

After sending another wink Hailey's way, Erik joined a group of people leaving the chalet, heading down the hill toward town.

"Why does that man talk so funny?" Natasha asked as they turned and walked toward the restaurant directly ahead of them.

"He's from New Zealand," Hailey explained. "They talk with a different accent. Maybe they think we talk funny too."

"I think he likes Miss Deacon. Don't you think so, Daddy?"

Dan pulled on the ski pole welded to the restaurant door as a handle. "I'm sure he does."

The edge of anger in Dan's voice puzzled Hailey. Where had that come from?

"Do you like him, Miss Deacon?" Natasha asked as

the door fell shut behind them, the warmth from the stone fireplace by the door washing over them.

"He's an old friend," was all Hailey would say.

Dan shot her a frown. "So will you be going out boarding with him?"

Why was he asking?

As their eyes met, a tingle of awareness flickered down her spine.

Why did Dan care?

And this was followed by a more tentative question.

Was Dan jealous?

Chapter Nine

"Try it again," Dan called out as he double-checked the connection of the booster cables and then stood back as Hailey tried to start her car.

Dan's truck and Hailey's car were the only vehicles left on the parking lot of the ski hill. Everyone else had long gone.

Exhaust from his truck and light snow swirled around him, lit up from the beams of his truck's lights. Darkness surrounded them, broken only by a few overhead lights on the parking lot.

If he looked over his shoulder, Dan could see the lights of Hartley Creek, nestled in the valley. Home was down there. A nice warm home.

He shivered and pushed his hands deeper in his pockets. He glanced back at his truck, where Natasha still sat, making sure she was okay. For the past twenty minutes they had been trying to start Hailey's car. But now all he heard from Hailey's engine was a faint clicking sound each time she turned the key in the ignition.

She finally stuck her head out the door of her car. "I'm not getting anything."

Dan stared at the engine, as if it would give up some secret.

"Do you know what's wrong?" Hailey asked, getting out of her car.

"My guess is you need a new battery," Dan said, giving a shrug. "It should have fired up right away, hooked up to my truck."

Hailey hunched her shoulders against the gathering cold, her eyes reflecting the light from his truck. "So what do I do now?"

"I can give you a ride into town," Dan said. "We can deal with this tomorrow." If he were completely honest, the idea of spending a little more time with Hailey didn't bother him either.

They'd had a lovely dinner. Casual. Relaxed.

And thankfully Erik had stayed away.

Dan had surprised himself with the flash of jealousy he'd experienced when he'd seen Erik grab Hailey. And when he winked at her. And when he invited her to come boarding with him.

"I guess we'll have to," Hailey said. She squinted up at the falling snow. "Though it will probably have a foot of snow on it by then."

"We'll take a shovel along," Dan said. He shivered again. "But we should get going."

"Sure. You must be freezing," Hailey said, giving him a grateful smile. "Thanks for your help."

"No problem."

As Dan coiled up the cables, he glanced Hailey's way, surprised to see her still watching him. It had been that way all evening, sitting across the table from each other. A casual glance that they both allowed to linger.

The occasional brush of their hands.

It was a like a slow movement toward the emotions

they'd shared that moment in the cabin. An easy shift into different territory.

He didn't want to think too hard about what was happening. He was tired of analyzing and watching. Right now loneliness was too familiar to him and he missed having Hailey in his life.

"We should get going, then," she said, finally looking away.

She got into the truck. He tossed the cables into his toolbox, then got in himself.

"Miss Deacon's car won't start?" Natasha asked, her face lit up by the lights from the dashboard.

"No. That's why I'm taking her home," Dan said.

"You should come to our place." Natasha bounced on her seat. "We can play a game together."

"I should probably go home," Hailey said. Did she sound reluctant?

Dan dismissed his dumb thoughts with a quick shake of his head. Now he was just projecting. However, the thought of going home and spending the evening alone with Natasha held less appeal than it once had.

"Do you have games at your place?" Natasha asked.

"I don't."

"Do you watch television?"

"No. I don't have a television. Mostly I read."

That much hadn't changed. Hailey was seldom without a book of one genre or another.

"And when I know how to read, I can read books too," Natasha said. She yawned, rubbed her eyes and heaved out a sigh. "I'm glad you came skiing with me, Daddy," she said quietly, taking his hand in hers.

"I'm glad too, punkin," he replied.

And he truly was. Watching Natasha's pleasure had relaxed an ache in his heart that had been there since Austin's death. Seeing her smile as she skied and turned on the very hill that had claimed his little brother had created a small shift in his view of Misty Ridge.

As he drove no one spoke, the fresh air and exercise having taken its toll on the skiers.

Quiet strains of music came from the radio and he was content not to say anything. He saw Natasha's head bob and then she shifted, laying her head on Hailey's lap.

Dan's thoughts switched to the times he and Hailey would drive back from the hill, both of them too tired to talk. They would go up to his place, share a cup of hot chocolate and some cookies his mother had made, share stories of amazing jumps, awesome runs and excellent snow with Austin and his parents. Just before dinner, Dan would bring Hailey home.

She always said how much she hated going home. Her mother was often gone and because Naomi and Shannon had moved away, it meant she sat in her apartment by herself.

She never invited him up and he never came. It was an unspoken rule between them. A setting of boundaries.

Boundaries he'd jumped across as soon as he'd left town.

The memory of Lydia was like a stain. And a reminder?

As he came to a stop at the first set of traffic lights in town he glanced over at Hailey again, his thoughts a jumble. He knew he was treading on dangerous ground and had been from the moment he'd confessed how his relationship with Lydia had come about.

But it was as if that confession had eased a strain between them. Had that confession been a mistake? Or had he simply created a space for a change in their friendship? How would that change look?

Hailey, gently stroking Natasha's hair, shot him a sidelong glance, then slowly turned her head as their gazes connected and held.

He didn't want to look away. When a smile spread across her features and lit up her face, he couldn't.

A horn honked behind him, startling him into action. He sped through the green light, made the turn at the alley and then into the parking lot behind the store. He turned off the truck before he realized he had planned on taking Hailey home.

He was about to start the truck again when Natasha's head bobbed up. "Are we home?" she asked, stretching out her arms.

"Yes, but I have to bring Miss Deacon back to her place."

"No. Please no. I want her to come and play a game with me." Natasha turned to Dan and clung to his arm. "Please, Daddy? I won't complain about bedtime."

That was almost incentive enough. Natasha was at her most creative when trying to avoid going to bed.

"I'm sure Miss Deacon wants to go home." To an empty apartment and a book.

"Please. Just come for a little while." Natasha turned her attention to Hailey. "Daddy doesn't like to play Snakes and Ladders with me."

Hailey hesitated. "Just come up for a bit," Dan said. Reality was, he wasn't ready for her to go either. "You can help me convince Natasha that bedtime isn't the worst thing that can happen to her."

Hailey laughed. "Okay. I'll come and play a couple of games with you," she said to Natasha.

But as she spoke, her eyes were on Dan.

A few minutes later Natasha and Hailey sat in the dining room while, in the kitchen, Dan stirred hot chocolate into three mugs. He brought the steaming mugs to the table and set them down beside the girls, then sat down with Natasha.

Hailey looked at the mug beside her then shot Dan a coy look. "Did you put seven marshmallows in?"

"Exactly seven and no more," he said in a mock stern voice.

Hailey smiled, and he knew she remembered how his mother would carefully parcel out seven marshmallows per cup. She never explained why seven, only that seven was exactly enough. No more and no less.

"Four, five, six. Goody. I get a ladder," his daughter crowed, swooping her game piece up the board.

"I think I'm going to lose this game," Hailey grumbled good-naturedly.

"That's okay," Natasha consoled her. "Maybe you'll do better the next game."

Dan laughed at her parroting of the same encouragement he gave her when she was losing. Hailey's laughter wove through his and once again their gazes connected.

And once again awareness arced between them. Was it simply old feelings coming back to haunt them? Or was this something new and present?

He stifled his questions, drank his hot chocolate and allowed himself to simply enjoy the pleasure of seeing his daughter happy. Of spending time with Hailey that wasn't heavy with conflict.

Hailey and Natasha played another game and, true to Natasha's promise, Hailey won this one.

"See, I told you that you would win," Natasha said, taking a final sip of her hot chocolate. She set the cup down and glanced at Dan. "I suppose it's bedtime now," she said morosely.

"I suppose you're right."

Natasha turned her attention back to Hailey. "Can you tuck me in bed?"

Hailey opened her mouth as if to protest, then, to Dan's surprise, she simply nodded. "Sure. I think I can."

Don't read anything into it, Dan thought, getting up to grab Natasha's pajamas. She's just humoring Natasha. But the thought that they might share a few moments together after Natasha was in bed made him hurry up.

Be careful. Don't get involved. You have Natasha to think of.

Dan pushed the concerns away as he pulled Natasha's ruffly blue nightgown out of her drawer. Hailey was simply an old friend and he looked forward to sharing some stories with her, nothing more.

There is no "simply" with someone like Hailey. You loved her once.

Dan clutched the nightgown as he leaned against the dresser. He was tired. He was lonely. He had been dealing with a lot of changes and disruption the past few months. He hadn't had a chance to catch up with any of his old friends. This was nothing more than that.

And before his thoughts could accuse him again, he strode down the hallway to the living room to get Natasha ready for bed.

Twenty minutes and three books later Natasha scrambled into her bed and pulled the blankets around her. "Miss Deacon, you have to tuck me in," she commanded.

"Pardon me?" Dan suggested.

Natasha bit her lip. "I'm sorry, Daddy. That was rude. Miss Deacon, can you please tuck me in?"

"I don't know if I can do it right," Hailey said with a grin.

"Yes, you can. You just have to push the sheet and blanket under the mattress. And then I'm all tucked in.

And then you have to sit on the bed beside me and sing my song."

"What song is that?" Hailey asked as she followed Natasha's instructions.

"The bedtime song my Daddy always sings to me." Natasha lay on the bed, the muted glow of the nightlight casting her features in shadow. But from his vantage point at the end of the bed, Dan saw her bright eyes flicking from him to Hailey, as if picking up on the sense of expectation lingering on the edges of Dan's consciousness.

"I'm in the dark here," Hailey said, sounding confused.

"Of course you are, silly," Natasha said with a giggle. "It's nighttime. Daddy, you have to start the song."

Dan cleared his throat, feeling suddenly self-conscious. He didn't have the best singing voice. But what made him the most self-aware was the fact that the song he always sang to Natasha was one Hailey had taught him.

She had taught him the song so they could sing it to their children after they were married. It was the song her grandmother had sung to her whenever she tucked her in at night.

Well, it didn't really mean anything. It was the only bedtime song he knew.

He kept his eyes fixed on his daughter as he started.

"Little one, safe in bed, God is watching your little head. God is holding your little heart, as the daylight now departs." He stopped and cleared his throat, but he sensed Hailey watching him.

He sang the other two verses and when he was done he brushed a kiss over Natasha's forehead.

"Are you sad, Miss Deacon?" Natasha asked as Dan straightened.

"It's a pretty song," Hailey replied, her voice wavering.

"My daddy said a very special lady taught it to him to sing to little kids."

"It's a good song." Hailey bent over and brushed her hand over Natasha's forehead. "'Night, sweetie," she whispered, then got up and hurried out the door.

Dan followed her out, but stopped in the doorway and waggled his fingers at his daughter, their last bedtime ritual. "Sleep well, sleep tight. Stay in your bed all night," he intoned.

"Until morning," she called back.

"Until morning," he repeated. Then he closed the door quietly behind him, waited a moment to gather his thoughts and then walked down the hallway to where Hailey waited in the dining room.

She stood with her back to him, cleaning up the game.

"I can take care of that," he said.

Her only reply was a careful sniff as her hands stilled their busy activity.

"You taught her the song," Hailey said, her voice subdued.

"It's the only bedtime song I know." Dan came to stand behind her and then, giving in to the impulse he'd been fighting all evening, put his hands on her shoulders and turned her to him.

A lone tear tracked down her cheek and the sight of it disarmed him. He could never handle tears, and Hailey cried so seldom that each instance pulled the ground out from under him.

She kept her eyes on the red game piece she was turning over and over in her hands.

"I'm sorry it made you sad," he said quietly.

She looked up at him then. "I can't believe you still remembered it."

"You sang it enough times to me," he said, eeking out a smile. "Made me memorize it."

The smile wavering over her lips lifted his heart. He gently brushed another tear away, his fingers lingering on her cheek.

"It's a good song," he said. "Natasha loves it."

"I'm glad your little girl got to hear it."

Your little girl. Not *their* child or children. The ones who were supposed to hear the song.

Regret clutched his heart. What could he say that he hadn't said already? But he couldn't let her stand there, her eyes rimmed with tears.

"I'm so sorry for how things happened," he said quietly, willing her to understand. "I'm sorry that you had to hear about me marrying Lydia from someone else."

"How could you tell me? We weren't in a good place then," she said, as if exonerating him.

Instead, it made him feel even guiltier over how things had happened after he left. And why he had left.

His heart stuttered as he pulled himself back from futile memories and mistakes that couldn't be changed. Leave the past in the past, he reminded himself. Doing otherwise served no purpose.

Right now Hailey stood in front of him, her sadness pushing at him.

"I can't change how things happened," he said, wishing he had the right words to say. "But I have to live in the present and deal with my responsibilities here and now."

"One of which is Natasha," Hailey said with a melancholy look.

"Yeah, Natasha is the biggest one and I'll do anything for her." He wished that hadn't come out like a threat. The fierceness of his love for Natasha always surprised him.

"You should be thankful for her. She's a sweet, precocious child. You're lucky to have her."

Guilt and sorrow pierced Dan like a knife. If things had gone according to his and Hailey's plan, maybe they would have a little girl by now. Or a boy. Or both.

He couldn't let himself go there. Life was what it was.

Hailey drew in a long, shuddering breath, her throat working as if she struggled to hold back her sorrow.

His fault, he thought, the knife taking a twist.

But he couldn't stand to watch her suffer anymore. He pulled her close to him, shielding her from the sadness and pain he had caused her. Tucking her head under his chin, he wrapped his arms around her, sheltering her.

"This is all a bit of a mess," she muttered against his shirt.

He had to agree. And yet, holding her close to him, he didn't feel that things were a mess at all.

For this moment, he felt as if everything was exactly right.

Chapter Ten

Hailey laid her head against Dan's chest, contentment flowing through her. It felt good to rest in his arms and be held up by him instead of being strong herself.

She stifled the warning voice telling her this was dangerous territory. How could it be? She belonged in Dan's arms.

She lifted her face and saw the broken longing in his gaze. A longing that mirrored hers.

They had lost and sacrificed enough, she thought. All she wanted from him was just one kiss. No more.

She lifted her hand, let it rest on his shoulder and then, finally, he lowered his head.

Their lips met in a slow, delicate kiss.

Dan softly drew away, his hand cupping her chin. When she saw the warmth in his eyes she realized how foolish she had been.

One kiss wasn't nearly enough.

She slipped her hand around his neck and drew him closer to her, clinging to him as if she was drowning and he was her only hope. They shared another kiss. And another.

Finally, she drew away, nestling in the cradle of his arms, wishing time would stop its steady turning.

"This feels so right," she murmured into the gentle silence cocooning them.

Dan's only reply was the slow rise of his chest as he took in a long breath. His arm held her anchored to him, his other hand rested on her head, his fingers tangling in her hair.

They stood this way for a long moment, neither wanting to be the first to break the embrace.

Then, a cough from Natasha's room brought reality into the moment.

Dan drew away, looking over his shoulder, but no sound followed the cough.

Then he turned back to Hailey, his fingers caressing her face, his eyes following their gentle path. "I feel like I should apologize, but I'm not sorry," he said.

Hailey closed her eyes, letting herself simply be in Dan's presence as the tangled and unraveled ends of her life slowly became whole.

"It just feels right," she said, catching his hand by the wrist, holding it in hers.

"It does," he agreed, pulling her close again. "I feel like I've come home after a long, hard journey."

His words settled into her heart, filling all the empty spaces that had hurt her so long.

But another cough from Natasha's room became a stark reminder of Dan's main obligation.

"I hope she's not coming down with anything," Hailey said, bringing Natasha into the moment, moving away from him.

"I think her throat is a bit raw from yelling so much today." Dan let Hailey go, but kept one hand resting on her waist, as if reluctant to release her. "She had a lot of fun. I want to thank you for that."

"And you? Did you enjoy yourself?"

Dan's slow, crooked smile told her all she needed to know. "Yeah. I did."

"I know Natasha is looking forward to going again tomorrow."

Dan brushed his fingers over her cheek. "Thanks for pushing me to let her go," he said. "You seem to know exactly what she needs. Every time."

His words created a flutter of happiness deep within her. "She's a sweet girl."

Dan looked over his shoulder, as if connecting with his daughter, then gave Hailey a rueful look.

"You know, I just realized I can't drive you home now that Natasha's in bed."

"I can walk. It's not far and I don't mind the cold."

"I'm so sorry. I wasn't thinking about how that would work for you."

It actually worked out fine, Hailey thought. But she reluctantly stepped away, unable, however, to look away. "I guess… I should be going."

Dan brushed his knuckles over her chin, then pressed another kiss to her forehead. "I'll get your coat."

Hailey wrapped her arms around herself as he left her side. She didn't want to leave, but at the same time she knew that they had played a dangerous game. Natasha was sleeping down the hall. What if she had seen them?

Would it matter?

Hailey pushed the unnerving questions aside. Natasha hadn't seen them. They didn't need to explain anything to her. Yet, as Dan returned with her coat, his eyes holding a hint of promise, she knew the situation between her and Dan had radically shifted.

The kisses they'd shared had changed everything. They couldn't go back to what they were before.

"Are you sure you'll be warm enough?" he asked as he eased her coat over her arms. "You could phone your sister and get her to pick you up."

Hailey could imagine what Shannon would make of this situation. After Dan had left the first time, Shannon had been furious with him for Hailey's sake. As a big sister she had consoled Hailey, dried her tears and told her Dan wasn't worth crying over. So what would Shannon say now, with the resentment of her own recent jilting by her fiancé still fresh in her mind?

Hailey didn't want her sister's bitterness to sully this moment.

"It's a beautiful winter night." Hailey pulled the front of her jacket together and zipped it up. "I don't mind walking for a bit." And thinking for a bit.

"Okay. But let the record show I feel really lousy about this," Dan said, stroking her hair off her face.

"Duly noted and forgiven," Hailey said, grinning up at him.

Then, to her surprise, he kissed her again. Hard. Then moved away from her to the door. "You better get going. You shouldn't be out on the streets when it's late."

"This is Hartley Creek. What could happen?" Hailey returned with a light laugh.

"Anything," was his succinct reply as he took her hand.

With reluctant steps she followed him and, when he opened the door, looked up at him again. She lifted her hand to his face, then drew away and closed the door behind her.

The air felt cool as she jogged down the stairs. At the bottom she shot a quick glance up at the windows, glowing yellow in the darkness. Dan's apartment. His parents' old home.

Hailey tugged her mittens out of her pockets, pulled them on, then headed around the building to the street.

Downtown was almost deserted, the lights casting cones of silver onto the street, illuminating the falling snow, which cooled her heated cheeks.

A few cars swished down the street, crunching through the gathering snow and as she passed the Royal, pulsating music pouring out as the door opened and people spilled out. Down the valley she heard the haunting sound of the train's horn bouncing off the hills as it came closer. It sounded again, louder this time, and Hailey heard the comforting rumble of the wheels on the tracks edging the town.

She smiled as she crossed the street at the corner. As a child the train's horn had become her way of measuring time. When she had to go home and when she had to go to sleep. It was a constant in her life and its melancholy sound seemed to underline her current emotions.

She followed the sidewalk, passing the chocolate shop with its tempting treats still in the display, the flower shop with its for-sale sign in the window and the bookstore, which held the promise of further adventures on its shelves.

She knew each business on the street and most of the owners. Though Hartley Creek could be classified as a resort town, it was coal and mining that had employed the majority of the residents for the last century. The town had its own industry, which created a solid community that didn't depend entirely on the ebb and flow of tourism.

And now Dan was a part of that community.

Dan, who had kissed her. Dan whom she had kissed back.

Hailey lifted her face, watching the heavy, fat flakes drifting lazily down against the darkness of the sky above. Each flake fell on her face like a cool kiss.

Dan's kisses were warm.

"Oh, Lord, what have we done?" she whispered, lowering her face as she traversed the streets of her old hometown.

And yet she couldn't muster enough regret to truly feel they had made a mistake. It felt so right to be in Dan's arms and to be held by him.

Could they do this? Could they really connect again? Start over?

Her thoughts moved like a slow, gathering storm. They had loved each other once. Obviously the attraction still hummed between them. Yes, things had changed.

You have plans. You have a job waiting for you.

But all that could change and would change if...

If what? If Dan decides he can now love you again? Do you trust him to follow through? He didn't once, he might not again.

He was grieving. He made a mistake.

And could make another one.

Hailey wanted to stifle her storm-tossed thoughts. Put them to rest, but the memory of her father's desertion hung like a shadow over her life.

Dear Lord, she prayed. *Help me to understand what I should do. What Dan and I should do. I'm confused, but I'm also happy.*

And she was. Happier than she had been in a long time.

She ducked down the next street and saw her apartment as the train rumbled a block away, then receded. Tomorrow is another day, she reminded herself. See what happens tomorrow. Take things one day at a time.

* * *

"I did a good job of skiing today, didn't I?" Natasha bounced up and down on the wooden bench of the rental chalet as Hailey helped her pull her snow-encrusted boots off. "And I'm glad we went on the big hill. I wish I could go all the way up. On the chairlift."

The chalet buzzed with the excited chatter of twenty grade one students and a few tired parents who had come to help. Hailey had already assisted a number of the children with their skis while Natasha waited patiently.

"The chairlift isn't that hard to learn, but you need to be a good skier." Hailey banged the snow off the hard plastic ski boots, set them on the rubber flooring, then gave Natasha her winter boots. "Put these on, missy, and we'll bring your skis back."

"Deanna said that I am a good skier. And that she goes up on the chairlift."

"That's very nice for Deanna. You had fun with her today, didn't you?" Hailey asked.

The past couple of days Natasha and Deanna had been skiing together, laughing and racing each other down the hill. Much as she and Megan used to. Natasha and Deanna had become good friends, which boded well for next week when Hailey hoped to transition Natasha back into the classroom.

"Deanna said that she goes to the movies," Natasha added, pulling her boots on as she made a lightning-quick change in topic.

"Movies sound like fun," Hailey said, pushing herself to her feet.

"Deanna told me there was a fun movie tomorrow night," Natasha said. "Deanna said I could go with her if I wanted."

"And who is Deanna?"

Dan's deep voice behind her made Hailey jump. She turned and when she caught his smiling gaze, her own smile blossomed.

"She is my friend," Natasha replied. "She's right over there, at the desk where we bring our skis back." Natasha jumped off the bench and ran over to Dan. "Why did you come here, Daddy?"

"I had to deliver a lift of Sheetrock to the Misty Ridge Lodge. So I thought I would stop by. Give you and Miss Deacon a ride home. Especially now that we know Miss Deacon's car won't be working for a couple of days."

Hailey pulled a face. "Try a week or more. The mechanic said he could get a secondhand starter but it would take five days to get here."

"Yay for imports. Guess you'll be begging rides from me until then." Dan's grin showed her he didn't mind the idea.

"Or my sister," Hailey added.

"Can we go to the movie?" Natasha piped up. "Deanna said we should go. I never been to a movie before. Hailey said it would be fun."

"Is that what Miss Deacon said?" Dan corrected, as he swung Natasha's hand, his eyes still on Hailey.

The flush heating her cheeks surprised her. To hide her confusion at seeing him, she bent over and picked up Natasha's skis, sliding them so the bindings locked together.

She and Dan had seen each other only in passing this morning when she'd arrived at his apartment to tutor Natasha. He had to get downstairs right away to deal with an influx of customers. He hadn't come up for lunch before the school bus picked up Natasha and Hailey to take them to the ski hill. So they hadn't had a chance to experience this new place they had come to.

And now he was here.

"Can we go, Daddy? Can we? Please?"

"I think it could be fun. But we don't need to talk about that now." Dan reached over and without a word took Natasha's skis from Hailey. "I'll bring those back," he said. "Natasha, you take your ski boots please." Then he turned back to Hailey. "I'll be back." His voice held a hint of promise and an echo of what had happened yesterday.

And sent her heart knocking against her rib cage. She wished she could be calmer about the situation. Wished she didn't feel this breathless eagerness each time she was around Dan. It was confusing and disconcerting.

And it made her feel like a high school kid again.

"I have to help the kids get on the bus." Hailey poked her thumb over her shoulder at the group of children behind her.

"I can wait." His added smile didn't help her inconsistent heartbeat.

As she walked toward the gathered children she had to calm herself. Get focused. Try to put the change in their relationship in perspective.

One day at a time, she reminded herself as she helped one little boy lift his skis onto the desk.

Ten minutes later fifteen subdued and tired grade one students were lined up at the bottom of the stairs by the bus parking lot, cheeks flaming red, drooping with weariness as they waited for the bus. A few parent-helpers stood watch, chatting amongst themselves.

"So why did Dan come to pick up Natasha?" Megan asked, joining Hailey at the back of the line.

Hailey sent a quick glance over her shoulder. Dan sat on a wooden bench, Natasha on his lap as he chatted with Tim, one of the men who did repairs on the skis and snowboards. He was sitting outside, drinking a cup of coffee. Hailey recognized him as an old classmate from school.

"Just being his usual protective self," Hailey said, keeping her words purposely evasive.

"I don't know about that," Megan said in a knowing tone. "Looks like he's paying more attention to you than Natasha."

Hailey stole another look and, just as Megan had said, though Dan had his arm around Natasha and was talking to Tim his eyes were on her. And he was smiling.

Megan caught her by the shoulder, her grin expanding. "Are you two a couple?"

"Not a couple," Hailey protested. Then, unable to keep everything tamped down, she said, "But we've spent some time together."

Megan squeezed Hailey's shoulder, barely able to contain her squeal of joy. "That's so cool. I was hoping—" She stopped herself there.

"Hoping what?" Hailey prompted, shooting her friend a puzzled frown.

Megan's eyes sparkled back at her. "Never mind."

And things came together. "You were playing matchmaker when you wanted me to tutor Natasha."

"Maybe. A little." Megan waggled her hand in a vague gesture. "And right now he is checking you out like he used to."

Hailey wished she could suppress her blush. Instead she turned her attention back to the children. "Cory, don't fall asleep, honey." She bent over and caught the little boy as he wavered on his feet. "Just hang on. Here's the bus."

And with a hiss of air brakes and crunch of tires on the snow, a long, yellow school bus pulled up in the parking lot.

The children came to life again and under the supervision of Megan, Hailey and the other parent-helpers, clanged up the metal stairs of the bus.

As the last child boarded, Dan joined her. "So, duties done here?" he asked.

Hailey watched as the doors swooshed shut behind the last adult, then nodded.

"Let's go then," he said.

But as the bus pulled away she caught Megan grinning out the window at them, giving her a discreet thumbs-up. Hailey hoped Dan didn't notice, but when she turned to go she caught his eyes flick from Megan to her.

And he was smiling.

"Can we go to the movie tomorrow, Daddy? Can we?" Natasha danced alongside Dan, hanging on to his gloved hand. His daughter's cheeks were pink from a combination of the cold air and excitement.

"Maybe," Dan said, playing along as he unlocked the door of the truck. "The store closes early on Saturday so we could."

"And Hailey can come," Natasha said before she got in the truck, her eyes shifting from Dan to Hailey and back.

Dan looked over at Hailey, who now stood beside him, her arm brushing his as she helped Natasha into the truck. "I think that might be a good idea," he said.

Kind of a clumsy way to ask her out, but Hailey's warm glance gave him hope.

"Yay. I'm so excited," Natasha shouted as she clambered into the truck.

Dan laid his arm on Hailey's, holding her back a moment. "That is, if you don't mind coming," he said, making the invitation more personal.

"I heard it was a really good movie," she said, her eyes flashing with humor.

"Four stars according to the paper," he replied.

"Sounds like a winner." Her smile grew and he felt a slow movement toward familiar territory. From the first day they'd acknowledged their attraction there had been an easy comfort between them. A sense of belonging that he never felt with anyone else.

"Are you going to stand there all day?" Natasha called out, clapping her hands like a queen summoning her subjects.

Hailey laughed and got in the truck, and as Dan walked around the front happiness mixed with anticipation bubbling up inside him.

He got in, put the truck in gear and as he headed out of the snow-covered parking lot his cell phone rang. Probably his father wondering where he was.

"Hey. What can I do for you?" he said as he spun the steering wheel of the truck toward the road.

"Dan. I'm so glad I finally connected with you."

A barb of dread hooked into his heart.

"Hello, Carla."

"I just thought I would call," Natasha's grandmother said, before he could say anything more. "See how Natasha is doing."

Checking up on him, he couldn't help thinking.

"Natasha is doing fine."

In his peripheral vision he caught Hailey's quick glance and Natasha's sudden interest.

"That's my gramma on the phone," Natasha informed Hailey in a whisper.

"We were wondering if we could come up for a visit?" Carla asked, in a deceptively reasonable tone.

Dan pulled off to one side of the road and parked. He would need all his attention for this phone call. He wished Natasha didn't have to overhear it.

Or Hailey.

"Can I call you back on this?" he said. "I'm kind of busy right now."

"Surely you can give me a simple answer."

Surely he couldn't because there was no simple answer. Natasha was settling into her life here. Having his in-laws over would disrupt the peace his daughter was enjoying and bring up old memories and pain for her.

Besides, he would be kidding himself if he thought this wouldn't become part of their campaign to get Natasha back.

He shot a quick glance over at Hailey, his mind shifting back to her conversation about the need to let Natasha deal with sorrow and Lydia's death.

But not yet, he thought. Not when things seemed to be moving to a better place in his life. He wasn't ready to analyze his and Hailey's relationship.

For now he knew it was right. And bringing Lydia back in the form of her parents would disrupt that too.

"I have to check my calendar. I'll call you back in a day or two."

"If we don't hear from you, then I'll call you as well," Carla said.

Dan tried not to see that as a threat. But as he hung up on her, he had to suppress a sense of foreboding.

He slammed his truck in gear and spun down the road.

"Everything okay?" Hailey asked.

Dan sucked in a deep breath, then backed off on the accelerator. No sense in getting themselves plowed into the ditch.

He eased out a tight smile. "Sure. Just fine. I'll bring you home and call you tomorrow about the movie. Maybe pick you up early and we could go for pizza?"

"That sounds like a great idea," Hailey said.

Natasha squealed with excitement. "Yay. We're going to have a pizza and movie night. That's rad."

Dan and Hailey both laughed and as they drove Hailey home he forced himself to relax. He didn't have to think about Carla and Alfred right now.

Help me, Lord, to take one day at a time, he prayed, *and to enjoy the day I have right now.*

Because no matter what, he couldn't suppress a sense of foreboding that, once Lydia's parents came to Hartley Creek, everything would change for the worse.

Chapter Eleven

"Do you think it will be a good movie? I hope it has a princess in it." Natasha wiggled in her seat, almost spilling the tub of popcorn on her lap.

"I don't think it does," Hailey said, pulling Natasha's tangled ponytail straight. All day Natasha had been taken care of by a young girl in high school but it seemed hair care wasn't one of Colleen's strengths.

"I don't mind. I think it will be fun no matter what." Natasha's gaze was riveted on the pictures flashing on the screen—advertisements and trivia games—and Hailey glanced over her head.

Dan grinned back at her and laid his arm across the back of Natasha's seat, his fingers within centimeters of her shoulder.

A light flutter of anticipation began in her midsection. Just as it had when she and Dan had gone to the movies. Except then they sat side by side, Hailey would lean her head on his shoulder and his arm reached all the way around her.

"Oh. Oh. I think it's starting," Natasha squealed, leaning forward as the lights dimmed. Sound blasted from the speakers surrounding them and images flickered on the screen.

They watched the trailers for upcoming movies and then, finally, the main feature started.

Anticipation curled in her middle as the movie studio logo came up with its triumphant music. How often had she and her sisters and cousins come here clutching their spare cash? Their entrée into other worlds—sailing across oceans with pirates, heading off into space, flying on horses across open plains—each adventure more amazing than the last.

Then, when she was older, tucked up against Dan's side living through drama, action, adventure and romance.

Dan's fingers brushed her shoulder. His touch was so light she might have imagined it. But sitting in the dark, with only his daughter between them, she had become hyperaware of his every movement.

She caught the sparkle of his eyes looking over at her.

They were flirting with each other. No other word for it.

And where would this go? What could come of it?

She quenched the annoying questions, lifted her hand and laid it against his, anchoring it to her shoulder.

But as they sat in the dark, connected, she knew they would have to talk about this. They weren't careless teenagers anymore, testing the waters of affection and attraction.

Natasha's presence was a potent reminder of what was at stake.

In spite of her reservations, Hailey kept her hand covering Dan's rough one as images flickered on the screen in front of them, a kaleidoscope of color and sound melding past and present. From time to time his hand would shift and she would look his way and they were young kids all over again.

Stolen glances, gentle touches.

She wished she could dismiss the swirling undercurrents. Wished she could simply pull her hand away and return to being Hailey Deacon, woman with a plan to leave.

But couldn't that plan change? Could she and Dan become what they once had been? Could she stay here?

As if he'd read her thoughts, Dan's hand slid below her hair and his fingers made slow, entrancing circles on the back of her neck. Just as he used to.

One day at a time, she reminded herself as shivers slipped up and down her spine.

All too soon the closing credits flowed up the screen. The houselights came up and Dan pulled his hand away from hers. Hailey blinked in the growing light and Natasha sat back in her chair, her expression rapt.

"That was so, so fun," she said, her voice quiet with awe. "Way better than television."

Hailey shot Dan a grin as she helped Natasha with her coat. "I'm guessing this is only the beginning of a whole new adventure."

"I can see my Saturday evenings flashing before my eyes."

"In Technicolor and surround sound," Hailey joked.

"Did you like the movie?" Natasha asked Hailey as she zipped closed the coat.

"It made me laugh," was all Hailey could say, because Dan had held her attention more than the story line playing out on the screen.

"I liked the part where the mouse said, 'Oh, no you don't, you rascal,' that was so, so funny," Natasha said, suddenly overcome with another fit of the giggles. "What part did you like the best, Hailey?"

As her mind scrambled for something she caught Dan's eye and saw his mouth quirk upward. He knew she was distracted but she wasn't letting him off easy.

"Why don't you ask your daddy what he liked the best?"

"Touché," was all he said, then he bent over to retrieve Natasha's popcorn bucket. "Do you want to keep this, munchkin?" he asked.

"I'm full," she said, placing a greasy hand on her stomach. "Can we watch the movie again tomorrow?" Natasha asked. "They said they are going to have it again tomorrow afternoon."

"We have church—"

"We have church tomorrow—"

As Hailey replied at the same time as Dan, she felt a flash of self-consciousness. She was Natasha's tutor, not her mother.

But the lines between the two were blurring. Which lent urgency to discussing their relationship. A little girl who'd had a lot to deal with was involved and they had better tread warily.

The thought was a sobering douse of cold water and Hailey turned away from Dan, moving out into the crowded aisle, joining the people leaving the theater.

"Hailey Deacon. Hold up a minute."

A familiar voice called out and Hailey turned in time to see Mia Verbeek, an old school-friend of hers, waddling up the aisle. Her short brown hair framed her face in a cute pixie cut. She looked sixteen but the four-year-old boy tugging on one hand and her mounded stomach proclaiming an advanced pregnancy told a different story.

"Hey, how are you doing?" Hailey asked, smiling at the sight of Mia.

"Same as last time I saw you. Pregnant," Mia said, pushing down on her stomach with one hand with a groan. "But we plug along."

"Where's Josh?"

"He's sick so I left him with my mom. Nico really, really wanted to come to the movie and I couldn't hit the matinee, so here we are."

"Hey, I heard rumors that you're buying the flower shop?" Hailey said, shuffling along with the crowd, leaving Dan and Natasha behind. "That's pretty ambitious." And puzzling. The last time she and Mia had coffee together, Mia was content to stay at home with her two boys, being a homemaker, a wife to Dean and getting the nursery ready for her twin girls.

"Girl's gotta do what a girl's gotta do," was Mia's ambiguous reply. Mia glanced back at the people coming up behind them. "So, I noticed you and Dan sitting together." Mia gave Hailey a broad wink. "Just like old times."

Hailey's mind shifted back to Natasha sitting between Dan and Hailey, a visible reminder of how different from old times their situation had become. "Not really. I'm just tutoring his daughter."

Mia playfully punched Hailey's shoulder with a fist. "You and Dan are like peanut butter and jam. I couldn't believe it when I found out he was back the same time you were, and now look at you two. I think you might be changing your mind about that job you were talking about," she added with a knowing grin.

Hailey felt a small lift of panic at the thought of her future changing because of what was happening between her and Dan. Did she dare change her plans? And if she didn't, what was she doing to Dan and Natasha?

Hailey pushed the future aside and gave Mia a quick grin. "I'm not making any plans one way or the other yet."

They reached the end of the crowded aisle and the crush of bodies dissipated as people moved into the foyer.

Mia's son, Nico, tugged on her arm, dancing from one foot to the other. "I have to go to the bathroom," he announced.

"Of course you do, after all that pop you drank. Hang on a few more seconds." Mia turned back to Hailey, her expression growing serious. "Speaking of plans, I'd love to get together with you again. I need… I just would like to visit with you."

Hailey frowned at the suddenly serious tone of her friend's voice. "Yeah. Sure. Just say when."

"Mommy. Please."

"I'll call you," Mia said, waggling her fingers at Hailey as she walked across the lobby, her son pulling her along.

"Was that Mia Strombitsky?" Dan asked, as he caught up to her, Natasha clinging to his hand.

Hailey looked back, unable to stop the silly flicker of her heart when their eyes connected.

"Yeah. Except she's Verbeek now. I hung out with her in high school. She's married now. Expecting twin girls."

"And I heard she has two boys already. That's a lot of kids," Dan said with a laugh as they walked into the foyer.

And as Hailey watched Mia negotiate the bathroom door a faint twinge of envy caught her. She'd always wanted lots of kids. Mia was the same age and already had four.

Hailey was still single and had none.

"Are you coming to our house again?" Natasha asked as they walked toward the outside door. "Are you tucking me in again and singing the special sleeping song?"

Hailey smiled down at the little girl as something deep and maternal moved through her.

"I'd like it if you came," Dan's deep voice added.

That was all she needed to hear.

A blast of cold, dark air greeted them as they stepped out of the warm movie house. Snow drifted down onto the cars parked in the parking lot of the movie theater, sparkling in the light cast by the streetlamps.

The air looked magical and as Hailey walked with Dan back to the truck, anticipation buzzed through her.

On the short drive back to the apartment, Natasha filled the silence with animated chatter about the movie, her favorite characters and what she would do if she ever met a talking mouse.

An hour and two cups of hot chocolate later, Natasha was tucked in her bed, cheeks shining from her bath, eyes glowing as she looked from Dan to Hailey. "And now you have to sing the song."

"Yes, your majesty," Hailey joked, settling down on one side of the single bed, Dan on the other. She rested her hand on the opposite side of Natasha and when Dan did the same, it was as if they created a sanctuary for the little girl.

And created a connection between her and Dan.

As they sang the song, Hailey felt her heart filling with a peculiar emotion. Affection for the little girl, but something deeper. Stronger.

Love.

Her voice faltered on the words, eliciting a puzzled frown from Dan. He shifted his hand to rest on her knee, giving it a light squeeze that did little for her equilibrium.

And as his eyes met hers, a promise glowed in their depths.

They got to the last verse and Dan's cell phone rang, bursting into the intimacy of the moment.

"Sorry," he mumbled as he pulled his phone out of his pocket and beat a hasty retreat.

Hailey finished the song, tucked the blankets around Natasha just the way she liked them, then giving in to an impulse bent over and kissed Natasha on the forehead.

It was the first time she had kissed the little girl and when she drew back, Natasha's eyes glowed.

"I love you, Miss Deacon," she said, suddenly sitting up and throwing her arms around her.

Her words were at one time both heartwarming and painful. Even while her declaration created an ache of yearning in Hailey's heart, it immediately made her think of what Natasha had lost. Lydia's death was the reason Natasha had attached to her so quickly.

Be careful, a voice warned her. *Tread very carefully with this little girl.*

Because she knew whatever she decided she would do in the future would have an impact on Natasha and her well-being.

"I don't think it will take her long to fall asleep," Dan said as he walked back to the living room.

Hailey stood in the center of the room, her hands fiddling with the ends of her scarf, as if uncertain what she should be doing. "That's good."

"Sorry about that phone call," he said, tossing his phone onto an end table in the living room. "Turns out I should have let it ring," he said with a heavy sigh.

"Bad news?"

He shook his head as he dropped onto the couch. He was thankful when Hailey followed suit.

He wasn't ready for her to go home. He wanted to spend some time, just the two of them. Just like old times.

"Actually, that was Natasha's other grandparents again. Lydia's parents. When they called yesterday I said I would call back, but things got busy today and I forgot. I knew they wouldn't." He shoved his hand through his hair, then dropped his arm along the back of the couch, his hand landing inches from Hailey's shoulder.

"What did they want?"

A weary sigh slipped out. "To visit Natasha."

"You don't sound pleased with the idea," Hailey said, tucking her feet under her.

"I don't know what to do about it. Natasha is still getting settled. I'm worried that them coming here will cause more problems."

Hailey twirled a strand of hair around her finger, her lips pursed.

"You look like you don't agree," Dan said.

"Your parents really enjoy having her around."

"They're thrilled. They hardly got to see her when she was little. It was hard enough for me to get my regular visits, let along bring her back here."

Hailey nodded, smiling. "They do dote on her."

"My father would give her every toy in the store if he had his way and my mother can't stop hugging her."

Hailey laughed, then lowered her hand, letting it rest on his. Her skin felt cool, soft, as he twined his fingers in hers. He wished his weren't so rough. "I know how much my grandparents loved us kids," she said, her voice quiet. "I remember my Nana telling me she would have done anything for us."

"And you would do anything for her," Dan said, tightening his grip on her hand.

"When I heard about her heart attack I couldn't come

back fast enough. I love her so much and can't imagine what my life would be like without her." Hailey gave him a trembling smile. "But at the same time, I sometimes wonder about my father's parents. Why they didn't contact my mother. I often wondered if they even cared about me and my sisters." She stopped there, biting her lip, looking away.

"You've never heard from them?"

"I've never heard from my father."

Her bitter tone surprised Dan. Hailey had never spoken of her father and Dan only knew that he had left her mother when Hailey was about eight.

"I used to wonder if they ever thought about us or wanted to see us." She pulled her hand away, lowering it to her lap.

The hitch in her voice surprised him. Hailey was always so tough. So sure of herself. But in the past few days he'd seen her cry. Twice. And now he was learning things that he'd never known before.

"I'm so sorry," he said, moving closer to her, putting his hand on her shoulder. "I never knew that."

"You don't need to feel sorry for me. I don't. It's just part of my reality." Hailey released a laugh, but kept her eyes down. "I think it's important, however, that Natasha doesn't have to deal with the same questions. The more people she has in her life that love her, the more secure she'll feel."

Dan blew out a sigh. "That makes sense, but I'm worried about the Andersons. They've been fighting for custody of Natasha ever since Lydia died. They're not scared to toss money toward a lawyer if it means getting Natasha back. Carla has never made a secret of the fact that they want Natasha."

"That's too bad," Hailey said. "It's sad when families resort to fighting instead of talking things through."

"For now, though, I think it's best if they keep their distance. They've seen enough of Natasha before, when Lydia had custody of her. I had to fight for every minute I spent with my own daughter. I'm not about to let that happen again." Dan let his hand rest on Hailey's shoulder, shifting himself a bit closer. "But I don't want to talk about the Andersons right now."

Hailey tilted her head to one side, her smile showing him her willingness to go along with the change in topic. "What do you want to talk about?"

Dan let his fingers twine in her hair as his other hand caught hers. "I think we both know something is happening between us. We've been here before."

"And yet it's different," Hailey said, finishing his thoughts like she used to.

"A lot different." He stroked her hand with his thumb, making gentle circles as he tried to find exactly the right words.

Then Hailey tossed her hair back and looked directly at him, holding his gaze. "Do you ever wonder where we would be if things had been… If things hadn't happened the way they did?"

"I tried not to. But lately it's been harder."

"Why?"

"Because I see you every day. And every day I'm reminded of what I lost."

He moved closer, sliding his hand up her arm, capturing her shoulder. "I'm so sorry for the way things turned out," he said. "But you need to know I've never forgotten about you. I thought about you all the time."

"But when I saw you that first time, you seemed so

angry. So remote." The confusion on her face was mirrored in her voice.

Dan touched her cheek with his forefinger, as if she was a bird that could take flight if he made the wrong move or said the wrong thing.

"I had to be that way. I had to protect myself."

"From me?"

"From what I felt for you." He stroked her face, then shifted his hand around the back of her head. "From what I knew I lost when I left."

"I'm glad you told me about Lydia," she said, stroking his arm. "It changed a lot for me. Explained so much."

"I was scared and I missed you like crazy." He didn't want to talk anymore. Words were getting in the way. He pulled her close and kissed her gently. She returned his kiss and then rested against him, cradled against his chest, held close in his arms.

This was how it should be, Dan thought, easing out a sigh as he pressed a kiss to her temple.

"I don't know the right words to use," he finally said, "but I feel like this is right. Having you in my arms, well, it feels like home."

He could feel her smile.

"I know what you mean."

They sat quietly, enjoying the moment.

Then, she pulled away, her expression serious.

"So where do we go from here?" she asked, folding her hands over each other.

"I'd like to say we can take it one day at a time," he replied, knowing they needed to have this discussion. "But I don't know if I have that luxury."

"Your life is more complicated now because of Natasha," Hailey said, voicing the words for him again.

"I have to think about her. She's my first priority."

He didn't know what else to say. Didn't know where they were supposed to go from here. They couldn't go back to the place they were before—two kids making all kinds of plans. They had to deal with the issues between them.

"I don't want to lose you again," Hailey finally said.

"I don't want to lose you either."

"Then we have no choice *but* to take this one step at a time," Hailey said quietly. "But to always keep Natasha's well-being our first priority."

Dan nodded. What Hailey said was sensible and mature. They had a plan.

So why did he feel as if he was missing something?

Chapter Twelve

"How did things go today?" Dan bent over and picked up Natasha's backpack from the floor of the school's hallway.

"Really well, didn't they, Natasha?" Hailey asked as she zipped up Natasha's coat.

Natasha nodded. "I made a clay mountain today," she said, demonstrating with her hands.

"And you did a good job," Hailey said.

Behind them a couple of children ran down the hall toward the double doors, screaming for the bus to wait, the excitement of Friday adding a shrill note to their voices.

"Tell your daddy what else you did today," Hailey said as she handed her toque and mitts to the little girl.

"I wrote in my journal. And Miss Tolsma is going to write back to me," Natasha beamed as she tugged on her toque and shoved her mitts in her pocket.

On Monday morning when Hailey had come to the apartment to teach Natasha, she had floated the idea of Natasha coming to school for a few mornings. Thankfully, Natasha had been excited about the idea. Then on Thursday she had decided, on her own, that she wanted to start coming for the full day on Friday, today.

However, that meant it was also the first day Hailey had seen Dan only for a few moments, this morning when he'd dropped Natasha off at school and now.

As Hailey straightened she glanced Dan's way. "Do you have a plan for her care after school?" she asked. Though they had seen each other every day, Hailey knew things would change for her and Dan once Natasha attended school every day.

"I asked Colleen, the girl that took care of Natasha last week, to come after school as well as Saturday," Dan said as he took Natasha's hand.

"That's good. I'm glad things are coming together." Though she had to admit she felt left out of the loop.

"They are, but, well, I missed you today," he said quietly, speaking thoughts aloud that she'd had of him too.

Hailey glanced at Natasha, who was looking straight ahead, seemingly lost in her own thoughts, then she looked back at Dan, her heart warming at his crooked smile and intent gaze.

"I missed you too," she said quietly.

"Do you want to come over for supper tomorrow night? Mom brought me a couple of casseroles today and I've got more than enough for the three of us."

"Tomorrow?" Hailey couldn't keep the disappointment out of her voice. "I promised my Nana and my sister I'd go out for supper with them. It's Shannon's birthday."

His expression mirrored her feelings.

"But I can come Sunday," she added.

Natasha snapped out of wherever she was. "Sunday? I want to go skiing Sunday."

"Sorry, honey," Dan said. "I am busy after church and can't take you."

"Hailey can take me." Natasha turned to Hailey with a winning smile. "Can you?"

Hailey looked down, recognizing the same breathless enthusiasm that had sent her, whenever she could scrape together enough money for a lift ticket, to Misty Ridge.

"I'm not busy," she said, but then glanced at Dan to make sure it was okay before she offered to take Natasha. The reluctance on his expression was a bit of a puzzle to her. "But maybe your daddy wants you to spend time with your gramma."

"I see Gramma all the time. Please, Daddy, can I go?" Natasha turned to Dan, pulling on his hand. "Then Hailey can take me home and we can have supper. Please, Daddy?"

Natasha scrunched up her face in the same pleading gesture Hailey had been subjected to from time to time.

Dan bit his lip, obviously reluctant, which puzzled her.

Then Natasha turned her pleading gaze toward Hailey. "Please tell my daddy to let me go."

Hailey held up her hands, giving Dan an out. "I'm not getting involved. If your daddy doesn't want me to take you, then that's the way it is."

Dan looked as if he was about to say something when Natasha pulled on his hand again.

"I'll be really good and I'll eat all my casserole tomorrow night and I won't spit out the mushrooms."

Hailey suppressed a laugh and even Dan's expression lightened.

"Okay. You can go," he finally conceded.

"Yay, yay, yay," Natasha called out, pumping the air with a fist, then released Dan's hand and danced around Hailey. "We can go skiing again. We can go skiing again." The little girl leaned against Hailey, looking up at her. "And then Sunday night you can come for supper because you can't come Saturday. And you can stay and sing me a song. And then you can kiss my daddy again."

Hailey went cold and taut at Natasha's words, her gaze flying to Dan's.

He looked equally shocked. She saw him swallow, as lost for words as she was.

"I saw you," Natasha said, frowning as if she didn't understand the moment of surprise holding Dan and Hailey in its thrall. "And it made me happy."

Well, that was a small blessing, Hailey thought. But still.

Dan pulled his hand over his face, then blew out his breath. He looked as surprised and agitated as Hailey felt.

"So are you coming Sunday?" Natasha asked, taking charge of the awkward moment. "You can come and pick me up after church."

"I guess so, now that it's okay with your daddy." Though she still sensed his reluctance.

Dan took Natasha's hand, then shot Hailey a quick glance. "So we'll see you Sunday after church?"

"I'll be by at about one," Hailey said.

He hesitated a moment, then said, "We need to talk."

She guessed he alluded to Natasha's little revelation and nodded. "Sunday evening."

"It'll be okay." Dan brushed his finger over her cheek, his light touch even more reassuring than his smile. "See you then."

As they walked away from her, and the door closed behind them, Hailey was surprised at the sudden jittery feelings gripping her.

She dismissed her concerns with a shake of her head. Sunday she would be spending time with Natasha. And then she would be having dinner with Dan and Natasha.

Just like a little family.

The thought erased the misgivings in her soul. Things were moving along step by step and they were moving to a good place.

* * *

"Are you sure you don't want dessert?" Hailey asked her grandmother from across the table in the noisy restaurant. Carter, Hailey's cousin, sat beside Nana and Emma sat beside him.

They looked happy, Hailey thought, watching as Carter bent his head toward Emma's darker one to catch what she said. Hailey's own happiness made it easier to watch the two lovebirds.

"I'm quite full," Nana said, "And until I can start walking more frequently, I had better watch my caloric intake."

"That might be a while before you can go walking regularly," Carter said, raising his head. "I heard the snow will be around until end of March."

Shannon shivered. "That sounds depressing. When I move, I'm going somewhere warmer."

"Move?" Nana perked up at that.

"In spite of not being able to walk, you've been feeling pretty good, haven't you?" Hailey asked her grandmother, making a quick switch in topic. Neither Shannon nor Hailey had told their Nana about their potential moves, knowing how much their plans would upset her.

Though Hailey was sure she wouldn't be moving anywhere.

We need to talk. Dan's words echoed in her mind, reassuring and mysterious at the same time.

"I'm feeling a bit tired yet, which disappoints me," Nana said, glancing around the table. "But sitting here in the restaurant with my grandchildren and grandchild-to-be makes my heart very happy." Nana turned her attention to her oldest granddaughter. "I'm so glad we could do this for your birthday, Shannon, and I hope we can do this many, many more years."

"I'm glad we could do this too," was all Shannon would say.

Hailey knew the reason for her evasive reply. If things went the way Shannon wanted, she would be gone once all the cousins made their way back to Hartley Creek. She had gotten a job as a travel nurse and was moving to Chicago. Hailey had been surprised her sister had taken the job. Up until a year ago Shannon had loved her job working as an emergency room nurse. Of course, she had also loved her fiancé, Arthur, until he'd called off the wedding two weeks before the date. The shame of that public humiliation had Shannon packing up to leave town. If it hadn't been for Nana's heart attack, Shannon would have been long gone.

And what about the job waiting for you? Hailey brushed the question aside. She wasn't doing anything about future plans until after Sunday. When she and Dan would have their "talk."

The buzz of conversation around them created lulling background noise. Beside their table sat a couple still wearing their ski jackets and pants, conversing in German. Across from them, a group of young people wearing the funkier clothing of snowboarders chattered about their exploits on the hill that day, various accents sparkling in their earnest conversation.

"I missed this," Hailey mused aloud, her hands wrapped around the oversize mug of tea.

"Missed what?" Carter asked, pulling a toothpick out of its plastic wrapper.

"The ambience of this town in the winter. All the different types and nationalities of people that come here to ski and board."

Shannon glanced around the restaurant and Hailey

saw a melancholy smile drift across her sister's mouth. "Yeah. I know what you mean."

"Things certainly have changed in this town since I was young," Nana said with a slow shake of her well-coiffed head as she looked around the busy restaurant. "I remember when there weren't nearly as many places to eat or hotels and most of the people that lived in this town were connected to the coal industry or the railroad."

"Lots of people still are," Hailey assured her. "It's a strong community. A good place to live."

This netted her a wry look from Shannon and Hailey guessed her sister would be asking her about her comment when she brought Hailey home.

"Speaking of places to live, have you started looking yet?" Shannon asked her Nana.

Since her heart attack, Nana had been looking at leaving the ranch she had moved onto as a young bride and purchasing a house in town. But to date, she hadn't found anything.

"I'm in no rush," Nana said. "But I don't want to talk about a house just yet. For now, I'm glad we could spend this time together," Nana said with a gentle look for each of her grandchildren. "Though I think it's time for this old lady to get home."

She lifted a finger to indicate that she wanted the bill.

Their waiter sauntered over, a study in indifference. "So ladies, is there anything else I can get you?" he asked, his tattooed hand resting on his hip, both eyes resting on Shannon.

"I'd like the bill," Nana said briskly, obviously unimpressed with his easygoing attitude.

"Of course," he said with one more lingering look at Shannon, then left.

"The service is getting entirely too casual here," Nana

sniffed. "And I don't like the way he flirted with you, Shannon."

Hailey nudged her sister with her elbow. "I don't think Shannon minded that much."

Shannon shot her sister an oblique look. "Not interested."

When their waiter returned, Nana and Carter had a mini tussle over the bill but Nana won out, as she always did.

Ten minutes later Hailey and Shannon were waving Carter's truck off, its taillights blinking at the intersection. Then watched it turn onto the road leading to the highway that would take them home.

"That was nice," Hailey said as she pulled her coat around her. A sudden wind had picked up, sending chilly fingers snaking down her back.

"I'm so glad to see Nana looking so much better," Shannon said, pressing the button on her keychain to unlock her car, which was parked down the street from the restaurant.

"She seems a lot happier, though I think a lot of that is just because she's got most of us around for now." Hailey ducked into Shannon's compact car and shivered as Shannon started it up. "I'll be so glad when my own car is fixed," she announced, her breath a white fog in the cold interior of the car.

"When is it ready?" Shannon asked as she put her car into gear. Her wheels spun, then gained traction as she turned onto the street.

"Monday. So I was wondering if I could borrow your car tomorrow. I'm taking Natasha to the ski hill."

Shannon shot her an oblique look. "You seem to be spending a lot of extracurricular time with Dan," Shannon returned.

Hailey hunched her shoulders, her hands buried in her pockets, wishing she didn't feel she had to defend herself. "I am still Natasha's tutor."

"Yeah, but you're not Dan's girlfriend anymore. And you used to talk as badly about Dan as I talk about Arthur the snake."

The only sound following her sister's comment was the squeaking of tires on the snow and the hum of the car's heater fan. Hailey knew Shannon was simply watching out for her, but she didn't want to hear her own misgivings spoken aloud.

"I'm just telling you to be careful," Shannon said, turning the fan down. "He's a guy and we both should know by now guys can't be trusted."

"I was the one that broke up with Dan before he left, remember?"

"Only because you wanted to beat him to it. Remember?"

Hailey did. After Austin's funeral Dan had retreated so far from her she'd known in only a matter of time he would finally sever their fragile connection before he moved away.

"It's different now." She spoke the words quietly, as if unsure of the strength of her emotions. "I feel such a strong connection to him. It just feels…it feels right."

"Feelings are all well and good, but you need to be smart about this," Shannon said as she turned onto the street leading to Hailey's apartment. "He broke your heart once before and you didn't even know why."

"It was because of Austin."

Shannon slowed and parked in front of Hailey's apartment. She looked ahead, her lips puckered in an expression of concern. Then she turned to Hailey, her long hair framing her face, the light from the dashboard casting her wide eyes and narrow nose into shadow.

"You know, I always thought that was a lame excuse on his part. He lost a brother, but you lost a good friend too. You were grieving too." Shannon was quiet, as if expecting Hailey to respond to that. "Has he said anything about why he left? What his real reasons were?"

Hailey pressed her fingers to her forehead. She didn't want to be confused or to go back to that horrible time when it had seemed as if her heart had been cut out of her chest.

"That's in the past. Why go there?"

"Because sometimes you need to go back before you can go ahead," Shannon said.

Her words struck a chord deep within Hailey's heart. She knew her sister was right. "But things are going so well." Hailey turned to her sister, feeling as if she had to explain. "I never cared for someone the way I care for Dan," she said. "You know that. I tried dating other guys, but it was never the same. Now, being with him, I feel like I'm whole again."

"And what about his daughter?"

"I think she really cares for me too."

Shannon's doubtful expression didn't shift one centimeter.

"I'm happy now," Hailey said, willing her sister to understand. It was as if she needed Shannon's blessing to eradicate the concerns roaming the deepest recesses of her mind. "Happier than I've been in a long time. Surely that has to mean something?"

"I think it does," Shannon finally said, reaching over and covering Hailey's hand, granting her a bit of reassurance. "But I'm just telling you to be careful. You really don't know why he left, or why he felt he had to leave.

I think you need to find out more about what happened before you move on. Besides, you have Natasha to think about. If this doesn't work out, it could be devastating for her."

Hailey nodded, knowing her sister was right.

Then Shannon squeezed her hand. "I'll be praying for you."

Hailey eked out a smile. "Thanks for that."

"I'll stop by tomorrow morning. You can bring me to work and then the car is yours the rest of the day."

"Thanks, sis." Then Hailey stepped out of the car, the chilly air cooling the heat of her cheeks. She fumbled in her purse for her keys, and when she had them in her grasp she turned and waved at her sister.

Shannon waved back, tooted the horn and drove away.

But as Hailey walked up the flight of stairs to her apartment, Shannon's words resounded in time to each footfall echoing in the stairwell.

Be careful. Be careful.

Chapter Thirteen

"You got everything you'll need?" Dan asked, handing Hailey an extra pair of bright red mittens with white maple leaves on them. "Snacks? Extra socks?"

Hailey nodded as she stuffed the mittens into the backpack sitting on the floor of the apartment's front entrance. "I think we're well provided." As their eyes met he caught an excited sparkle in her gaze.

He and Natasha had slept in this morning and missed church. As a result he'd been dogged with guilt all morning. But underneath his guilt crept an uneasiness that had nothing to do with missing church and everything to do with Natasha going on the ski hill with Hailey. But he had to let her go. He didn't want Hailey to think he didn't trust her with his daughter. Especially not after allowing her to go with the class.

That was different. That was an organized trip.

Dan shoved his hand through his hair, then grabbed the back of his neck. "Okay, then. I guess you should get going."

"Not yet," Natasha called out, lurching to her feet, her movements hampered by her snow pants and coat. "I have to get my wings."

"You won't need them, honey," Dan said, shooting Hailey a pleading look to help him out.

"But they'll help me ski better," Natasha complained, already heading off to her bedroom.

"One of these days she's got to stop wearing those silly things," Dan muttered as she left.

"I'll let her wear them for a couple of runs, then convince her she can ski without them," Hailey assured him. "She doesn't wear them to school, so that's a good thing."

"I suppose I should be thankful for small blessings," Dan said.

Hailey zipped up the backpack and stood. "So, I'm ready to go."

Dan nodded, his previous misgivings returning. "So you'll be careful, right?" The question burst out before he could think about it.

Hailey's light frown bothered him, but he couldn't help himself.

"Of course I will."

Still he hesitated.

"She'll be okay," Hailey said. "Please don't worry about her. I'll take care of her like she was my own."

Dan experienced a precarious happiness and, at the same time, a thrum of concern. He and Hailey. Was he making a mistake?

But as his eyes held hers, he felt that what was happening between him and Hailey was right and true.

He also knew that since he'd kissed Hailey, the restlessness that had been his constant companion since he'd left Hartley Creek had settled.

Hailey glanced past him, then her expression grew even more serious. "Has she said anything more about… about what she saw?"

"You mean us kissing?"

"Yeah. That."

"No. And I haven't had a chance to talk to her about it." He heard Natasha rattling around in her drawers and decided to let her root around on her own for a few more moments. He turned back to Hailey, trying to figure out the best way to express what he wanted to say.

And at that moment her cell phone rang.

Hailey drew it out of her pocket, glanced at it, then turned away from Dan to answer it.

"Yes. This is Hailey Deacon... Oh, hello. No, it's fine to call me now. I realize you're probably busy during the week." She shot Dan a look of concern, then took a few steps farther into the house, going around a corner.

To give her some privacy he went back to Natasha's room to help her out. The room was an explosion of clothing and toys. "What happened here?" he asked Natasha, who was on her knees, head in her closet, as she tossed clothes and shoes over her shoulder.

"I can't find them," her muffled voice called out, close to panic. "They were from my mommy and I can't find them."

Dan walked over to the closet and pulled Natasha to her feet with a swish of her snow pants. Her face was beet-red and her hair a damp tangle. Poor kid was cooking-hot, wearing her ski clothes in the house.

"I think you left them in the bathroom the last time you wore them," he said. "In the cupboard where the towels are."

Natasha sniffed and when she grinned Dan knew she remembered too. "Thanks, Daddy. I don't want to lose them. They came from my mommy and they are special."

Her comment about Lydia brought up his misgivings. He felt as if he and Hailey hovered on the cusp of something that would change everything for his daughter. He needed to know where Natasha was emotionally before he and Hailey made any kind of commitment.

The word resounded in his mind as he knelt down, looking directly into his daughter's eyes.

Commitment. Was he ready? Were he and Hailey really heading in that direction? He tested the thought as he brushed a few strands of hair back from his daughter's red face.

"Honey, remember you said that you saw me and Miss Deacon kissing?"

Her expression shifted and she gave him what could only be described as a flirty grin. "Yes. I did," she said, clasping her hands in front of her and twisting back and forth.

"How did you feel about that?"

Natasha lifted her shoulders and giggled. "I felt happy." Then she leaned closer, whispering. "Are you and Miss Deacon in love?"

How did she know this stuff?

"We like each other" was all he could say for now. He didn't know if he dared mention love yet. Not in front of his daughter and not even to himself.

As for Hailey, there were moments he was sure she sensed his misgivings. At times he felt as if his life was complicated and tangled and he wasn't sure how to find the ends and make them whole. He often felt much of his uncertainty hearkened to the past, but what good would going back do? He had already told Hailey about Lydia. Austin's death was far in the past and had no bearing on his and Hailey's relationship.

"Now can we go get my wings my mommy gave me?" Natasha said, tugging on his hand, pulling him into the present.

Dan pushed himself to his feet and went to the bathroom to find his daughter's precious wings.

Interesting that Natasha had no trouble melding her past and present—Lydia and Hailey. As he pulled the glittery wings out of the laundry basket he wished it were as easy for him.

When they got back, Hailey held her phone, frowning at it as if it had just given her bad news.

"Is everything okay?" Dan asked, hurrying to her side. "Is it your grandmother?"

Hailey shook her head, looking up at him. "No. It was the school that offered me that fall job. They want me to come earlier."

She looked as if she expected something from him, but he wasn't sure what to say. Did he dare encourage her to reconsider taking the job?

Were they even at that point?

Your daughter saw you kissing Hailey. You know you care about her and she cares for you.

Once again it was as if they stood across from each other with a space between them that he had to figure out how to cross.

"Can we go?" Natasha called out, rescuing them both from the uncertainty of the moment.

"Yeah. Sure," Dan said, turning to her. He bent down and kissed her on the cheek. "You be careful and listen to Miss Deacon, okay?"

"I will," she assured him. She gave him a quick hug, then with a rustle of snow pants and jacket, walked over to Hailey, tugging on her hand. "Let's go," she said.

Without another look at Dan, Hailey pocketed her phone, grabbed the knapsack and headed toward the door.

"You forgot to say goodbye to my daddy," Natasha said. "You can kiss him too if you want."

Dan groaned inwardly, but Hailey didn't seem flustered by his daughter's comment.

"See you later, Dan," she said, her smile flickering at the corner of her mouth.

"Have fun, you two," was all he said.

And as the door closed behind them, he realized they hadn't finalized their plans for tonight.

With a swish of her skis and a spray of snow, Natasha came to a halt in front of Hailey, executing a picture-perfect parallel stop.

"That was excellent," Hailey said, clapping her hands. "Very good."

Natasha beamed up at Hailey. "I'm a really good skier."

"You are."

"When can I use a snowboard like you do?" she asked, pointing her skis downhill for her next turn, arms up, knees bent, showing perfect form.

"When you know everything there is to know about skiing," Hailey said, following Natasha, the sun sparkling off the snow on the hill. "That's how I started."

They had moved from the learning hill to the bunny hill. Natasha had easily mastered the T-bar and was quickly gaining confidence going down the longer hill.

"But I know a lot," Natasha said, flashing Hailey a grin over her shoulder. "And I bet I can go on the big hill."

"I don't know about that," Hailey said. Though she was sure Natasha could easily navigate the most basic green run, she was hesitant to follow through.

Especially with Dan's warnings to be careful ringing in her ears.

"Deanna went on the big hill," Natasha announced as they quickly came to the bottom of the bunny hill. "I saw her going up with her mom and dad. And she doesn't ski as good as me."

Trouble was, that wasn't an idle boast. Natasha had more control and could stop much more quickly than Deanna could, but Deanna was with her parents, who were responsible for her.

Natasha was with Hailey, who was no relative.

But you kissed her father.

Though Hailey suppressed that thought, embarrassment still heated her face.

"I know, but I promised your dad I would take care of you."

"Natasha. Natasha."

A little girl's voice rang out and Hailey turned to see a lime-green dynamo come barreling toward them. Deanna.

She snowplowed to a stop in front of them, her hands flailing as she tried to catch her balance. She grinned at them, pushing her helmet back on her head. "That was fun," she announced, then turned to Natasha. "Are you going on the chairlift too?"

Natasha made a face of disgust. "No. I'm 'posed to stay on the bunny hill."

"You can come with me," Deanna announced, turning and skating with her skis toward the chairlift.

"Hey, hold up, Deanna," Hailey called out. "Where's your mom and dad?"

"They were with my brother. They know I'm here. I told them on the radio." Deanna held up her handheld radio to show Hailey, then shoved it back into her pocket and got in the lift line.

"Honey, you can't go on the lift by yourself," Hailey said, trying to stop her. "Come back here."

"I been already. I know how to ski." Deanna got in line, working her way to the front.

Deanna was not competent enough to go on the hill by herself and Hailey doubted the liftees would stop her. Hailey couldn't believe her parents let her get ahead of them like that. She looked from Natasha to Deanna and made a sudden decision.

"Deanna, wait," Hailey called out. "We'll go with you."

"Yay," Natasha yelled, already heading toward the lift.

Thankfully, Deanna stepped out of the line and let Hailey and Natasha catch up to her. Deanna was even more headstrong than Natasha. If Hailey went along, hopefully she could control Deanna and prevent potential injury.

As they moved to the head of the line, Hailey laid down the law with Natasha's friend. "Deanna, you have to listen to me. If you don't, I'll take away your lift ticket and you won't be able to ski anymore," she warned, using her sternest voice.

Deanna glowered at her, but thankfully, from previous run-ins with Hailey in the classroom, she knew Hailey meant business and would follow through.

"Okay," she said.

When they got to the front of the line Hailey maneuvered the girls, pulling them along with her hands, and got them in place. The cables of the lift creaked, the wheels hummed, then the chair came around. Thankfully the liftee slowed the approach of the chair even more and helped Deanna on while Hailey tended to Natasha.

Then, with a whoosh, the chair swung away and off the ground. Hailey settled the girls in and lowered the metal bar with a clunk. Okay. This was it. They were committed now.

"I'd like you to call your parents on your radio," Hailey said to Deanna, once they were underway. "Tell them where we are."

Deanna nodded, pulled the radio out of her pocket and pushed the call button. "I'm on the Crow's Nest chairlift with Miss Deacon," she said into the radio. She released the button and a female voice squawked back. "Okay, honey. Make sure you're back at the chalet at three."

And that, it seemed, was that.

"Look behind us," Deanna said as she shoved the radio back in her pocket. "We can see Hartley Creek."

Natasha looked around and gasped. "Look how high we are, Hailey." Below them lay the town, the buildings small squares along the grid of the streets, the river bisecting the town in a snow-covered ribbon of white.

"I can see my daddy's store." Natasha pointed, her movements making the chair swing.

She turned to Hailey, a huge grin on her face. "Thanks for taking me up here. I'm so excited."

Hailey smiled back and though she was glad Natasha didn't seem frightened, she sent up a prayer for safety for all of the girls.

They hung suspended in space; the only sound was the creak and hum of the motors pulling the chairs along. As their chair headed toward the top of the hill, the usual sense of anticipation gripped Hailey.

As long as she could remember she'd spent every winter weekend on this hill, either boarding or helping with the lifts to pay for her boarding. It was like her second home and it was where she and Dan had first declared they were a couple.

Her heart shifted at the thought of him and she wondered if he would ever come on the hill again. He used to have the same passion she did, the same sense of adventure. She couldn't imagine living in town and not ever going on the hill.

She wondered if he would ever get over Austin's death and, once again, wondered why it had put so much distance between them. But he never mentioned Austin's name and never talked about his brother, and she guessed that part of Dan's reluctance to let Natasha on the hill was rooted in Austin's death. Yes, Austin was his brother, but surely he would have gotten through the worst part of his grief after seven years?

When they got to the top of the hill, the dismount went smoothly and Hailey took a moment to set the girls straight as she strapped her other foot into her binding.

"Okay, girls. You have to listen to me, right?" Hailey said, putting on her sternest voice. "We are taking the easiest run, but you have to make sure you go all the way back and forth across the hill so you don't end up going too fast."

Natasha nodded and Deanna just shrugged.

"Remember what I said about your ticket?" Hailey warned Deanna.

"Yeah. I'll listen."

"Good. Now, this isn't hard, Natasha. It's like the bunny hill, only longer, so you have to stop once in a while for a rest. I'll go first and you follow me and do exactly what I say, okay?"

They both nodded and with another prayer to settle her own concerns, Hailey headed out. She looked back and first Natasha and then Deanna followed her.

After the fifth turn, Hailey allowed herself to relax. Both girls listened and did what she told them and took their time going down the large hill. By the time they got to the bottom Natasha was so excited she wanted to go immediately again.

So they did.

Natasha was in her glory and as they started down the hill for the third time she was laughing and relaxed. Another skier is born, Hailey thought, watching as Natasha made her turns a little sharper, angled herself down the hill, gaining speed.

But, thankfully, she always listened to Hailey.

Halfway down the run Hailey stopped at the edge to wait for Natasha and Deanna and to check her helmet. As she unbuckled it, she turned, and looked up.

Natasha was halfway across the open space when Deanna, who was about two turns behind, made a sharp turn and came flying down the hill. She was a blur of neon-green.

And she was out of control.

One foot lifted off the ground as she tried to make a turn to slow down. But she was moving too fast. She tried again, arms flailing. She avoided hitting a mother with her little boy, avoided an older man, but kept coming.

"Turn, turn," Hailey called out, unable to do anything else. The little girl was uphill from her. All Hailey could do was yell instructions and hope Deanna didn't plow into anyone as she tried to slow down. "Snowplow, push on your downhill edge, push, push."

Deanna tried to regain control and managed to form a snowplow. She wouldn't make it, Hailey thought, watching in horror as Deanna headed straight toward Hailey and the trees behind her.

No time to kick off her board. All Hailey could do was try to position herself to slow the girl down.

Deanna came right at her, Hailey reached out and scooped her arm around Deanna's waist. The momentum of the little girl's speed pulled Hailey off balance. They landed together, rolling down the hill, a collision of arms and legs and skis. Snow showered over them, covering Hailey's face, blinding her as she hung on to Deanna.

Hailey heard Deanna screaming as she tried to get her board under her to dig in the snow. Finally, after what seemed like an age, they skidded to a halt. In the melee Hailey had lost her helmet. Melting snow covered her face and slid down the back of her neck and pushed up the front of her jacket.

Deanna lay against her, sobbing, one ski off her foot, the other still attached.

"Are you okay, honey?" Hailey asked, hurriedly brushing the snow off her face, blinking it out of her eyes, trying to look at Deanna.

"I'm scared," Deanna wailed.

Then Hailey cranked her head around.

Natasha. Where was Natasha? Hailey yelled her name, her head whipping around as she tried to find the little girl.

"I'm here." Natasha's voice was a tiny, wobbly sound from just above Hailey.

Hailey craned her neck. Relief sluiced through her when she saw Natasha sitting on the snow a couple of feet behind her.

"Hailey. Your face," Natasha called out, pointing. "You've got blood on your face."

Hailey reached up and touched her face with her gloved hand. But she couldn't feel anything.

"Are you all okay?" A woman's voice called out as a skier came to a stop beside them. When Hailey looked up, the woman's eyes grew wide and with a few quick flicks of her ski poles, she was out of the bindings of her skis.

And as Hailey blinked again, she realized that it wasn't melting snow running down her face. It was blood.

* * *

"So you haven't seen them all afternoon?" Dan asked one of the liftees working on the small chairlift situated beside the bunny hill.

"No, man. Sorry." The kid whipped his head back, tossing his shoulder-length hair back from his face, his multipierced ears glinting in the sun. He caught the chair coming around the turn, held it and helped a couple of giggling young girls onto it. "I saw them for most of the morning. Next thing I know she booked it for the Crow's Nest."

The main chairlift going up the hill.

Dan pushed down his panic as he walked back to the chalet. Hailey knows what she's doing, he told himself. It would be fine.

Standing by the stairs leading to the chalet, a middle-aged couple waited for him. The woman wore a thin wool blazer over a skirt and leather boots and despite the sun pouring down on the mountain, she shivered, the silk scarf around her throat offering her scant protection from the cold.

The man had his hands pushed deep into his wool top-coat, his groomed and graying hair glinting in the sun.

Mr. and Mrs. Anderson. Lydia's parents. Natasha's grandparents. They had showed up at the store twenty minutes ago, demanding to see Natasha. Immediately.

Dan had explained that Hailey would bring her back when the hill was closed, but they couldn't wait to see their granddaughter and make sure she was okay.

Thankfully, his parents were able to take care of the store. So he'd led the Andersons here. And then started looking for Hailey and Natasha.

"Did you find them?" Carla asked as he walked across the snow-packed ground toward them. "We checked the rental shop, but they hadn't returned the equipment and they weren't anywhere in the main lodge or the coffee shop or the restaurant."

"It's a big place. We could easily have missed them," Dan said, squinting against the sun glinting off the snow as he looked up the main hill.

The run coming directly toward them was the easiest on the mountain. If they weren't on the bunny hill the chances were good they were on that one.

He would have a few words to share with Hailey if that were the case. Though he hadn't specifically said that Natasha couldn't go down the big hill, it had been assumed.

Skiers and snowboarders in brightly colored coats and pants flowed down the hill, all coming from various runs, funneling toward the main chairlift. But Dan couldn't spot Natasha's bright red suit or Hailey's distinctive red-and-orange coat.

He looked over toward the bunny hill again, checking all the bodies going up and coming down but there was no one he recognized.

"What's going on over there?" Mr. Anderson asked, pointing one gloved hand toward the main run.

Dan turned and his heart flopped in his chest.

A little girl wearing a neon-green coat and pants was being led by a woman on skis. And behind her came Natasha and Hailey. Hailey had lost her helmet and she was holding something against her forehead.

Was she hurt?

"Wait here," he told the Andersons, and with his blood rushing in his ears he ran across the hill, kicking up lumps of snow as he went.

"What happened? What's going on?" he called out as he came near the little group.

"Daddy. Daddy. Hailey had an accident. Deanna ran over her," Natasha called out. "She's bleeding."

Something deep in his gut downshifted, like a truck hitting black ice. Dan's eyes flew back to Hailey holding a bloody cloth to her forehead.

"I'm okay," she called out, obviously picking up on his panic. "I'm fine."

She turned to the woman holding Deanna's hand. "Could you make sure she connects with her parents?"

The woman frowned. "You should get that cut looked at."

"It's not a big deal," Hailey assured her. "It's already stopped bleeding. Please, just get Deanna to her mom."

The woman glanced at Dan, obviously assuming he was taking over, then she nodded and she and Deanna skied farther down the hill toward the lodge.

"What happened? Is Natasha okay?" Dan hardly knew what to ask first, his heart still thudding in his chest. "Where's your helmet?"

"Natasha is fine. Deanna went out of control and I caught her and we tumbled a bit." Hailey gave him a quick grin that, he guessed, was supposed to reassure him.

But his emotions had gone through a horrible turmoil and he couldn't focus on any one feeling. As he looked down, his thoughts jolted backward and ice slid through his veins.

He and Hailey had been in the same place when the ski patrol had come off the mountain carrying Austin's body.

Now Hailey, the woman he had put in charge of his daughter, stood in front of him, blood dripping down her face as all the worst scenarios ran through his mind. So close. So close.

His emotions exploded.

Chapter Fourteen

"Natasha, Grandma and Grandpa Anderson are waiting. Take your skis off, go to them and wait for me with them," Dan said.

Hailey heard the chill in Dan's voice and an answering shiver grabbed her neck.

Natasha seemed to sense her father's anger and without so much as a whimper or pout, bent over, popped her skis off and walked down the hill where an older, very well-dressed couple stood. Lydia's parents, Hailey presumed.

Then Dan turned to her, his hazel eyes cold, deep lines bracketing his mouth.

"What were you thinking, taking her down that hill?" he snapped.

Hailey's own misgivings crowded in her mind at the anger in Dan's voice. "She did really well. And she wanted to go. She's a capable skier."

"I thought I told you to keep her on the bunny hill?" Dan kept his voice down but the ice in his gaze and the fierceness of his voice buffeted her like a blizzard.

"She's going to ski the main hill sooner or later, Dan. And I was with her the whole time." She reached out to him, touching his coat sleeve with her hand, trying to bridge the gulf that seemed to yawn between them. "She's a good skier, Dan. And nothing happened to her."

Dan looked down at her hand and Hailey saw the blood streaked on it. She pulled her hand back, curling her fingers against her palm.

Dan swallowed but didn't meet her eyes. "This place is too… It's… She's not coming here again."

Hailey heard the finality in his words, but then her own anger kicked in.

"Really, Dan? You would keep her from the most popular thing to do in this town? Where her friends will be every weekend? Don't you remember how much fun we used to have here?"

"Used to," he said, chopping the air with his hand, as if slashing past away from present.

Hailey glanced down at the bloody cloth now twisted around her hand. The cut on her forehead still stung, but the cold air probably kept it from feeling worse.

"You're upset about me and Natasha because of what happened to Austin, aren't you?" she asked, trying to understand the relentless current of his anger. When she looked up at him again she almost fell back at the cold fury stamped on his face.

"That's in the past. It's done. We're not talking about that."

As she held his flinty gaze, realization moved like a slow storm through her. Shannon's warnings about Dan's lack of communication after Austin's death flickered and gained strength. "And that's the trouble, isn't it? We've never talked about Austin."

"What's to talk about? It's basic. He got lost. He died." His gaze cut away from hers as he shoved his hands in the pockets of his coat.

But he looked away as he spoke and his voice caught on his last word.

Hailey felt as if she was within inches of grasping something that had eluded her for seven years. "I don't know if it's that simple," she said. Then she moved closer, fear skittering through her abdomen. It was as if she and Dan were staring across an abyss.

No way that was happening. Not again.

Her sister's warnings about Dan rang once again through her head, along with every other concern that wove in and out of their relationship.

"Dan, I know something important is happening between us. I don't want to lose that. I'm happier now than I've been in a long time. I don't think I'm imagining what you are feeling either."

"You're not," was his reply, and in his eyes all traces of anger had been replaced by a broken, longing gaze. "I lost too much when I lost you."

"And I don't want to lose you again," she pleaded. "But I feel like I am. And I think it has everything to do with what happened in the past. What happened with Austin."

They were surrounded by the sounds of happy laughter and shrieks of pleasure backed by the steady hum and thump of the ski lift picking up skiers and boarders. But it was as if they were captured in their own moment in time.

How could she get through to him? She felt on the verge of discovering the one thing still standing between them.

"When Austin died, I lost so much as well." Her voice broke as she reached out to him.

Dan looked at her and in his eyes she only saw emptiness and sorrow. "And that's part of the problem," he said as he took a step back and away from her.

She fought down her panic, sensing his physical movement was an echo of his emotional withdrawal. *Not again, please, Lord, not again.*

But how could she get through to him?

"Dan. We would like to go," Mrs. Anderson called out.

Dan shot a look over his shoulder, then looked back at Hailey. "I gotta go," he muttered, but Hailey didn't release him right away. Surely whatever Mrs. Anderson wanted could wait a moment?

"Please don't walk away from me," she pleaded.

His mouth set in grim lines, Dan glanced from her to the Andersons, who were now walking toward the lodge.

"Don't throw those ambiguous statements at me and then walk away," she said, pressing on. "I'm not letting you leave me again. I need you to tell me about Austin before you leave."

Dan shot her another anguished look, but then, without another word he turned and strode away, each step he took away from her falling like a hammer on her heart.

Dan stared at his cell phone for what seemed like the hundredth time. Should he try to call her?

What could he possibly say to her when his fear at seeing the blood dripping down her face had been like a blinding storm? In that moment so many things had come together. He knew how much he cared for her. He knew how much she had also lost when Austin died.

And he knew how little he deserved to hold Hailey's heart.

But he hadn't had time to sort it all out. Not with the Andersons and their threats to take Natasha hovering behind him.

After leaving the hill, they had all driven to Cranbrook, an hour and a half's drive from Hartley Creek.

The Andersons had flown there from Vancouver and had rented a hotel suite there.

Dan wasn't letting Natasha go with them on her own, so he had come along. Now it was late evening and Carla and Alfred Anderson were tucking Natasha in for the night.

Dan dropped his head against the chair in the hotel suite, staring sightlessly up at the ceiling. His head ached and his thoughts were a tangle of worries and fears. His concern over the Andersons' unexpected visit battled his struggle with Hailey's anguished gaze as he walked away.

You should have told her.

And how could he in the few minutes he had? And even worse, what would she think?

If she cares for you it doesn't matter.

Dan wished it were that easy. As she had said, when Austin died, she had lost something too. As had his parents.

As had he.

Too much sorrow, he thought, dragging his hands over his face. Too much pain and grief on his conscience.

The door of his and Natasha's bedroom clicked shut and Alfred Anderson came out, his smile relaxing his features. "She's quite the girl," he said as he folded his suit jacket in half and laid it carefully over the chair. "Pretty precious to us."

Dan tried not to see that as a veiled threat and instead decided to take it at face value. "I know. She's very precious to me too."

Alfred sat down in a chair across from Dan, then sighed heavily. "I know we should have warned you we were coming, but Carla and I got scared."

"About what?" Dan said, a knot forming in his gut.

"You know what Natasha means to us," Alfred said,

leaning back, looking every inch the successful businessman he was. Dan tried to keep his cool and not feel
intimidated by a man wearing a suit worth more than
his truck. "We need her in our life. We can't function
without her."

Dan felt as if Alfred's words sucked the center out of
his world. But he waited to let Alfred play his hand before reacting.

"We know you love her so I'm hoping you understand
that we love her as well," Alfred continued. "And we miss
her." Alfred's voice broke on that last word.

Dan felt a flicker of surprise at the unexpected emotion Alfred let slip past his businessman's facade. But as
he watched Alfred lean forward and drag his hand over
his face, Hailey's words slipped back into his mind. Her
comments about her grandmother's relationship with her
and how important that was.

"I'm sorry about that," Dan said. "But I needed to give
Natasha a chance to settle in to her new life." Dan put
extra emphasis on the last phrase, as if to underline the
fact that Natasha's life was in Hartley Creek.

Then Alfred looked over at him and Dan saw the an-
guish in his eyes.

Please, Lord, Dan prayed, *let Hailey be right about the
Andersons and let me and my worries be wrong.*

"I know that Carla has been pushing to get Natasha
back with us," Alfred continued. "But you have to understand that my wife is a very frightened woman." Alfred
pushed his hand through his hair, rearranging its neat
waves. "Lydia never gave us much time with Natasha—"

"She didn't give me much either," Dan put in, leaning
forward as if tensing for battle.

"I know. I gathered as much. But you have to understand she is our only granddaughter."

"But she's my daughter and I think that would hold more clout in court."

Alfred pulled back, looking surprised. "Of course it does. We don't want to take her away from you."

"That's not what I understood from Carla."

Alfred got to his feet, his expression pleading. "When you first took Natasha away, we thought we would never see her again. Carla got desperate and overreacted and I apologize for that. She would apologize as well, but she's too proud. We know Natasha is your daughter and we know you love her. All we want is some time with her. A visit now and again."

"So you don't want custody of her."

"No. Never."

That wasn't how Dan had read the situation, but Alfred's sincerity kindled the tiniest spark of hope in his heart.

"When you say now and again, what were you thinking of?" Dan asked.

"A couple of weeks in the summer. Maybe part of the Christmas break or Easter break. We'd like to come down a couple of times a year." Alfred held his hands up in a gesture of surrender. "We're open to whatever you want to give us. We have so much love to give her. Please, just give us something."

As Alfred pleaded, Dan's shoulders lowered, the tension easing out of his neck. Hailey was right, Dan thought. And she was also right in saying Natasha could not have too much love in her life. It was obvious the Andersons cared for Natasha with the same intensity his own parents did. "I think we can come to some type of agreement," he said.

Alfred blew out a sigh. "Thank you for that, Dan. That's all we want. That's all we ever wanted."

Then the bedroom door opened again and Carla walked into the room, smoothing down the wrinkles in her shirt. "She's full of stories, that girl," Carla said as she settled into a chair. Her lips tightened as she looked at her husband, then at Dan. "I missed her. I missed her more than you can know."

"Dan and I discussed this already," Alfred said. "We'll be able to see her from time to time."

Carla gave a tight nod then leaned back in the chair, one manicured hand slipping over her face. Then she turned to Dan. "I had quite the chat with Natasha. She talks a lot about this Hailey girl." Carla tilted her head to one side in question.

"Hailey. Is she the girl who was injured at the ski hill?" Alfred added.

Dan nodded, trying not to think about the terror that had clawed at him when he had seen the blood on Hailey's face. How that same terror made him blow up at her. He knew he had overreacted but who could blame him after what had happened all those years ago?

He pushed those thoughts aside. He had been struggling to move on for the past seven years. The past was over. He had enough to deal with in the present.

"Hailey is Natasha's tutor," Dan said, "And yes, Natasha is quite fond of her."

"And you?" Alfred asked.

His question dove into Dan's heart. He was more than fond of Hailey, but how could he say this to Lydia's parents?

And were he and Hailey still "dating"? After leaving her with her questions ringing in his ears? With his own pain coming back to haunt him?

"I don't know if I should be talking about Hailey to the parents of my ex-wife."

Alfred glanced at Carla, who lifted her shoulder in a light shrug, as if telling him to go ahead.

Alfred cleared his throat, then leaned forward. "We want to talk to you about that."

Guilt clutched at Dan again. "I know how our relationship started wasn't ideal—"

"That's not what we want to talk to you about," Alfred interrupted. "Lydia was the kind of girl who always went her own way, did whatever she wanted. I'm fairly sure whatever happened between you two wasn't one-sided."

Dan could only stare, dumbfounded, even more confused. "What are you trying to say?"

Alfred folded his hands over his chest, his intertwined fingers tapping on his silk tie. "We know how difficult things must have been with you and Lydia. She was our daughter and we loved her but—" Alfred's voice broke and he glanced toward Carla as if asking her to help him out.

Carla then leaned forward, her hands resting on her knees. "Since Lydia was a child, she followed her own path. Did her own thing and many of the things she did were either to spite us or to show us she didn't care what we thought. I spent hours worrying about her—where she would end up and whom she would end up with. When she met you, well, we thought her life had taken a turn for the better. We thought she had finally come to a good place." Carla cleared her throat, lifting one hand and letting it fall. "While we weren't thrilled about how your situation began, we realized that mistakes get made." Her words were meant to reassure, but they also drew up Dan's old guilt over his and Lydia's lapse in judgment.

"I'm so sorry about that," he said.

Carla waved off his apology. "Goodness knows I'm not in any position to stand in judgment of you. I know my own behavior through all of this has not been stellar. But all of that faded away when we saw what a calming influence you were in her life. We were so thankful you married her."

Dan felt as if the center of his world shifted on its axis. He had felt nothing but shame about his marriage and the subsequent breakdown, and now his in-laws were telling him how happy they were he married Lydia?

Carla then twined her fingers around each other, lowering her head, and shot him a pleading glance. "When you got divorced, we lost something precious and we also lost some of the hopes we had for Lydia. We had hoped you two would get together again, but over time we knew that wasn't happening. However, we thought you believed what Lydia might have said about us. She disliked us so much and fought with us so much we thought she would have influenced your opinion of us as well. So when Lydia died, we thought you would take Natasha away from us permanently. That's why I said... Made the threats I did."

Dan heard the fear and sorrow in her voice and, as his gaze held hers, he saw the glint of tears.

Hailey was right, he thought again.

His heart stumbled over the thought of her. She was right about Carla and Alfred.

And maybe she was right about a few other things.

He pulled his attention back to what Alfred was now saying, fighting his own desire to call Hailey.

"We do want you to know we are so thankful for the bit of stability you brought to Lydia's life." Alfred leaned forward, pleating his tie. "Though we didn't see a lot of our daughter, we were fully aware of how hard you tried to make the relationship work. You were probably the best thing that ever happened to her. And we also saw what a wonderful father you were to Natasha. How hard you worked to take care of her." Alfred shot a quick glance toward Carla. "And again, I'm sorry for the antagonistic attitude we showed you. Please understand how desperately afraid we were that we would never see Natasha again. We overreacted and we know that now."

"I would never take her away," Dan said, still trying to absorb what Carla and Alfred had told him about Lydia. What they had given him with their encouraging words. Did they really think he was the best thing that happened to their daughter? "But I was afraid too. I didn't want to lose Natasha. Because she's one of the biggest blessings in my life."

Because his other blessing was Hailey.

The thought of her sent a shaft of pain plunging deep in his soul. He wanted to call her. He didn't dare call her.

"I'm glad we could clear this up," Carla said, resting her hands on her knees, leaning toward him. "I know we put you through a lot and I don't blame you if you can't forgive us, but I'd like to ask anyway."

Dan pushed his own worries aside as he held her earnest gaze. Felt her pain.

And the anger and fear he had felt around the Andersons faded away in the face of her sorrow.

"As a Christian I know I've been given forgiveness for so much more. How could I not forgive you?"

Carla sat back in her chair, her smile bemused. "Lydia said that about you. That you were a man of faith."

"Not as much as I know I should be," Dan said, feeling a flush of regret for the times he held God at arm's length. "And I feel like I'm kind of stumbling along. But I know where my hope is and I know that, as I said, I've been forgiven for my own sins."

"Well, I know we haven't made things easy for you," Carla said. "So I thank you for your forgiveness."

Dan held her gaze, surprised at the release he felt at her words. The release of the burden of his anger. He couldn't help but feel amazed at how things had changed in the past few minutes. How the atmosphere had shifted from antagonistic to understanding.

But what was more surprising was how easy granting forgiveness became when the truth surfaced. When the Andersons had admitted some of their own wrongdoings.

As those last words settled in his mind he felt a jolt of shock. He hadn't struggled with forgiving the Andersons when they had asked. Not when he saw their own struggle with the consequences of their decisions. Forgiveness had been easy to allow when the truth was on the table.

Could Hailey feel the same if he told her everything? Could his parents?

Dan shot a glance at the clock and got up from his chair. "Please excuse me, I'd like to go tuck my daughter in." And then he had a few phone calls to make.

As Dan walked toward Natasha's room, his step felt lighter, his heart less heavy. He thought of Hailey and he sent up a prayer.

Show me what to do, Lord. Please give me a chance to fix things between us.

He waited a moment, hoping for some miraculous answer or maybe even to hear his phone ring, with Hailey on the other end, laughing and telling him she forgave him for leaving her behind at the ski hill.

But nothing.

Natasha lay in bed, beaming at him. "I'm so happy to see Gramma and Grandpa Anderson," she said, weaving her fingers together. "I missed them."

"And they missed you, punkin," Dan said, sitting on

the edge of the bed, relief easing the stress in his shoulders. This part of his life, at least, was working the way it should. The Andersons weren't his enemy. Not anymore.

"Can you sing me our song?"

Our song. The one Hailey meant for our children. Dan faced a surge of fear and desolation. What if she never wanted to talk to him again? What if she was going to take that job and leave immediately?

He pushed his questions aside. He couldn't deal with them right now. He had asked God to show him what to do. For now, he had to leave the rest in God's hands.

Dan sat down beside his daughter, pulling her close. He drew in a slow breath, then sang the song, surrounded by memories of earlier times. More innocent times.

As he sang, Natasha's eyelids grew heavy, sleep finally claiming her. He held her a moment longer, inhaling the little-girl smell of her freshly washed hair, the brand new flannel nightgown Carla had brought along for her.

But as he laid his little girl down onto the bed Alfred and Carla's words resonated through his head.

You were the best thing that had happened to Lydia.

Could that really be? Could the relationship that was ignited and instigated by his guilt over Austin really have become a blessing? Could an association that had rung the death knell on Hailey's love for him—could God have used it for good?

He pinched the bridge of his nose, trying to reorient himself. For so long he had seen his relationship with Lydia as a failure, and it had become a reason to stay away from Hailey.

But he'd had it wrong. He'd taken on something he shouldn't have. He'd let false guilt stand in the way of his love for Hailey and in the meantime he'd hurt her and betrayed her again.

"Don't walk away from me." Her words echoed in his mind. Though he knew he had to go with the Andersons at that moment, at the same time he had left her. Had left her with questions he knew he didn't dare answer.

He covered his face with his hands, turning to the one source of strength and forgiveness that had always been in his life.

Please, Lord, he prayed, *I've prayed for forgiveness for Austin before. I'm asking for it again. Help me to feel it. Let me find a way to talk to Hailey. To explain. Let me find a way to let go of the guilt between us. And help her to understand.*

Chapter Fifteen

Hailey dropped her knapsack on the floor and rolled her neck, easing the kink out of it. The first day of the school week had been long and tiring.

And depressing.

All morning she'd felt as if she was waiting. Every slam of the classroom door, every glimpse of a man's figure, set her heart into high gear. But neither Dan nor Natasha had shown up and Hailey had resolutely forced herself not to go digging through her knapsack to find her cell phone to call him.

She walked to the frosted window of her living room, pressing her heated forehead to the chilly glass. From here, if she angled her head just right, she could see the ski hill. And if she moved a foot to the right, she could catch a glimpse of the top left-hand corner of the brick building that housed Dan's hardware store and apartment.

She pushed herself away from the window and grabbed her knapsack. All morning she had resisted the urge to call Dan. She wasn't chasing after him. Especially when he hadn't called to talk to her either.

Was it over between them?

She wasn't sure. She just knew what she had gone

through the last time he had walked away from her and then not called. She wouldn't allow that to happen again.

With a toss of her head, she grabbed her knapsack. She was calling that lady back. Telling her she was taking the job. This time she would be the first to leave Hartley Creek.

She walked into her bedroom, dropped her knapsack on the bed and, as she did, she saw her Bible lying on the bedside table. Last night she'd been too tired and too overwrought to read it. She reached for her knapsack to get her phone.

Don't call yet.

So what do I do instead?

Think about this. Pray about it.

Easing out a sigh she picked up her Bible and, on impulse, turned to the passage the pastor had read in church yesterday morning. Before she'd gone to get Natasha. Before everything had fallen apart.

She looked down at the Bible and started reading at verse 5 of Psalm 36. As she read, her hand clutched the necklace her Nana had given her, as if anchoring herself to the stories of the past while she dealt with the present.

Your love, Lord, reaches to the heavens, Your faithfulness to the skies. Your righteousness is like the highest mountains, Your justice like the great deep. You, Lord, preserve both people and animals. How priceless is Your unfailing love, O God!
People take refuge in the shadow of Your wings.

Hailey rested her finger on the passage, reading and re-reading them. *Your righteousness is like the highest mountain.*

She lowered her head, pressing her fingers against her

eyes. *"Please, Lord,"* she whispered. *"Help me to trust in Your faithfulness and Yours alone. Help me to know that Your righteousness and Your love are more secure and strong and powerful than the tallest mountains surrounding our valley. Help me to know that Your love is more secure than any man's."*

She felt a sob catch in her throat as she thought of Dan. She kept seeing him walk away from her, leaving her with echoes of Austin once again resounding between them.

Left behind again.

Those words had a nasty curl to their edges and part of her didn't want to believe it. Yes, Dan probably had a good reason for leaving and she imagined that his controversy with the Andersons had much to do with the physical distance he had put between them.

But he had left her in other ways as well. He hadn't called. He hadn't tried to connect.

But neither have you. A cord of three strands is not easily broken.

The words resounded through her mind. She had separated herself from Dan as surely as he had separated himself from her. She didn't go after him, or give him the benefit of the doubt.

Yes, her father had left her when she was a child, and yes, Dan had left her once before.

She clutched her necklace again, thinking back to her ancestor August. A man who had swallowed his own pride and made the trek back to the woman he loved. He had chosen love.

Maybe she needed to make some move herself.

With this resolve burning in her soul she took her backpack and upended it to get her phone.

This time she was not idly sitting by and letting Dan set the conditions. She was not allowing the cord they had been weaving to be torn apart again. Before she called back to take that job, she was calling Dan to give him one more chance to make things right between them.

But five minutes later, with every pocket searched and every item in her backpack sorted on her bed, she realized her phone was not here.

She got up and checked her bed. Checked the floor. Then she remembered tucking her phone in the pocket of her coat after the school had called her to see if she could come sooner. She ran to her snowboarding jacket and shoved her hands in the pockets.

Nothing.

She leaned back against the door of her apartment, still clutching her jacket. Where could her phone be? How could she have lost it?

She mentally retraced her steps from the time she'd put the phone in her pocket until she'd realized it was missing. And then realization dawned.

When Deanna had run into her on the ski hill, her phone must have fallen out of the pocket of her jacket into the snow. But what were the odds of her finding it again?

She didn't care. She had to try. She needed to know if he'd been trying to call.

She quickly changed into her snow pants, swapped her school shirt for a merino wool top, shrugged on her jacket, snagged her snowboard and headed out to the hill. Thankfully, her car was finally fixed so she had her own transportation.

The sun eased its way down toward the horizon when she got off the chairlift at the top of the run she had taken Natasha and Deanne down only yesterday. She stood there a moment, allowing the waning warmth of the sun to ease away the chill that had enveloped her soul since she'd watched Dan walk away. When she found her phone, she would know if he'd really meant to abandon her.

The hill was quieter than yesterday. Most of the weekend tourists were back in Calgary, Lethbridge, Cranbrook or wherever they had come from.

She twisted her board downhill, then let gravity do its work. The wind whistled through her hair as she carved quick turns, the snow spraying out from her board with each twist of her body.

She missed this so much, she thought. But more than anything, she missed doing this with Dan. Her heart stuttered at the thought of him.

And as she neared the spot where she was sure Deanna had run into her, she slowed down, praying she would find her phone.

Praying there would be a message on it from Dan.

She came to the area and loosened her bindings, stepping out of her board. She looked over her shoulder, trying to recreate the scene. The odds were not in her favor. How many people had gone over this spot since? But it was close to the trees and maybe. Just maybe.

She first walked a circle around the area, going into the trees, then back onto the hill. Nothing. She started kicking up the snow in the vain hope she would find something.

Nothing.

This was silly. Just go to the chalet and call him.

Maybe she needed to take a leap, here. Trust that going back to Dan was right, whether or not he'd come to his senses.

Searching for her phone was obviously futile. She knew her pride was getting in the way.

She walked over to her board, stepped in the bindings and then as she bent over to tighten them she caught a flash of metallic pink winking back at her. She pushed the snow aside and with a triumphant grin, pulled her cell phone out of the snow.

She pushed it into her shirt against her stomach to warm it up, her heart beginning a nervous pounding. What if the phone was broken? What if Dan hadn't called her? She took a deep breath. She already knew what she had to do, regardless.

When the metal no longer gave her a chill she pulled the phone out and hit a button that woke it up. The screen flickered, wavered and then shone back at her.

Twelve missed calls.

With trembling fingers she checked the call log. One of the calls was from Shannon. One from her Nana.

And ten were from Dan.

She sat down in the snow, her legs giving way, her heart fluttering in her chest. He hadn't left her. He hadn't forgotten about her.

Then the phone sent its tinny song ringing into the silence. Hailey started, her fluttering shifting into pounding.

She glanced at the call display.

Dan.

"Hello," she said, frustrated with the weakness of her voice.

"Hailey. Finally."

Did she imagine the relief in his voice?

"Where are you?" he asked.

"I'm on the hill."

Silence followed and she found herself tensing, curling her toes up in her boots, clenching a fist.

"Can you wait there for me?"

"Okay." She hated how shaky that single word sounded.

She cleared her throat, got a grip and continued. "Where do you want to meet?"

"Top of Monnihan?"

"On the hill?" Dan hadn't been on the hill since Austin died.

"Yes. If that's okay."

She hardly dared think what this might mean.

"Yeah. Sure. I'll be waiting."

"I'll be there in about half an hour."

She took a quick glance at her handset. "That's cutting it close. Crow's Nest chairlift shuts in forty-five minutes."

"I'll be there. Just wait for me, please?"

She wanted to ask why, but that would waste time. So she simply said yes, and disconnected. When she put the phone in her pocket she made sure to zip the pocket shut. Then she pushed herself to her feet, trying to work her head around what was going on.

Dan was coming to the ski hill.

"We're closing the lift down." The liftee held up his hand as Dan came up to the Crow's Nest Chair.

Dan slipped on his gloves, his heart still pounding from running all the way from the ticket booth. He caught a few breaths as he watched the chairs still moving up the mountain, holding skiers. He held up his ticket and looked the kid, much younger and about a foot shorter, in the eye. "I bought this ticket five minutes ago. The girl who sold it to me said the lift would be running for another fifteen minutes."

With a rustle of his baggy snow pants, the kid shifted his weight, snapped his gum and shrugged. "Yeah, but that's only for the people on the chair already. I'm not letting anyone else on."

Dan stifled the urge to grab the kid and throttle him.

Hailey was waiting and he wasn't letting her down. Not again. He looked up the hill, then slid a bit closer to the kid, smiled down at him. "I've been skiing and boarding on this hill since you were in diapers. I know this lift doesn't shut down until four and it ain't four."

The kid just stared at him.

"I'm getting on the lift."

"You can't."

"Try and stop me."

Dan pushed himself past the kid and jumped onto the first chair that came around.

"Hey, you can't do that," the kid yelled. "I told you it was closing."

Dan ignored him, knowing the kid wouldn't stop the lift, not with all the other people still on it, though he had to suppress a laugh at his own daring. For someone who routinely drove five miles an hour under the speed limit, paid his taxes even before they were due and always came to a full stop at a stop sign, this was daring indeed.

And he didn't feel the least bit sorry.

Hailey was waiting for him.

He wanted to call her, to make sure she was still there but resisted the urge. Anything he had to say to her from here on had to be said to her face.

The lift creaked and groaned as his chair headed toward the top. The muted humming of the cables pulled back memories of hours and days spent on this hill. He looked below him, watching the more adventurous and reckless kids, skiing and boarding down the packed snow below the lift. Their laughter and squeals reminded him of the adventures he and Hailey undertook.

In spite of his resolve, memories of Austin wove themselves through them.

Seven years later, memories of his brother, of that day,

could still sting and accuse. He struggled to put that aside. Then he sat back in the chair and did the only thing he could while he waited. He prayed.

After what felt like hours, he finally got to the top of the hill and slid off. No sooner had he touched the ground, the lift creaked and then groaned to a halt.

Dumb kid shut it down early anyway. But Dan didn't care. He had made it.

He tightened his bindings, and looked around a moment, orienting himself.

Seven years later. As he stood on this first ridge of the mountain, it felt as if he had never been gone. The angle of the lowering sun cast waiting shadows. The day was winding down.

Below him he saw the town of Hartley Creek. His hometown. The place he had run away from all those years ago. He was back now and he was back on the hill.

In spite of the weight of what lay ahead of him, he felt euphoria build as he pushed himself off, snow swishing under his board, the cool air whistling past him. He faltered a moment as he caught an edge, regained his balance, and then he was carving down the hill, shredding snow, heading off toward Monnihan.

Where Hailey waited.

Just then Dan caught a flash of orange as a kid zipped past him on his snowboard, almost cutting Dan off. He resisted the urge to yell at the kid to be careful, then frowned as the boy headed directly toward the ropes marking off the area that was off-limits.

The boy didn't look back and without hesitation lifted the rope and ducked under.

"Hey, where are you going?" Dan called out.

The kid looked back over his shoulder. He couldn't

have been more than fourteen or fifteen. Younger than Austin was.

"Come back here," Dan called. "That area is out of bounds."

The kid turned, then with a swish of his board, disappeared over the white ridge. Dan hesitated a moment, wondering what to do. He thought of Hailey, waiting for him, then thought of the kid heading into an area that he knew would be dangerous.

You haven't boarded in ages. You'll just cause more problems.

But Dan couldn't ignore the voice in his head that nagged at him. What if something happened to that kid?

Dan glanced down the hill one more time, apprehension over Hailey fighting his need to at least keep an eye on the young boy. He made his decision, then ducked under the ropes and followed the tracks through the fresh powder.

The boy was going fast. Dan had pushed himself beyond his comfort level, but was pleased to feel his old skills returning. He was never the flashy boarder Hailey was, but he always managed to stay ahead of her in powder.

He carved over, cut a quick turn to avoid some trees, then hit an almost vertical slope. His heart jumped in his throat as he made his way down, his every nerve on alert, his heart lifting in his chest.

He caught a glimpse of orange, yelled again but the boy didn't slow down. Dan pushed himself to go a little faster to keep up.

He maneuvered past a clump of trees, heavy and white with snow, cut a sharp curve and then stopped.

He couldn't see the boy anywhere. Frowning, Dan scanned the hill again, following the tracks.

Then ice flowed through his veins. The tracks led to a tree and then disappeared.

Dan pushed off, heading straight down the hill, the wind whistling past him. He struggled to maintain control, adrenaline surging through his arteries.

He got closer and his suspicions were confirmed. All he could see sticking out from the snow around the tree was the edge of a snowboard. The boy had fallen into a tree well, a deep snow depression around the tree, and was now probably lying upside down, covered in snow. Dan stopped, took his board off and carefully approached the tree well.

"Can you hear me? Don't move," Dan called out. "Don't move at all. You'll just shake down more snow. Just lay still."

His heart plunged when he heard a muffled cry. The boy was still alive.

If he didn't pull the boy out soon he would suffocate. But if Dan wasn't careful he would end up stuck himself.

"Listen to me. Don't move," Dan repeated. "Stay calm. I'll get you out but you can't move." Dan went below the well, grabbed his board and shoveled snow away from the hole as fast as he could. "Don't move," he called out while he worked.

Dan forced himself to breathe, to make his movements steady and sure but his limbs felt like they were moving through syrup, his hands couldn't go fast enough. Thankfully, the boy's snowboard was lodged in the snow like an inverted bridge, preventing him from going farther down into the tree well. This high up the snow base was meters thick and the open area under the tree was also that deep.

Dan pulled, and when he felt a shift, he pulled harder. Finally, after what seemed like hours he managed to drag the boy free.

"Take a breath," Dan urged, rolling the boy onto his back. "Just relax and take a breath."

The boy, his face crusted with snow, coughed, sputtered, gasped and coughed again.

Dan sat back in the snow, his limbs like limp spaghetti. He had to breathe himself. Had to force himself to relax.

Thank You, Lord, he prayed as he drew in another shaky breath.

The boy coughed again, then jerked to a sitting position. "What happened?" he gasped, glancing wildly around as if getting his bearings again.

"You fell into a tree well." Dan forced himself to breathe again, his thoughts a jumbled whirl of relief, prayers and beneath all that a slow stirring of anger.

"A what?" he asked, his voice a timid sound.

Dan's anger grew. "You went boarding out of bounds and you don't know what a tree well is?"

The boy coughed again as he shook his head and Dan could see that his face had turned as pale as the snow they sat on.

"See how the branches of these spruce trees flare out?" Dan asked. "They're like an umbrella and keep the snow from gathering under the tree so there's this open space under the branches that forms a pit. This mountain gets an average snowfall of nine hundred seventy centimeters—that's thirty-one feet if you don't do metric. The snow around the tree is powdery. You get too close to the tree and you get sucked into the snow and dumped, usually upside down, in a hole deeper than you are tall. And there's a bunch of trees in these out-of-bounds areas, all of them with a well around them." Dan heard his voice rise and stopped himself.

The kid looked scared enough. He was still breathing heavily, his eyes wide and dark.

"What if you didn't follow me?" he asked, his voice wavering with fear.

Dan held his gaze a beat, as if to underline what he was about to say. "You would have died from suffocation because there's no way you could have gotten out of that well on your own."

It didn't seem possible for the boy's face to grow any whiter but it did. He blinked a couple of times, before giving in, dropping his face into gloved hands with a sob.

Dan watched him for a moment, then, taking pity on him, moved closer and put his hand on the boy's shoulder, giving him a hard squeeze.

"You're okay."

The boy dragged his gloved hands over a face streaked with tears. "Thanks. Thanks for saving my life."

The words shifted something deep within Dan as the reality of what had happened only now seemed to settle. If someone had followed Austin, would he still be alive?

"What's your name?" he asked the young boy.

"Jeremy. Jeremy LeBron," the boy said, his voice still shaking.

"Well, Jeremy, you okay to keep boarding?"

Jeremy glanced back at the tree well and the disturbed snow around it and drew in a shaking breath. "I don't know."

"You'll be okay if you follow me," Dan said, getting to his feet. He didn't want to take the chance that the ski patrol would come and find them. They had to get back to the main hill before it got too dark.

Jeremy slowly got to his feet, wavered a bit and then nodded.

"Okay. Let's get you down the hill." He glanced around to get his bearings. Near as he could tell, if they traversed the hill they could hit the mountain at the top of Monnihan run.

And hopefully Hailey would still be waiting there. He pulled out his cell phone to call her to let her know. His heart sank in his chest. No bars. No reception.

He tucked his phone back in his pocket, then pushed off across the hill, Jeremy right behind him.

Please, Lord, let Hailey still be waiting, he prayed.

Chapter Sixteen

Hailey pulled her knees close, digging her board in the hill. She'd been sitting here, at the top of Monnihan run, for twenty minutes now. Dan should have been here long ago.

She glanced at her phone again, wondering if he would call her. Wondering if she should call him.

He knows exactly where you are, she thought.

So where was he?

Hailey glanced down the hill, now empty of skiers, the chairlifts swinging lightly in the ever-present mountain wind. In a couple of minutes the ski patrol would make their last sweep of the hill, urging all the laggards down to the bottom, checking for injured skiers and boarders.

The sun was easing down toward the mountains. Soon it would be dusk.

How long should she wait? Should she wait?

He'd said he was coming.

But behind her confident declaration came a chilling thought. What if he changed his mind? And on the heels of that, what if something had happened to him?

Hailey felt a flutter deep in her stomach as she looked down the empty run below her. She could see the figures of the last skiers and snowboarders standing at the bottom of the hill, done for the day.

Please, Lord, let Dan come.

She felt as if all she'd done since Dan had called her was send up simple, formless prayers. Because she wasn't sure what to pray for.

She pulled out her phone and checked but there was nothing.

The familiar swish of a board caught her attention and her heart. She spun around and then with a spray of snow, a red-coated ski patrol stopped by her. Though he wore a helmet Hailey recognized Jess Schroder, a fellow boarder whose father owned the ski hill.

"Everything okay?" Jess called out, looking down on her.

She wanted to smile up at him and say yes. She wanted to believe that Dan wasn't here simply because he was late.

"Have you seen Dan? He's wearing a blue coat, black pants, riding a black snowboard?"

Jess leaned on his poles and pushed his goggles up on his helmet, his blue eyes squinting against the glare off the snow. "No, sorry, Hailey. Haven't, though I've got a couple of guys checking out some tracks that went out of bounds about hundred feet above here."

Hailey hugged her knees, chewing on her lip. Was that Dan? She dismissed that thought. Dan would never take a chance like that. He knew she was waiting.

"But sorry to say," Jess said to her. "The hill is closing. You've got to get to the bottom."

Hailey reluctantly got to her feet just as Jess's radio on his shoulder squawked.

"Yeah. Jess here," he said.

"Got a couple of guys here, heading toward you. Looks

like one of them ended up in a tree well," the tinny voice over the radio replied. "We're following the tracks to make sure they get onto the hill okay."

Hailey wanted to grab Jess's radio and ask who it was. What did they look like? Where were they?

"I'll wait," Jess said.

"Can I wait too?"

Jess looked down on her from his considerable height, pursing his lips. "Yeah. Sure."

Hailey wanted to hug him but contented herself with a quick smile.

She turned to the trees edging the run, her heart pounding in her chest, willing, praying for someone to come out.

The air grew cooler and a few flakes began drifting down.

"Supposed to get primo powder up here tomorrow," Jess said, leaning on his poles. "Be great for the Cat skiing."

Hailey wrapped her arms around her waist, unable to make small talk with him, her entire attention focused on the trees. She didn't know where the late skiers would come out and she didn't know if one of them was Dan. All she could do was watch and send out small, unspecific prayers.

Please, Lord. Please, Lord.

And then she saw a figure burst out of the trees, duck under the rope marking the boundary, then turn and hold it up. He wore a blue coat and black pants. Hailey's heart turned over and she pushed off just as a young boy came out from the trees and ducked under the rope Dan was holding up.

"Dan. What happened?" Hailey called out, heading

directly toward him, her heart dancing against her ribs, relief and happiness battling with each other.

"Jeremy here ended up in a tree well," Dan said as the young boy came to a halt beside him. His coat was crusted with snow and Hailey could see the fear still etched on his features.

Jess was beside them, pulling off his pack.

"You okay?" he asked the kid, then turned to Dan. "Nothing broken?"

"Nope," Dan replied, drawing in a deep breath. "He's okay far as I can tell."

The boy shook his head and turned to Dan. "This guy saved my life. I thought I was going to die."

"You would have if you'd been on your own," Jess said, his deep voice full of reprimand. "Let's head down the hill. We'll check you over at the bottom."

Just then the other ski patrol members emerged from the trees.

"We'll all go down together," Jess said. He looked over at Dan and Hailey. "You'll have to come too."

Hailey nodded, then glanced at Dan, relief sluicing through her. He hadn't forgotten about her. He hadn't abandoned her.

They said nothing as they carved their way down the hill. They were just about at the bottom when Dan caught Hailey by the arm.

"I need to talk to Hailey," Dan said, when Jess stopped, shooting him a questioning glance. "And I want to do it up here. On the hill."

Jess glanced up and down. The chalet was within view. "Okay, but I'll be watching to make sure you make it down."

"Fair enough," Dan said.

Hailey felt a thrum of anticipation as the ski patrol

took Jeremy farther down the hill, disappearing over a ridge, then reappearing at the very bottom.

Dan dropped down onto the snow and pulled Hailey down beside him. "Hey. So. Here we are. Full circle."

A silvery fragment of happiness, bright as the sparkling snow around them, pierced her heart.

"Hey, yourself," she returned. "Are you okay?"

"Trying to be," he said, pulling in a wavering breath. "Seeing that kid upside down in that tree well took ten years off my life." He pulled his helmet off and rubbed his eyes with his fist. Then he drew in another breath and looked over the valley below them. "In spite of that, I missed this."

Hailey's questions and thoughts tumbled over one another, all demanding to be spoken. But she kept quiet and waited for Dan.

They sat for a few more moments, as if letting the time between them catch up to this moment, this completing of a circle of events that had sundered their lives.

Then Dan reached over and ran his fingertip above the cut on her forehead, now covered with a couple of Steri-Strips. "Are you okay?"

"I'm fine. It stung a bit but Shannon said it wouldn't scar. Not that I care about that," she added, in case he might think her vain.

Dan let his finger drift down her face, then, to her disappointment, he withdrew his hand, and turned his eyes back to the valley.

Hailey let the moment lengthen, knowing that after all these years, Dan would need some time to begin. For now, she was content to be beside him, sitting on the ski hill.

"I don't know where to start," he said finally, his words quiet. "I'm not sure exactly what to say."

Hailey swallowed, then said, "Why don't you start with Austin?"

"That's probably the best place to begin." Dan waited a moment, then turned to Hailey. "Remember how we got separated on the lift that day?"

She nodded. "You and Austin ended up together with some girl and I was trying not to be jealous."

A melancholy smile tweaked his lips. "You never needed to be jealous."

Hailey returned his smile, his words like a gift.

"Anyhow, when Austin and I got to the top," Dan continued, "I told him to find some friends to go boarding with. I wanted to be alone with you. I had something important I wanted to ask you."

Hailey couldn't help it. Even after all this time, her heart beat with a sense of expectation.

"But Austin didn't want to go. He wanted to be with you." Dan looked down at his hands, shaking his head lightly. "I don't know if you ever noticed, but my little brother had a huge crush on you."

This was news to Hailey. "No. I had no idea."

"That's why he always hung out with us. I guess he was hoping, somewhere along the way, that you'd notice him or that you'd get rid of me and go with him." Dan stopped there, pressing his lips together. He blinked once, dashed his hand over his eyes and eased out a slow breath. Hailey sensed how difficult this was for Dan but also knew they were on the verge of something important and necessary to their relationship.

That last word caught in her mind, full of hope and possibilities. But she caught herself. Just wait. Just wait.

"I was mad at him because all day I'd been trying to get rid of him and he wouldn't take the hint. I had… I had a ring I wanted to give to you. A promise ring. A way of letting you know you were mine." He paused again and Hailey clung to his words, holding them close. "Anyway, Austin wasn't getting the hint and I was getting more and more frustrated with him. So while we waited for you I told him that I wanted him to leave us alone. Take a hint and take a hike and stop being so ridiculous about his feelings for you. That you would never have anything to do with him. I didn't hold back." He paused, lowering his head in his hands. "I'll never forget the look on his face when I said that. He looked as if I had punched him in the stomach. Then he pushed off and the next thing we knew, he was gone. And the last thing he heard from me were those hateful, awful words that probably caused his death."

Dan's voice broke and Hailey felt all the pain and guilt Dan had been carrying around all those years.

And suddenly it was as if the sun had come from behind the clouds, illuminating all the doubts and concerns she'd had all those years.

"So that's why you pulled away from me? Not just because you lost Austin but because you thought you caused his death?"

"I kept going over and over what I said to him, wishing, praying I could back up and do it all over again. It was like every word I said was a punch that pushed him to the edge." Dan stopped, his voice cracking. He cleared his throat and continued. "I couldn't talk about it either to my parents or you. I couldn't let you find out what kind of person I really was. The only way I could deal with what I did was to push you away too."

Hailey felt her own regret move slowly through her, picking up emotions as it gained strength. "And I broke up with you. I couldn't be bothered to understand. To understand or to wait until you got through this all. I'm sorry."

He turned to her then, taking her hand in his, covering it, his eyes holding her like a tack. "Don't apologize. You have nothing to apologize for. I told you I was leaving Hartley Creek, what else could you do?"

"I could have been more understanding…but I was scared. Scared that you were leaving me like my father did. That's why I broke up with you. Because this time I wanted to be the one to do it first."

Then Dan caught her face in his hands. "So much pain and sorrow…" He let the sentence trail off. "So much misunderstanding."

His eyes held hers, delving deeply into her soul. "I'm so sorry for everything. Would you forgive me?"

She held his broken, longing gaze and her heart leapt in her chest. "I have nothing to forgive you for and everything to love you for."

Then, to her surprise, he pulled her closer, lowered his head and caught her lips in a cool, gentle kiss. A kiss which connected them and calmed the sorrow and hurt of the last few days.

He pulled away, then pressed his now-warm lips to her cheeks, her forehead, then her mouth again.

Hailey clung to him, her soul singing with joy and wonder.

This was right, she thought. This was how things were supposed to be.

He finally pulled away. "I love you, Hailey Deacon. I love you so much. Always have." He sighed. "I've got so much more to tell you, so much more to talk about. I want to spend the rest of my life loving you. Telling you what you mean to me."

Hailey's heart skipped. Had she heard him right?

He kissed her again. "I hope I'm not jumping the gun, but I don't want this to end, ever. I want you to marry me."

Hailey closed her eyes, letting his wonderful, loving, amazing words rest in the silence. Letting them register in her heart.

Then she looked up at him, her smile threatening to split her face.

"Yes. My answer is yes."

He cupped her face, letting his fingers trace her features. "You are amazing to me, Hailey. I've learned so much from you."

"Well, that's a good thing, I guess. I am a teacher after all."

He grinned at her, then kissed her again.

"I'll have to go talk to my parents next. Tell them what really happened with Austin." He paused and Hailey heard the pain and regret in his voice.

She cupped his cheeks, turning his face to hers. "Dan, Austin made his own choices. You don't have to take that on. He didn't have to go down that run. You didn't push him down there, just like no one pushed that boy you just rescued down the hill. He had made his own choices too."

Dan pressed his lips together, as if still not sure.

"You've taken responsibility for seven years," she said, hoping, praying he understood. "You told me what happened and I wasn't shocked or angry. I know your parents won't be either. They're so happy you're back in their lives. You and Natasha. That's enough for them."

Dan shot her a grateful glance. "Part of me knows that. The Andersons asked me to forgive them for trying to take Natasha away."

"And did you?"

"Yeah. I did. And it wasn't that hard after all."

Hailey ran her fingers down his face, cupping his chin in hers, his whiskers rough against her hand. "Forgiveness is freedom and I know your parents, once they hear the truth, will not even think they have anything to forgive. I think they'll be glad to have the Dan they have always loved, completely back. Nothing can bring Austin back, but you didn't cause his death."

"I think a part of me always knew that," Dan said. "But I couldn't forgive myself. And when that happened, I compounded that mistake with many more."

"But you're here now," Hailey said. "And I'm here. And you just saved a young boy's life. And maybe, if someone had been watching out for Austin like you were watching out for that kid, he might be alive too."

Dan looked at her again and she saw the beginnings of understanding in his eyes.

"I'm looking forward to starting over," she continued. "To taking care of you and Natasha."

Dan's grin expanded, and he caught her in a fierce hug. "You are such a blessing. I'm so thankful that God gave us another chance together."

This declaration was followed by another kiss and then another.

Hailey pulled back and looked down over the deserted hill, letting the peace of the moment wash over her.

Her heart sang and she folded her hands over Dan's. "Can we pray together? Right here?" she said.

"I'd like that."

Hailey tightened her grip on Dan's hand then lowered her head, drew in a breath to center herself and began.

"Dear Lord, thank You for this mountain that brought us great joy and sorrow. Help us to find our way through the sorrow. Thank You for Austin and the blessing his life was for all of us. We miss him, but we also know that he

*is now with You. Help us through our pain and sorrow
and guilt. Thank You for using Dan to save that boy's life.
Help us to embrace Your forgiveness and show us that
always and everywhere, our lives are in Your hands."*

She stopped, her own throat thickening as she thought
of Austin and the sorrow and guilt Dan had been carrying all these years.

Dan squeezed her hand and then he began, his voice
quiet and subdued, but, at the same time, holding a power
that resonated with Hailey.

*"Thanks, Lord, for Hailey. Thanks for family and the
town and community we're a part of. Forgive me, Lord,
for what I told my brother. Forgive me for how I treated
him."* He stopped a moment, then continued. *"Thanks
for covering our mistakes. Thanks for feeling our pain.
Thanks for Your love."*

Dan stopped and Hailey whispered an *"Amen."*

Neither said anything, as if unwilling to break the
holy moment.

Finally Hailey drew in a long, cleansing breath and
gave Dan a smile. "That's the first time we've prayed
together," she said.

"It's a good way to start what we're going to finish."

Hailey nodded, peace washing over her. Then she
looked backward, up at the mountain, and she smiled.

"Okay, what's putting that look on your face?" Dan
asked.

Hailey's smile grew. "According to my Nana, the ridge
behind us is the one that August Beck came over when
he came back to Kamiskahk."

Dan followed her gaze and a smile crept across his lips
as well. "Very appropriate then, isn't it, that I proposed
to you right here."

Hailey turned back to Dan. "He made the right choice when he came back."

Dan dropped a cool kiss on her forehead. "I'm glad I made the right choice too," he said. "I'm glad I came back."

"So am I." She kissed him back, then wrested her gloves out of her pocket, glancing around. "We're losing our light soon. I guess we better get going before Jess kicks us off the hill."

Dan grinned and touched the end of her nose. "Won't be the first time," he said.

"Race you to the bottom?" Hailey popped up to her feet and slapped the snow off her pants.

"I'm too rusty to do any racing," Dan groaned. "I'll be lucky to get to the bottom in one piece."

"Hey, I know a good snowboarding instructor. Could give you a few lessons," Hailey said with a wink.

"She already has," Dan said.

Then, together, they made their way down the hill. Toward Hartley Creek. Toward Natasha.

Toward home.

* * * * *

Amos Burkholder looked out over the Millers' fields to be plowed in the spring. He couldn't help but think of them as partly his. Of course, they weren't his fields, and he might not even be here to do the plowing and the planting. But if he was, he would take pride in that work.

Bartholomew Miller appreciated everything he did around the farm, so Amos worked harder than he ever had at home.

Bartholomew had never had a son to help him with all the work around the farm. How had he run this place without sons?

But on the flip side, Amos's *mutter* had been alone doing the house chores, cooking, cleaning and laundry for six men. How did she do it without help?

On the far side of one of the fields, a woman emerged from a bare stand of sycamore trees nestled next to a pond. She walked across the field.

The woman came closer and closer.

Deborah.

Where did she go all the time? She had disappeared every day this week and would be gone for hours. He was about to find out.

With her head down, she didn't see him approaching. He stepped directly into her path a few yards in front of her. When it looked as though she might literally run into him, he cleared his throat.

She halted a foot away. She was so startled to see him there, she appeared to lose her balance. Her arms swung out to keep herself upright.

Looking for inspiration in tales
of hope, faith and heartfelt romance?

Check out **Love Inspired**® and
Love Inspired® Suspense books!

New books available every month!

CONNECT WITH US AT:

Harlequin.com/Community

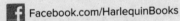 Facebook.com/HarlequinBooks

Twitter.com/HarlequinBooks

Instagram.com/HarlequinBooks

Pinterest.com/HarlequinBooks

ReaderService.com

Love Inspired®

LIGENRE2018

Inspirational Romance to Warm Your Heart and Soul

Join our social communities to connect with other readers who share your love!

Sign up for the Love Inspired newsletter at **www.LoveInspired.com** to be the first to find out about upcoming titles, special promotions and exclusive content.

CONNECT WITH US AT:

Harlequin.com/Community

 Facebook.com/LoveInspiredBooks

 Twitter.com/LoveInspiredBks

LISOCIAL2017